The

DARK ROOM

ALSO BY JULIA CAMERON

The Artist's Way: A Spiritual Path to Higher Creativity

The Money Drunk: 90 Days to Financial Freedom
(co-authored with Mark Bryan)

Vein of Gold: A Journey to Your Creative Self

Heart Steps: Prayers and Declarations for a Creative Life

This Earth
(poetry by Julia Cameron and music by Tim Wheater)

Blessings: Prayers and Declarations for a Heartful Life

The Artist's Way at Work
(co-authored with Mark Bryan and Catherine Allen)

The Right to Write

The

DARK ROOM

■

JULIA CAMERON

CARROLL & GRAF PUBLISHERS, INC.
NEW YORK

Copyright © 1998 by Julia Cameron

All rights reserved

First Carroll & Graf edition 1998

Carroll & Graf Publishers, Inc.
19 West 21st Street
New York, NY 10010-6805

Library of Congress Cataloging-in-Publication Data is available.

ISBN 0-7867-0564-7

Manufactured in the United States of America

For Tray

The

DARK ROOM

Chapter one

——■——

I know that if I am going to tell you this story, I am going to have to give you the pictures. Pictures are hard for me, and some of them may be hard for you, too. That's only human.

Let me start with an easy picture: me. I'm forty-seven years old, Black Irish, although you might say gray. Once, in a cocktail bar in Las Vegas, a drunken waitress whispered to me, "I know who you are." I couldn't wait for her to tell me, and after a while, she did. "Sean Connery," she giggled. I laughed too. If I looked like him, you'd think I'd know it. The guy I see in the mirror is my job—a homicide bull, twenty-three years with the force. Over six feet, over two hundred, solid, nothing glamourous—at least to my eye. The glamour must have been the rented tuxedo I was wearing, in Vegas for a friend's wedding.

Another picture. I am in the station house, at my desk, in a room I experience as sound and smell. Too many phones, too many computers, the smell of bad coffee and too many men in tight quarters.

A police station isn't much like you see it on television. We don't usually have hookers in micro-miniskirts draped across our desks. Or female undercover cops in their undies, either. What we've got is a lot of paperwork, dirty ashtrays, dirty cups, and, now that we've gone modern, diet Coke cans and computer terminals.

I've got seniority and what passes for a corner office in a cop's life—my very own glassed-in partition with cartoons, fingerprints, and a couple of vagrant gum wads separating me from the bull pen. I work, and my men work, in plain sight—which made the next set of pictures the focus of considerable interest.

First, you have to picture her. She was tall and expensive with blond hair, a pale oval face, and violet eyes—the color they say Elizabeth Taylor has. I wouldn't know, but maybe Sean Connery does. She wore a white silk shirt with a plunging neckline, a safari jacket, and side-slit skirt in expensive gabardine. I placed her as a high-ticket call girl, the kind who looked like a million dollars, all of them hers.

"They were a mistake, that's all. He was a mistake." The blonde sent the photos skittering back across my desk.

You might call them art shots, but in the murder I was investigating—the extraordinarily violent death of one Jack Nesbitt, photographer—the pictures were a clue. They'd arrived at the station earlier that morning by special messenger. They came in an ordinary envelope, and when the desk sergeant opened it, he found himself staring at a pair of shapely breasts—perfect breasts—several shots of them, all torso to chin, headless and anonymous except for the inscription inked across the back of each; "These are the breasts of Violet Winters. Ask her about Jack's death." That, and a phone number.

The desk sergeant got the messenger to reveal the sender's identity only as "some fancy doctor's wife up in Highland

Park." When the photos got to Oscar Gomez—I was out—he took one look at them and dialed the number they gave, demanding that their owner, Violet Winters, get into the station house "Immediately, for questioning."

Gomez was a notorious letch. I came in just as Violet Winters was storming out. Gomez had questioned her, all right.

"Get her!" Gomez yelped at me like she was a con going over the wall. Reflexively, I shot out one arm and grabbed her by a tawny elbow.

"What are you doing?" she demanded.

"What are you doing?" I countered.

"She's here for questioning on the Nesbitt case. She's a suspect," Gomez volunteered. Poor Gomez. He looked like a cartoon cop—hopping mad as he thrust her nudie shots at me and repeated, "Here for questioning! About Nesbitt!"

"So I'll question her," I said. "Won't I?"

"Oh, all right," Violet Winters sighed with exaggerated patience. I led her to my desk, where she settled in on the guest chair like she was doing David Letterman.

"Those are your—"

"Tits? Boobs? What do you cops call them? Yes, they're mine. Were mine."

She lit a cigarette, or, rather, put one in her mouth and waited for me to light it.

Where do women like this come from? I wondered. Actually, I knew the probable answers to that.

A. A broken home (She missed her father.)

B. Poor white trash (Prostitution was her way out.)

C. More money than I'd ever seen.

Something, dough or desperation, had given her that cool, that aggressive air of entitlement. That, and those breasts.

In the photos—as in life, no doubt—they were large, round, perfect. And now she wanted them back.

"The pictures are evidence."

"Evidence of what? That I was a dumb kid? That I did whatever the son of a bitch wanted? That somebody up there likes me?"

She had a sense of humor. That, as much as the legs, the hair, the hungry eyes and mouth, that could do a man in. She knew it.

If I am not the best homicide dick in the world, I'm one of the best in this town. And this town is Chicago, where they give tours of murder sites. "Right over there, in that alley by the movie house, that's where they got John Dillinger." I've worked patrol. I've worked tac, I've worked sex crimes, and I've worked vice. I did an undercover stint for three years. By the time I made detective and moved over into violent crimes, I'd already seen a few things.

I tell you this so you understand that when Violet Winters threw me, I was not a man accustomed to being thrown.

"Evidence of what?" she repeated.

"That you knew him."

"You mean that he knew me. . . . Maybe he didn't. Maybe his ex-wife just has a grudge against me. She's the one who gave you those shots, isn't she?"

"I'm not at liberty." But she was right. His ex-wife was now a fancy doctor's wife in Highland Park.

"Too bad. Looked like you could have been fun . . . once upon a time . . . years ago."

"You still can't have the pictures."

"Well then, neither can you. So give them back."

I gave her what I hoped was a stern look. I slid the photos into my drawer.

"Not those pictures. The ones in your head."

I winced. Across the station room floor, I caught Gomez staring at me—watching me with her, the blond goddess, his idea of prime pussy, the reason he couldn't think straight enough to do his goddamn job. Among the force, Gomez's sexual obsession was the butt of jokes. He fancied himself a Latin lover. The rest of us thought he was a hopeless putz, following his dick wherever it led him, like it was a dowser's wand and he'd die without a drink of water.

"Maybe we could start again," the blonde was saying now, "with the facts." Wasn't that my line?

"The facts?" Ah, yes, the facts. "Your name is Violet Winters. That's spelled? Like the flower and the season?"

"The facts about Jack," she interrupted my poetry. "I'm assuming he's dead. . . . I heard that."

This "Jack" was her lover, her once lover, at least. In that distinction, she could evidently join a cast of thousands, all of them young and nubile.

On the case of John "Jack" Nesbitt, photographer and cocksman extraordinaire, I had expended ninety-plus hours. This week. I wanted to solve the crime. But not because Nesbitt was a nice guy. In ninety-plus hours no one had told me that. I wanted to solve the crime because it was my job, and, twenty-three years after my vows to love, honor, and do it, I am still faithful.

"Gomez didn't fill you in?"

"Fill me in? He was too busy trying to feel me up. He wanted to look at the dirty pictures, probably take some himself."

"Instead of your mug shot." She didn't laugh at my joke. She glared at me like I was a mistake, birth to death. "Gomez hit on you?" I managed to ask.

"Of course Gomez hit on me. And that's where you came in. My hero. Able to interrogate tall blondes without a single throb."

Where did she get that mouth? I didn't know whether to

tape it shut or volunteer to be a cigarette. I settled for a glare of my own. That got her attention.

"Okay . . . Jack's dead. We know that much. And I'm a suspect. I am a suspect, right? Your pal read me my Carmen Miranda. 'Yew hat a rite too remayn sighlent' "—her accent was pretty funny—"And so I'm here, and you want to know—"

"The nature of your relationship with the victim."

"We fucked a lot. He made good coffee and a bad margarita. We smoked hash instead. I liked his hands. He talked dirty and was sort of helpless with his lust. I liked that. In the end, he couldn't leave her, so I left him."

"And the pictures?"

"My mistake, dumb move."

"Not so dumb. You can't see your face in any of them."

"Yes, dumb. What did he need me for once he had the fantasy? I was dangerous and the fantasy was much safer."

"Maybe not. Whoever killed him took his hands off— and—" I stopped, wanting to spare her the gory details. Just for a second, I thought I saw something fragile moving under the ice.

In the photos of the scene you got the whole ugly picture played out for you. The bloody phone dangling from the wall, the bloody doorknob he couldn't grasp to turn, the dead bolt he'd used his teeth on, chipping an expensive cap, not that he cared at that point.

Our coroner, Dr. Harold Myerling, was very thorough. He got the graphite on the teeth from the pencil Nesbitt tried to dial with. He got the tooth and the way he chipped it, all right. He got the probable sequence of events and missing parts: hands first, then death, then castration. He had determined that the paper cutter, with its three-foot blade, was, as it appeared to be, the murder weapon.

"Go on," she pushed me. But I didn't think I was wrong about the flash of fragile I had seen. She knew I'd seen it, too, and so she toughened up and pushed. "Go on," she said again.

But Gomez was edging closer, annoyed at me for pulling rank, convinced it all had to do with getting a little nooky, not with solving a crime, not with doing our job. I glared at Gomez, who glared straight back. The blonde watched us like a game show. Gomez backed down. I was the boss.

"He can't help it," Violet Winters scolded me. "Some of them are like little boys. All they want is the candy."

I wondered if all Jack Nesbitt had wanted was the candy. And which kind? He was a cokehead, we knew that, but even for a coke killing, his was particularly brutal: the slow and thorough death that comes from bleeding. He'd tried to call for help, while someone watched—that was the reconstruction, anyhow. Someone hated Nesbitt so much that they'd lopped off his hands—paper cutter as weapon—and then watched him try to save himself before letting him die.

I told Violet Winters the abridged version of the crime. I did mention the paper cutter and the overall savagery of the events.

"Jack had a lot of enemies," Violet Winters abruptly volunteered. Like a good girl. That's like.

"Why do you say that?"

"He wasn't a nice guy. Not to me, not to most people. Certainly not to most women."

"He was your lover."

"My mistake."

"How long a mistake?"

"Oh, at least a foot."

"They said that, too. Even dead, they noticed."

"He'd be so pleased."

"I meant, how much time? How long were you together?"

"I told you, we were never really together."

"Miss Winters," I glanced at the file and Gomez's note. "I'm talking about carnal knowledge."

"I thought you'd never ask." She flashed me a look that was like looking a mile straight down.

"You could make this a lot easier if you'd cooperate."

"That's what Jack used to say if I didn't get off instantly."

"I'm sorry about that." Why was I apologizing for a dead man's bedside manner? A dead man with a cock so long, they called him The Hose?

"They called him The Hose on the street," I told her—as if she didn't know.

"They called him that everywhere," she scoffed. "He liked that. Even if it was really for his blow habit, not his cock."

"That's not our information." It seemed to me I knew more about Jack Nesbitt's sex life than I did about my own.

"You're telling me he even fucked the cops? Because I'm telling you, he fucked everybody—me, her, her little sister, your brother, your mama. . . . He was disgusting."

Violet Winters stubbed out her cigarette with a hand that was shaking. She tried to make it look like righteous rage, but I was getting that flash again: fragile, handle with care.

"I'm sorry," she said. "It makes me furious even now."

"He was very famous." I thought I'd state the obvious. Chicago is a town that hates and fears celebrities. This sends most of them packing once they attain a certain status. Nesbitt was the exception. He bloomed where he was planted, getting more famous every year—doing artsy posters for the film festival, the blues festival, the Taste of Chicago, a restaurant fair.

"Jack was famous for being disgusting."

"So, did the fame turn you on? Is that it?" I heard myself

sounding angry—at her or at Nesbitt, at the whole decadent scene. I knew Nesbitt had been a fixture for years at the Playboy mansion until Hefner got too famous for Chicago and left for the coast.

"What the hell did you like?" I demanded. Even to my ear, I sounded righteous and paternal. What's a nice girl like you, etc. Ever since his death, I'd heard nothing but orgies, sex shows, three-ways, AC/DC. Violet Winters caught this and gave me what might have been a straight answer.

"I told you. It was his hands. Oh, he was a great photographer, a real artist. Or didn't you know that? Is that relevant?"

"It wasn't a very artistic death, Miss Winters. So, you were telling me how long."

"Six months—six months, maybe a year."

"Two years."

"Why'd you ask me, if you knew?"

"A little test."

"To see if you could trust me? A man like you would never trust a woman like me. You like them short, a little frumpy, and dependent."

I winced. She was describing my wife, my now ex-wife, Gloria. Then I noticed her eyes on my bulletin board: the wife, the kid, myself five years younger. The photo was fading. "My family," I told her unnecessarily. I didn't say the photo was a remnant of happier times.

She wasn't interested. In fact, she was leaving.

"You know where to find me. You even know what I look like."

With that, Violet Winters got to her feet, and then did some more. She was really that tall, nearly my own height. Taller, in heels.

"Are we finished, Miss Winters?"

"Dr. Winters, if you don't mind. And I've got some

appointments, so I'm afraid we are finished—but you can always call me." She slid a card across my desk. Thick, snowy, and expensive. It read: Pediatrics, Children's Memorial Hospital, and her name.

The rookies, Chaworski and Lynch, were watching us like TV. Gomez was sniggering at me from across the room, but I let her go. Six feet tall, snow-blond, a doctor, for crissake, with the mind of a hooker. I let her go because I didn't want to, and that had me worried. It was time, I decided, to close up shop and go see my friend Jamie.

Chapter two

———■———

Jamie Hackett was my best friend—was/is/will be. Womb-to-tomb. Same parish, St. Angela's. Same block, 1200 Parkside. Not to mention same chip on the shoulder, same amount of time in juvenile hall as I spent in pre-seminary out at St. Mary's of the Lake. Just long enough to turn me around from a life of virtue and into a cop, just long enough to turn him from his life of crime into a life of legalized violence as a boxer. How he got from boxing to fine arts remains a mystery. The known fact is that he's always liked to draw and, as he put it, "I just moved on from graffiti."

Jamie is my brother, my historian, my rabbit's foot. He knows my story and my path. When I stray too far in what he thinks of as the wrong direction, he gives me a shove back on track. Sometimes he gives me a shove just to give me a shove.

Jamie's place, the Tattooed Zoo, is South Loop, neoindustrial, very trendy. He's trendy himself these days. Tattooed, bald, rich. I love him anyway. So does the New York arts scene, whatever that is.

I found Jamie in his usual getup: backwards bandanna over

his bald pate, muscle shirt, old jeans. He was what I would call halfway across a painting the size of a bad auto accident and largely the same colors. Power art, the critics called it. A kick in the balls, Jamie preferred.

He wanted the skinny on the Nesbitt case. I told him about the nude photos of Violet Winters. Then I told him about Violet Winters in the flesh.

"Elliot Mayo and Violet Winters, imagine that," he said.

"You know her?" Jamie knew pretty much everybody. He indulged in a form of negative social climbing, following the players, just not playing the game. He was like a handicapper who never placed a bet.

"Violet Winters, that's interesting," he dangled.

"What do you know?" I bit.

"What can I tell you? She's into artists. Gives her something to classify besides viruses. Why don't you introduce us?"

Jamie threw this out to see if I liked her. I did.

"Fuck yourself, Jamie." For years he had slept with any and every woman I introduced him to.

"You say the nicest things, but I don't have the forty-foot schlong your friend Nesbitt had." Jamie dangled this as more hot gossip.

"I've heard all about it, even the coroner."

Jamie laughed. He knew about Dr. Winters. He knew about everybody. He even knew about Jack Nesbitt's cock. I waited for the story.

"It's true. I swear to God. He and I got into this scene. Christ, it was years ago. A couple of Swedish girls. This black hooker turned chanteuse. A coke party at Danny Merton's. The kind everybody ends up in a pile. They thought I was pretty hot, but then Jack pulls that thing out, and I was over. They were impressed."

"Can't you talk about anything but Dick-and-Jane games? Jesus Christ, Jamie."

"You came here to talk about Dick-and-Jane games, remember? What did I know about a certain Dr. Winters? A certain Dr. Winters and Jack Nesbitt, the late, great, et cetera? See his obit?"

"Clipped it."

"Kinda hard to see a guy's work overshadowed like that."

"He was so good?"

"Yeah. A great photographer, a great fucking photographer."

"That's what she said."

"She should know. Hey, it's good to see you." Jamie and I had been missing each other. We'd been doing it for months. I told myself it was coincidence, but it was pure avoidance. I was avoiding Jamie because I was avoiding me and my pain. Gloria, my wife of twenty-plus years, had left me. Left me for another man. A man I knew. At least that was the recent rumor.

There are those who would say she left me years before the event. Jamie would say that. And had. But as long as she slept under my roof, as long as our son slept peacefully down the hall, I told myself we were together and things would get better. When you have a child, you want to believe things like that—at least I did.

I met Gloria the week of my father's funeral. She lived next door to my cousin Charles and came to the wake as his friend. She asked him about his "cute cousin." Me. Even then Gloria knew what she wanted. And in those times that was a lot to me.

"I loved her once, didn't I?" I asked Jamie after our troubles became chronic.

"You thought you did," he said. "It wasn't a good time for you."

I remembered. My father's death seemed impossible to me. I missed his company in death in a way I had seldom enjoyed it in life. There was so much I wanted to ask him. But he carried his answers, if he had them, to the grave. Within six months of his death I followed his fading footsteps into the force. Once there, I loved it.

I never decided to be a cop. I came into the idea the way a man engaged to one woman falls suddenly and irrevocably in love with her sister. In my case, I jilted the law. I didn't mean to do it. My father was a cop and it killed him. I was, he always said, "too smart for a cop." Maybe I am, but my father loved his job, and that is what he really taught me.

As long as he was alive, we both pretended I'd be a lawyer, a step up he wished for me and maybe for himself. With his death, I met Gloria and, in a sense, I met myself. The law faded from my memory—if not from Gloria's.

Jamie cleared his throat.

"I've been kinda holed up," I told him lamely.

"Even when you're here you're still not here. She really left you."

"Looks that way. She threw me out. Four months ago. Then she set a moratorium on my visiting Zach."

"What?"

"She wanted time out for them to normalize as a household. He was having nightmares, she said, and she thought it was his worry about my job. That's what she said, anyhow. To anyone who would listen. Now, though, I could get joint custody. At least I think I could."

"Right. Under the circumstances. So I hear." Jamie heard everything. People dropped by his studio just to catch up or to put things on the circuit. In another life, he was probably Hedda Hopper.

"You've heard she's shacked up with somebody? . . ."

For the three months since Gloria's departure, I had buried myself in work. My partner of fourteen years, Jack Carney, had suddenly developed colon cancer and had gone to Arizona to die in the sun. He'd left me with a room full of rookies and a workload that let me submerge myself. I'd used work as a narcotic to keep from missing Zach—and the precise details of Gloria's defection.

"Gomez."

"No. No way."

"They've been seen out and about."

"Gomez?"

Couldn't my ex-wife do a little better?

"Maybe he changed his stripes," Jamie helped me out. "Maybe—"

"He's still a cop. That's no life for a kid. Gloria always said it wrecked her nerves. Maybe it's bad for Zach, too. That was her whole rationale for my not seeing him these three months—he needed to 'detox' from my high-adrenaline job. When I thought of him having nightmares, I had to go along with her."

"Maybe."

"She got a therapist to agree with her, Jamie . . . I only went along with it because if she was right, then I owed it to Zach. He's the point here. Anyway, I'll probably settle for joint."

I had promised myself one thing, insofar as it was possible. Zach would not be harmed by this divorce. I would speak no ill of his mother, her choice in consorts, her life. I would not use Zach as a weapon or engage in warfare at his expense.

That meant that I would not fight for custody if my custody would harm him.

"She's really with Gomez?" For years Jamie had tweaked me about Gloria's alleged weakness for Latin types—a line of teasing grounded in her crush on Julio Iglesias, a crush she shared with half the women on the planet, evidently. Now Jamie acted like Gloria and Gomez were a big surprise—and they were.

To me.

"That's the rumor."

"Gomez probably started it." Jamie was being kind. Not his long suit.

"Gloria probably started it. Fantasies of Latin love. She always said my preoccupation with my job made me less than attentive. Hell, something did. But I thought it was her endless worry."

In her determination to marry me, Gloria had seemed strong to me as a young man. Only later did I see that it was closer to desperation, a grasping at security, that came from fear. Gloria's scenarios for catastrophe were many and varied. If a cop sees the potential for human evil nightly, Gloria watched it daily—both prime time and daytime. In her overheated imagination I was her young, feckless boy bride set loose in a dangerous world.

And Gomez? He was such a lousy cop, maybe he did excel in the sack. The thought made me jealous.

"Miss her?"

"No."

"Why do I believe you?"

"It's been over a long time."

In a sense, Gloria and I had raised each other and, judging by the result, neither of us had done a good job. Like a lot of young men, I'd used my wife as a sounding board for my self-doubts. Nothing wrong with that, with the right woman. Wrong with Gloria. Years later, she played my self-doubts back to me free of charge. I felt older and steadier. That just made her madder and louder.

"People change, Gloria. I know what I'm doing."

"What if you're wrong? What if . . . ?"

When Gloria married me, she believed in what I believed: I had a future in law, not in law and order. My father had been a cop, and I would have told you watching his life chilled any need to repeat his sins in mine, but life is more interesting than that. As Gloria and I found out.

As I've said, my father wanted me to be a lawyer, and I planned to be a lawyer. Ever since the Jesuits failed to make a priest of me, I saw law as a clerical form of religion, one to which I was called. I worked my way through a fine Jesuit college, got accepted at a fine Jesuit law school, married Gloria the summer before, the summer after Dad died, and as a fill-in, took a temporary job at Area Six. That's right, I was a typist. Twenty-three years later, I'm still at Area Six, and still at sixty-five words a minute. I lose about a word a year.

"What do you mean?" Gloria said when I told her I wanted to be a cop. "I thought you wanted to be a lawyer."

"So did I. But I don't. I like what I'm doing."

"What you're doing is typing."

She was right about that, but if I joined the force, it would change—for the better, I was sure. For the worse, Gloria was sure.

"For better or worse," I reminded her, and joined the force. I have regretted this decision in no substantial way. On my annual birthday drunk, I mourn my lost law career. Three hundred and sixty-four other days, I go to my sometimes terrible job a happy man. In this, I am as truly blessed or cursed as the man who says rapturously of his difficult wife,

"But I love her." After each new heartbreak, you hear it again. "But I love her."

And I do.

I believe in right livelihood. I believe in form follows function. I believe I was built to be a cop. Gloria says I'd have been a good lawyer, too. Maybe. But I'm a happy cop. When I was little, my mom told a nursery story about knowing your place. It ended with the line "You make a wonderful donkey, but a terrible lapdog." I see myself as that wonderful donkey. My wife saw me as a mule—or maybe a horse's ass.

"Miss Zach?"

Jamie brought me back to the present with a question like an uppercut to the kidney. It didn't just hurt. It pierced me. I knew he was inviting me to take the cap off my emotions, but the pain made me nasty. I cut him short.

"What the fuck do you think? I miss him like my right hand—not that we should mention hands right now."

Jamie took the cue and changed the subject to murder—which was nothing compared to divorce. "It was pretty gruesome, even in the papers." He was adding gore to his painting.

"It sure was."

"Chopped off his hands?"

"Chopped off his hands first—his weenie second. His forty-foot weenie."

"Jesus. I wanna ask you how you know that."

"The things a cop knows would fill a library."

"So stay away from that blonde. You're not ready for her."

"Did I ask?"

"Date a nice little secretary, a desk bunny. R&R. Wading, you know? No deep water."

"You should talk."

"I did. I don't know you all these years for nothing."

All these years. With ten off for bad behavior, years when I was newly married and he was nearly always drunk. Since he stopped drinking and drugging three years back, our friendship has enjoyed a renaissance. I drop by and don't have to scrape him off the floor. He's Jamie again, the funny guy he was before I went straight and he went to hell for a decade.

"The druggie's life was very interesting," Jamie liked to kid. "I'm sure if I remembered it, I'd be fascinated."

Well, I remembered it. I remembered hauling Jamie out of bars and abandoned cars, taking him blankets the winter he spent in a doorway.

"Leave me the fuck alone, Elliot," Jamie would say. "I'm a hoping to die alcoholic."

Finally I left him alone because I couldn't stand the pain anymore—not his, mine. I couldn't stand to see him one more time with the razor blades of pain behind his eyes. Three months later, as Jamie tells the story, an angel came to visit him in that doorway and "I understood I had to change."

It was DTs, I'm sure. Some people see a white snake, a white rat, Jamie saw an angel. When it told him to stop, he listened, and now he listened to me.

Jamie forebore telling me to shut up, except for one memorable occasion, when he told me the simple truth: Gloria had done for me what I couldn't do for myself, and the marriage was over.

"Can I use your phone?"

"Need to tag base?"

"I thought I'd see if I could take Zach to dinner. The moratorium's over."

Zachary wasn't home, but Gloria was. She said that Zachary was out shooting baskets with a friend of theirs. It was wonderful, she said, the way some people found time for children.

I did not take the bait. I wished her a good night and asked her to have Zachary call me. Then I got off the phone, calm, and calmly put my knuckles through Jamie's Sheetrock wall.

"What are you going to do?" Jamie asked me, meaning, about Zachary.

"Whatever is best for Zach. Meanwhile, go back to work," I told him. I did.

Chapter three

It took me a week to surrender. One night about nine, after a day full of dead-end calls and frustration, I thought about how the case wasn't going anywhere and where I'd like to go was out to dinner with a tall, pale blonde with violet eyes. Bad idea, I told myself and the empty station room. Any objections? I asked. None were voiced.

"You did call!" the charming doctor greeted me when, just as she suggested I would, just as Jamie feared I would, just as I shouldn't have, I called.

"I've got a few more questions for you."

"Bullshit. You want in my panties."

"You're a suspect. You're not in the clear."

"Oh, neither are you. Who is? I say, scotch and steak. I want a real meal, Detective."

"I strike you as a snack, Doctor?"

"Oh, goody, you are going to be fun. Jacky and Johnny's at ten?"

It was a new spot for some old players.

"I'll be wearing a badge."

"Then I'll leave my undies on."

I got off the phone and thought about calling Jamie. To be accurate, I got off the phone and thought about not calling Jamie.

I knew what he'd say, "Don't do it/you're not ready/what about professional ethics?"

I'll tell you what I told me about professional ethics. Interviewing her was professional ethics. If Gomez interviewed her, he'd only want to fuck her, and he was probably already getting his Latin nuts off with my ex-wife. No doubt about it, I was the man for the job. I could handle it, be fully professional, even if it was off hours—just to get her relaxed. See if she'd let anything slip.

She did.

The dress was red and it let everything slip . . . and slide . . . and I was in trouble instantly. When I got to the restaurant, the doctor was already there, ensconced in a dark back booth. Brand new, but not to look at it, Jacky and Johnny's was a dark, smoky kind of place, 1940's B movies, and Dr. Winters glowed like a pearl in the half-light. She greeted me with a languid wave, then gripped my hand hard and held it.

"My point of reference is the hands," she said, "like that little dent where your wedding band should be."

"She left me."

"In the last week?"

"I'm a slow learner. She's living with that Latin guy you liked so much at the station."

"Ouch."

"I couldn't get the ring off."

"Use soap."

"That a surgical procedure?"

She had her shoe off, spikes this time, and was rubbing her toes along my shin.

"I'm an old man, Doctor."

"I can see that."

"And a homicide cop. You don't want to play with me." Her feet thought otherwise. One was nudging at my sock.

"This how you got involved with Jack Nesbitt?" The first foot stopped. The second foot kicked me in the shin.

"Ouch. Broke my toe."

"You're breaking my heart." Why was I being so unfriendly?

"That was easy." Why was she being so unfriendly?

Safety, I decided. We either found it or needed it with each other. Maybe both. The doctor coiled back in her chair and kissed a cigarette. I made the pilgrimage to light it for her. It seemed only fair, since we were the only two adults in America still smoking.

"If we've got to talk about him, let's do it after I eat. Right now I've got an appetite."

As if signaled, Johnny came to take the order. He had on his year-round tan and his summer whites, an expensive linen suit that looked to my eye like flour sacks. He was nothing if not a trend setter. When *Miami Vice* made a star out of Don Johnson, we kidded Johnny about missing his callback and losing out to a cheap imitation. I'd known Johnny Vanilla for years, since before the Mafia money set him up in three swank joints and made him a big deal with a life sentence. I think of Johnny as a handsome man, the kind a woman would want. The doctor looked at him like he was a dirty plate.

"Johnny, Dr. Winters." I tried to soften the blow.

"Enchanted, Doctor." He looked at her like a meal. It crossed my mind they'd been together. This wasn't hate at first sight.

"The New York strip, rare, baked potato, bleu cheese on

the salad. And another one of these." The doctor lofted her scotch glass.

"She gets down to business, doesn't she?" Johnny wasn't liking this much.

"Double that, Johnny. Winning at the races?" I nodded at his pricey decor.

"Come on, Elliot, I'm a new man."

"I'll bet you are."

"I'm dry," the doctor interrupted.

"I'll bet you are," said Johnny.

"Hey," I chastised Johnny, my attempt at chivalry. Had I heard him right?

"I can take care of myself," the doctor said, "and I certainly don't need protection from this gumbo."

"Listen, bitch—"

At that, the doctor put a hand on her steak knife and I put a lid on the whole thing.

"Johnny, if you don't mind, the doctor and I are just leaving. Tab me."

I got the doctor by the elbow, she carried her shoes, and we were on the street just in time to save her Porsche from a kid with a crowbar. He read me cop from a hundred yards.

"Love these night spots, don't you? I hate it when I get triggered like that." She was stepping back into her stiletto skyscrapers. It occurred to me that they were weapons in the war between the sexes; that she dressed to kill because to her it was kill or be killed between men and women. But it was one thing to realize this and another to deal with it. You might think I was jealous.

"That was pretty. Old boyfriend?"

"Are you kidding? I like a man with some mileage, not just the chrome. Johnny Vanilla's a showboat. I hate flashy men."

"I guess that makes me your type."

"Maybe. I liked you better when you were married."

"I'm probably still married. It's a habit."

"So's what I do."

"And what is that, Doctor?"

"The flirting. The bullshit. Dr. Feelgood, that's me. Leave 'em laughin', but leave 'em."

"Why are you telling me this?"

"I think you had it figured out."

"Maybe. Or maybe this sincere line of yours is one more come-on."

"You are suspicious, Detective Mayo."

"Cops are suspicious people, Doctor. It's natural and necessary."

We were at her Porsche. My unmarked was parked conveniently right behind it.

"Your car or mine, Detective?"

"Mine's bigger."

"That's what you all say." She was back to her shield of banter and innuendo.

"Or we do Harry's?"

Harry's was half a block away, a hot dog stand with one table near its only window. We had shipwrecked dinner. It was late and I was starving.

"I'm hungry," I told her, taking her by a sleek elbow. She shook me off.

"Don't grab me. Don't ever grab me."

"I'm starving. And I didn't grab you. I took your arm. Chivalry isn't always an insult, Doctor."

"Oh, all right. We could let our cars get to know each other."

The doctor was heading into Harry's. From the back she looked like heaven.

"Stop staring and buy me something with mustard," the doctor ordered, looking back at me like the Coppertone girl.

Harry looked at me with new respect. Even in red, the doctor was a class act, and Harry's usual clientele was junkies and whores and what he called "double winners"—whores who were also junkies. I've known Harry for twenty years. Occasionally he's been very helpful, and I've never abused the privilege.

"Two footlongs—everything?" The doctor nodded. I'd known she would.

"Fries, rings, and a malted—two malteds."

"Trying to pass your cholesterol test with high grades?" She was laughing.

"Be careful, Doctor. You're sounding like you care."

"That's the hard thing about my job, Detective. You know what you know." Which didn't stop her from tapping out a cigarette.

"Same problem with mine, Doctor."

So there we were, two professionals out on the town. The fun was gone from our little date, and I thought it left when Johnny did.

"So. I was the setup to get Johnny back, is that it?"

"Don't flatter yourself. It was something else. A needle dick like Johnny sees competition in Mr. Universe—maybe."

She was right, of course. An over-the-hill homicide cop would not be Johnny's idea of competition.

"What else?"

"I was thinking about Jack."

"That's why we're here, Doctor. To think about Jack."

"Is it? I was hoping you'd had an ethics slip and were looking for a hot time."

"Come on, Doc. Homicide is a hot time." Now I was picking up her style. She didn't like that much.

"I don't think a paper cutter would go through that bone. I cut and saw a lot, a whole lot. Even in surgery I'd use what you'd probably call a hacksaw. The wrist can be a tough mother to get through. Hold that ketchup, okay?"

"Ready to eat these things?" Harry had our order up, and it looked like a bad idea. I rounded it up while the doctor guarded our cars. I was bloodying up the fries and the rings. "Sorry."

"Guilt by association."

"I'd have thought you'd be immune by now, Doctor."

"Same to you, Elliot. Can I call you that? Are you ever immune when it's someone you know?"

"Why don't you call me Detective, Doctor, and I'll call you ma'am."

"Too generic. Cop talk. Try 'sweetheart.'"

"Doctor, I can't call you sweetheart."

"Then try Violet. It's my name. Think of my eyes." She batted them. She was right.

"I think I'll call you Doctor, Violet."

"With a name like Violet, I had to compensate."

"I'd noticed."

"The act worked for a long time. If a woman comes on strong enough, she can scare off almost anybody—except maybe a homicide cop who comes on like a softy."

Having laid in that little grenade, Dr. Violet Winters, just like her card said, began nibbling at her food. She made it look like a forced march.

"Trying to be a good girl? You don't have to clean your plate with me, Doctor. And you don't have to flirt with me, either."

"I can't get the thing with Jack out of my mind."

"Sounds like you miss him."

"Are you crazy? I wanted to kill him." I felt my cop tugging at my stomach lining.

"You want to tell me who you're protecting, Doctor? You're already a suspect, and making you a better one doesn't fool me. I'm too old."

"You are too old. Why didn't I notice that before?"

The doctor suddenly had at the french fries, ketchup and all. She ate them like there was gold in the bottom of the cardboard carton, if she just got there fast enough.

"Are you a puker?" Her head shot up. Good.

"Pardon me?"

"It's my experience a girl eats like that, she's stuffing something—"

"I'm just hungry."

"Right. And I'm Cinderella."

"Don't psychoanalyze me, Detective. I can diagnose my own eating disorder. Right now I would call it hunger."

The doctor acted true to her word. Two minutes more and she was the scene of the crime. Red dress, red face, red hands, ketchup everywhere—and a look of contentment in her eyes. I handed her a napkin.

"Food never does it for me," I told her.

"Stop treating me like I'm twelve." Just for a minute, she did look twelve. Just for a minute, yes she did, all six glorious feet of her. My cop tugged at me again. Ask, it told me.

"Those pictures, Doctor. When were they taken?"

"Jesus, Elliot! I'm talking how and why they did it, and you're stuck in when." She sounded like I'd made bad love to her.

"When?" I pushed. I knew paydirt when I didn't hear it.

"Some afternoon. A couple of afternoons. It was his thing."

"The year, Violet." She looked at me like a cornered

rabbit. The mask was gone. The kid I'd seen a minute before stared me in the face. Oh, Jesus, I thought. No wonder she acts tough. A bone is always tough in the broken places.

"I was—" she started lying. It was in the pause.

"Eighteen?" I helped her.

"No."

"Sixteen?" I pushed her.

"No."

"Fourteen?" I cornered her.

She saw that I knew, and she broke. Her tough girl came apart in pieces.

"Hate crying," she said. "I hate crying in public places. I was twelve. He was my art teacher. Get me out of here."

I waved Harry good night, tucked her under my arm, and took her to sit in the unmarked, where we'd have a little privacy. She cried big, hiccuping sobs, like a little girl. I patted her shoulder. I put my arms around her and rocked her. I wanted to kill a dead man. Even dead, Jack Nesbitt was twenty-five years her senior, twenty years mine. I didn't just want to find his killer anymore. I wanted to kill Jack Nesbitt myself.

"It's over," I said. "The worst is over and you survived it."

"Did I?" she asked through tears.

"Sure you did." Even to me I sounded glib. The tabloid reporter at the scene of the crime: "And how does it feel, Mrs. S., to have seen your only son die a horrible death before your very eyes?"

"You're real good at it, aren't you?" Violet sniffed. She wiped her runny nose on a long, golden wrist.

"It's my job."

"How'd you know?"

"I don't know. A hunch. I call it my cop."

"I never told anybody."

"You don't think they knew? What about your mother?"

She rolled her eyes. "Mother," she spat out. "You're thinking lace curtains, aprons, cookies after school. Think again."

"Somebody must have known."

"Oh, later they did. When we had our official affair. That six-month thing I told you about? Two years, minimum. They all knew then."

"What was that about?"

"Revenge, I thought. I could hang him out to dry. What a joke."

"I'm not sure that was it."

"I've got a therapist, thank you, Detective. I've done all the necessary work. I'm a survivor, not a victim, et cetera. I know about repetition compulsion. I don't need you to analyze me. I've been analyzed. So fuck off."

"Thought you never told anyone?"

"Anyone real. Therapists don't count."

"That sounds like a come-on, which means it must be time for me to go home."

"This is a real bad time for you to have professional ethics."

The doctor was back to her adult self. One long leg was working on one of mine. I caught Harry watching us through the window, amazed. He'd known me for years as a straight cop. That helped me do the undoable.

"Say good night, Doctor. It's bedtime, not playtime."

"Speak for yourself, Detective. I've got places to go and people to see."

"Walk you to the car?"

"No, thank you. You look too tired to be useful."

Chapter four

———■———

"Heard you had a hot night, boss. Devil with a red dress on."

Gomez was on me. It was early and we were both in the station house before reveille. Maybe my wife was having the same effect on him she had on me. Maybe Gomez would be a good cop after all.

"I had a few more questions."

"Gotcha. Like, is this it, baby? You like this?"

"Gomez, I would not push it if I were you."

"Whatever you say, boss. If I was you."

He had me. Twenty-three years on the force, and when you got me riled, under my tough-cop act was still the snotty-nosed little boy the Jesuit fathers had worked on. They hammered it into me: "If I were you, Elliot. Subjunctive. A situation contrary to fact. It always requires were."

That was it in a nutshell: a situation contrary to fact, and it had me by the balls, and Gomez knew it. In Dr. Violet Winters, long-legged, lava-mouthed, a suspect, I had found myself a real femme fatale. She was young enough but old enough, and last night she'd been a twelve-year-old kid. Busting her that way, I'd felt like Einstein when I needed to be Sigmund Freud.

Which was what I was doing when Gomez's snitch saw me. Word travels fast.

My plan, going into the station early, was to spend some quiet time poring over the pictures in Nesbitt's file—not the pictures of Violet. Knowing she was twelve and an early bloomer scotched those photos for me. I was interested in the photos of Nesbitt himself. I was thinking about the doctor's opinion.

As my friend Jamie always tells me, cop photos are art. They use them a lot in movies these days, so I guess they must be.

But I wouldn't know. What I see, looking at shots like the ones of Jack Nesbitt, is that people are capable of anything, and not a lot of it is pretty. Now, maybe if the shots were color I'd "love that red," as Jamie says. Blood in black and white is a gray smear.

There were gray smears all over the walls of Jack Nesbitt's, near the locked door and near the phone, especially. The killer came and went through the skylight, a lot of trouble unless you're doing it for effect, which they must have been. The back window on the fire escape would have been easier and less visible. Not that we had a witness on the rooftop entry. As Gomez said succinctly in his notes, "No witnesses of nobody seeing nothing, not before, not after, not during." And during could have been a while. As I'd told Jamie, and the papers were now telling the world, Jack Nesbitt bled to death, and not because he was trying to.

No hands, no dick, no chance. All of this carnage accomplished, to our coroner Harold Myerling's estimable satisfaction, by a paper cutter. A smooth fit—but not to Dr. Winters.

Always listen to a suspect was a rule of mine. Elliot's homicide rule number one. Suspects suspect things, and they're often right. And so, I was sitting at my desk, contemplating Jack Nesbitt's gray smears, when the call came in.

"Hey, boss."

It was Gomez, sounding respectful for once, or scared. I looked at him and wondered if this was the time to ask him about him and Gloria. Or if he thought I knew. But he'd have to tell me. I wasn't about to give Gloria the satisfaction, or to put Zach in the middle. Gomez shifted uncomfortably. He even looked a little pale. I must intimidate him more than I know, I thought comfortably. No such luck.

"Pick up the phone," he finally interjected. "Looks like we've got another one." He sounded like this was a surprise.

"What do you mean, another one?"

In Chicago, counting murders is like counting flies. Another murder was no surprise.

"One of those serial guys."

"Christ, Oscar! You've got a brain like a tabloid. It's a technical term. It means a stranger killing strangers for no motive. It does not mean a strange killing."

"No hands, no clues, no dick," Gomez shot back nervously. He was scared. "Two in a row. That is strange, you ask me."

"Another one?"

"That's what I am telling you!"

For the first time in twelve years of knowing him, I almost liked the little prick. Another dickless corpse was enough to scare any man, cop or not, much less a Latin lover. If Gomez was nervous, so was I. Cops see a lot, hear a lot, and we develop at least the necessary amount of what the good doctor would dub immunity. Cop or not, I was not immune to dickless corpses.

"I'm on my way," I told Gomez. "But this still doesn't make it a serial killer. Maybe it's two different guys with the same modus operandi. Maybe it's one guy with two grudges and a motive. Maybe it's a business partnership gone south. We don't know yet. And if you think you do, we'll never solve this thing." If there's one thing I hate, it's premature theories.

"Yeah," he said. "Would you like to know where you're going?"

As it happened, I had been there before.

It was eight o'clock in the morning, but the crowd outside Jacky and Johnny's was thick. At my age I look like what I am, a homicide bull, and I don't need to show badge to part the Red Sea. The crowd was comprised of equal parts likely victims and perpetrators. "A neighborhood on the way up," they were calling this part of town. What the real estate ads don't say is "on the way up from hell."

I pushed through the bottle-green smoked-glass doors and into the swank interior. In broad daylight, with all the lights on, the place still looked like a movie set. Of course, that was the whole point. A marketing ploy. Make the joint look like something they liked—say, *Casablanca*—and then cash in on their associations.

"Here's Johnny," caroled bald little Roger Rogaine, our photographer, as I came through the door. I used to get ticked by his humor, but over the years I've understood it to be a necessary defense for a job like his. And he's good at his terrible job.

"Here's Johnny," he sang again, and this time I realized he was bowing me toward something behind the bar, the long, polished teak bar, costlier than anything but the drinks.

"Thanks, Roger." I took the cue. I headed around the bar.

"It's slippery," he warned just as I rounded the end and stepped into a lake of blood that used to belong to Johnny. "A bloody Mary," Roger joked. "A real bloody Mary."

Handless and dickless, Johnny Vanilla was lying flat on his back on the floor, behind his own cash register, which was standing openmouthed, like it couldn't believe what it saw.

"Boss?" Roger was still working on his pictures. "If you'd give me a shout when you find his hands."

"I'll just hit the head." ("Are you ever immune when you know them?" Violet Winters had asked me. The answer was no.)

Normally I've got a solid stomach, but normally I don't know the victim. Also, normally, victims still have their dicks on. I could feel my own balls searching for a hiding place. The men's room door was locked, and I noticed the floor outside was sticky.

"Get that bathroom door down/don't let the press in yet/ Roger better get back here," I barked.

They got the door down. Johnny's penis was in the sink. "Here's Johnny" was written on the mirror in lipstick— lipstick the color of blood. Evidently "Here's Johnny" was going to be the obit phrase. The bathroom's skylight was broken, and the top of the toilet lid. Someone liked showy exits.

I wiped my mouth on the winding towel and ran into Gomez on the way out. He was the color of a flour tortilla. In the bathroom mirror I had seen an aging man with a kicked-in look in his eyes. A year ago, unhappily married, complaining every inch of the way, I'd been a contender.

I tried to imagine who could kill Johnny with such obvious hatred and relish. The first person who rushed to mind was Dr. Violet Winters. If I knew one thing from their exchange of the night before, I knew she hated Johnny Vanilla. What I didn't know was why.

"I hate it when I get triggered like that," she'd said. "Triggered" was a sinister word.

"I've got places to go and people to see," she'd said. Was Johnny Vanilla one of them?

Chapter five

◼

When I got back to the station after the press and getting Johnny into an outsized baggy and at the coroner's, I had two calls I wanted and some hundred others to get in my way. Jamie Hackett had called me, and my son, Zach, had called me back. I was glad Zach still needed me now that he was all but living with that colorful father figure, Oscar Gomez. Since it was still school hours, I called Jamie first. I called his gallery, then his pager. He got back fast.

"What do you think about Johnny?" he wanted to know. "Is it true they couldn't find the hands?"

"I think it was a Mafia hit," I told him, "a copycat. They're just trying to confuse us." I didn't know yet why I thought that, but I did. "I'm not calling this a theory. But I'm not calling it the same guy, either. The lipstick bothers me. 'Here's Johnny' on the mirror? I didn't notice any jokes at Nesbitt's."

"I hope you're right. I like the Outfit a lot better than some crazed, dick-happy butcher."

"A little nervous?"

"Every man in Chicago is grabbing his nuts with both hands," Jamie said. "How about a frosty tonight?"

"I'm working late," I whined. "I'd love to be really working, but instead I'm returning calls to our beloved press establishment. All I need is for someone to breathe the words *serial killer,* and I'll spend weeks playing beat the press. A reporter used to work on a case. A reporter used to work on a story, not just phone up the cops. Do I sound bitter?"

"You're breaking my heart, Elliot. Try me about eleven."

"Right."

Chicago is supposed to be a great newspaper town, and maybe it was once. I remember when I started on the force, there were reporters who were better cops than the cops. I used to call them to learn homicide. Those guys are gone and the papers are full of celebrities, and half of them are reporters themselves—if you can call what they do reporting. The part of my job I hate is dealing with the boys and girls of the press. They don't know what they're talking about anymore, and they'll print almost anything. Give them a case with a celebrity in it—and Nesbitt qualified as one, as did Johnny in his glamour-boy way—and they will write whatever crosses their little minds. If you don't watch out, they'll have you saying it. At the best, they'll have you denying it.

"Looks like some antihomosexual thing," one guy got me on the line, "doesn't it?"

"Not particularly," I told him. "And don't print that."

My second call was an underground paper wondering about a feminist plot.

"You've got to be kidding," I said. "Don't print that. This isn't the movies."

Caller three, a certain Big Name Columnist, wanted to know if I thought there was a trend toward sexual killings as a whiplash effect from the fear of AIDS.

"What does that mean?" I asked. "I'd be pretty hard pressed to work up a theory like that," I told him.

"But you wouldn't rule it out?"

"Hell, I wouldn't even think of it. I'm too busy trying to solve the things."

And so it went, so many phone calls from the press, no time to work on the case. No time for my own suspicions instead of theirs. I wanted to call Dr. Winters and ask a few tough questions. Questions like "Will you go to bed with me?" And "Did you kill Johnny Vanilla?"

I was thinking about Dr. Violet Winters, when my phone rang still again. I wanted to shoot it, but I answered instead.

"I hear you think the killer is a feminist homosexual," said a woman's voice.

"Screw you," I snapped. Let her quote me.

"That was my plan for last night, but we got derailed."

Ah-hah. This was one call I did want.

"Haven't I told you a million times not to call me at the office, Violet, Dr. Winters, sweetheart?" I was so obnoxious, my manly heart swelled.

"I know, boss, but I just admire you so, and you're so big and strong and quotable," she laughed. We both liked this little game of ours.

"The whole thing with the press always makes me think of Lyndon Johnson."

"How's that?"

"It was early in his career, a close race down in Texas, and he calls his advisers in and says, 'I've got an idea. Let's tell the press he fucks pigs.' His advisers squeal, 'But, Lyndon! He doesn't fuck pigs!' 'I know that and you know that,' says Lyndon, 'but let's see the bastard deny it.' "

We were both laughing by this time. I was almost in a good mood. Gomez was eyeing me suspiciously. Maybe Dr.

Winters couldn't cost me my job, but she was hell on my concentration. And why was she chasing me?

"Are you chasing me, Doctor?"

"Yes, Detective, I am."

"Why are you chasing me?"

"To get to the other side? I hate being a suspect. Can I see you tonight? I've got this thought—"

"I've got a drink date with a friend of mine—hell, join us. His name's Hackett. About eleven."

"That boxer-painter guy? Sounds like a real character."

Maybe Jamie was right about her and artists, or maybe he was better known than I thought—famous even in Chicago, where you had to leave to make it.

"That's the guy. The place is Tattooed Zoo—"

"South Loop. I got it. I'll meet you there." She was off the line.

After that Zachary called to say he would love to see me but, a friend of theirs, Oscar, was taking him camping. I promised him a Cubs game, which I hate, but in my sudden competition with Gomez, it seemed appropriate. Zach sounded like he missed me, and I told him that I missed him sixty times. That was an understatement.

How did they do it? I wondered—those fathers who left their kids and never looked back? Hell, I stared back, and I wasn't even leaving. Just the sound of his voice set off a slide show of memories—as well as the sure knowledge of the memories I was missing now. Loss caught me by the throat, and my voice came out harsh and gruff.

"Are you obeying your mother?" I sounded like an ogre— an ogre with a heartache.

"She's ignoring me."

"What does that mean?"

"You know. She's always busy with that guy." We both knew his name was Gomez.

"You like him?" I was struggling to sound neutral, no putting Zach in the middle.

"He's okay. After we get back from camping, he says he's going to take me to more Bulls games. Lots of them."

"Hey. That's great."

Half of me was processing Zach's news for Zach himself and half of me, the cop, was processing the news about Gomez for me. Bulls tickets were so scarce to get your hands on, Michael Jordan had to play to get his. In order for Gomez to be scoring Bulls tickets, lots of them, he had to be on the take. Unless his sister had married a player.

"Obey your mother."

"Yes, sir."

"Have fun camping."

"You're not mad at me?"

"Why would I be mad at you?"

"I wish I was going with you, Dad."

"Hey. I just want you to have fun. It's okay to go with— it's okay."

I got off the phone feeling gutted.

About five o'clock I got a call from Myerling. He wanted to talk about Johnny Vanilla. He sounded uncharacteristically urgent. I agreed to meet him for a drink.

Harold Myerling was an all right guy, which in his line of work made him an ethical giant. All the stuff you've ever heard about how the corpses are tossed around, just a piece of meat, no respect—those stories are true, but not with Myerling. At God knows what cost to himself, he has always managed to stay connected to the idea that the human flesh he deals with was once a human being. When that flesh has been shot, sliced, strangled, molested, burned, staying attached to its once-upon-a-time humanity must be a painful business. I know that's why the others numb out. It's anesthesia, like Roger Rogaine and his dumb jokes, a defense mechanism.

Harold Myerling did it the hard way. He unzipped a body bag like the spirit was still in there. "Jesuit talk," Jamie would call this. One night, drunk—my idea, not his, he was humoring me—Myerling told me he had a calling, that the dead would sometimes talk to him, even tell him their dreams. I didn't want to hear this. Like his staff, I wanted to forget the dead had ever had dreams, much less dreamed on somewhere. I've drunk with Myerling since then, but very cautiously.

We met at the Billy Goat, a newspaper bar popular with writers from both the *Trib* and the *Sun-Times*. The Billy Goat is located directly underneath Michigan Avenue, a part of the maze of underground streets that form a subterranean delivery system for the Loop. Myerling claimed they had good sandwiches there. I ate a pastrami on rye—my usual attack of appetite brought on by grisly details.

Myerling's scenario was dick first, hands second, then death. I listened to Myerling for a long time, drank while he ate, and then looked at my watch and realized I was late. By then Jamie and Dr. Winters could be newlyweds.

Chapter six

———◼———

Chicago specializes in greasy weather. I emerged from the Billy Goat with a pastrami sandwich in my stomach and a greasy feeling all over. It wasn't raining exactly, but it wasn't not raining, either. The humidity was somewhere close to a hundred percent, and the pollution filled in whatever chinks of dry air were left. I moved through something damp and gritty I hesitate to call a summer night.

"It's the dick-first part that gets you," Jamie said when I got there. I got to Jamie's slightly hammered from fatigue and two drinks with Myerling. I found him and Violet laughing together like *I Love Lucy* reruns.

"Oh, Violet."

"Oh, Jamie."

You get the picture. I hated it. This time Violet was wearing blue jeans, cowboy boots, and a denim shirt. She looked like the Marlboro Man in drag. I was relieved about that, since Jamie responds like any man would to red dresses, spike heels, and late-night hours.

"I'm afraid I'm just a little—"

"Sideways?" The doctor was a quick study.

"We knew the guy twenty years," Jamie explained.

"Then you knew he was a real sweetheart," the doctor said.

Jamie and I both looked at her. Was she saying Johnny deserved it that way? Could anybody deserve it that way?

"He was all right," Jamie said.

"Yeah," I agreed.

"Inside information, that's all," said the doctor—just what I'd been afraid of.

"You mean you fucked him?" God bless Jamie, straight for the hoop.

"Are you kidding? I ran a group for battered women and— I can't really go into it."

"She's right," said Jamie. "I'd forgotten that shit. Remember, we were kids, he was always roughing up the girl?"

"Frank's sister," I suddenly remembered. "I guess Frank broke him of the habit, so to speak."

I was remembering like yesterday Johnny with double knee casts and a sudden attitude shift.

"They never lose the taste for it," the doctor was saying.

I sensed our second late-night rendezvous heading the way of the first, but she was right about the taste for it not leaving them.

I said before the things a cop knows could fill a library. I should have said a garbage dump, or a capacious sector of hell. Cops know things other people don't want to know. We know that with certain things, the worst things, they'll do it again, or at least want to do it again, or try to do it again.

I was beginning to think Dr. Winters knew some of the same things a cop knew. I didn't know what details she had about Johnny and some woman or women he'd abused, but I knew to my bones she was right about Johnny and his thing with hurting women. Even in front of me, even with my job, our twenty-year acquaintance, the appearance of a dinner date, he'd called Dr. Winters a bitch.

"And he said I was 'dry'." She interrupted my thoughts.

"Johnny. Last night," I explained.

"Nice guy. Famous last words," joked Jamie. Violet shot him a look he should have ducked at.

"Just kidding." Jamie, uncharacteristically, was backpedaling.

I was beginning to think that Dr. Winters was not a good mixer, not with my circle of acquaintances, when she suddenly pulled a harmonica from her back pocket and ran up and down the tones a few times.

"Icebreaker," she said. "Make up the verses as we go." With that she was off and running.

> "Well, we've got a stiff named Nesbitt,
> "And if you've read the obit,
> "You know the bastard died a bastard's death.
> "Now we've got a dead Johnny,
> "We'd all think of him fondly,
> "But he was a louse who liked to beat—"

She stopped short. I finished.

"His spouse?"

"Confidentiality. Got to watch it with rhymes. Get too busy with the rhyme scheme, you tell the truth. You try it."

Call it exhaustion or Myerling's scotches. I did try it. I went barreling right into it.

> "Met a girl named Violet.
> "Hope to God that she's not violent.
> "Has she led a life of crime,
> "Or just of slime—?"

"Thank you." Violet was laughing. Jamie was staring bug-eyed at my antics.

"No interrupting him," Violet insisted. I went on.

> "Met her on a killing,
> "The worst kind, it was chilling.
> "Still, I found her pretty thrilling,
> "All the same—"

"Quite a tenor. Haven't heard that since grammar school." Jamie was trying to bail me out. I was grinning like a goon, proud of my rhymes and even a little proud of the reason for them.

"You're a nice guy, Elliot," said Violet Winters.

"Be careful, that's usually followed by a 'but,'" Jamie warned.

"It is followed by a 'but,'" Violet illustrated. "You're a nice guy, Elliot, but you look exhausted, so let's go home to bed."

"I think that's an exit line, sport," said Jamie like I was his slow younger brother.

"He gets it," Violet defended me.

I got up to go, and that's when the doorbell rang.

It was Gomez. My favorite. I thought he was supposed to be off in the north woods somewhere, camping out with my kid. Instead, he was standing on Jamie Hackett's doorstep, looking like he'd been hit by a truck.

My kid!

"Tell me," I said. "I know it's about Zach."

"Glad I found you."

"What is it?" I grabbed for Gomez. The doctor grabbed for me. She yanked me back and Jamie held me there. Maybe it was the liquor. Maybe it was the way I'd felt about Gomez for a long time. Maybe it was that some part of me knew he was there about Zach and I wanted to kill the messenger.

"Your boy, he's in the hospital. An accident. I'll drive you." Gomez was floundering. He looked scared, whether for me or because of Zach, I didn't know. I didn't care.

"Get the fuck out of here," Jamie snapped.

"Which hospital? I'll drive him. I'm a doctor," Violet said. Gomez stuttered out the hospital and fled.

"They're good there," Violet assured me. With that, Jamie tucked me into her car.

"It's kind of weird Gomez came for you," Jamie said, but I didn't really think about it.

Chapter seven

———■———

Some people who have near-death experiences talk about time slowing down. They say their life passes before their eyes like a movie. They say they watch it with clarity and gain a deep understanding of what is important.

Driving Lake Shore Drive on the way to Zachary's bedside, I had the experience they describe. I wasn't near death, but for all I knew, Zachary was. Maybe the experience I had was really his. Although I knew the doctor was driving close to a hundred, the lights on the shoreline, the distant lights of the boats on the water, all moved by slowly, like fish sliding past in an aquarium. Images moved through my consciousness the same way. I didn't see my life, but I did see Zach's: his dark, narrow head at birth; his golden curls by the time he was a year: his first crew cut and a baseball cap as he rode his new tricycle and fell on the sidewalk, splitting his lip; Zach with an armload of puppies at the children's petting zoo; Zach on a two-wheeler . . .

We left the drive at Fullerton, jagged east for two blocks, raced up the tree-lined street edging Lincoln Park, avoided being hit by a wide-turning bus, and slid into a spot by a hydrant. Then we were at the hospital.

The doctor had me by the elbow. Her badges and wherewithal, not mine, got us past the desk, down the corridor, up the elevator, down the next corridor, into a hospital room. My son's. He started crying when he saw me, telling me he didn't mean to do it. He didn't mean to.

"What, honey?" He didn't answer me or couldn't. I thought maybe he had run out into traffic, although I saw no casts, nothing that looked broken.

The nurse didn't answer for him. Gloria was in a chair by the window, rocking back and forth. Nobody was telling me anything.

Zachary was wearing a hospital gown open down the back. I took him in my arms.

"Can't somebody get him some pajamas?" I snapped, like pajamas would fix it.

"I'm Dr. Winters. What's the diagnosis?" Violet, even in her cowboy boots, got to the answer.

"Corrective surgery," the nurse said quietly. "Tomorrow morning." She handed Violet a chart. I watched her face darken and then clear by an effort of will.

"Elliot, why don't you step into the hall with me for a second?"

"Let him find out the way I did," Gloria suddenly spat out. "Let him find the blood."

"I don't understand."

"I didn't mean to do anything, Daddy—" Zachary started crying again. Gloria moved to the bed and sat beside him, glaring at me across the wings of his back as she took him in her arms.

"I didn't mean to, Daddy. I didn't, I didn't—"

"Of course not, Zach. Bad things just happen sometimes."

I reached across to stroke his back, but Gloria gathered him defensively to her bosom.

"Why don't we step outside for a minute," Violet Winters suggested. Her voice, if not her clothing, held a surgeon's authority.

"I'll go in a minute," I said. "As soon as somebody gets this kid some decent pajamas. Can't you see he's freezing?"

"Shock. Shock makes them shake," said the nurse.

"Pajamas, right," said Gomez, who had appeared.

"There's a pair in my overnight bag," Gloria began. She started crying.

"It's going to be okay, Zach," I told my son. I couldn't see anymore. I couldn't hear anymore. He was the whole world just then. I wanted to sing to him. I reached over and touched his hair.

Zachary struggled to pull himself away from his mother's embrace. He was trying to act grown-up. Gloria stiffened, and moved from the bed back to her station by the window. Now I sat on the bed. After a minute, Zachary moved into my arms. I saw Violet shaking hands with Gloria, handing her a Kleenex. I heard her say "doctor," like that explained everything. My son, my only son, was shaking in my arms.

"Did you see the Cubs won, Dad?" he asked me. "Mom says I can get Air Jordans when I get out."

The wings of his shoulders felt chilled. I wrapped the sheet higher on his back. Nobody had told me anything yet. Then I noticed that Violet was signaling for my attention. She was standing out of Zachary's line of vision and mouthing one word: RAPED.

Rape. I'd seen it happen to grandmothers, to teenage girls, to mothers. I'd heard all the rhetoric that makes you understand: Rape is about violence, not about sex. Rape is about power, not about seduction. Rape is—

The reason my son was shaking and we were all there and surgery was scheduled for the morning. He must be doped up, I realized. He must be torn, shamed—

Shamed. Rape is about shame. About rage, about—

"Your wife would like to talk to you. I'll sit with him." It was Violet, talking to me from far, far away. Zachary heard her.

"I'm Dr. Winters," she said. "I'm a friend of your daddy's."

"You look like a cowboy."

"I do, don't I? Can you play a harmonica?"

Violet gave me a nudge, and I came to. Gloria and I stepped into the hall. Abruptly, she stepped into my arms. She smelled dear and familiar—like my wife. "I'm glad you're here," she said, talking into my badge. She was shaking, just like our son.

"How, Gloria? When?"

I got the story in pieces.

Zachary had gone camping with Oscar Gomez. Gloria had gone to visit her cousin. They all got back about the same time, but Zachary was locked in the bathroom when she came home. He wouldn't come out. He wouldn't open the door. He was crying. Oscar got him to open the door. Good old Oscar.

Zachary was standing funny. He couldn't walk right. She found a bloody towel, bloody underpants. She thought maybe something in gym. Oscar said no. "It was a man," Zachary told Oscar, who in turn told Gloria. "He grabbed me."

Gloria garbled the rest, who called the doctor, somebody—how they got to the hospital, somehow.

"Is anybody looking for this guy?" I knew I wanted to find him. "Where did this happen? At the park?"

"We don't know who it is."

"Gloria, it's rape."

"If he'd told us sooner."

"What do you mean? I thought you came home and found him crying?"

"I did, but . . . the towels were old."

"What are you saying?"

"It first happened two months ago. That's what we think. It just happened again. The therapist felt there was more than one occasion."

"What? What therapist?"

"His therapist. Zach didn't tell us at first. Maybe he knew him. His therapist says—"

"How long have you known about this?" I grabbed her by the shoulders.

"A little while." She looked frightened, and she should have. "Elliot, I got him a therapist. I did all the right things. I knew if I told you, you would take him away from me, and you weren't supposed to be seeing him anyhow."

"You were hiding this from me!"

"I think Zachary was hiding this from both of us, Elliot. Obviously, if it happened more than once. It could be the cause of his nightmares. His guilt."

I almost hit her. Now she was saying—implying, anyhow—that Zach had somehow asked for it. Sex games at nine? With somebody old enough and big enough . . .

"I'm doing the best I can, Elliot. But if he knew the person and encouraged him—"

"So what if he knew him, Gloria? Does that make it different? He's a child. The other person was an adult. That's rape."

I was yelling. This was his mother talking. How had I come

to marry her? She was blaming Zachary. What was she doing when our son was getting molested?

"You stupid, stupid, stupid . . ." I was yelling. Now I was blaming her.

I got that in mid-shout and broke off in a sort of strangled growl. I heard harmonica licks from somewhere.

Gomez stuck his head out of Zachary's room. I'd thought he was on the pajama run. He stepped into the hall, right between us, saying, "Everything okay, sweetheart?" To my wife.

What could be okay? Our son had been raped. Bloody towels, hospital room, corrective surgery. What kind of monster?

"Elliot? He wants to see you," Violet stepped into the hall to tell me. "They've given him something to put him under for the night."

"And you can be back at six when he goes in. Oscar will stay with me. I've got the cot." Gloria had it all planned.

"You need to sleep a couple of hours," Violet told me. With Zachary listening from the room, there was no place for argument here. "They've got him on some strong stuff, so hurry."

I ducked back into Zachary's room. He lay flat on his back, his arms in their white hospital gown spread out like wings. I bent down and kissed him on his cheek. It felt cool, papery, and dry.

"It's all right. He's just sleeping." Violet had me by the arm. "You'll be back when they wake him."

"I'd like to stay."

"You may need some reserves for this. Tonight he won't know who's here."

"All right."

Now it was my turn to get comforted. Violet winked at me gently. "I think he's going to be a natural on harmonica."

I crept from the room into an empty hall. Gloria and Gomez had gone to the cafeteria for coffee. Dr. Winters patted my arm and kissed me on the cheek.

Somehow in the course of one evening, she had shifted from suspect to caretaker, from femme fatale to Florence Nightingale. Just because she was kind to my son did not mean she was kind to Johnny Vanilla, I reminded myself. When Jack Nesbitt died, somebody sent me her pictures, I reminded myself. Somebody thought Dr. Winters was a suspect, and I better not forget that.

"Let me get you home," the doctor said.

Chapter eight

———■———

Home?

When Gloria left me, I just couldn't ask my son to move out of his home. If I couldn't be there, at least the house could father him. So Gloria and Zach, and now Gomez, it seemed, had my brick bungalow house on the Near West and I had a bachelor's lair in a newly built high-rise on the edge of Greektown. I should have known I'd hate it.

We picked up my unmarked at Jamie's, filled him in since he was up and working, then headed for my place, where I offered Dr. Winters a drink. Her status as "suspect" was fading again.

"No, thanks. I'll meet you at the hospital, but you need some sleep."

"I guess so."

"Go to bed, Elliot. This isn't your fault. It's nobody's fault but the guy who did it."

"Sure you don't want a nightcap?"

"I am sure."

"Good thing. I couldn't fuck you with a borrowed dick tonight." Now, there's charm, Detective Mayo.

I was trying for bravado. She smiled weakly and stepped into her Porsche. I watched her taillights clear the corner, then turned and rode the elevator up to my plate glass window and three hours of sleeplessness on my living room couch. I listened to sirens instead of the stereo and told myself that any minute I would either go into the bedroom or I would fall asleep where I was.

From my window, ensconced on my fake leather couch, I could watch the show called Chicago. I was the eighteenth floor, high enough to see distance and low enough to see detail. The night my son got raped, I wanted to stand at my window with high-powered binoculars and a rifle. I wanted to watch the streets for some pervert, catch him, and when he made his move, pick him off. What I really wanted to do was turn back the clock, go home, go back to my miserable marriage and Gloria's ever-so-long-suffering bed—more fun, doubtless, with Gomez in it—go back to a time when I was sad and trapped but my son was safe and happy.

Those times did exist. I know that, although they seemed as distant as the Crusades, as likely as Scheherazade. The good old days: only the occasional murder, and that usually with a motive behind it. None of your serial killers cruising the highways like scavenging sharks. None of your Texas chain-saw massacres or Chicago's own John Wayne Gacy, killing for kicks, disposing of kids in such numbers and for so long that you had to conclude they were disposable, and that's why nobody was searching a long, long time before there were thirty-three of them, thirty-three teenage boys "disposed of" in a basement and backyard right in Chicago.

I told myself I should be grateful Zachary wasn't one of them. I told myself a lot of things, things designed to assuage my guilt. Gloria left me, not vice versa, I told myself. I tried to see Zach and she wouldn't let me, I told myself. I didn't know he was in trouble and she didn't know the kind of trouble. I told myself that last over and over. I could not afford to think of Gloria as the enemy. Boyfriend or no boyfriend, it was a hard time for her. A divorce was hard for anybody. Her judgment and focus were probably impaired by stress. She had gotten Zachary a therapist when she thought his nightmares were a signal. All she had missed was what the signal meant.

The sirens calmed down when the sun started up. So did I. At dawn's early light, I showered, shaved, pretended I had slept, and drove myself back to the hospital.

Chapter nine

—■—

The doctor met me as promised. I came up the hospital walk and saw her waiting for me in the lobby. This time there were no cowboy boots, no slinky red sheath. She wore an elegant pearl-gray suit and a manner of consummate professionalism.

"We should go right up," she said, taking my arm. "He's probably in pre-op already."

We rode the elevator to the sixth floor in silence. Small talk escaped me, and so did a great deal else. My sense of Dr. Winters as a suspect was eroding yet again. Seen on her professional turf, any thought of her as a marauding murderess seemed ludicrous. She exuded competency, calm, even virtue.

So did the man striding toward us down the hall as the elevator doors opened—a big, silver-haired, genial man.

"It's Dr. Crutcher," Violet said. "He's excellent."

"Who?"

"Dr. Crutcher. The surgeon."

"Good morning. You the father?"

"Yes." I stepped forward and offered my hand. The surgeon held his aloft.

"Already scrubbed. I insisted they reach you. A little meddling, I suppose, but a father has his rights—or should have. Oh, I'm Malcolm Crutcher. I'll be doing the needlework."

"Elliot Mayo, Dr. Crutcher."

"Pleasure, Detective."

Crutcher laughed and gifted me with his ivory smile. I knew that face from the society pages. Malcolm Crutcher was quite a fixture on the arts and philanthropy circuit. He chaired a big children's charity and had some power position with the Art Institute board. Crutcher's reputation did precede him, just as he might have hoped.

"What will you do?" I asked him. "How complicated is this?"

"It's routine. Very routine actually. Let me worry. You just relax."

"Now, there's an easy directive," I told him.

"I'll let you know how it went, but these things are simple—just like taking a little tuck."

With that, Crutcher vanished toward the operating theater and I stared numbly into space.

"He's good," Dr. Winters informed me, taking my arm. "I've sent him many cases. Your boy's in very good hands."

Seated on the Naugahyde chairs next to the coffee station, I learned some of the things that doctors know that even cops can't imagine.

Corrective rectal surgery is not uncommon, Violet told me. Corrective vaginal and rectal in little girls. The usual gloss is that the kid was exploring, playing doctor, and somehow managed to rip himself wide open—not likely.

"They say with a bottle or a cucumber," she laughed

bitterly. "Fortunately, it's a fairly simple repair—not unlike an episiotomy."

"A what?"

"That snip they like to make for an easier delivery. You know, repair of the birth canal."

My stomach was crawling around inside me. The doctor was talking rips, tears, and large foreign objects. It was my son in there on the table, ripped and torn. The foreign object was some guy's cock.

"I've done my share of it myself," Dr. Winters was saying. "The worst is when you know, or you're pretty damn sure, that the person responsible is right there with you, the concerned dad or mom who just can't imagine how this happened to little Billy—and for the second or third or fourth time. At least the authorities are getting better."

"We are?"

"You cops aren't the only authorities. I mean the state agencies. They finally accept that incest exists and nice people do it."

"Nice people. Think there are any of them left?"

Dr. Winters didn't answer because Malcolm Crutcher stepped out then to say Zachary was recovering nicely and he'd be "good as new."

I doubted that.

Chapter ten

There were no nice people at Johnny Vanilla's funeral, or if there were, I didn't see them. Half the old neighborhood was there—the half that had made it this far—and the rest of the crowd was the uptown clientele he'd been so proud of, a lot of slick suits and champagne blondes. A lot of sick curiosity, if you asked me. Which nobody did. I wore a suit and tried to act like I wasn't working.

I expressed my condolences to Johnny's ex-wife, Esther, a North Shore girl who'd given Johnny a couple of miscarriages and a lot of her money before he connected up with the kind of cash he needed and she'd given him a quick divorce. Smart girl, Esther. She'd known when to fold her cards. I kissed Johnny's mother and called it a tragedy. I was glad his dad was gone a few years now, because this would have killed the old man for sure. I thought a little about how a man like Charles Vanilla, a workingman, could have raised a son like Johnny Vanilla, an angle shooter from the cradle, on the make since elementary school—which was where I'd made his acquaintance, Jamie reminded me as they were lowering the coffin. I'd seen him slip in dressed like a grave digger with his bandanna and working clothes.

"This is about what Sister Clarasine expected. Remember how she'd call Johnny a bad seed? Think maybe she predisposed him to a life of crime?"

Jamie was kidding.

"That, or she was just a great handicapper."

"Hmmm."

I jerked my head to where Father Damian was mouthing his usual platitudes. At sixty-five, he'd run out of new material forty years earlier, when Jamie and I served as senior altar boys at the nine o'clock Mass and Johnny Vanilla, a novice, was already stealing from the collection plate.

Johnny was the thief. Father Damian knew he was the thief. We all did. Father Damian had heard his confession about being a thief, Johnny bragged, but he counted on seal-of-the-confessional confidentiality. Jamie and I talked about beating the crap out of Johnny, but we didn't because of his father and because "he'd grow out of that junk."

But he never did.

When Johnny Vanilla died, Father Damian was the only one who acted like it was surprising. Maybe he'd forgotten all those confessions, or maybe the seal of the confessional had struck him dumb in more ways than one.

Jamie and I kicked dirt side by side listening to Father Damian describe nobody we'd ever met, certainly not our boy Johnny.

"A pillar of his community, a comfort and strong right arm for his mother, Maria . . ."

I thought Jamie was going to start giggling if he kept it up. Of course, Maria Vanilla wept as though every word were true, as though her son John Anthony had ever been anything but a heartbreak to her, to her late husband, to anybody, ever, who'd trusted a word he said through those golden smiles he traded on.

"He should have been a movie star," Gloria told me once. We were eating at Johnny's first joint, one Esther's money had bankrolled. I got it about Johnny and women—or about Gloria and Latin lovers, for that matter.

Father Damian was up to the holy water and shovel of dirt when Big John made his appearance. I saw his limo oozing up the cemetery curves, when Jamie whispered to me, too loudly, "D'Amato decided to show."

"Good business."

The timing was a little gauche, but I'd been expecting D'Amato, the family money behind Jacky and Johnny's and my prime suspect. I'm sure he knew that. John D'Amato emerged from his limo dressed in Armanis and carrying a single red rose. One of his flunkies carried a dozen more to press on poor Maria.

"He was a good boy," I heard D'Amato say, kissing both of Maria's wet and wrinkled cheeks.

"A good boy. Almost like a son."

Then the flunky handed her the roses and D'Amato tossed his, slowly and deferentially, onto the soft brown loam being used to cover Johnny. I caught his eye as he headed for the car. He's been expecting me, his look said.

As Mafia hoods went, D'Amato was a class act. Not the Armanis, not the roses—that was show. I'm talking about business. He didn't get into the worst of it—the crack, the guns to kids in projects—and it cost him money. I respected him for that, if you can be said to respect a man who restricted his illegal activities to whores, numbers, gambling, and "leveraged" real estate deals. In a sense, D'Amato was a throwback. He didn't like drugs, wasn't interested in joint ventures with the black dope dealers or the Latins. In a sense,

Big John D'Amato was just a neighborhood guy who'd made it—and according to his own lights, within the rules. That was my make on him. That was everybody's.

The only misstep I'd ever seen him take was his fondness for Johnny Vanilla. Even there, there was a reason. The one piece of success that had eluded D'Amato was fathering a son. He and his wife had four girls. He and his longtime mistress had another—a boy would have won her John's divorce. He really wasn't kidding, John D'Amato, when he told Maria Johnny was like a son to him. It was the closest he got.

Which didn't mean he wasn't still a suspect. Personal affections aside, if Johnny had crossed him at business, he'd have done whatever was necessary. When I told Jamie a Mafia hit, a copycat, it rang true to me. Nodding to John D'Amato, I didn't rule him out. I considered it well in the realm of possibility that Johnny Vanilla's killer was joining me in paying my respects.

I scanned the crowd. I got a nod from Judge Ricky Noonan, a neighborhood guy. Jerry Delancey, the snitch, was there. Also Tommy and Trudy and a few other regulars from the Hub. I saw a heavily veiled stump of a woman that I recognized as Angela Remo's mother, D'Amato's sister. For a second I thought I saw Violet Winters. I started toward her, but the crowd shifted, moving between us. I paid my respects to Johnny's mother. When I looked up again, the blonde was gone.

Chapter eleven

———■———

The Irish have a sweet tooth. In my case, it's more of a sweet fang. Working on a grisly murder serves in some backward fashion to whet my appetite, and what that appetite is really for is sugar. Maybe a spoonful of sugar makes the medicine go down. I do know that a double hot fudge sundae seems to help me to digest unpalatable facts.

Leaving Johnny Vanilla's funeral, I had a real craving for a double hot fudge. The cemetery was a mile and a half from my parents' home, right down the road from my cousin Charles's. I decided to pay an impromptu visit and see if I could lure Charles into being a partner in crime.

I rang the bell at my cousin Charles's bungalow, the bungalow that had belonged to his parents.

"You're early." Charles answered the bell, and then, "Why, Elliot! I was expecting a client. But come in, come in."

Charles was an accountant who ran his flourishing business out of what was once the dining room and sitting room of his home. He worked at the large oval cherry table where

I'd enjoyed many holiday dinners. No one, not Charles and not his clients, seemed to find this arrangement odd.

Maybe it was Charles's domestic personality that made the arrangement seem normal. "Betty Crocker with a beard," Charles described himself, and although the beard was really a mustache, the description was accurate.

"I won't keep you, Charles. But I will take a glass of water."

"Water? I've got coffee, tea, homemade lemonade?"

"Lemonade." Charles loved to fuss.

"This guy is always late. I don't know why I put up with it. My goodness, Elliot, you do look dreadful. Sit down. Let me see if I can find you some cookies."

"Actually, I'm in the mood for a double hot fudge, and I stopped by as a near occasion of sin."

"Yes, yes. You've always been a lower companion as far as my dining habits go."

Charles pinched his waist, which was expansive. There was, as there always had been, a softness to Charles's physique that had made him the butt of grade-school jokes. Poor Charles. The last to be picked for team sports. He compensated by a mind kept fit by *New York Times* crossword puzzles.

"I guess you heard about Zachary." My mother knew, and if my mother knew, the world as she knew it knew. That would include Cousin Charles.

"Yes, yes. I heard. I'm so sorry."

"He doesn't remember anything, Charles."

"It's just as well. Ah! Here are those macaroons." Charles was rummaging in his freezer. "Unless you'd prefer English toffee bars? Aunt Helen's recipe."

I loved English toffee bars, and said so.

"They may be a little tricky to defrost in the micro, but I'll give it a try."

"Great."

"Who does Gloria think it is?" Charles asked.

"Screw Gloria. She made it sound like Zachary asked for it. She thinks it's someone he knows."

"Maybe it is."

"Come on, Charles. My son does not exactly consort with known—" I stopped short.

"If you were going to say homosexuals, Elliot, I would have to set you straight. Child molesting is not a homosexual predilection. Not that some homosexuals don't do it, but it's something else entirely from being gay. Child molesters, straight or gay, are into power. It's the power, not the sex, that's the issue. Oh, damn! I've melted these." Charles took the plate of molten toffee from the microwave. "Want to try it over ice cream?"

I nodded.

"Molesting an innocent child. I've got no stomach for it— and I certainly have no stomach for you acting like it's a homosexual crime."

"Calm down, Charles. Did I say that?"

"You almost did. And I've been working on your consciousness for years!"

This was true. Charles and I were very close, and always had been. When he chose to officially come out as a gay, I was the family member he first told. As far as I know, I am also the only family member who believed him. The rest took it as a whim, a passing phase. The fact that the phase hadn't passed after twenty years did nothing to rock their denial.

"Here's your ice cream." Charles slammed down the bowl on his kitchen table.

"Oh, for God's sake. Let's change the subject, Charles."

"Why? For all I know, next thing you'll be accusing me."

I stared at Charles in amazement. In his coming-out announcement, Charles had made it clear that his ideal of homosexual love revolved around lofty platonic ideals and a certain standard of physical perfection approximating Adonis. Hardly a taste for young boys. I doubted I was manly enough for Charles.

"That witch of a wife of yours wouldn't let him go to the zoo with me. And you know how Zachary loves the zoo!"

"Gloria?" Charles nodded, tears in his eyes. "She wasn't letting him see me, either, Charles. I'm sure she didn't mean—"

"Oh, yes, she did."

"Maybe so. She's not always a very enlightened woman."

Charles was dabbing at his eyes. I was swabbing up the last of a creditable hot toffee sundae, when the doorbell rang.

"Oh, dear. That must be my eleven o'clock. Are my eyes all red?"

"Not really."

"Could you let yourself out the back, Elliot? I wouldn't want to give my client the wrong impression."

"This isn't Mr. Right?"

"No, no, I'm afraid not. He's had fifteen years to make his move, and nothing. Do I really look all right?"

"You look fine. I'll let myself out."

"Don't forget to set your dish in the sink."

With that, Charles fussed with his shirt and headed to the front of the house. I heard his effusive greeting all the way back in the kitchen, but I fought my impulse to sneak a peek at Cousin Charles's Mr. Right.

And yes, I set my dish in the sink.

———■———

Despite the help from Charles's toffee sundae, I still couldn't figure Johnny Vanilla. A gambling debt? I'd have heard about gambling. A crime of passion? Call me sexist, but lipstick or no, I didn't believe a woman had done that to Johnny. To my eye—blind, maybe—it looked like an Outfit hit. Mob guys indulged in the most flamboyant killings. Meat hooks, freezers, car trunks—they're routine. What you don't read about are the dicks-in-mouth, the tongues cut out, the digits missing. The Outfit is big on sending messages, and how they do it is body language. Dick in mouth: You fucked me. Tongue cut out: You talked. Digits missing: It's not your pie. Johnny Vanilla's death fit with this code. Dick in sink and hands gone. What did that mean?

Chicago settled into a week-long heat wave. Brownouts were frequent as air conditioners ran on high and tempers ran on red alert. I put in ninety hours of useless digging on Johnny Vanilla. Nobody knew nothing. At least I asked them. I even asked Big John D'Amato. I called him up just like a citizen.

"Let's get together for a little chat," I said. I pictured Big John thinking this over in his "office" over on Taylor Street. I knew him to spend his days doing business from the back of an Italian restaurant, officially closed until dinner.

"Are you drunk, Detective?"

"A short chat."

"Are you crazy?"

"I'm getting nowhere on Johnny Vanilla."

"Which makes me a suspect?"

"Come on, John."

"He was like a son to me."

"So cut me a break."

"Why? Are you like a son to me?"

"I hope not, John."

He laughed at that.

"You got balls, Detective. Phoning me up."

"You're an American, John. I can call you. Dope?"

"I don't answer questions. You want Q and A, you get a subpoena."

"I thought girls, weird sex."

There was a silence, a long silence. Bingo.

"Leave it alone, Detective. He was a good boy."

"So help me out."

"Leave it the fuck alone."

I thanked Big John and we ended with neighborhood pleasantries. Or tried to.

"His dad was good to me, John . . ." I said. "He'd want me to get to the bottom."

"His dad was good to everybody, Detective. Leave his son rest in peace. Do us both a favor."

"It's my job, John."

"Yeah. Some job."

"I like it."

"I guess you do."

"So call me if anything comes to you."

This was a sore point.

"I'll call you if I grow wings."

John D'Amato was cooperative after his fashion, according to his code. I knew he'd call me right after he'd polished his toenails.

For my part, I came away thinking that Johnny Vanilla's sexual life had been a source of problems for D'Amato. I'd hit on something with the phrase "weird sex," and my next question was, how weird?

I thought I knew where to find the answer.

Chapter twelve

———■———

Esther Vanilla, or Esther Newton Vanilla Newton, Johnny's ex-wife, agreed to see me. To her it was all part of being responsible.

I'd met Esther once or twice back when Johnny was running his first restaurant and she was in love with him and playing hostess to class the joint up. Esther was nothing if not classy, and she was slumming when she hooked up with Johnny—not that she thought so at the time.

Back then, Johnny hung the stars and moon, and Esther polished them for him. Her money, or her father's money, had put Johnny in business for himself. You'd have thought he'd invented the wheel for all the modesty he displayed.

"Not bad, eh?" I remembered him asking me and Gloria, indicating his restaurant and his new wife in the same backhanded sweep. I wondered, driving to Esther's home nine years later, if he'd used that backhand on her.

Esther Newton lived in Winnetka now, in a gracious Georgian showcase with good landscaping as manicured as Esther herself.

When I pulled into the drive, a yard boy was tidying up under the azaleas. I walked past him along the curving flagstone walk to the front door, trying not to step on the border of tiny purple flowers that grew between the stones. When Esther Newton opened the front door to me, she was not the same beauty I remembered. She was even lovelier, serene now instead of merely chic.

"We've met," I said as she showed me into her living room.

"At the Hot Spot," she agreed. "I never forget a customer. How's your wife?"

"We're divorced."

"Sorry."

"Nice place." The room looked floral, and so did Esther. She was blooming without Johnny.

"It's a relief. Johnny's taste ran to chrome and glass. Drink?"

"Coffee."

"Of course. How silly. You're working."

Esther disappeared and came back with coffee, cookies, a pie.

"Still in the restaurant business," she joked. "Or maybe I should have been a flight attendant. Coffee? Cream, sugar?"

"Black. With pie." I liked this lady.

Esther cut a slice of what looked like homemade apple. I caught myself wondering how a nice girl, et cetera, got caught up with Johnny Vanilla. Might as well start at the deep end.

"I'm sorry about Johnny."

"Thank you. It's really not necessary."

"Is this your genteel way of saying he was a son of a bitch?"

"Something like that."

"Well, then. Who do you think did it?"

Esther was pouring coffee for herself. She poured carefully and added cream and two sugars before she answered me.

"Rationally, I have absolutely no idea," she said. "Not rationally."

"And irrationally?"

She stirred her coffee. She stared out the window at the azaleas. She smiled thinly when she spoke. "Irrationally, I thought it was a woman."

"A woman. Why would that be?" I hung out the question and waited.

"Well, maybe it's just revenge fantasies, but Johnny . . . How much do you know about me and Johnny?"

She sipped her coffee. The cup shook. I let her have her sip and just raised my eyebrows to say, "Go on."

"You know I paid for his first couple joints? You know I left when he and John D'Amato found each other? You know I almost died?"

"I heard you had a miscarriage, maybe two."

"You call them miscarriages. I call them murders. He beat the first one out of me. The second time, he helped me down the stairs."

"You never pressed charges?"

"I thought it was the coke. He had a real habit for a while. Used to hang out with some guy he called The Hose. Like vacuum cleaner. He'd come home—when he came home—wired for sound and real nasty. Whatever they did together, it left him in a bloodthirsty mood."

"But it wasn't the coke?"

"Not the second time. I started trying to leave."

"How'd you get out?"

"You'll laugh. It was pretty smart."

"Try me."

"Johnny didn't want to divorce me, but I knew he had a

thing in place with D'Amato. He didn't need me anymore, and I definitely didn't need him. I went to D'Amato and said, 'I'm divorcing Johnny. Make him let me go. I'm not Catholic. I'm not good for him. Johnny wants children. Help me.'"

"You're right. It was shrewd. Johnny got his partner and you got out."

"I had to. I had my dreams, too."

From the back of the house I heard a child's voice.

"Yours?"

"Finally—and with great difficulty. Come to Mama, Lillian."

Esther held out her arms to a tiny Asian girl in a pale yellow sunfrock. Lillian toddled to her mama.

"Lillian, this is Elliot. Elliot, this is Lillian."

"Hello, Lillian. Esther, you've been very helpful."

Esther showed me the door and Lillian waved me bye-bye.

Esther thought it was a woman. I thought that was a revenge fantasy, but maybe not. What I wanted to know was what Johnny Vanilla and Jack Nesbitt did together besides coke.

One of the things I learned, working sex crimes, was that in the same way a coke habit could make for some odd companions, a sex habit could do the same thing. It creates a sort of grid, an interlocking network of people connected only by their addiction.

I remember when coke first struck Chicago in a big way, when it went from being an underground, bohemian musician's drug to being a commodity in demand with thrill-seeking suburbanites. Violence went along with it, and at first we couldn't figure the thing out: What was a nice, white, middle-class high school boy from Grayslake doing turning up dead in a urban housing project on the South Side? The answer was drugs.

After a while we knew that, and when we ran across a weird grid—how does this black hospital orderly come to know this Junior League Highland Park matron?—we began to look for the drug connection between them.

It was the same with sex and sex clubs. A taste for certain sexual acts might very well introduce two people whose only point of social contact was genital. Raid a Chicago strip joint and you came up with farmers from Des Moines, stockbrokers who lived in the Hancock Building, guys who drove delivery trucks. The same is true with adult bookstores, with gay clubs, with hookers, male and female.

I headed back to the city along Lake Shore Drive. I took the long curve past the giant cemetery south of Evanston, thinking less about the dead than the living. Esther Newton had helped me, but my cop was tapping out stop-look-listen. Something didn't add up. I was still looking at the sex angle.

I passed Howard Street and headed into Rogers Park. Ten blocks in, I pulled onto Estes and took it to the lake. I know there are Chicagoans who love the lake, swim in it, sail on it, run by it, bike by it, treat it as a recreational facility. I use it to think.

I left the unmarked and walked out to the grubby waterline. The lake was a silver slab stretching east to Michigan. Johnny beat Esther, Esther stayed. Johnny beat Esther, Esther went to Johnny's partner. She got her divorce, Johnny got his Mafia money, and Big John D'Amato got . . . ?

Bingo: weird sex. Big John D'Amato got an earful of Johnny Vanilla's kinky tastes, and a blackmail lever if he wanted it. Smart girl, Esther.

I got back to the unmarked just in time to see a pit bull peeing on my front wheel. A young Latin gang kid getting his rocks off. Big mean dog, big mean chain to "teach the dog."

He still looked scared when I said, "Hey, you. Kid!" He grabbed the dog and ran.

I drove to the gas station in the elbow of Sheridan Road where Devon meets the lake. I called Esther Newton.

"Esther? Detective Mayo here."

"It was nice to see you, Detective. Did you forget something?"

"Weird sex, Esther. How weird?"

There was a very long silence. I let it grow.

"He liked choking," Esther said. "He liked you real stoned and out of it, half dead practically, and then he'd pretend to choke you."

"You've been a sport. That Lillian's pretty special."

"Thanks, Detective. And, Detective? Don't call me back if you can help it."

Chapter thirteen

———■———

I called Violet Winters at her office. She was in surgery, I was told, and would get back to me. I asked that she meet me at nine at P.O.E.T.S., an underground bar on Division Street. It was owned by Ronnie, an ex-cop, and offered me some protection, if not anonymity. It was time to ask the tough questions.

"I feel like I've been called to a summit meeting," Violet said, sliding into my booth. This time the dress was hyacinth silk and matched her eyes. "Am I here for the third degree?"

"Maybe," I allowed. "I need to ask you some questions."

"If it's marriage, I'll get back to you," she joked, "after about three scotches."

I signaled the waiter, who arrived with the speed of a rush hour bus. Meanwhile Violet and I looked each other over.

"You look tired, Detective."

"I'm just old."

"I like grown-ups."

"You were in surgery?"

"Tuesdays."

"You make it sound like laundry."

"After a point it is. I clean up society's stains, blots and tears. . . . What is wrong with this waiter?"

"Ronnie! Scotch rocks," I called across the room to the bar, where Ronnie was swabbing up spilled beers.

Violet Winters looked tired herself. She was thinner than I remembered and even more pale. Her eyes were surrounded by dark circles, and I thought I saw a shadow in them. It looked like fear.

"I need to ask you some tough questions."

"Don't sugar-coat it. Just give me a minute to numb out, okay?" Violet's drink arrived and she sipped it. "Shoot," she said.

"Where were you on the night of Jack Nesbitt's murder?"

"I don't know."

Violet faced me across the table. She held her scotch glass in both hands.

"Where were you the night of Johnny Vanilla's murder? After you left me, that is?"

"I don't know."

"What do you mean, you don't know?"

"I mean I don't know."

"You're a professional. You don't keep a desk calendar?"

"I've been having trouble."

"Trouble?"

"Trouble remembering."

Violet looked at me with those moist hyacinth eyes. Her pale skin had a faint slick sheen. She was sweating, I realized—sitting in the blast of air-conditioning, sweating.

"Are you drinking?" I asked.

"These aren't alcoholic blackouts. I wish they were."

"What, then?"

"I think they're some sort of flashback."

"To what?"

"I don't know. I just sort of disappear."

"CAT scan?"

"A tumor would be good news. I had the CAT scan. No dice."

"What's your theory, Doctor?"

Violet took a long, deep breath and looked at me. She gripped my hands in hers across the table. "It's possible," she said, "that I am a multiple. If I were treating me, that would be my first guess."

I tried to remain calm. I forced myself to meet her eyes as I stroked the backs of her hands with my thumbs. Her skin felt waxy, and her hands shook.

"What, exactly, is a multiple?" I was thinking—*Sybil, The Three Faces of Eve.* I told her that, and she smiled grimly.

"Basically," Violet said. "It's a coping device. When the personality cannot handle an intolerable trauma, it may create another personality that can handle it. It's a little like building a closet and putting something away."

"Do you think you are a multiple, Violet?" Even asking the question, I felt a glassy calm icing over my emotions. I was matching Violet's clinical tone with a clinical detachment of my own.

"I don't think so," she answered after a long while. "It's more likely something is trying to surface. Something I missed in therapy. Whatever it is, it's something so terrible, I am disassociating from it."

"That's quite a set of options."

"Yes. Are you going to take me in?"

"No. It's presumed innocent, Violet. I've got nothing to link you to the scene of a crime—nothing but motive in both cases."

"Lots of people had motive, Detective. We're not talking about two boy scouts."

"That's why we're having this drink instead of taking statements, Doctor."

"That's quite a set of options, Detective."

"Exactly. By the way, Doctor, what were you doing at Johnny Vanilla's funeral?"

"Don't scare me."

"What were you doing there?"

"I said, don't scare me. I wasn't there."

"Sure you were. I saw you," I told her.

"Wait. Just a minute." She dug out her purse, opened it, took out a date book, and thumbed it frantically.

"It was last Tuesday."

"Exactly! I couldn't have been there. I was in surgery."

She showed me her little book with "surgery" penciled in.

"Seeing is believing," she said.

"Exactly. I saw you at that funeral."

"Not possible, Detective."

"Maybe not, but seeing is believing, and I know what I saw."

"I'll put you in touch with my staff. Of course they'll say I was in surgery—I was."

Ronnie was watching us closely. I could almost hear him wondering the nature of our connection. I was wondering that myself.

"Who else was there?" Violet asked.

"Mainly neighborhood—Jamie, Judge Ricky Noonan—"

"Sounds like a Native American name," Violet interrupted. "Judge Ricky Noonan. Chief Who-Laughs-Out-Loud. Farting Bear."

She gestured toward the bar, where big, bearish Ronnie did look like a constipated grizzly.

"What about me?" I asked.

"Solemn Bear," she answered. "Thorn-In-Paw."

"Pain-In-Butt, Doctor. That's you. Care for another?"

"Surgery tomorrow."

"Anything tricky?"

"No. I do the easy stuff—tonsils, adenoids. Anything complicated goes to Crutcher. He's a master craftsman."

"Sounds a little callous applied to flesh and blood."

"We doctors are a little callous, Detective. Just like you cops."

I signaled Ronnie for the check.

They found Johnny's hands in a Dumpster. The Dumpster was on the Near North Side, just off Lincoln, near Altgeld—in the very alleyway where Dillinger bought it. Maybe it was an homage. Some industrious alcoholic, scavenging for beer cans to recycle, had landed right on them. They were missing one finger.

It must have been a sobering experience.

I rode over and looked at the Dumpster, not because I expected to find anything. It was behind a Mexican restaurant and next to a pocket park that suburban skinheads were fond of. You could find them there every weekend pretending to be gang members.

I paid my regards to my North Side comrades and headed down to meet Johnny's hands at Myerling's. We were assuming they were Johnny's hands.

I cut south on Halsted and passed just west of the Cabrini Green projects. At North Avenue—which naturally runs east–west—I spotted a young gay hustler. The kid couldn't have been older than fifteen. Black and nervous, dressed in a pair of leather pants and a silk shirt open to the waist. I watched as a BMW sedan pulled over and the kid leaned in to set his price. The right one, it seemed. The driver leaned across and opened the passenger door—he looked like a family man in his mid-forties—and the kid hopped in and directed him to take a quick left and head down into the factory area. I figured the guy had a fifty–fifty chance of getting mugged as well as blown when he got there. Hustlers usually work five blocks farther west. This kid was probably a decoy for a gang from the projects.

I wondered how long he had been turning tricks. Working vice, I had run into hustlers who claimed to have started at Zachary's age. I learned to believe them.

Zachary was home from the hospital. I had come to realize that my invitation to the hospital that night had been a calculated move aimed at defusing my anger. According to Gloria, Zachary was now in intensive therapy, but still unable to retrieve the details of what happened to him. I had violently mixed feelings about that. As a cop, I wanted him to remember. As his father, I wanted him to forget. Gloria said the therapist opposed hypnosis. I felt that was just as well. Let the events slide back into the darkness from which they came. Let Zach emerge into the sunny childhood he deserved. He was a normal child. What had happened was an aberration, no fault of his own.

Above all, I wanted Gloria to keep her interpretations and innuendoes out of it. Except for essential information, I hadn't spoken with her since the hospital hallway. I didn't want to say anything I would regret. Meanwhile, I bought Zach a VCR and all the Disney movies on tape. For good measure, I rounded up all the classic westerns I had loved as a boy—*Red River, She Wore a Yellow Ribbon,* and *Fort Apache*— and I dropped them by, along with the outsized color TV I had bought for my bachelor life and neither watched nor needed. When Zach called to thank me, I thought his voice was slurred.

"Percodan," Gloria told me. "For the pain." Her voice sounded slurred with pain as well.

Harold Myerling didn't want to talk about Johnny's hands. He wanted to talk about the Nesbitt case.

"I've been thinking," he said. "About that paper cutter? I am not sure it could have done the job. Not without more damage to the bone. A surgical saw may be our weapon."

"C'mon, Harold. You're a careful man. I've never known you to reverse yourself this way."

"Let's just say I performed a few little tests."

I thought of the Warren Commission and their tests with human corpses to assay the condition of the bullet said to have killed the president.

"I'm not sure I want to know what tests."

"No. Probably not."

"May I ask why you performed these tests?"

"Doubt."

"Ah. Thanks, Harold. All this time I've been looking for a guy armed with a paper cutter. You've really widened the field."

Myerling laughed. He printed the severed hands quickly and efficiently, and I took the nine prints back to check them against Johnny Vanilla's.

They matched. I called Jamie and told him the good news.

"So come over," he invited. "Unless you're seeing that blonde."

"I haven't spoken to Dr. Winters recently," I told him. "She's back on my suspects list."

"I'll bet she is," he snorted through the phone. "Most wanted."

"Not these days. I'm avoiding her. And her sex in general, I might add."

"This too shall pass. Come on over."

The city was heating up for its summer crime barbecue. The humidity had to be ninety-plus. You might as well stand in a bucket of warm beer. Heat lightning was flickering out over the lake, great sheets of dull light blinking on and off like a broken neon sign. Ah, Chicago.

I headed over to Jamie's thinking that the thing with Zachary, or maybe the things with Nesbitt, Vanilla, and Zachary, had resulted in my sex drive dropping to zero, beyond zero, into the negative numbers. I'm sure this is a textbook reaction. I know it is. I've read the textbooks.

Not for nothing did the Jesuits save me from the streets and shepherd me through St. Ignatius and then Loyola before I joined the force. My neighborhood excels in two splendid species of urban manhood: cop and robber. The Jesuits had helped me make a choice and blessed me with a lifelong reading habit that enriched my street education and gave me a name for some of it, sometimes a Latin name. Confronted with my depressed sex life and my aborted affair with Dr. Winters, I called it coitus absentus interminus.

"Oh, shit" is how I put it to Jamie when he opened the door with a paint rag in one hand and a Coors in the other. "All I need is you drinking."

"Not for me, for you," he said. "You're still waiting for me to tie one on, aren't you?"

"Maybe."

Jamie led the way to the back of his studio, where carnage was in progress on an eight-by-ten canvas.

"It's been three years. Have a little faith."

"I've got nothing but faith. What I could use is some charity."

"Maybe you could get some from the good doctor."

"My dick's in hiding these days," I told him, back to my sex life. "I'm just not interested, and I'm avoiding her—or it is."

"It'll be back," he assured me. "Hope springs eternal, and so does the cock—at least so far."

He was throwing what looked like blood at the base of a canvas, swabbing it with a rag tied around his tennis shoes, and then glazing what was left with a tiny torch. Hopping around on one foot, bobbing and weaving with the torch, he looked like a madman or a shaman. I tried his powers of augury.

"Think she likes me?"

"The doctor? Shit, yes. Or else she's guilty."

"There's a swell thought—which I've been entertaining anyway."

"She's an entertaining broad."

That was one way to put it. For the past week I'd been running through my images of her like flash cards. Would the real Violet Winters please stand up?

Suspect identifying her breasts, as per photo by Nesbitt.

Lady in red, tracing a foot down my skin, trashing Johnny Vanilla.

Same lady, same night, confessing to Nesbitt molesting her at age twelve, the age she looked when she said it.

Same lady, Marlboro-style, playing harmonica for me and Jamie, playing angel of mercy for my son.

Same lady, new game, now playing hide-and-seek with her own memory.

"She's a toy for grown-ups," Jamie warned me now. "Like a loaded gun."

"Hey. I never even kissed her."

"That's your problem. Besides, it's ones like that that bust your balls. Remember Elizabeth Minerini?"

He named a redhead who led me a merry chase before marrying big. I still had a soft spot for her. I'd see her Sundays at St. Angela's, all dolled up with her two little girls, beaming at the goon she married. I lusted after her three long—and need I say hard?—years in college before it dawned on me "not tonight" was "no," just nicely.

"I can be a slow learner."

"The doc's like a fucking bar exam, you ask me."

"Did I?"

"You should have."

"I never touched her."

"You keep saying that. My theory is, you should have. That way, it's lousy and you're over her."

We both knew this theory was hogwash. What were the odds of sex with Violet Winters being lousy? Now, there was a dangerous line of inquiry.

"What's a regressed pedophile?" Jamie threw this one out just as he lobbed another glob of his red at the canvas. The paint and the question both oozed in front of us.

"It's a guy who—why do you ask?"

"No reason."

"Right. I really believe that."

"Just give the answer. Save the psycho-schmycho."

I kicked the answer around, settled for short form. "It's a guy who does kids but doesn't see anything wrong with it because in his mind he's a kid himself. Regressed . . . pedophile. Get it?"

"Hell, no. I don't get it. Do you?" Jamie asked.

"So what's the scoop? You didn't just pull the question out of the air."

"I ran into Nesbitt's dealer at a benefit, the Doctors' Ball. Carson Stoufley was his name. He said that he heard that someone said—"

"That Nesbitt was a regressed pedophile."

"How'd you know?" Jamie stared at me. I felt faintly pleased.

"He sure as fuck was a child molester," I volunteered. "Whether he thought he was a child himself, that I don't know."

"No shit. How'd you get that?"

I turned the question aside.

Jamie was impressed with me again. I didn't tell him about Violet Winters, victim and now survivor. Let him think I'm super sleuth.

"Why do you go to those things?"

"What things?"

"Benefits. Don't tell me you ever sold a painting there."

"Sure I have—indirectly. This one had good food, and the guy who ran it is on the board at the Art Institute. He and I had a nice chat about beefing up their contemporary collection. He was a real knowledgeable guy. A doctor."

"Malcolm Crutcher," I informed him, a knowledgeable guess.

"Very good," Jamie conceded. "Is this town getting smaller, or are you getting better?"

"Fish in a barrel. I just met the guy myself. He was Zachary's surgeon."

"Seemed like a nice guy—claimed he liked my work. And what about Crutcher's wife? She's a real dish." Jamie all but smacked his lips.

"Never met her. Never met Crutcher socially. I was standing in a hospital corridor hoping my son would survive. But Dr. Winters says he's good."

"Now, there's a recommendation."

"Come on, Jamie. What have you got against her?"

"She gives me the creeps, the way she looks at me. Like I'm a snack or something."

"I'm sure there's more than one woman who'd say you made them feel that way. She's just turned the tables."

"So I'm a sexist pig. So what?"

"I like her, that's what."

"Elliot, you like anything that gives you a sense of danger. Why do you think you're a cop?"

"Save the psycho-schmycho, social climber."

"How's the kid?"

I told him about Zach's amnesia—"Repression, right?" and the possibility of hypnosis.

Jamie had an edge to him, an edge I seldom saw even when he was "power painting" or "slinging the shit," as he called it.

"What's eating you?"

"He's my godson." The words were spat out.

Suddenly, I got it. Jamie was feeling guilty. Like something he could have done would have changed things for Zach. I made my speech, the one I practiced on myself.

"Jamie. It's not your fault. It's not Zachary's fault. It's nobody's."

Jamie was not convinced.

"Maybe if I'd seen him more—I was kind of an absentee godfather, don't you think? First I'm drunk, then I'm doing my brilliant career. Maybe if I'd spent a little more time—"

"Some sick fuck wouldn't have grabbed him? I doubt it. Besides, you saw him a lot. I saw him a lot. Hell, Oscar Gomez saw him all the time." I stopped, sounding defensive even to me. "I know how you feel," I said finally. "I wish I'd seen him more or better. I wish I hadn't holed up in my work when things got bad with Gloria. But we're not talking a dearth of father figures, Jamie. We were there—just not there at that moment, and that's what hurts. But he had a plethora of father figures."

"Plethora," Jamie snorted. "You and that Jesuit talk. I'm surprised they didn't turn you into a lawyer." He was winding down.

"They might yet."

"I'll commit crimes and you defend me. How does that sound?" With Jamie's temper, it sounded all too plausible. I made a joke of it.

"Keep painting like that and we've got a great defense. Total insanity. Jamie was now lying on his back, scooting his stocking feet across the canvas. "If anybody saw how you do this, they'd never take you serious. Next you'll be making snow angels."

"Next I'll be counting sheep. Go home, copper. You're yawning."

"What was the name of Nesbitt's dealer again?"

"Carson Stoufley. Real Gold Coast guy. You'll see."

"That's my plan."

Chapter fourteen

———■———

I went home. I opened my mailbox and found a crisp linen note that read "Why are you avoiding me?" I also found Johnny Vanilla's finger. The note was from Violet Winters.

You're probably thinking, guilt by association. So was I. True, the note was tightly sealed, and the finger came in a cheap white envelope, taped, no return address. But they were in the same place at the same time, my mailbox, and that was circumstantial evidence. Or an ugly coincidence. Or a setup.

If I knew one thing, and I knew several, I did not want that finger or its appearance in my mailbox making its way into the paper. Despite my basically adversarial feelings, I have grown adroit at steering the press away from whatever trail I am pursuing. My experience is that a trail tends to disappear when you shine a spotlight on it. The glare of publicity obliterates details instead of illuminating them.

Over the years, I've developed a strategy. On the first few calls, they get obdurate, homicide bull charging them, "And don't print that." If they keep calling, I bring out the cooperative cop who explains that it's only with their cooperation that I can smoke things out. "I don't like it when you guys get too specific too fast. People tend to leave town."

This approach panders to their feelings of power, yet leaves me free to do my work. The wild theories die down, the stories move to page three or six or even nine, and we at homicide get back to business instead of just answering phones.

As a rule of thumb, if not finger, the gorier a case, the stickier the press. If they got word of that finger in my home mailbox, the case would get personal, very fast, on a very public level. "KILLER GIVES ELLIOT THE FINGER." I learned years before that being named Elliot was not an advantage, at least in Chicago.

"You named for Eliot Ness?" I was asked once a case.

"Actually, I'm named for my uncle."

"Your uncle's Eliot Ness?"

And so on. I spent more time denying a relationship to Eliot Ness than I did passing my academy exams. And with the Ness thing, I flunked.

"You related to Eliot Ness?" I got asked once too often by a cub reporter at a press conference.

"Sure," I said. "He's my sister."

"His uncle," somebody sang out from across the room.

"Can we get off this thing?" I asked. The answer was no.

The next day in the paper I was Eliot Ness's nephew. They printed a retraction, but nobody ever reads those. I've been Eliot Ness's nephew ever since. I try to look on the bright side. My mom nearly named me Ignatius. Forced to choose between "Iggy" and "Eliot Ness's nephew," I've done all right. Which did not mean I wanted a headline.

"KILLER GIVES ELIOT NESS'S NEPHEW THE FIN-GER."

I took the finger straight to Myerling, called him at home from the phone in the parking garage, and promised him it was worth his trouble.

"No more dead bodies?"

"Well, in a manner of speaking—"

"All right, all right." He hung up.

Myerling beat me to the morgue. He was inside, flicking on the lights, when I arrived with Johnny Vanilla's finger.

"I guess they weren't after the rings," I said, shaking the finger out of its envelope so it lay like a tiny corpse in the center of a stainless steel table.

"Have you ever seen one before?"

"Finger? I got ten of them myself."

"The ring. You probably got it back because they knew what it was."

"What is it?"

"A power ring."

"Don't start on me, Myerling. This isn't the comics." I was thinking Spider-Man, Flash Gordon. Myerling, just as I feared, was thinking something else.

"You looked at the ring?"

"Of course: heavy gold, filigreed design. I figured I'd get it back from you. I didn't want to try and take it off him myself."

"You don't want it. Believe me."

"C'mon, Harold. Don't get strange. It's just a ring."

Harold didn't argue with me. He just opened a locker, took out a jar of what looked like soap "salts," filled a medical basin with water and salt, and said, "Soak your hands a couple minutes. I'll get the ring off."

I didn't want to watch Harold digging and gouging the ring

off Johnny's finger, so I watched my own hands soaking in Harold's brine.

"Primitive but effective," Harold said.

"I feel like I'm getting my nails done, Harold."

"Give it a couple of minutes. How does it feel?"

I hadn't been thinking about how it felt, but I had been thinking about how it looked. Dr. Winters was right about the ring dent on my left hand. Other than that, they were standard issue male hands, on the large side, a little thick. You wouldn't take me for a pianist, and neither had Sister Clarasine, although she'd labored with me on piano lessons for all of third grade.

"How does it feel?" Myerling repeated.

I flexed my fingers. They did feel good. The little salt bath was relaxing.

"This Epsom salts?"

"Mainly. I doctor it a little."

"Am I done yet?"

Myerling was dropping the ring into a salt bath all its own, and I swear I expected to hear it fizzle. "Power ring," he said.

I felt something stirring way back in my mind, a shadow. What? Myerling picked up the cue.

"Remember that stuff downstate? The state park near Marion? Those kids?"

I remembered. It didn't start as our case, but it ended up that way: A bunch of artsy new pagan environmentalists decide to hold a solstice celebration in the woods. They go prancing around buck naked and stumble on a pile of dead chickens. Chickens without their heads on, then a goat without its head on, then three little boys without their heads on. One boy was from Chicago, a runaway, and I'd been called in.

My view of the crime differed from that of the locals. I was the hotshot Chicago rookie. They treated my opinions like jokes. Maybe I had looked like a joke to them. Zealous, I'd brought in a tracker, coon dogs, and an unwelcome idea: There were more children than we had found—five in all, and two were still missing. Three children were dead. A fourth child had vanished into thin air. A fifth child had left tracks leading deep into the state park, ending at the edge of a cliff overlooking a shallow river.

Yes, I remembered. I remembered the way I had felt, working with the tracker, tracing the child's steps to cliff edge, a limestone lip, where the child had fallen or leapt to the water below. I remembered the way my career and my confidence had gotten smashed up when my theories—to me they seemed totally real—had been dismissed by the older cops. "We've got a bad enough mess without you inventing more." I remembered slinking back home, shamed, discouraged, and rattled. I hadn't trusted myself the same way after that.

"Remember?" Myerling nudged.

"Yes. I remember. I remember the ones we don't solve."

"Then you recognized the design?"

"I hadn't, but I do now. Thank you, Dr. Freud."

Talk about repression! They found the bodies in a circle of stones, lying on an elaborately contrived design. That design was made with painted pebbles. In Johnny's golden ring it was made with the jeweler's knife. The design was a pentacle, a five-pointed star bound by a circle. The bodies were laid out one to a point.

"Your friend Johnny was into some dark stuff," Myerling said ominously.

"What are you saying? Like satanism? That's the buzzword these days."

"I would have left it at evil. You know that's *live* spelled backward, right?" Harold was serious.

"Harold, I hate this bullshit. I went to grammar school with the guy. He was an altar boy. Maybe he got the ring in a pawnshop, won it at poker—"

I was awfully open-minded. Not about to be drawn back to a theory I couldn't prove. I shook the water off my hands and Myerling handed me a towel. Then he handed me a glass jar he'd filled with his miracle salt.

"I want you to use this every night on this case. Half a cup in a hot bath."

"I take showers."

"Call me if you need more."

"Myerling, I haven't taken a bubble bath since I was ten and my mom walked in."

I tried to hand him back the jar, but he was doing something with Johnny's finger.

"Just a minute and let me get you the ring," he said.

"I'll get it." I started to scoop it out of the water where he had it soaking, but Myerling whirled on me and hissed—that's the only word.

"Stop!"

He took the ring from the beaker with a set of tweezers. He laid it in the center of a piece of snow-white silk he'd produced, evidently saved for such occasions, and he then pointed to the silk triumphantly.

"Look!" He tapped the tweezers on a grayish stain.

"Must have been wet."

"It's not wet, Elliot. It's evil."

"Karmic grease, is that what you're telling me?" I was joking.

"Something like that." Myerling was dead serious.

He put the ring in the silk, put the silk in a new, clean envelope, and handed it to me.

"I don't need to tell you. Take it straight to evidence. And I'd sleep with a Bible overnight."

"A Bible? Harold, I don't have a Bible. I'm a swinging bachelor now."

As luck would have it, Dr. Harold Myerling, a good Jew, had a spare Christian Bible—St. James, not Catholic, but close enough. He placed the envelope in the Bible and sent me out the door feeling like a Jehovah's Witness.

I went straight to the station and gave the ring into the custody of Officer Chabrol. I went home. I went to bed. I did not take a salt bath. I dreamed of being chased through the woods and woke, soaked with sweat, three hours later. The Bible was lying open on the bedroom floor. I'd left the Bible dead center on my living room coffee table, I could swear to you. And I've never been reported to walk in my sleep.

I found myself thinking of Father Aloysius Bremner, S.J. Back when I was deciding to drop out of pre-seminary, it was Bremner who had assured me that God's will involved my happiness—which might not be found in the priesthood. "We all serve God in our own ways," he told me. "God needs policemen just as much as he needs priests—not that some people don't think we're the same thing. . . ."

And so, faced with karmic grease, *live* spelled backward, and sleepwalking Bibles, the thought crossed my mind to call him. Just not at five A.M. The last I knew he was running some Jesuit retreat house in the country. I would ask him about power rings and evil. Or maybe I'd just ask him to pray for me—not a thought I'd had in many years.

Chapter fifteen

——————■——————

There's nothing like a sleepless night to make you want to get an investigation over with fast, and that was my plan heading over to Carson Stoufley's by dawn's early light. The crowd at Holy Name Cathedral was just leaving eight o'clock Mass when I drove past on my way to the Gold Coast.

Carson Stoufley lived in one of the elaborate rock piles Chicagoans built at the turn of the century. Big, gray, grace-less, it looks like a fortress, not a home, and I probably qual-ify as part of what it's intended to keep out. Chicago has always been an elitist town, despite its pretensions to the contrary. Stoufley's manse was one version of the neighbor-hood turfs the city is built on.

If you don't know what I mean about Chicago neighbor-hoods, I'll tell you: If you're born and raised within a certain radius—the Near North, say, or the Near West—that is your country and your fortress. You can leave it, but like an ex-tended family, it never leaves you. Neighborhood loyalties and expectations will trail after you. So will the reputation you had in fifth grade. Stoufley's rock pile just off Astor Street was a neighborhood joint, that's all. Instead of Ignatius, he went to Chicago Latin, but we were really just two Chicago guys and both of us knew it. Or I wanted to think we did.

When I rang Carson Stoufley's bell, I was shuffling through a stack of messages I'd grabbed at the station. Carson Stoufley opened his door, and I opened my wallet to show badge. He was politely surprised—and faking. He'd been expecting me.

Stoufley showed me past the potted cacti—palms were out, it seemed—and into a side room filled with tropical plants, exotic birds, and breakfast.

"Coffee? Croissant?"

I accepted. Stoufley seemed to enjoy fussing. He was a good-looking man by anybody's standards, even Hollywood's. He had the look of a forties matinee idol, and could have been quite the ladies' man if that was his preference.

"One lump? Two? Sweet'n Low?"

"Black."

It was the fifties, not the forties: Charlton Heston, I realized—the same granitic jaw, aquiline nose, stony cheekbones. Stoufley wore blue jeans, a soft denim shirt, some kind of pale moccasin. He was tan and his eyes were the aqua of a swimming pool at night. Taken with the house, or even without it, he was a dazzling specimen. The question, or one of the questions, was—of what?

"I must say you look like a homicide cop," he said in case I'd missed the return scrutiny across the rim of his coffee cup. "I'm very visual," he went on—a little nervous? "Of course, that's good in my line of work."

Carson Stoufley was an art dealer. He might prefer "collector." The facts were he had made a considerable fortune catering to and educating the whims and fancies of his cronies from Latin School and their cronies from the club, the board, the bank, the street. Chicago was a town full of money, but just like everything else, it liked to stick to its own neighborhood. Old money and new money mingled but didn't mix. Carson Stoufley was old money. Jack Nesbitt was his long-time client, and a subject he was determined to handle with delicacy. That was not my plan.

"Good coffee?"

"Who do you think killed Jack Nesbitt?"

"Killed?" Stoufley's coffee cup clattered. "How stupid of me. Sorry. It's all rather upsetting." For Charlton Heston, this guy was doing a good Janet Leigh. "I respected Jack. I respected his work—"

"I heard you called him a repressed pedophile."

"Ah. Yes. That may have been a bit of an exaggeration." The rattling cup again. "I was about to say, I respected his work but always found he had some—let's say, unsavory companions."

"Companions or habits?"

"Both."

"And you knew this?"

"I suspected."

"You suspected? Why did you suspect?"

"Why, his subject matter, of course."

What I knew of Nesbitt's subject matter was the classy nudes he shot for New York magazines and coffee table books. Evidently, I'd missed something. "Could you be more specific?"

"More specific. Well. He worked in the same territory as Helmut Newton. You know, the perversely erotic nude with a hint of bondage. . . ." He made it sound like a dessert.

"Go on."

"Maybe Newton on the left, Mapplethorpe on the right, to give you a map."

"Mapplethorpe?"

"The homoerotic image."

"Ah. You are Nesbitt's executor? I'd like to see the images you're talking about. A picture's worth a thousand words, et cetera."

"There's a massive volume of work. Jack was quite prolific. It's not even catalogued yet. You must know his studio is crammed with work, work in progress, a disaster area, not categorized, I'm afraid."

"Regressed pedophile sounds pretty categorized to me."

"Ah. Yes. I suppose it does. I overstepped myself. He had a leaning, you see?"

"A leaning?"

"A proclivity."

"What you're telling me is he fucked kids?"

"Younger people. I'm afraid so. At least, the work would indicate—"

"You never reported him?"

"He was my client." Abruptly, Carson Stoufley was actually crying. "I wasn't sure. No one was sure. . . ."

I thanked Stoufley for his time and his coffee. I left him sniffling among his outsized houseplants and tried to get out of his presence before the bomb went off. Unless I missed my mark, Stoufley was a purveyor of kiddie porn, Nesbitt's kiddie porn. I needed to get out of there before he knew I knew that. I wanted a search warrant and I wanted it fast. I wanted to seize Jack Nesbitt's estate and lock it up before it disappeared.

With luck, I could catch the state's attorney, catch a judge, and make it over to Nesbitt's all by the same afternoon. I needed some luck on this case.

■

Maybe I'm a sucker for leather-bound books and mahogany—an "education junkie," as Jamie kids me. But when I go to see a judge in chambers, I'm impressed. Even if that judge is little Ricky Noonan. Prematurely silver like many of the Irish, Noonan looked as distinguished as a Hallmark greeting card for Father's Day—until you noticed the streetwise twinkle still hiding in his eye.

I went to Peter Abramson, the state's attorney, and then I went to Judge Richard Noonan.

I'd known Ricky Noonan since before he was Judge Noonan, before he was lawyer Noonan, before he was altar boy Noonan. He was in Johnny Vanilla's class and I had playground and crossing guard duty the year he started kindergarten. He never wanted to wait on the curb. Evidently, he'd grown more cautious lately.

"You couldn't go with something a little more focused?"

"I want it all. I want everything. Rafters to sewers."

"That's pretty broad."

"I want it all. Nesbitt was into some dark stuff, and maybe his murderer is hiding in some inky corner."

"Mmm." Noonan usually gave me pretty much what I asked for if he could. Not this time. This time he had his reservations. "We still need to show cause."

"Porn."

"You're kidding. Elliot, the Jesuits really got to you. Nesbitt's work is art, not pornography."

"You haven't seen the stuff, Ricky."

"It's a pretty fine line—art photography and porn. I don't want any flack like the National Endowment for the Arts mess. I won't give you carte blanche for a witch hunt, Elliot."

"Kiddie porn. He was a sick son of a bitch."

"We all are, Elliot. Didn't the Jesuits get that fact across the bridge?"

I let that pass. I didn't want to get into that, not even with Ricky Noonan. If he hadn't pressed, I'd never have told him what I was after. You couldn't be too careful. Rule number two of a good homicide cop is never rattle before you strike.

I headed back to the station to touch base and get myself a backup. I had an ominous feeling about going to Nesbitt's, and over the years I've learned to listen to those feelings. Looking around the bull pen, I saw a lot of worthy men— Daley, Chaworski, Lynch, my star rookies. Since I'd been partnerless six months, I'd been rotating rookies, but couldn't see using any of them. Maybe I was sensitive about what had happened to Zachary and embarrassed by what- ever images we might find—images of what had happened to him. The very thought made me both queasy and explosive. I decided to go alone. I'd just hit the men's room, splash some water on my face and—

I stopped to take a whiz, and there was Gomez.

The grief over Zachary had bonded us.

I could see that in his own clumsy way Gomez the putz actually loved my son. Like any other parent, I have a hard time hating anyone who loves my kid. I told Gomez where we were going and what we were after.

"Those fucking sons of bitches." He put a fist through the men's room window.

"Me, I hate that shit."

"Who doesn't, Oscar?"

"Pussy"—he pronounced it poo-say—"that's one thing. Kids is something else."

He was my man.

"Boss," Gomez said. "You didn't see me, eh?"

I handed him a wet handkerchief for his knuckles and we headed out. We aimed crosstown through traffic that seemed, collectively, to have gotten up on the wrong side of the bed. It was a twenty-minute drive over to Nesbitt's place, but Gomez and I traveled light-years.

"He's better last night. No dreaming," Gomez said. He looked at me sideways to see how I would take his having news of my son. The fact that it was good news helped.

"He used to dream when he was little," I told Gomez. "When he was two or three, he'd even sleepwalk. I used to think it was my stuff he was picking up on. I'd have a bad case and he'd have bad dreams—my bad dreams, it seemed like sometimes."

"Kids are so funny," Gomez said. "I always wanted some—maybe forty or fifty, you know?"

I laughed, then put my foot in it. "What's stopping you? The way you fool around, you should have a dozen by now."

There was a moment's silence.

"Hey, man. That's history," Gomez protested. "Me as pussyhound. Not anymore. No more, amigo. I tell my friends don't send me any, I'm not interested. I tell them don't come to me to find it. I don't know where it is anymore. I got mine at home."

It was a long speech. For Oscar Gomez, it was an oration. And there was more.

"Boss, I know what you think. I know I deserve it. I fool around. I even take advantage on the street. You know that. But no more. You know? I am a happy man. So we can't have kids. We have other things. Love."

"Sorry," I said. Gloria had had her tubes tied. It wasn't my fault. It was her idea, but riding with Gomez, I felt like I should have stopped her. I'd tried, but not very hard. And she wasn't my property, or his.

"One kid without a father is all I could handle," Gloria used to say, talking about the dangers of my job. I know I should have been better with her about the fears, but I didn't know what to do about them. The danger went with the job, and I couldn't imagine not having it. Whatever else he must offer her, Oscar Gomez must have somehow managed to make Gloria feel safe.

"It's okay, man," Gomez said. "What the hell. I love her." That got me between the eyes. For the first time, I saw that his relationship with Gloria wasn't about me and him and some macho ownership game. It wasn't even about me and him and Zachary. It was about him and Gloria. He loved her. I wondered if I ever had.

We were at Nesbitt's.

"It's sealed, right?"

"Right."

I wondered if Gomez's cop was going off like mine was. Even before we tried the door I had that feeling I know to listen to. I don't think civilians have it. Firemen say they do. It's a sixth sense, an instinct, "a grace," Myerling or Father Bremner might say. My cousin Mike, the fire fighter, calls his a voice, St. Michael, "because of his fiery sword." Whatever you call it—and I call it "my cop"—mine went off at Nesbitt's door.

I had the keys, but it opened at the touch. What pounced was the smell.

"Shit, no," said Gomez.

Once you've smelled death, you know it anywhere, and death was waiting for us somewhere at Jack Nesbitt's. We drew our guns, held our breath, and headed in.

There was a bucket of something awful that used to be

human sitting in the middle of Nesbitt's studio floor. I didn't want to look, and neither did Gomez. So we looked. The head of Carson Stoufley looked back.

Gomez lost it into the kitchen trash. My stomach stayed where it was. I was wondering who Stoufley talked to after I talked to him. Or who had seen me come and go. I noticed motion. Flies had found the paper cutter blade. I could hear Dr. Winters telling me the blade was not a guillotine, no matter what it looked like—which it did. I could hear Harold Myerling saying a surgical saw was more likely. Either way, Stoufley's head was present and accounted for while Stoufley's body was missing.

I counted back: out of Stoufley's by eleven-thirty, downtown by twelve, over to Abramson, who'd taken early lunch, so I waited, then over to Noonan, back to the station, over to Nesbitt's—three hours, three and a half. Three hours, broad daylight, daylight still. I looked up: The skylight was open. I swear it was.

"Hey, Gomez!" I pointed. . . . The skylight was closed.

I ran for the back window. It was sash-locked. I broke it with my gun. The glass came apart in jagged sheets, not a breakaway like in the movies.

"Careful," said Gomez.

He was right. This was real glass, not stunt stuff. Of course it took me too long to pick the glass out, and by the time I got out and up the fire escape, the roof was empty— and the skylight was open again.

"Hey, Gomez—Oscar—call in the guys," I shouted through it. The roof was covered with fine white pebbles. There were two tubs of geraniums and a lounge chair. Near the lounge chair was a pack of matches. Jacky and Johnny's.

Does it surprise you to know that Nesbitt's studio was ransacked? File drawers gaped open and files were missing.

Stoufley had said the work wasn't categorized, but the killer clearly knew what he was looking for, and probably where to find it. I got the creepy feeling that Stoufley's murder was incidental, more a diversion than a stand-alone crime.

When you catch yourself thinking murder is cover-up, you know you are dealing with something deadly, something that is *live* spelled backward.

Chapter sixteen

———■———

A new murder is usually good for all bets off in my personal life, but not this time. I had an unbreakable date, the one I'd made to see the Cubs with Zachary. I didn't care that messages were piling up. I didn't care if the press made me into a monkey. I left the station with the phones all singing after making two calls, one to Myerling and one to Dr. Violet Winters.

"Get my note?" she asked. To hear her voice, she was all innocence, not a "possible" multiple who might have left Vanilla's finger with one personality and left her little note with another. I was spooked, and when I am spooked, I always act tough.

"It's the drift I didn't get. We're not dating, Doctor. I'm solving a crime—or trying to solve a crime. That makes for a busy schedule."

"I thought you'd call me." She sounded wistful.

"You thought wrong."

"Dinner?" She was nothing if not persistent.

"I've got a date with Zachary."

"Cubs?"

"You got it. How'd you know?"

"He told me at the hospital. . . . Great kid, Elliot."

No matter which way she came at it, Dr. Winters could get to me. Liking my kid was probably the world's fastest way to make me like her. Hell, it had even worked for Oscar Gomez.

"I've got a question for you."

"I hope you want a yes."

"How do I find Nesbitt's ex-wife?"

For a minute, I thought she'd hang up on me. After a long time, she said, "She lives on the North Shore, married to a fancy doctor. I'm still mad about the pictures she sent you. She must have wanted to get even with me all these years."

"I know that much. What's her name these days?"

Dr. Winters sighed. "I should have told you sooner. Crutcher. Mrs. Malcolm Crutcher. She's legit these days. I suppose I should have told you she was Mrs. Crutcher sooner?"

"Maybe."

"I didn't want her to trash me. I guess that was a lie of omission."

"I'll say. Thanks for the note. Let's try for a drink tomorrow . . . call it research."

"Oh, sure. I'll have my secretary phone you with an appointment." She laughed. "Why not Billie's tonight at ten? We can pretend it's tomorrow."

One thing about Dr. Winters. Somebody had taught her how to close a deal.

"All right," I told her. "But it's past my bedtime."

"Now, there's a romantic note."

She clicked off.

———■———

The Cubs did nicely, but what I remember of the game is the way Zachary kept his hand curled in a fist inside mine—for the whole nine innings. Before his accident, which is what I found myself calling the attack, he'd been outgrowing such little-boy behaviors. Not anymore. Now he was on me like a shadow. Gloria said it was the same with her and Gomez. I promised him a sleepover for the weekend, told him his teddy missed him, the one he's given me to sleep with when I moved out. His "sleepover teddy" when he visited.

"Dad? Did anything bad ever happen to you?"

"Some things, sure. Bad stuff happens to everybody."

Did that sound casual enough? I didn't feel casual. I was straining to catch something behind the words. I was straining to catch sight of what he had forgotten. I didn't want him to remember, but I wanted to know: How bad was it?

"Why is that, do you think? Why does bad stuff happen?"

"I'm not sure."

This exchange happened in the bottom of the ninth. A good thing, or I'd have missed the whole game. As it was, I stepped into deep water.

Why did bad things happen? Who the hell knew? I had had this conversation before, practiced it, in fact, like every other human faced with a tough piece of road. Usually I had it with other adults. Talking to my son, I wanted to ask, "How bad a thing, son?"

Because I couldn't ask him that, I asked if he wanted another hot dog, a T-shirt, a pennant. Popcorn? A Coke?

"Dad, you're spoiling me," he finally said, nailing it. But he never let go of my hand.

We were crossing Clark Street, along with about a thousand other people, when I felt him stiffen. I looked down and he was staring straight ahead into the crowd.

"What is it?" I tried to scan for whatever he had seen. I saw fans, vendors, after-game traffic.

"I just remembered something."

"What?"

"I don't know. It was—" He pointed to a display of Cubs jackets, hats, and T-shirts. "Shiny. Like that."

"What about it?" I asked.

"I don't know," he said miserably. "Something. Could we just hang out for a while, Dad?"

"Let's walk a ways, that okay?" We'd taken the el to the game.

"I can walk, Dad. I'm fine."

With that, Zach and I set off west on Addison. After about three blocks, we turned south onto a quiet, tree-lined street of two-flats with Cubs banners in the windows and gay little strips of garden out by the sidewalk. The air was heavy, and you could smell the trees even above the bus fumes and the faint smell of rotting garbage that signals summer in the city.

"It's nice, Dad."

"The street? It's a nice street, yeah."

"C'mon, Dad!"

"What? I miss something?"

"It's nice seeing you."

"Oh."

Zachary sometimes talked to me like I was the child. It was a game we had—at least I liked to think of it that way instead of as the tone he'd learned from his mother.

"Maybe we could find some ice cream," I suggested.

"I'm sick of ice cream. That's all they gave me at the hospital."

"Some hospital, eh? Not even steak and eggs. I guess ice cream's out, then."

"Dad—" this time it was Gloria's patient tone—"I ate three hot dogs and a Snickers."

"Okay, I get it. I'll just have to get a Dove Bar for myself, later." Dove Bars are a Chicago concoction, ice cream and chocolate, as heavy as a gold brick.

"I don't know what I'm going to remember if I do remember."

"That must be scary."

"Yeah. Dr. Hauser says I don't need to remember, not for a long, long time."

I would call Dr. Hauser, I decided.

We walked the long, green blocks all the way to Belmont, where I hailed a cab. "Take us to Buckingham Fountain," I told the cabbie. As a toddler, Zachary had loved that elaborate fountain almost as much as the zoo.

The cabbie took us south along the lake, past Navy Pier, past the yacht club to the long, formal park. We sat on a bench at fountain's edge and watched the lake go from blue to silver. We watched the city lights and the fireflies flickering on in the early evening dark.

I didn't know what to do for my son but to give him time.

"Dad," he said as the water splashed softly and we sat together in the gathering dark. "I'm scared to see the pictures if I remember."

"I know, son," I told him. And I did.

I get pictures. Like I said when we started, everybody does, at least some of the time, and they can be hard. It's an occupational hazard for cops. Like black lung disease for miners.

When I first started working violent crime, I thought the pictures were because the particular crimes were so horrific.

Take the call we got to go to North Lincoln Avenue, a hooker motel, "screaming and things breaking. Room Eleven." The manager sounded scared.

We got there in under five minutes. The screaming had stopped and blood was running out from under the door. I tried the door—you'd be surprised how often they're not locked—and a gun went off. Then there was just silence.

"Police officers. Come out with your hands up, or we're coming in."

Nothing.

We went in and found a nude woman lying on the floor— half of her. The other half was in the bathroom, where the guy with the gun was waiting for us. He had a chain saw.

"We were playing," he said, and then lifted the gun, real slow motion, and blew off his head.

The pictures from that one nearly killed me. I'd get her pretty little legs, no torso. Her torso, no legs. His head blowing apart. I thought the pictures were going to kill me. They'd come while I was driving, when I was in the shower, while Gloria and I were making love. They liked to visit just before sleep—anytime, really, when I was relaxed and my mind wasn't focused. They drove me crazy.

For some reason, I got it in my head that I was the only one who had them, that they meant I wasn't going to make it as a cop. I had the pictures and I hated the pictures and I felt guilty about the pictures. In a grim way, it reminded me of fighting "impure thoughts" as an altar boy. It was like that old joke: "Don't think about pink elephants." "What are you thinking about?" "Pink elephants."

That was the first time I had an unusual conversation with Harold Myerling. We brought the bodies over, the pieces of the bodies over, and Myerling received them like we were unloading Chinese jade.

I saw the care, the respect, the delicacy he used, and it scared me a little. He saw that.

"Worried you're going to have pictures?"

"Pictures?"

I was astounded. Somebody was actually talking about it.

"What I do is substitute. The minute the picture starts, I change the slide."

"I don't get it."

"Change the slide. I made myself a set of alternative images, scenes that make me happy. I pop in one of those. You need about ten, and they have to be good ones, the stuff you really connect to, safe, happy, peaceful, et cetera."

"Thanks."

Myerling gave me a little nod and smiled. "It works for me."

It worked for me, too. I spent about a week working up my set of alternative slides, and the next time I got pictures, I used them. They were simple conversions.

Bloody torso . . . convert to . . . the Grand Canyon trip with Dad.

Bloody head splattering . . . convert to . . . snow falling softly on the steeple of St. Michael's.

You get the idea. Myerling's technique helped me enormously. Over the years I learned others, learned that other cops got pictures and had their own tricks. One guy I knew went to a hypnotist and learned a trick: When he brought his thumb and index finger together he would see the Swiss Alps, not the carnage Chicago had just spewed out.

Some guys use the alphabet. Some use multiplication tables, or chanting. You had to come up with something, or the pictures would take you down. My son was afraid of his pictures—and so was I.

Chapter seventeen

———■———

"It's called a blip," Zach's therapist, Alice Hauser, explained to me. Her phone voice had an annoying nasal tone. I called her after I dropped Zach off.

"What exactly is a blip?" I pressed her.

"It's almost like a subliminal image, a flash, a tiny piece of film. A blip is the memory bleeding through. Sometimes all you get is blips. Sometimes they're first and then you get the whole memory."

"I see."

"Elliot? May I call you Elliot? You sound upset."

"Of course I'm upset. I haven't seen my son in months. He gets raped or molested or whatever you and my wife are calling it. No one tells me until they have to at the hospital, and I'm also in the middle of a murder investigation."

Did that sound upset enough to her therapeutic ear? She put on a soothing tone, like I was a mad bomber she was trying to keep from pulling the pin.

"I know you're busy right now, but maybe you should

come in once or twice, talk about it. If Zach thinks it will upset you, he's not going to remember—or tell us if he does."

I could see the sense in this. I made an appointment. As directed. Not that she could see me for another two days. She had her busy schedule. I was just a cop.

Like a lot of cops, I have a hard time respecting doctors because of how they testify on the stand. I think "psychiatrist" and "fool" almost in the same sentence. I know it shouldn't be that way, but that's what happens to you if enough bleeding-heart doctors undo enough cases.

I'd like to believe in remorse and redemption—I have seen the rare case of it—but what I see is recidivism. Rapists rape again. Thieves steal. Violent people grow more violent, not less, incubating their next crimes in our penal system. "Lower companions," the Jesuits used to call it. "Near occasion of sin." What was a prison, really, except a community of low companions decreasing each other's morals further still?

I should be careful about such thoughts. But if psychiatrists would try thinking along these lines, a lot of needless tragedy would be averted. It all came down to one question and two answers.

Q: "Do you think he will do it again [rape, murder, arson, steal, child-molest]?"

A: "Yes [cop]."

A: "No [therapist]. I hope not."

Nonetheless, I was going to see a therapist, one Dr. Alice Hauser, in two days. And I was going to see another doctor, Violet Winters, in two minutes. She had managed to talk me into dinner after all. Dr. Hauser was for Zach's sake. Dr. Winters was for my sake—or maybe for truth, justice, and the American way.

In the meanwhile, I wanted an expert's opinion.

■

I phoned Dr. Malcolm Crutcher at his office, expecting him to be long gone. To my surprise, he answered the phone himself. When I identified myself, he was cordial.

"Hello, Detective. Yes, I'm still downtown for some damn meeting, an Art Institute thing. I swear that place takes more of my time than my medical practice. What can I do for you?"

I didn't exactly know the answer to that. Crutcher waited out my hesitation.

"I think I need to see you," I said. "I want some expert guidance about Zachary. Any chance I could take a few minutes?"

"Well, where are you? I've got an hour or so. All I was doing up here was watching the sunset."

I told Crutcher where I was, about twenty blocks west of him, and he suggested we meet in the Santa Fe Bar. It was a swank watering hole, midway between his office and the Art Institute.

"You can park under Grant Park," he began to tell me. I cut him short.

"I'm a cop. I can park anywhere," I told him. He chuckled over that.

Where I parked, five minutes later, was in a bus stop, near a hydrant, in front of the entrance to the Santa Fe Bar. I'd made record time across Lake Street, and I expected to gather my thoughts before the good doctor arrived.

So much for expectations. Dr. Malcolm Crutcher had snagged a prime booth and was sipping a scotch when I arrived. I settled in, ordered a drink, and searched for words.

"My son's seeing a therapist named Alice Hauser," I started in. "I was wondering—"

"Excellent choice. I'd recommend her myself."

"It seems my son doesn't remember much. Dr. Hauser says—"

"Very common. All for the best."

"But he's getting these blips."

"Ah . . . They can be very disturbing."

"We could do a regression, but Dr. Hauser's opposed."

"There I completely agree with her. Why stir up the water? Let your son remember—if he remembers—at his own pace, Detective. After all, he's more important than whatever crime occurred. I'd be damn sure I wanted that regression for his sake, not mine, before I did it. Another scotch?"

Crutcher signaled for another round while I processed his opinion. I'd asked for it, after all.

"Sorry to be so blunt, Detective. I guess I'm just an old goat, and some of these newfangled techniques strike me as dangerous. The mind's a delicate thing. Dr. Hauser's conservative, and no charmer in my book, but she's sound when it comes to practice."

"There's one other thing, Dr. Crutcher."

"Ask away."

"I heard your wife was formerly married to Jack Nesbitt."

Crutcher flushed. When he spoke to me again, he was clearly furious.

"If I'd known this was about my wife's past, I'd have come to your office instead of meeting you for a drink."

"Now, just a minute, Dr. Crutcher. Nobody's talking about your wife's past except as a means to an end. I've got a murder to solve, and she might shed some light on it."

"What's to shed? Jack Nesbitt was one rotten son of a bitch, and I got her away from him. Forgive me for saying so, Detective, but some people deserve their bad ends. Jack

Nesbitt hurt Ilene. I don't think she needs to be reminded of those pains."

"Your wife sent some photos to us, Dr. Crutcher. I don't know if you know that."

"Those shots of Violet Winters? I'm sure Ilene thought she was doing you a favor. As you may have gathered, I believe in leaving the past lie, and Dr. Winters is a valued colleague of mine now, but I'm sure my wife felt Dr. Winters might be a worthy focus for your investigations."

"What are you saying, Dr. Crutcher?"

"You'll judge for yourself, Detective, but my wife doesn't think Dr. Winters can be trusted."

As always, it all came down to who do you trust? Malcolm Crutcher trusted his wife, even if he didn't approve of her actions. On some level, I trusted Violet Winters and did not entirely trust Malcolm Crutcher. He had a secret, I thought— evidently at the same moment he decided to share it with me.

"One more thing about your boy and those regressions," he said, lowering his voice. I leaned forward across the table to catch his words above the hubbub of the bar. "Leave well enough alone and the boy will heal. Let nature take its course. He'll forget about it. You'll see."

I must have looked dubious, because Crutcher grabbed my arm and spoke with some urgency as he continued. "I know what I'm talking about, Detective. I don't intend this as a matter for public consumption, but as a boy, I was molested myself. Know what I did? Forgot all about it. Didn't even remember it until I was long out of med school. I ask you, do I seem fixated? Do I seem damaged? Now, some son-of-a-bitch Freudian could argue that my profession is a fixation of sorts, but I bet that's true of many doctors. You know what they call us?"

"They?"

"The therapy crowd."

"Ah. What?"

"They call us the wounded healers. I'm trying to tell you your boy will be okay. The mind's a remarkable, resilient thing, Detective."

I thanked Malcolm Crutcher for his time and did not volunteer the information that I was leaving to meet Violet Winters. Crutcher had reassured me on Dr. Hauser's plan of treatment for Zachary; he had underscored my own sense that Violet Winters was fragile or volatile or both. What he had not done was settle my sense of disquiet.

Chapter eighteen

—■—

Dr. Winters and I had agreed to meet at Billie's, a dangerous move, no doubt. I saw too many movies growing up
to think a piano bar and a beautiful woman weren't a dangerous combination. I wasn't disappointed. This time the dress
was black, very covered up, and so were the shades she was
wearing. She had a table for two in the darkest recesses of the
bar, and she waved to me like she was bidding discreetly.

"A woman of mystery?"

"Something like that."

She didn't take the glasses off when I sat down.

"What is this? Your Jack Nicholson imitation?" I was
proud of the line.

"They make me feel invisible."

"They make you look conspicuous."

"Not by comparison."

My cop elbowed me in the abdomen. I reached over and
lifted off her glasses.

"Don't," she said. Too late.

Dr. Violet Winters had a shiner. The kind of shiner makeup

can't disguise. It was her right eye—which made the assailant a probable leftie, unless it was a door.

"Door get you?"

"I don't know."

"What about that lip?"

Her lips were puffy, and not from too much kissing. Somebody had beat her. In the blue-silver light of the bar, her white-gold hair looked silver. This case was aging her.

"I don't know about the lip. I don't know about any of it."

"You weren't there? Come on, Doctor. I'm a big boy. If you're into kinky sex, you can tell me."

"I don't even know where 'there' was."

"One thing about you, Doc. You're interesting."

"What's interesting about a bad drunk?"

"You're telling me this time it was a blackout?"

"I don't remember. I think maybe I was drugged."

The doctor took out a cigarette and lit it herself. She puffed it stiffly, like her upper lip hurt.

"Don't smoke that thing if it hurts your lip," I told her.

"Leave me alone. I'm addicted. And give me back my shades. Got any aspirin?"

I asked the waitress for bar aspirin. She said, "That's illegal," and I said, "It's okay, I'm a cop." Two aspirin materialized and a glass of water with fizz in it. Behind her sunglasses, the doctor looked grateful.

"You're kind. That's why I sent you the note. I like you, Elliot. I used to like me."

She sounded so miserable, so kidlike, I took her by the hand. Like Zachary, she didn't want to let go.

"I guess this thing with Jack has really kicked my butt. Those pictures—I was back in that apartment on Roscoe with my mom's johns in and out. I was that kid again, hadn't escaped yet, wasn't the distinguished professional you see

before you tonight. I took it kind of hard, and so I told my-
self, take a long, hot bath, have a drink, relax . . . and then
I wake up looking like this. It makes me feel a little crazy. Did
I slip in the bath? Did somebody hit me? Right in my own
home? There's a scary thought. Did I do this to myself?
There's an even scarier one."

"Take it easy." She was scaring me, too.

"And then I read about Carson Stoufley, and you don't
return my calls, which said 'emergency.' "

"Wait a minute. Your calls?"

"I left at least three of them. Didn't you pick up your messages at the station?"

"Shit." I remembered the stack of messages I'd scooped up
and taken with me to Carson Stoufley's. He'd offered me
coffee.

I'd taken a cup, set my papers on the table, taken out my
notebook—Dr. Winters's messages and the rest of my calls
were back there at the pepper shaker, unless Stoufley's killer
had taken them. He'd have my son's name, Violet's, Gloria's—a who's who of my near and dear—even a number for
my cousin Charles.

A chill walked my arm.

"What'll it be?" I asked her. "Scotch or a hot milk?"

Just then the piano man started up "It Had to Be You,"
and Dr. Winters and I started laughing. She wasn't a suspect,
I decided. It was not seeing her that was pulling at me.

"You're okay, Elliot."

"What'll it be? Scotch or hot milk?"

"What about your place or mine? You could call it protective custody."

If there's one thing I love, it's a woman who does your
rationalizing for you. "Even for protective custody, my place
is a mess."

"And mine's so perfect, you'd never forgive me. Please, Elliot. I'm scared. Tomorrow I'll wake up and go home and we'll pretend it never happened."

"Now, there's a plan."

So we went to my plate glass window, with a stop at a Greektown package store for "a fifth of milk." On the way up in my elevator she asked me in a small voice, "Do you think somebody could have gotten in and drugged me right in my own house?"

"Could have? Yes. But it's not likely," I told her. "What's likely is that you were more tired than you knew, the drink was stronger than you thought, and you took a fall."

"I'll try to believe that," Violet said. Just as the elevator doors opened, she leaned over and impulsively kissed me.

"I hope you're not thinking serious sex," Violet was saying as we stepped up to my door. What I was thinking about was putting her to bed, someplace safe.

"No, no, I hate that kind," I told her.

I unlocked the door and stepped aside. For some reason, my door was jammed. The doctor gave it a little shove. That struck me funny.

"Here, let me get it." I pushed with my shoulder like a linebacker.

Oscar Gomez was the reason my door wouldn't open. He was sitting with his back against it and a surprised look on his face.

"Oscar! He's my wife's lover. Ex-wife."

I was feeling for a pulse. So was Dr. Winters. She had the throat. I had a wrist. Nothing.

"Somebody knew what he was doing," Dr. Winters said. "I wonder if they knew to whom?"

Oscar was really dead. He had Zachary's sleepover teddy

bear in one hand, and a note peeked out from where he'd sat down. I pulled out the note.

Elliot,
Sorry, Zach couldn't find his bear. Gloria gave me a key.
Oscar

"He came for my son's teddy bear. I better call Gloria."

"We better call the cops."

"Violet, I am the cops."

"Then figure out who wanted to kill you."

She had a point, and it was sinking in just like the ice pick in Oscar's chest. I felt sick, and not just for Oscar—for Gloria and Zach. I called the station and told them about Gomez.

I called Myerling and he asked me, first off, about the ring. Where was it? Had I put it in evidence?

"Fuck the ring. I put it in evidence, what do you think? Harold, I do not believe in power rings, karmic grease, or whatever."

"Just checking." Myerling said he'd be over. "Stay in a well-lit place, would you, Elliot? Unless you think they were really trying to kill Gomez instead of you."

Ten minutes later, Daley, Chaworski, and Lynch all came through the door together, guns drawn. I guess when the scene of the crime is your boss's place, it makes you a little nervous.

"What are you guys doing? Put away those guns."

"You okay, boss?" It was Lynch, the smartest and sweetest of my rookies. Daley and Chaworski were shooting looks at Oscar, trying to determine the cause of death. As weapons go, an ice pick is very . . . picky. Very little blood. You have to look for the handle. As Dr. Winters said, somebody knew what they were doing.

Dr. Winters had her shades back on, and she was sitting on my couch, methodically sorting my laundry: light, dark, colored. She acted like this was normal. I suppose, compared to everything else, it was.

"I do it when I get nervous."

"Go home."

I caught Lynch glancing over at us. His look was a question I wasn't comfortable with just yet.

I wasn't hiding her, exactly. I was hiding me. I didn't want my ethics questioned then.

"Go home," I repeated.

"But—" She didn't look stubborn, she looked scared, but my place, not hers, was the scene of a crime, so I shrugged her off.

"Lock your doors. I'll call you."

So she left. That gave me time to call Gloria. Zach was asleep, she told me. They'd found his other bear under the bed.

"Breathe," I told her.

"Could I speak with Oscar?"

"No. That's why I called."

She caught her breath.

"It was very fast. I'm sorry." And I was.

"What am I going to do? How am I going to tell Zach?"

"Worry about yourself, Glo. Can you call your sister or something? I'll tell Zachary in the morning."

"I can't believe it, Ell. He was so good to me. So good to Zachary. Always taking him on outings and everything. He made us feel safe."

"He loved you, Glo. I can tell you that much. He was trying to become what you wanted."

"Why, Elliot? Why?"

"They must have been after me."

"I wish they'd found you." She hung up.

I got off the phone and closed Gomez's eyes. I'd tell My-erling I'd done that.

"You know, boss, this is going to take a few hours. Maybe you want to go somewhere and sleep."

Maybe I did, but first I was feeling sorry for hustling her out of there, sending her home unescorted. Besides, I needed somebody to talk to. In the morning I would have to tell Zachary about Gomez and face the fact I'd broken Gloria's heart not once but twice.

Chapter nineteen

—■—

Violet Winters lived just west of Greektown, not far from Jacky and Johnny's, on the edge of hell, you might say. It was an area of lofts and factories and rehabbed factory lofts, "convenient to the Loop and LaSalle Street," as a Realtor might say.

Because it wasn't safe and wouldn't be for ten years minimum, all the showy condos and converted lofts made a show of just how safe they really were: well-lit parking lots, alarm systems, elaborate coded lobby doors—a joke among cops, and among robbers, too, since it was while you were punching your seven-digit code that they got you.

Violet's building on Green Street had the full regalia: video-cams, even a dozing guard with a dozing Doberman right at his feet. I knew her address because, like most cops, I was very good with numbers. It's a skill you get after years of radio transmissions laced with static and the consequences of get-it-right-the-first-time-or-maybe-somebody-dies-maybe-a-cop-maybe-even-you.

Sixty-six Green was the number Gomez took when the

poor bastard first tried to question her about the nudie pictures and the nature of her relationship to the late Jack Nesbitt. He'd got the numbers right, there was V. Winters on the register next to the phone—but something in his tone had set her off and that's how I got into the loop.

Enter the knight in shining armor, "I'll handle this." Which was what I was still trying to do three weeks and four deaths later when I rang her doorbell at two A.M.

"It's me. Elliot."

"What a nice surprise."

"Are you okay?"

"Get up here. Top, then left." She buzzed me in.

I don't know about you, but I think we men are a laugh riot. "Are you okay?" I'm asking her, when what I want to do is bury my head in her chest and say, "I'm not okay. Hold me."

Violet Winters read me like a book.

"Poor baby. Thanks for coming to check on me."

She was wearing a white terry-cloth robe and white men's pajamas with pink piping, some New York designer's idea of sexy, like Jockey for girls, as if lingerie weren't the only way to go.

"Sorry." I sort of stumbled across the doorway.

"I'm sorry. I look like a ten-year-old at sleepover camp in these things."

"They're nice."

"Poor Elliot. I'm going to make you a bath and a drink. Rémy?"

What was this thing with baths? First Myerling, and now her. Did I look dirty or something?

"I hate baths."

"You'll love it. C'mon. We'll play house."

She took me by the hand. The bathroom was about the size

of my apartment. You could swim in the tub, and there was even a bar. I surrendered. I'd take a goddamn bath.

"It's nice in the daytime, or when it's raining. The skylight—oh, my God."

We both looked up. The skylight was standing wide open, and I sensed that one second earlier somebody had been watching us.

"Obviously, you're the one they're after," Dr. Winters declared with the clarity of her second stiff Rémy.

We'd checked the roof, the fire escape, the parking lot. We'd woken up the guard and his Doberman, who'd seen nothing. "And he's a real warrior, let me tell you," the guard had said. The Doberman still looked drowsy if you asked me.

What it all boiled down to was what looked like a robbery attempt—unless you had a recent history with skylights. I began to feel that I was dealing with a master criminal, not just a murderous thug. I was dealing with a man who could open an apartment like a can opener.

"They said it would take a blowtorch to get that skylight open," Violet complained.

"I'm sure that's what they used."

"Really!" For once, I'd impressed her.

"If we've got the technology, they've got the technology," I lectured her. "It's my homicide rule number three: Never underestimate your opposition. I got it from Mike Ditka."

"Well, Detective, I appreciate the primer, but you're obviously the one they're after."

"Why obviously? This is your place, not mine. You're the one who knew Jack Nesbitt."

"Oh, everybody knew Jack Nesbitt."

"Not me."

"Elliot!" Violet reached for my hand and held it captive.

"Don't scare me. I knew him years ago. Before he was notorious and I was respectable. And I am respectable."

With her shiner and men's pajamas, Violet Winters was starting to look nonrespectable. This struck me as a good thing. That might have been because we were both exhausted.

"Real respectable," I teased her. Now she was rubbing a bare foot on my shin. I captured it and nibbled along the arch.

"I have worked very hard to be respectable . . ." she managed to get out before she surrendered. The way to a woman's bed is through her foot, which is something none of the books ever tell you. The foot is Africa—underexplored, wild with possibility, a lot more remote and adventurous than a breast, a thigh, an ear.

"I do have this thing with my feet," Violet purred.

She took me by the hand and walked me toward the bedroom. I don't know what I was expecting, but not the white eyelet teen-queen heaven, canopy and all, that was Violet Winters's bedroom.

"It's so—"

"Pretty?"

"Girlish."

"So am I, Elliot. In secret. But before I can join you, I have to check in with my service. Sometimes I have about a million messages, so this may take a while."

She patted the bed, told me to lie down and she'd be right back. I remember sipping my drink, savoring the afterglow. I remember thinking what a comfortable bed she had, what a comfort it was to be there. I remember thinking how many messages she—and all doctors—must have. . . .

When the alarm went off it was seven A.M., and her side of the eyelet didn't look slept in. Out in the kitchen, I found brewed coffee and a note on that violet paper:

You needed to sleep and I needed to go in to work. Can I have a rain check? V.

Do I have to tell you I was disappointed—and relieved? She was still—technically—a suspect and I had still not technically—taken her to bed. There was also the guilt factor. Call it too many years of Catholic education. How would I have felt? Facing my ex-wife Gloria's grief wreathed in the morning-after of another woman's bed?

Chapter twenty

———■———

"I wanted it to be you."

Gloria pounded me with both fists. Zach was inside sleeping, and she and I were on the back porch that Jamie and I had built the summer she was pregnant with Zach and wanted a place to sit in the sun. Maybe I had loved her once upon a time. That was ten years ago, and the porch sagged in places because I never kept it up. "I wanted it to be you, oh, Elliot. . . ." Gloria was sobbing now, terrible, heartrending sobs. I patted her hair. "Oh, Elliot, it's not fair."

"No, it isn't fair."

Gloria believed in fair. She always had, despite all evidence to the contrary. Fair was at the basis of most of her grievances with life. It wasn't fair other women had husbands who came home at five and she didn't. It wasn't fair, I remembered now, that the neighbors had a porch where their baby sunned and we just had a patch of dirt yard. It wasn't fair. . . .

We used to fight about it. As if, had I just agreed with her that all things should be equal, it would make things fair—or more fair, at least. Then she'd have had an "understanding" husband even if he didn't come home at five, make more money, go to bingo with her Thursdays at St. Angela's. All she wanted, Gloria used to say, was for life to be fair. But life isn't fair, and never will be.

"It wasn't fair," I agreed with her now as she wept against my shirt.

"It wasn't fair they got Oscar. He loved me," Gloria sobbed.

I knew what she meant. Life isn't fair, and Gloria had loved me more and differently than I loved her. Loved me, perhaps, the way Oscar loved her. It was a trick of the lens. I was smarter, stronger, better in Gloria's eyes than in my own. She expected a lot of me and I disappointed her, but I was grateful, in a way, for those expectations. To be taken so seriously gave me something to live up to—unlike the love that gives you something to live for. From the few things Oscar had said to me about Gloria, I knew that through his eyes she was more beautiful, more special, more worthy than through mine. He "really" loved her—or loved a more lovable version of her than I had ever provided. It wasn't fair.

"Hey, you guys, what's going on?"

It was Zachary, barefoot, in pajamas, curious. It must have seemed like old times—his mother crying, me stiff and distant.

"Oh, Zachary! Zachary!"

Gloria reached for our son, but I stepped between them and scooped him up. "We've had some bad news," I told him. "Oscar got killed on duty last night."

I didn't say "Oscar got killed in my own apartment, where I should have been." I didn't say "Oscar went for your bear and that got him killed." I didn't want Zach putting two and two together and coming up with his fault.

"Really?" Zach was blinking in the bright sunlight, still

sleepy, unable to take it in. "Look at the cardinal." A bright red bird had settled on the homemade bird feeder Zach and I had made together one summer over the Fourth of July. "And there's his mate." A second, less-colorful bird had flown to his side.

That set Gloria off again. I patted her shoulder and headed inside with Zach still riding my hipbone. "What about bacon and eggs?"

But the phone was ringing, and when I answered it, I was who they were looking for.

"Myerling says to call him right away, and there's press all over the place, boss." It was Lynch. "Maybe I could stop by there later if that would help—"

"We'll see. I'll be there in twenty minutes."

Zachary was listening intently. He was sitting at the kitchen table doodling on a Post-it pad. I grabbed the pad to jot down Myerling's number. It wasn't the one at the morgue. I didn't want to call with Zach there.

"Hey. That's my picture."

"Sorry, champ." I'd written right over his doodle.

"Can't you stay for breakfast?"

"Not this time. Tell your mommy I'll call her later."

"Dad?"

"Zach?"

"It doesn't feel real."

"No. That's okay for now."

"Okay." He was back to doodling.

"Gloria? I'll call you later. I've got to go back in."

I called this in the direction of the back porch. I knew she would say it wasn't fair.

Myerling was waiting at Harry's when I got there. Harry was busy at the grill, and Myerling was fidgeting by the window.

When I'm dumb, I'm dumb. I told Myerling I put the ring in evidence. I would have sworn I did, which is why I trust witnesses to lie no matter how hard they try to tell the truth. What Myerling told me when I called him at the mystery number was that he'd found the ring in Gomez's pocket when they brought him to the morgue, and that he had to talk to me. Okay. I was ready to talk, but Myerling wasn't.

"Maybe we should take a walk."

"Harry's okay."

"Let's walk."

I got a Coke to go and fries, and Myerling acted like we were watching continents form, although the whole order took maybe three minutes.

"You don't get it, do you?" he said when we were outside.

"I don't care about getting it, I'm trying to solve it, which nobody seems to notice, Harold."

"You haven't taken the baths."

"No."

"You didn't put the ring in evidence."

"Yes, I did."

"Ever make a mistake like that before?"

"No."

"See what I mean? Something's affecting you."

"You can call it the devil, Harold. I'm going to call it stress. Things fall through the cracks."

We were walking north past a motley collection of winos and bottle stores. Urban renewal, my ass. We did not fit in, we would be remembered, but I was the cop, and Harold the coroner had chosen our venue.

"I wanted to talk to you about Gomez."

"Ice pick, right?"

"Wrong. A kris."

"What's that?"

"A ceremonial knife with a wavy blade."

"You're saying Gomez was a human sacrifice?"

"I'm saying he had the ring in his pocket and the kris through his heart—that's all."

"That's not all, Myerling. I know you twenty years."

Myerling sat down abruptly. We were at a glass-free stretch of curb. He gestured for me to join him.

"We could have done this in my car."

Myerling didn't answer. For a minute he didn't say anything at all, leaving me time enough to appreciate just how uncomfortable cement could be on my buttocks.

"C'mon, Harold," I said finally. "Spill the beans."

"Okay," he said. "I saw this coming. I saw it when I picked up the ring."

"C'mon, Myerling. Don't give me you 'saw' it."

"There was death in that ring. Death in its past and in its future. I saw it."

I looked at Myerling sideways. Maybe he'd been working with corpses for too long. Maybe he'd stepped quietly around the bend a while ago and none of us had noticed.

"I know what you're thinking."

"What?"

"That I stepped around the bend a while ago."

His exact words. I felt a chill creep up my arms and my shins.

"Galvanic skin response," Myerling said with satisfaction, pointing to where the hair on my forearm stood at attention. "You know I'm telling you the truth."

He was right about that. My inner cop was paying close attention, elbowing me to do the same. "It's the truth. It's the truth," my cop was telling me, practically jabbering. I surrendered: Myerling was telling me the truth, no matter how unlikely it seemed to my rational mind.

"Okay," I said. "You saw it. Did you see anything else?"

"Yes," Myerling said. "Woods."

"You've already mentioned that one," I said. "The night I brought Johnny's finger in. You asked me if I remembered those kids in the state park. They were in a woods, remember?"

"No, this wasn't about the kids. This was you—running."

I coughed and spilled my Coke. Myerling pounded me on the back. "Swallow wrong?"

"I dreamed it. I dreamed it the night I put the ring in evidence. I don't remember my dreams very often, but this one was so clear. There was a full moon and I was running with a sound in my ears like a drum or a—"

"Human heartbeat? Terror is what you were hearing, Elliot."

"Yes."

"What else?"

"Why does there have to be a 'what-else'? You read minds, is that it, Harold? I've known you twenty years, and now I find out you read minds. I should take you around with me like a bloodhound. You could just tell me who the guilty parties are and save us all a lot of time and trouble."

I was babbling. Myerling heard me out—gently—and then he asked again, "What else?"

"It's too crazy."

"Try me."

"The night I took the ring?"

"Yes."

"The night I dreamed the thing about the woods?"

"Yes."

"I left the ring in evidence but took the Bible like you told me. I left the Bible in the living room."

"Yes."

"When I woke up from that dream? The Bible was by my bed."

Myerling crossed himself.

"I thought you were Jewish."

"You still don't get it."

"I'm a lucky man."

"Elliot, you need protection."

"I'm a cop. Who'm I gonna call? Ghostbusters?"

"Spiritual protection."

I got to my feet just as a red pickup rounded the corner. I grabbed for Myerling and got him up, too, barely. The pickup sailed into the package store window right behind us. If I hadn't stood up—Myerling was peeking in the pickup's broken window.

"Muy borracho," said the driver just before passing out.

"Let's get out of here," Myerling said to me. We hotfooted our way back toward Harry's joint.

"What about 911? I should at least write the guy a ticket— I should—" I was half kidding.

"You should get yourself just what I told you, some spiritual protection. And take those baths." Myerling wasn't kidding at all.

He slid behind the wheel of his Lincoln Town Car and waved me good-bye. Evidently, he had concluded I was a dangerous place.

Chapter twenty-one

Back at the station, everything was about what I expected: balls-out total chaos. Somebody had tossed a painter's tarp and a "don't disturb" over Gomez's desk—as though he were a suspect, not a victim, as though he were sleeping, not dead. Lynch was on phones, and from the look of it, he was toasted.

"Hi, boss."

"The press?"

He mimed strangling someone midair. I knew just what he meant.

"They come up with any good theories?"

Lynch relaxed a little. "They do that a lot?"

"It's their thing."

"Well . . ." He looked queasy.

"What?"

"I got this one call that said you were involved with a secret cult. . . . I told them you were a practicing Catholic."

Lynch thought it was funny—or tried to think so, until he

saw my face. I looked put out, and I knew it. I did not need a whacko religious fanatic.

"What kind of secret cult?"

"Actually, I told them to call you back." He looked guilty.

"That was smart. Good work." He looked relieved.

My cop was screaming at me. This case was getting very out of hand very fast.

It wasn't the death toll I was thinking about. It was the information flow. Except for Myerling, who was as silent as his customers when it came to the press, I had talked "cult" to nobody. Left to my own devices, I'd never have thought cult. That was Myerling's call, or maybe Chabrol down in evidence.

I had turned the ring in. I had given it to Robert Chabrol, who signed it in without much ado.

"Vanilla's," I had said.

"Mmm."

He'd written out the ticket while I caught the sports update. I remembered it now. I called down to Chabrol just to verify, planning some cock and bull.

"He's out today. Been out a couple days. Hepatitis or something."

My cop was sinking a pylon into my stomach lining.

I thought of Myerling. Maybe he was right. Maybe I was late to the party and did need spiritual protection.

"Look something up for me. A couple days ago, a ring, under Vanilla."

The line was quiet for a long time. My cop enjoyed a stroll through my intestines.

"No, sir."

"No what?"

"No ring, sir!"

"What's the paperwork say?"

"No paperwork, sir."

"You don't— Never mind."

I got off the phone without asking him for an addresss for Chabrol. I'd get it myself. Never rattle before you strike.

Before I checked out Chabrol, I had a personal call to make. I was an alumnus in good standing at St. Ignatius, and I used that and my full title to convince the secretary who answered to track down Father Bremner for me.

"It could take a while, Detective."

"I'll hold."

She left the line and I used the time to shuffle through my messages. At eleven-fifteen that morning, I'd had a call from Father Aloysius Bremner, S.J.

"I'm afraid I don't have a number for Father Bremner," she said. "If you'd call back Monday—"

"Thank you. I've found the number."

By then I was paying the kind of attention Myerling wanted me to. What were the odds of my getting a call from Father Aloysius Bremner? The first such call in fifteen, maybe twenty years? I would say zero, discounting a miracle. And I am an agnostic when it comes to miracles. I call them coincidence.

I dialed the number on the message, asked for Father Bremner, and wasn't even surprised when he said he'd blocked out time for me anytime after nine that evening. "It's about an hour's drive, make that an hour and change."

I straightened up my desk and made a stab at looking productive. I wanted to check in with Zachary, touch base with Jamie, get back to Nesbitt's, get a look at Stoufley's Nesbitt portfolio, make sure someone was dealing with Gomez's family and the financial arrangements, call back Violet Winters and thank her for her hospitality, get flowers for Gloria, and remember to eat something. I started with Jamie. As far as I knew, he didn't even know about Gomez.

"Yeah. Jamie here."

"Where do you want me to start?"

"Skip Gomez. Gloria called me. I got Zach right here."

Two birds with one stone. "Put him on."

"Hi, Dad."

"Hi, Zach."

"You coming over?"

"For a few minutes."

"Dad?"

"What?"

"Could you take me to some Bulls games?"

Poor Gomez. I wanted to say "Easy come, easy go," but Zach wasn't usually that kind of kid—although all kids probably are at least some of the time.

"We'll have to see. Tickets are hard to come by."

"But we've already got ten tickets, Dad. Oscar told me."

My cop grabbed me in a tight fist.

"No kidding. Then I guess we can. Tell Jamie I'll be maybe fifteen minutes."

I got off the phone and went straight to Oscar's desk. I pulled off the tarp and the don't disturb sign.

"His sister's number," I said over my shoulder to Chaworski. I made a show of riffling the Rolodex. Looked in the center drawer, lifted the blotter. Bingo. I found the tickets in an envelope embossed "Jacky and Johnny's."

Now it came clear to me. So much for Oscar's spontaneous and heartfelt speech about reformation. Reformation, my ass. Unless I missed my guess, the tickets were a payoff for services rendered to Johnny Vanilla. Just what services, I didn't know. What I did know is that both men were dead, and that the deaths were connected. It occurred to me that sex was the possible connection.

A taste for strange sex was like any other addiction. The hunger led you further and further into exile. If a junkie would turn a trick to cop a bag of dope, what would Oscar Gomez do to keep himself supplied—and not just with Bulls tickets? If Vanilla had a taste for street girls, maybe Oscar had an itch for the uptown kind that Johnny knew. Gomez must have been pimping for Johnny Vanilla. Hadn't he said as much? There was a scary thought.

A second, scarier thought intruded. If I had mentioned "cult" to nobody, what were the odds of someone calling, out of the blue, to mention "cult" to me?

"Hey, Lynch," I shouted across the bull pen. "What did the guy sound like?"

"What guy, sir?"

"The one about the cult. Did you notice anything?"

Lynch thought for a moment. "Actually, yes. I did notice something. His voice was, I guess you'd say, gentle."

"Gentle? You mean quiet?"

"Not so much quiet, exactly. More like soft. Almost feminine."

"But it was a guy?"

"I thought so. It was sort of velvety."

"Thanks."

I thought about Violet Winters's voice, its smoky, whispery quality. Was she the one who had called to say "cult"? Killers have a peculiar relationship with the cops who chase them. Sometimes it gets intimate. A game of hide-and-seek or a ghastly dance. If Gomez was pimping from within the department and the killer was phoning in tips, this investigation was getting very intimate very fast. What did I expect? I had a murder right in my own apartment.

Chapter twenty-two

The Lady of the Lake Retreat House is a glory: redbrick, three-storied, built in a figure eight enclosing two court-yards with fountains. The place reflects the deep pockets that were once the perks of Mother Church.

"In dealing with spiritual law you learn to ignore the odds." Father Bremner was chuckling as he led me down a long, echoing hallway toward the library.

To me as a young man, Father Bremner had seemed old twenty years ago. Now that I was an older man, I was sur-prised to notice, Father Bremner seemed remarkably youth-ful. Lithe, fitter than I was, even at sixty plus, he walked with the quick, catlike grace of a born athlete. His hair was snow white, close-cropped, almost military. I thought of the phrase "A soldier of Christ." Bremner looked like a soldier, all right, a retired officer with laurels galore. I mentioned the coinci-dence of his call. He shrugged it off.

"I just found I had the itch to call you."

"I'd been thinking about you, Father."

"Hmm. I find that happens."

The library was a fine room, paneled walls, towering book-
cases, mullioned windows, even a fire.

"I know it's summer, but so often a chill is spiritual, don't
you think?" Father Bremner talked as though the spiritual life
were a matter of fact, daily and observable as the weather.
I'm sure for him it was.

His forty-five years "with the order," as the Jesuits put it,
gave him security like my twenty-plus years "with the force."
I imagined that to him I was a spiritual rookie, that he saw
me coming the way I did Lynch.

"Pull up a chair." The temperature outside was in the mid
sixties, but he had correctly diagnosed my chill.

"I've been working on these murders," I began, then
looked around me.

"We're alone. You can talk."

So I talked. I told him about Nesbitt, about Johnny Vanilla,
Stoufley, and Gomez. I told him about the missing finger, the
lost and found ring, the sleepwalking Bible, and about Myerling's vision. I told him about my dream, the crank call
about secret cults, my divorce from Gloria, the attack on
Zachary—even my attraction to Violet Winters.

I talked for an hour. Father Bremner added a log to the fire.
We watched it catch fire, then I talked for nearly an hour
more. Once, a younger priest came to the doorway to offer us
tea. We both declined, although Father Bremner asked him to
see if there were brownies left, and two good glasses of milk.
A few minutes later he was back with the order.

"My vice," Father Bremner said cheerfully. "My own recipe."

I paused long enough to devour two brownies and down
the milk. Outside the window, the wind picked up and the
leaves made a soft shaking sound like the rustle of vestments
from high Mass.

I had come to Father Bremner for advice. I had expected to lay out the skeleton of my problem, or my situation, and listen to him analyze it. That didn't seem to be what he had in mind. Every time I would wind down, he would say "Go on," and I found I could go on, that I wanted to go on, that I wasn't nearly finished. When I got to my guilt about Gloria and my grief about Zachary, the tears came. Not manly tears, but great torrents of them. I couldn't even protect my son. It broke my heart.

I suppose you could say I confessed. I remembered what he'd taught us twenty years before in theology class; a definition of sin as "missing the mark," a shortfall rather than a deliberate evil. By that definition, I was definitely due for confession. No matter what area of my life I looked at—cop, father, husband, would-be lover—I seemed to be missing the mark.

The tears subsided as abruptly as they'd come. Father Bremner handed me a white linen square and offered me the last of his second brownie. I gulped it like a kid.

"Go on," he said.

Now I told him about the shadow of some sort of cult with those kids in the park years ago. I described the pentacle, the ritual feel to the crime scene, and the two missing children whom I alone believed to exist. I mentioned the way they had haunted me through the years—as Carson Stoufley's severed head in a bucket, the bloody paper cutter blade as a terrible, death-dealing sword might do in years to come. I told him about Johnny Vanilla's blood on my shoes, Violet being raped at twelve by her teacher, Gloria and how she wished it were I who was dead. I spilled all of my terrible secrets in no particular order, and why? I didn't quite know.

"You might want to add a log." Father Bremner indicated

the fire. I realized he was settled in and ready to listen all night if need be. "Just add a log, Elliot," he instructed.

I selected a piece of cedar, which burned with a smell almost like incense.

"Comforting, isn't it? The old smells."

Father Bremner read me coming and going. I wasn't ready to make Mass every Sunday or go back with Gloria into our empty marriage, not that she'd want me, but I did feel in some important sense that I had come home. Not to Mother Church, but to a father. I thought of what a friend who'd gone to 'Nam had always told me—that he needed his dad to know the horror he'd seen and done and to forgive him.

"I'll pray for you," Father Bremner said simply after I'd finished. I don't know what I expected him to say. I don't even know exactly why I went to see him, or why he summoned me after all those years, but I do know that after he told me he would pray for me, I felt immediately, immeasurably better. "Spiritually protected," Myerling might say.

"Somehow, I don't really get the impression this all has to do with Satan," Father Bremner remarked as he showed me into my unmarked in the courtyard outside the retreat house. "Although I suppose he's always got a hand in it."

I was heading back into the city, enjoying the midnight lull on the freeway, when it hit me: Where's the money? If Father Bremner saw the hand of satanic evidence in most mortal mischief, my own experience as a cop was that Satan's hand was usually to be found counting the money.

"Where's the money?" I knew the question—which didn't mean I had the answer.

Chapter twenty-three

———■———

Violet Winters was waiting for me when I got home. She was camped in her Porche outside my high-rise, asleep at the wheel, earphones in place. I rapped on the windshield. She opened her eyes but didn't jump.

"Catching Zs?"

"Get it while you can."

"What are you doing here?"

"I was jumpy. I even tried to borrow a dog."

Of course she'd be jumpy. I'd meant to check on her, thank her for her hospitality. I did that much now.

"Oh, you're welcome. Besides, it's your chance to return the favor."

I didn't argue. I even felt a little jumpy myself. I was a big boy, but I hadn't been looking forward to a night where Oscar Gomez had died.

"He's a friendly ghost." Violet Winters read my thoughts. "And besides, your place hasn't got a skylight."

She was right about that, which didn't mean I let her go in with me. I went alone, gun drawn, and found my boys had done a very nice job. The scene of the crime, a.k.a. my apartment, looked as it always had—no messier, perhaps even a little neater, thanks to Dr. Winters's folded piles of laundry.

I retrieved Violet from the hallway. "Aren't you going to carry me across the threshold?"

What the hell. I scooped her up and carried her past the spot where Oscar Gomez died. Violet Winters and I had indeed crossed a threshold. I knew it was risky. I knew it was bad professional ethics, and I also knew, as Oscar Gomez said to me of Gloria, "It's all right. I love her."

If you're picturing anything torrid, Violet Winters was back in her cowgirl gear and looked like the tomboy she probably once was. Her shiner was still in evidence, smaller and lighter, just a sinister bruise that looked like bad eye makeup.

"Sorry about my dropping off last night."

"You drank some of the same scotch I had the night I got this." She brushed a fingertip along her eye. She looked exhausted.

"You're saying it was doped?"

"There was enough meprobamate in that scotch to have killed me if I'd been a serious drinker. When it hit you like that, I got it. I mean, I like to think I'm an attractive woman . . . and when you snoozed off, I thought, Either I am losing my edge or this stuff is doped, so I took it to the lab."

"And you are an attractive woman, Dr. Winters."

"An attractive woman who was doped, beaten, and not even robbed."

"Some people do it for kicks, but I think this time is more dirty pictures. I'm sorry about that."

"You're sweet, Elliot. Can we have something that's not sick? I'd like that, I think."

I took her by the hand and led her into the bedroom. The

Bible was on the table by the bed—hardly a great seduction prop.

"Didn't know you were religious, Elliot."

"I'm getting there."

I wasn't ready yet to tell her about the floating Bible, Myerling's vision, or my trip to visit Father Bremner. Just at the moment she didn't look ready to hear any of it. She looked like a kid herself, like Zach, rubbing her eyes, stifling a yawn.

"I'll get you some pajamas."

"Thanks. I'm really flunking in the femme fatale category."

"Hey. We've had enough fatalities for a while."

I gave her my never-yet-worn Father's Day pajamas and half my bed. I went into the kitchenette, and by the time I got done with ice trays and water and J&B, I came back and found her out like a light. So far we weren't stars in the carnal knowledge department, but to tell you the truth, it didn't bother me. Sleeping, Dr. Violet Winters appeared young and wistful, neither a victim nor a suspect. She looked like a beautiful woman, and—I promise—my friend.

I tucked my blanket under her chin. I wasn't tired anymore. I knew where to find the money: Blackmail was a lucrative business, but not nearly as lucrative as pornography.

Chapter twenty-four

For a hot night with a full moon, it was quiet in Chicago. My scanner didn't crackle more than a hundred times. Violet Winters was sleeping in my bed, I was officially off duty, but my insomnia ruled me and I turned on my scanner for company.

After tucking the good doctor in, I took my J&B and retired to my couch. I wasn't in the mood for David Letterman and his East Village devos. What I needed was clarity, not more sexual confusion.

If I could link Carson Stoufley to Jack Nesbitt, and link both of them to a pornography ring—my plan before Stoufley was so rudely decapitated—then I had a motive for my murder. If I could link Vanilla and Gomez to the same ring, I had a motive for all my murders. The problem with doing any of this was that I had no proof. As Ricky Noonan had been quick to point out, there was an awfully thin line between art photography and pornography, and most people thought of Jack Nesbitt as an artist.

Noonan owes me, I told myself. He'll have to let me search

Stoufley's. I was comforting myself with this thought, when the scanner crackled about a flash fire and a possible bombing in The Golden Spike, a gay bar on North Halsted Street. From my plate glass window, I could just make out the blaze. Down below me, fire trucks were surging north from their base at Webster on Oz Park's northeast point.

On impulse, I picked up my phone and dialed my cousin Charles. The Golden Spike was hardly his style, but I was dialing before I thought it through.

"Hello?" My cousin's voice sounded velvety with sleep, as if his unconscious were throaty-voiced Marlene Dietrich.

"Sorry, Charles—"

"Elliot?" Now it was my cousin's voice as I knew it. "What are you doing calling me at three A.M.?"

"Sorry. My scanner picked up a fire bombing at The Golden Spike—"

"Oh, my God!"

"I didn't really think it was your style, but . . . I dialed before I thought."

"Don't worry about it. Nice to be cared for. Thanks."

With that, Charles was off the line. I stood there, phone in hand, replaying the call that I'd just made. My cousin's voice had sounded gentle, had sounded velvety, had sounded just like the voice that rookie Lynch had described.

"You are losing it, Elliot," I told myself, "if you really think your cousin Charles is making anonymous calls to you about secret cults."

I stretched out on my Naugahyde and repeated to myself the fiction that Ricky Noonan would be cooperative. Of course he would. We were old, old friends. . . . I just wanted a little favor.

■

"No," said Ricky Noonan. "No way. I think you're miles off base, and I can't see giving you carte blanche to rummage through a dead man's effects."

I'd found Peter Abramson, the state's attorney, first thing in the morning and managed to catch Ricky before he got to the bench. We were in chambers. He was suiting up. He had an athlete's build and energy. All I wanted was a search warrant for Carson Stoufley's. Since Stoufley was dead, that seemed simple enough.

"Show cause," Ricky snapped. We were in chambers. He was fussing with his robe, which looked badly pressed.

"Pornography, same as Nesbitt," I told him.

"And I told you that pornography to you may be art to somebody else. For all I know, you're Archie Bunker on art."

"Come on, Ricky. We're talking about murder. I need that warrant."

"Courker would never forgive me," Ricky said.

"And who, exactly, is Courker?"

"Stoufley's executor. Nice-guy lawyer. He golfs Thursdays just like I do. His group usually tees off right behind mine." I was the one getting teed off. Ricky Noonan was sounding awfully Gold Coast. Not wanting to offend the artsy set—

"Ricky, Jesus Christ— What does he care if I search his dead client's house? Why don't we at least ask him?"

Ricky knew I had him cornered. He muttered about privacy, about letting the dead rest, and then gave me the name of Courker's law firm.

"If he says okay, okay. I'll give you what you want. But I still don't like it," Ricky warned.

"Since when are you Mr. Conservative?" I couldn't resist asking.

"Drop it, Elliot. Don't push me. If Courker agrees to it, you're in. A favor." With that, Ricky Noonan swept from his chambers.

Chapter twenty-five

———◾———

Carson Stoufley's lawyer, Sherman Courker wore a pin-striped suit, rep tie, wing tips. Even a near crew cut, as if even his hair had his father's 1950's values. He carried some extra weight, about a person's worth. He also carried a larger than normal quotient of curiosity.

I met him at Stoufley's rock pile. He'd agreed to show me through with startling alacrity. "I've always been curious," he'd said on the phone. Waddling slightly, he led the way.

"I don't know what you think we're going to find. Carson was totally aboveboard, always, a wonderful guy."

"Nasty death for a wonderful guy, Sherman."

I followed him past the cacti, past the tropical plants in the breakfast room, past the kitchen quarters to a small staircase at the rear.

"A little eccentricity," Sherman said. "He called it his cave. I was never invited to see it." He sounded miffed.

Courker was leading the way, with some difficulty, down a narrow staircase with rough stone walls. Every ten feet or so, just above eye level, there were electric sconces of overwrought wrought iron. The whole place looked like the set from a bad Dracula movie. The door at the bottom featured heavy studded nails and a pirate-style padlock. Courker opened it with a key. I half expected Bela Lugosi to meet us. "The cave" was eccentric, all right.

"You have to understand, I've never been down here myself. I kept a key for him, of course, as his executor, but I can't say I really— Oh, my."

Courker was babbling, as well he might. The cave stretched off in all directions, an entire underground complex larger than the house above it.

"This is something, isn't it?"

"The question is, what?"

"Well, archives, of course. That's what Carson always said. Although what Carson said and what he meant—"

Courker was getting on my nerves. I suggested he have a seat while I poked around. He was glad to rest. I left him seated in an outsized chair, the sort Nosferatu was so fond of.

It amused me that Stoufley's secret life contained a taste for kitsch. This was a secret life, all right. Upstairs, Stoufley's home was *Architectural Digest*. Down here it was Gothic, even silly. The walls were all rounded, bulbous with irregularities, like a cave in an amusement park made from papier mâché. The main room, or cavern, was some forty feet across. It featured an outsized fireplace at one end, the end where Courker was seated, and at the far other end, a smallish wooden door. It was locked.

"Got a key for this?"

"Oh, yeah. Sorry." Courker struggled to his feet.

"Just toss it."

The key came skittering across the floor.

"Into the dungeon," I joked.

The small door opened into a small room, stark white with

a large steel trestle table dead center with a photographic scrim suspended alongside it. My cop turned a slow somersault in my stomach. A battery of outsized lamps and a large, locked silver camera case stood in one corner.

"Carson stored some things for Jack. Sorry if I startled you."

It was Courker looming in the doorway. For a big man, he'd been quiet as an overweight cat.

"That about it?"

"No."

Along one wall were large metal storage cabinets. The kind with narrow drawers used for storing art, maps, architectural renderings, that sort of thing.

"Those are just extra prints and things."

"Courker, if you don't give me some time and space to do my job, I'll have to ask you to leave."

"Whatever you like," he sniffed. "I had thought you might appreciate my guidance."

For Christ's sake, he was sulking. I forgot how much people liked playing cops and robbers. Sherman Courker wasn't trying to be a pain in the ass, he wasn't even trying to protect his client, he just wanted to be included in.

"What the hell. Give me a hand, then." He looked thrilled.

We started with the top drawer, first cabinet, and we worked slowly and methodically, one print at a time. Even to my eye, some of them were beautiful. Nesbitt's forte was the human nude, and he rendered them with a sense of mystery and mastery that frankly awed me.

"He was awfully good, wasn't he?" Sherman shared my sentiments.

We were on the third cabinet, third drawer, when we found what I was looking for. I'd suspected it since the night before, driving home from the retreat house. I knew it for certain when I spotted the little room with its trestle table and scrim. Did I say the table was outfitted with straps and stirrups?

The third cabinet was ordered in a progression I'd noted as we worked through the second. Gradually, a plate at a time, Nesbitt's work was darkening, growing kinkier. What had begun as classical scenes of the nude form slowly and inexorably darkened into something else. A slight contortion of the torso, a scarf-bound waist suggesting bondage. The play of black and white tones, then black and white skin tones, interracial couples, then couplings—all executed with the meticulous craftsmanship for which Nesbitt was famous. "A master of the shadow," I remembered one review. That was putting it gently.

The final and bottom drawer of the third cabinet—there were four—opened with difficulty. One print had wedged itself at an angle against the slide. I eased my hand in to dislodge it. Something sliced my finger.

"Ouch!"

"Don't bleed on them. They're valuable."

"So am I, Courker."

"Of course, Detective. I only meant—"

"Relax. It's just a paper cut."

I shook the drawer a little, then tried again. It slid open. Staring back at me, with one drop of blood speckling her breast, was a woman's torso severed at the waist. Courker involuntarily gasped.

"Why—it's fake, of course. I wonder how he did—"

If it was a fake, I couldn't tell. For all its technical perfection, the image was as chilling and clinical as any Roger Rogaine had ever shot for me.

"How do you suppose he managed that?" Courker was still sputtering.

"Quite a trick."

I shuffled rapidly through the rest of the drawer. The shot was one of a kind. I suspected it was there by accident, lodged up and out of sight until I dislodged it.

"One torso," I said. I turned to the fourth cabinet and tried the top drawer. Locked.

"Can't get it open?"

"Locked. I'm assuming you've got a key?"

Courker fished in his pocket. He came up with an entire ring of Stoufley keys.

"Let's see . . . gate, front door, back door, garage, cave— what a name—archives, that's here, ah—" He'd arrived at a small key.

"Let me try." I jiggled, twisted, forced. Nothing.

"Oh, well, probably more of the same. Do you think? I'd love to look through everything at our leisure, but I am due in court."

"Probably just more of the same." I wanted Courker to relax and cooperate. "Could I borrow that key ring over-night?"

"Why, I don't think Carson would—but then . . ."

"Carson's dead, and that's the crime you'd be helping me solve. You can have them back tomorrow. I just can't see wasting more of your time. You're a busy man, and you've already been generous."

Courker was going for it. People usually fall for the you're-so-important-why-don't-you-get-lost routine. Flattery will not only get you where you want to go, it will usually get you out of it.

"Well, all right. But if you find anything unusual . . . any-thing I should know about, you'll tell me."

"Of course. You're the executor. There's an investment to protect."

"Well, then, actually, I am running late to a state occasion. Partner's son's bar mitzvah."

"Better scram—and I'll call you."

I pocketed the keys, walked Courker to the door, let him out, and locked me back in. The front door was a key lock from the inside. Carson Stoufley was a cautious man, but a dead one. The odds were that his murderer knew him all too well.

After Courker left, I went back down to Stoufley's cave, into his archive room and directly to the fourth cabinet, which unlocked neatly. I pulled out the first drawer.

There was Violet Winters. She was twelve years old, naked, and very beautiful. She had a woman's body and a look of such gravity on her face, such sorrow, I understood suddenly that it wasn't just art that had made Nesbitt hide her face in the other shots, the ones I had seen at the station. Nesbitt hadn't wanted to see that face, to see those child's eyes looking at him with such reproach.

The shots of Violet had a progression that didn't surprise me. The top dozen were arty nudes—nubile young girl, the body as objet d'art. From there the shots moved further and further from innocence. The final shots of Violet were child pornography. The one that haunted me was an image of Violet kneeling, with an anonymous cock, an enormous cock, resting against her forehead. So that was Nesbitt's forty-footer. And that was what he'd used it for—children.

Drawer by drawer, child by child, the depth and perversity of Nesbitt's obsession was revealed: first young girls, then young boys, drawer by drawer, younger and younger, more and more sexually explicit, more and more bondage.

For years I had known the rhetoric: Pornography is about power, not sex. But nothing brings that idea home the way a single photograph can. Picture a tiny child tied in place while an adult male lowers himself—

You get the picture, and Nesbitt had taken thousands of them. I went quickly through the last few drawers. I could feel a terrible sickness settling on me as acrid and dank as sweat: These were children.

"New pussy." "Buttonhole." I'd heard the street slang for kiddie porn, but they didn't begin to convey the reality.

I pulled open the last of the drawers.

First shot up: A young boy, no older than Zachary, was being sodomized in crystalline detail. I slammed the door shut, locked the cabinet, made my way lock by lock, backward, to the street, fighting gorge the entire way.

Out on the street, I could smell myself reeking like an animal. My chest hurt. My stomach was heaving. Sweat was running down my legs and they were shaking. If I were a hypochondriac, I would have called it a heart attack. Myerling had given me a word for it: kriya, a sort of soul seizure, a bout of spiritual sickness, you might say a fever. Chilled, soaked with sweat, and trembling, I, a cop of twenty-plus years, was suffering the effect of human evil.

I turned into the alley. I pressed my back against the cool stone of Carson Stoufley's house. I closed my eyes. Even without what happened to Zachary, I would have been shaken. But the thought of Zachary turned my reaction into resolve.

"Hey, man. You okay?"

I opened my eyes to see a slick young man, early twenties, eyeing me the way I wished a woman would.

"Get away," I managed to spit out.

"Yeah. Sure. Only trying to help." He backed off like he saw something in me that frightened him.

He did, and it was rage.

Chapter twenty-six

When I stepped out of the salt brine, my bathtub was filled with water that was charcoal gray. I thought of the gray smudge on Myerling's silk. I was going around the bend, and I knew it. Salt baths, spiritual protectors, visions. All of this was exotic stuff for a Chicago cop. Eye of newt if you asked me, but no one was.

To Father Bremner I was a rookie, a spiritual rookie. Hell, to Myerling I was a spiritual rookie. Not to be a total jerk, I was used to being the one with the answers—or at least the one with the procedures for getting the answers.

Still, "A good cop is open-minded" was my own rule number four. And so, in the interests of being open-minded, and because I ached all over like I'd been beaten, I thought of Myerling's salt bath and called it an Epsom soak.

Yes, it felt wonderful. Myerling had left a message saying set bowls of salt in the corners of your house, and feeling experimental, I'd done that, too. The apartment was having its salt bath, I was having mine, and when it was over, I felt clean for the first time since the whole episode had started.

"As within, so without," Myerling or someone had written on the flyleaf of the Bible. Did I say I was up to my chin in hot water and reading Psalms? I was. Don't ask me to explain the impulse. If I had to, I'd blame it on Father Bremner, on sanctifying and actual grace.

The point is, when I stepped from the tub, I left the water an ashy gray. You'd have thought I'd been working the coal mines. I guess it's fair to say I was.

When I said before that cops know things that other people don't, I suppose it sounded arrogant. If it is, call it the arrogance of experience, the earned knowledge of a life's work.

Some of my earned knowledge was the gray in that bathwater. Knowledge isn't always about seeing the light. Sometimes it is letting yourself see the dark.

Jungians call it the Shadow, the dark or unacceptable self. The self with fears, dark passions, unseemly desires. As a young cop, I had wrestled with my own shadow, wrestled hard enough to need to name it. "My Jesuit side," as Jamie called it, had sent me skittering to the books. It's a primitive instinct, the need to name something to counter its power. Adam named the plants and the animals as a sign of his dominion over them. In the Old Testament, the Jews worshiped a god who would not let them speak its name: Yahweh.

At twenty-eight, wrestling for the first time with the shadow, I had gone to the books to get a handle on it. A spiritual undertow I called it then. I watched it claim my friend and partner, Frankie.

To be brief with the story, we were working vice. Our beat included a string of stripjoints on the edge of Greektown. After a while, the girls knew us, we knew the girls. We knew who did dope, who hooked a little. It was information, part of the job: knowledge, not power. At least for me.

For Frankie, it was different. It had a pull, an undertow, as

I said before. As we would learn some new scrap of street talk, he would seize on it, turn it over like a rock, hoard it. I was gathering knowledge. He was collecting it. To him, it was power. Knowing things made Frankie feel one-up on people. I can't say when I first realized this, but I knew something was skewed. But I'm getting ahead of myself.

We knew two girls, Rose and Jackie, knew them well enough to have watched their rise from novice strippers to headliners, from pawns, if you would, to queens. Frankie had a thing for Jackie. I called it a crush, but obsession is what it came to.

He said that what he was interested in was her power, the way she twisted men into needing her, into panting, ringside, slipping twenties, fifties, whatever she would "let" them give her into her G-string as she danced.

"It's an addiction," Frankie said about the other johns, not seeing it was an addiction in himself. Not seeing it the way I saw it, the leaning into the fire, the slip from "knowledge" into obsession, from curiosity into jealousy.

"She should go straight," Frankie would tell me.

"Why? She likes what she's doing."

"She should settle down. It's dangerous, some guy could go nuts over her."

To my eye, some guy already had.

"She gets off on it, Frankie. Leave her alone. You don't want to play."

But he did want to play, and he used his precious knowledge to leverage his bets. Jackie's act suggested to him—and probably to everyone—that Jackie was into bondage. Frankie got into it himself.

"You know about *True Detective*."

"Everybody knows about *True Detective*, Frankie."

"Strong stuff."

True Detective, for the uninitiated, is porn disguised as cops and robbers, grisly whodunits where the what-they-done was awful: tied her up or down or filleted her or hacked her up.

"Disgusting stuff," I told Frankie, and meant it. He couldn't hear me because the shadow had him and he was sliding under. Calling it knowledge, exploration, doing his job, Frankie was walking further into the dark country he shared with Jackie. She was his prey, or he was hers. It was never clear to me. They played their games, worked out their "power" arrangement. What was clear to me, when Jackie was found in a Dumpster, still bound, still gagged, still warm, was that Frankie was somehow responsible—Frankie and the shadow and an "accident."

Ever since Frankie, I have been wary of the shadow, wary of the way that darkness can call itself "knowledge" and insist that you explore it. It's been said that great explorers are all men of obsession, that the search for, say, the source of the Nile chose its participants, lured them with fame, with immortality, above all with "final knowledge," until the beasts, the disease, the fear or their simple hubris in the face of the shadow led them to overextend themselves, to trust their knowledge, when what they lacked was wisdom: the simple wisdom of knowing when to stop.

What I saw in those drawers at Carson Stoufley's was a man who had fought with his shadow, underestimated it, and lost. Crossing an invisible line, sober alcoholics call it in cozy retrospect. Unfortunately the line does not present itself to us. It does not say "To here is safe and beyond here lies addiction, madness, death. Beyond here you will be hooked, no matter what you tell yourself. The shadow will have you."

The answer to the question of how evil can I, a basically decent man, be is: More evil than you can yet imagine. The truth the shadow hides from us is that there is no automatic limit, final boundary, no place we can say, with absolute certainty, we would recoil. By the time we get there, we may be ready to go further.

I am certain that's what Frankie and Jackie discovered playing *True Detective* games. I know that's what Jack Nesbitt found. Trick or not, it's the thought that counts. Never duel with the shadow: Elliot's rule number five. And none of us is immune.

Nesbitt's pictures were almost addictive. I was with him there for a while. The next time, would I go one shot further? Would the line I drew today have moved? I knew that it would. Knowing that made me feel vulnerable.

Although it felt different to me now, my first encounter with Dr. Winters had made me alert for the presence of the shadow. The sparring, the ego play, the desire to win—these were the shadow's lures. So were my rationalizations: "Just once. I can handle it. It's business . . ."

Surrender, not control, is how to deal with the shadow. Never challenge it. Never test it. Never flirt with it. The shadow always wins.

"The shadow always wins . . ." I caught myself slipping under between that thought and the twenty-third Psalm: "Yea, though I walk in the valley of the shadow . . ." I stepped from the tub and saw the gray of my shadow there behind me.

Chapter twenty-seven

———■———

"Visitation rights." As if he weren't my own son. What about fathers' rights? What about just plain missing him? Why couldn't affection, not legislation, set the schedule for our times together? I know I am not the first father who has wondered these things.

Zachary and I were at Lincoln Park Zoo. We had been there an hour, enjoying the oasis of green, the talking trees whispering to each other above the distant traffic, the chatter of monkeys, and the shrieks of children.

Zachary was more quiet than usual, and I had to fight my own impulse to fill the quiet with chatter. What I needed to do was listen. Just in case Zachary needed to speak.

In awkward silence we visited the great apes, shivered at the slithering reptiles, stood on a little rise and watched the zebras cavorting in their wooded paddock. Zachary acted mute until we got to the bears. We were watching three polar bears have at each other with boisterous slaps of water, huge sheets of it swept up by their giant paws, when he suddenly piped up.

"Do you believe in guardian angels?" Zach asked.

One of the bears was clambering to the plastic shore. He stood and shook himself, arms outstretched: a big, snow-white, dangerous angel. Zach was absorbed in watching the big bear. Like me, he could not quite fathom the idea that a polar bear was dangerous. It looked too playful.

"Yeah. I guess I've got an angel. Why?"

"I have a guardian angel." Zach said this in the same tone he might use to reveal possession of a particularly hot baseball card.

"You do?"

"Yeah."

"What does this angel look like? That guy?" I hooked a thumb toward the bear, snowy white and magnificent.

"No."

"Well. That settles that. Don't give me any clues or anything."

"My angel's skinny," Zach said. "And blond, like your friend."

"What's his name? Gabriel? Raphael?"

"Nah. My angel has a regular name."

"And what's that?"

If he heard me, he didn't answer. Zach dropped the theological speculation, retreating into his thoughts, oblivious to the pandas, the jaguars, the antelope all coexisting much the way Chicagoans did—uncomfortably trapped in close quarters, convinced of one another's murderous intents. We did go back to the reptile house and see "the world's largest serpent," a giant anaconda with an ominous lump in its middle.

"Dinner," I said.

"Do you think it hurts?" Zach asked.

"It's probably pretty quick."

"I think it hurts."

"Probably so."

"I came here with Oscar. Did you know that? He liked the snakes."

He would, I thought, but didn't say it.

"I'll bet you made Oscar pretty happy."

"He said I did. Dad?"

"What?"

"Do people turn into angels when they die?"

"I'm not sure, Zach. But I know who we could ask. I know this old priest whose specialty is things like angels. He lives out in the country and makes great brownies and goes fishing a lot. I guess he's pretty good."

"Could we go sometime?"

"Sure. I'd love to take you fishing."

"To ask him about angels, I mean."

"Sure."

After his question about the angels, Zach was back to silence. I had time to devise one of my non-theories about his sudden interest in guardian angels: He needed one, and found the idea of an invisible protective playmate very comforting.

I knew how he felt.

Chapter twenty-eight

———■———

I rang the doorbell at Dr. Malcolm Crutcher's house in Highland Park in early evening. I'd waited for rush hour to pass before making the drive. Crutcher's house was in the expensive, well-zoned "woods" behind the Ravinia music park. The doorbell tinkled, and so did the strains of Oscar Peterson floating to me from the music pavilion half a mile away.

"Free concert," I said to Mrs. Malcolm Crutcher as she opened the door. "A house full of music."

"It can drive you crazy. Can I help you?" she asked, not merely from politesse. I was staggered, jaw agape, and knew it.

The woman who opened the door to me, or Malcolm Crutcher's wife, Jack Nesbitt's ex-wife, was a woman I'd last seen as a severed torso in Carson Stoufley's drawer.

"Do I know you?" she asked.

"No such luck," I steadied myself. After all, she'd recovered. So would I. "I'm Detective Mayo, Chicago homicide."

"This must be about Jack. Come in, won't you?"

Mrs. Malcolm Crutcher was a tall drink of water—Evian, no doubt. Younger than I'd expected, younger than she'd looked as a severed torso, although that kind of thing ages you, I suspect. Then again, Highland Park was a town full of doctors, and perhaps Dr. Crutcher numbered an excellent plastic surgeon among his friends.

"You can call me Ilene," said Mrs. Crutcher, a phrase that always struck me funny, as though there were some other names I was not allowed to use—Mary or Patty or Eleanor.

"Can I get you a drink, or don't you drink on duty?"

"Since you put it that way, Ilene, I feel obligated to decline."

Might as well call her on her nonsense. I found myself feeling adversarial, even hostile. I was about to blame it on the shadow and his favorite sexual game of cat and mouse, when I remembered it wasn't just high-octane pheromones. That was dangerous enough, but there was something more dangerous at play here. Ilene was an expensive-looking woman older than Violet by a few years, but the same general type: a knockout blonde, tall as a ski slope, with tits like the Alps and legs wicked as any slalom run. An embarrassment of riches, you might say, but remember, this was the woman who sent Violet Winters's nudie shots into the hands of the police. That she'd done it with malice aforethought I didn't doubt.

Ilene Nesbitt Crutcher gave off the scent of trouble the way the smell of leather gives away the price of a car. Mess with me and you'll pay for it, her label read. A jealous woman in love with a philandering man, she'd blamed Violet for his roving eye, and she wanted to blame her still for what Jack's vagrant lust had done to her pride.

"Jack wasn't a very nice man. Perhaps you've heard that."

"Go on." I was using Father Bremner's trick: Just let them talk. "Lovely house, by the way."

Ilene Crutcher accepted a compliment the way a haughty maître d' took a tip, thank you but no promises.

"Sure about that drink?" She wanted me to talk.

"It's after hours. One scotch." I could oblige her.

Ilene Crutcher was at the bar, an expensive thing in a room full of expensive things. The fake Monet over the piano looked real.

"Nice painting."

"Monet."

So it was genuine—or as genuine as Ilene Crutcher herself. "I don't know what would have happened to me if Malcolm hadn't saved me," she was saying.

"Somebody else would have saved you."

"You say the nicest things."

"You're that kind of woman."

"I'll take that as a compliment. It's true, men do like me."

She served me cleavage and a scotch. It looked like we were going to be pals.

"Malcolm's a real sweetheart," she went on. "Not an ass-hole like Jack—despite his line of work."

"I'm sorry?"

"Proctologist, remember?" She was showing off her sense of humor. She'd decided she liked me. For the record, women often do. I've never been sure what to do about that, which amuses Jamie.

"You're supposed to fuck them," he would say, exasper-ated by my hesitation. For myself, I've always felt my hesita-tion is what attracted them in the first place. And that was the way with Ilene Crutcher. I knew what she was after: that spark of interest that said, "I'm a grown-up, and you're a grown-up, so we can't, but I'd love to." I wasn't giving her the satisfaction, and it was annoying her. A woman like Ilene likes to be validated.

"What a terrible job you have."

"Not really."

"But you must meet a lot of interesting people."

"Not really."

This wasn't what she wanted to hear, and it made her get straight with me for a minute.

"I wasn't sad the son of a bitch died. I wasn't sad about how he died. I could quibble about timing, why now and not fifteen years ago, when I really hated him, but all in all it was a good thing."

"Ouch."

"He hurt me."

"Poor baby."

"If you're going to be disgusting, you can finish your drink and go. You have no idea what he put me through."

"I have some idea."

"I doubt it. Jack was a user. He used everything and everybody. He'd promise you the moon and then deliver—"

"A picture of it?"

"I get it. You admire his work."

"Not particularly."

"Good. Because I've had that up the ying-yang, let me tell you."

"So tell me, who else, besides you that is, wanted Jack Nesbitt dead?"

She laughed. Just let me try to get to her through all of Malcolm's love and money. So I asked her again.

"Who else, besides you, Ilene, wanted Nesbitt dead?"

"Oh, God. The line forms around the block."

"Forms around the block?"

"Forms to the left and goes around the block. Whatever that dumb expression is."

"Just a few thoughts."

"All right. Carson Stoufley. John somebody. D'Amato. Maybe."

"That's a big maybe."

"Sorry. You asked me to speculate." She didn't sound sorry. "And then there was this girl he dumped, Violet Winters. Dr. Violet Winters, if you can believe it. A real little whore. She'd been chasing him since she was ten or something."

"Normally, blame is placed on the perpetrator, Mrs. Crutcher. Not the victim."

"I find it hard to think of Violet Winters as anybody's victim. She is one tough cookie. She always was. 'Prematurely sexualized,' my husband calls it. Jack liked that kind of thing. 'The far side of kinky,' I called it. The King of Kink. That's what you want for the tombstone."

"You weren't into it?"

"Never. Let him fool around with his little obsessions."

"You weren't threatened?"

"Hardly. You see, he could try whatever he wanted, he wasn't going to find anything better."

"Sitting on your groceries?"

"To be vulgar about it."

"What about that torso shot?"

If looks could kill, I'd have been fatally wounded. "I let him talk me into it—"

"Some talk."

"To tell you the truth? When I saw it, it scared me."

I was glad something could.

"I told Malcolm about it. He said it was sick."

"Now, there's a diagnosis. So you were seeing Malcolm when you were still Mrs. Nesbitt."

"I was seeing him *as* a doctor."

"And why was that, you don't mind my asking."

"But I do." She squirmed, slanted her eyes away. "Oh, all right. Hemorrhoids. This is a fun conversation."

My cop was having a field day. Hemorrhoids? No way. Prolapsed rectum. Corrective surgery, more likely.

"Let's go back to Carson Stoufley. Best of friends."

"Jack thought so, too, but Carson was robbing him blind."

"Not Carson! Good upstanding rich boy Carson? That gives Jack a motive, not him."

"Oh, Jack took care of that. When he found out, he seduced Carson's lover, took pictures of him, of them together—very personal pictures, if you know what I mean. Of course, in the show, they were called art. Well, it broke Carson's heart. Oh, everybody acted like it was a big joke and let bygones be bygones, but it broke Carson's heart, let me tell you."

My cop was tugging at me to pay attention here.

"You sound almost fond of Stoufley."

"Why, of course I do. I always was. We were both Jack's victims, you see. It gave us something in common."

"So you kept up with Stoufley? After the divorce, I mean?"

"Not really. It was too awkward, but I always thought he was a lovely man. 'Nother little drink?"

"No thanks. I'm the designated driver."

"I'll tell Malcolm you were quite the gentleman."

"A load off his mind, I'm sure."

"Now, now. I'm very trustworthy, Detective Elliot."

So is a snake, I was thinking. Sooner or later it bites you. Malcolm Crutcher may have rescued her years ago, but in her

mind Ilene Crutcher was still a victim, and victims feel justi-
fied in anything they do.

"Thanks for everything," I said. "And tell Malcolm he's a
lucky man."

Do I need to say I wanted her to think I thought so? We
parted friends.

Dr. Malcolm Crutcher saw me the next morning at his downtown office, an expensive suite on Michigan Avenue. After a
brief wait, I was shown into the inner sanctum. Malcolm
Crutcher's office was furnished better than most homes. It
featured a small Monet, a large couch, the lake gleaming
dully half a mile below and beyond the windows, and a pale,
ice-blue carpet that matched. All in all, the office looked expensive, reassuring, solid, and charming, like Malcolm
Crutcher himself.

"Detective? Great to see you. The boy's doing well, I
hope?"

"I hope so, too."

"Oh, I'm sure." Crutcher came toward me hand outstretched, a big, charismatic guy more like a politician than a
surgeon.

"Heard you saw the wife," Crutcher said, all affability but
letting me know he ran the show. "Thought you'd want to
see me, too. She can be pretty inarticulate about all that." He
was scolding me, in his way, for putting her through it again.

"She was married to him, Doctor. It was my job to talk to
her," I explained.

"I'm sure it was. I call that marriage her trial run,"
Crutcher joshed me, man to man.

He was a charmer, no doubt about it, but then, most Michigan Avenue doctors were. The charm factor supported their

inflated fees. Still, Crutcher struck me as better than competent, insightful. I wanted his take.

"Your wife wasn't so much inarticulate as bitter. What was your impression of Jack Nesbitt, Doctor?"

"My impression? Terrific artist, sick guy."

"I guess your wife had a tough time of it." I wondered how much Crutcher really knew.

"She did, but that's all in her past," Crutcher said firmly. "You'd be amazed, Detective, how a helping hand, offered at the right time, can change a person's life. That's what I like to think I'm doing with those kids downtown—offering them a hand up, letting them put the past behind them." I could hear him saying the same thing to Ilene herself. He was a persuasive man. It was easy to see how his wife and his patients would view him as a protector against all their troubles.

"She saw you first as a doctor, she said."

"I'm not at liberty . . ." Crutcher shrugged apologetically, asking for a little professional courtesy. I couldn't afford to extend it.

"Tough job, eh?"

"Just like yours, I'll bet."

Under his nice-guy manner, Crutcher was tough. Very politely, he'd assessed my job and said, "Don't fuck with me." My cop was paying close attention. No wonder the former Ilene Nesbitt felt safe with him. As Zachary's father, I'd trusted him. Now, as a cop, I felt different. Crutcher's veneer was smooth and difficult to penetrate. His social manner made it hard to get to the truth. Or perhaps his truth was better dressed than most.

"Do much reconstructive surgery?"

"Some."

"Child abuse, that kind of thing?"

"Not often, Detective. Hernias are more often my line."

There was a soft, melodious chiming. It went on and on.

"Excuse me," Crutcher said. He picked up his desk phone, and the chiming stopped.

"Yes?" He listened, shook his head.

"They queuing up?"

"I'm sorry, Detective. They are queuing up, and now I've got an emergency. If there's anything I can do for you . . . Take a card from my girl on the way out. I'll tell her to give you my home line, too. Sorry I don't have more time. And, by the way, I think you were right to be conservative about the work with your son."

With that, Malcolm Crutcher dismissed me. He was smooth. As I got to my feet, he was back on the line. "Helen? Give the detective a card and my home line, would you?" He got off the phone. "All set," he told my back.

At reception, Helen had a card waiting for me. She was a big woman, nearly as big as Crutcher. They could have been brother and sister.

"Thanks," I said. "Hear the doctor does a booming business in reconstructive surgery. Heard he's the best."

"Well, yes. He's very good at it. The best there is, in fact. That's true. Why else would he be so busy?"

"Thanks, Helen."

I took the card and the information.

Riding the elevator, I chided myself for resenting Malcolm Crutcher's social ease. Maybe it's really his money I was resenting, his unshakable sense of privilege. I try to be fair. I try not to think of the rich as different from you and me, but a guy like Malcolm Crutcher can be just a little too wonderful. What was it about him that made me feel like a cockroach?

The elevator opened on street level, and crossing the lobby I got a good long look at myself in a gold-speckled decorative mirror. What I saw made my reactions to Crutcher entirely understandable.

Crutcher and I were the same age, same height, and same build. There the resemblance stopped. He was a silver-haired social lion, tennis-fit and well barbered. I was the grizzled beefy guy who looked like pinochle was his most strenuous sport. Crutcher was everything the magazine life said a man should be: the guy in the Johnnie Walker Black ads who drove the stylish car and made the winning investments. Me? I was the law, the guy in charge of helping Crutcher keep everything he'd won around him. I was Crutcher's protection against thieves and murderers, and guys like me who were jealous and wouldn't mind seeing a big-shot doctor take a fall.

No wonder Crutcher was nice to me. He knew I was jealous.

They always did.

Chapter twenty-nine

O scar Gomez was buried out of Our Lady of Pompeii instead of St. Angela's. He was buried three full weeks after his death because Myerling held on to the body for his own reasons while the Gomez tribe used the extra time to gather in Chicago from barrios across America.

The Gomez tribe was large and unvaried: all short, all stout, all looking like extras from a movie about the Incas. Oscar's mother, sister, cousins, and uncle all wore black. They resembled a group of beetles, round-shouldered and skittish even in their pain.

I knew the mother, had met the sister, had tried to help one of the cousins to make the force. He had not succeeded, having been arrested in a rather spectacular fashion for cocaine possession the night before his induction. A bad technicality got him off. He nodded to me now, Oscar's dark twin, although maybe Oscar was darker than I thought.

Gloria, Zachary, and I stood together. I'd wondered how she'd want to play it. She was playing it, I soon learned, as

Oscar's widow. I had been transmuted from ex-husband into family friend. I accepted the demotion gracefully.

Zachary wore a tight, slightly glazed expression. It was a curious expression. It made him look like a little old man. He kept his hand balled in a fist tucked into mine. I realized that in the weeks prior to the funeral, Zach had been able to put Oscar into limbo—dead but not really dead. Now Oscar was really dead and Zachary was shaken.

"Breathe," I told him. "Take a few deep breaths."

"Dad." Zachary was angry with me for treating him like a child. He nodded toward the officiating priest as if I should understand to be silent. Listening to the oratory, I was more speechless than silent. Oscar could have been a general for the sendoff he got.

"We are here today to honor a fallen warrior, a brother, a compadre who gave his life for all of us, for this community, to make our world a safer place. To those who knew him, Oscar Gomez was a gentleman, although he lived in a violent world and it took his life. . . ."

The priest was good, but I had to smile, remembering Gomez's fist through the men's room wall. Next to me, Gloria was weeping inaudibly, her public grief as private as a queen's. Good for Gloria, I thought. Good for Gomez. Good for anybody who finds a little love in this world.

The crowd was about what I expected—Lynch, Chaworski, Daley, the guys from the station, Gomez's family, Harry, Harold Myerling, and then, surprise of surprises, in the back of the church sat Big John D'Amato.

"He was a good cop," D'Amato said as I passed him on the way out. I took the remark for what it was intended, a sign of respect. Somehow it had been borne home to me recently that Lynch, Chaworski, and Daley, even Gomez for that matter, were my "boys." I headed my "family" as surely as D'Amato headed his.

I still didn't know what he was doing there.

Gomez's sister, a stump of a girl, sang the Ave Maria in Latin. Other than the homily, the service was in Spanish. Gomez's coffin was gay as a fiesta float. Gloria survived the ceremony. Only once, when she seized my hand as they closed the casket, did I think she might lose her composure. She didn't, though, and what I got at that moment was my first glimpse of the outsized diamond she was wearing on her ring finger, left hand. I didn't just see the diamond, she cut my knuckles with it.

How did Oscar Gomez, I wondered, afford an engagement gift like that? Maybe that's what John D'Amato had been doing there. I pondered it on the drive to the cemetery. I pondered it as we laid Oscar to rest.

A few Bulls tickets from Johnny Vanilla—okay, call it a return for a few favors. But a diamond as big as the Drake? Oscar had to be into something involving big money. I came back to my notion of Nesbitt, Stoufley, Vanilla, and a porno ring. That was big money. Could Oscar have had a part? Or maybe it was blackmail, or dope, or—maybe I just didn't know.

Several headstones over, I saw Dr. Violet Winters—or someone who looked an awful lot like her, a trim, androgynous figure dressed in khaki pants, hightop sneakers, a T-shirt, satin ball club jacket, and a cap. One more costume. This time she looked like a racetrack figure, a shill. Nice of her to pay her respects. I'd have talked to her, but just as we were tossing earth on Oscar's grave, she faded into the crowd.

———◼———

Don't ask me why I stayed at Gomez's graveside after all of them, the priest, the family, even the grave diggers, were gone. I'd placed Gloria and Zach in a car with Oscar's mother and turned back to wait until I was quite alone. Maybe I wanted to apologize. Maybe I wanted to say thank-you. Oscar Gomez had filled my shoes, and now he filled what should have been my grave—except that my son had missed his teddy bear.

Goddammit, Oscar, I wanted to tell him, you little fuck, you were almost a good man, Oscar, you stupid SOB. What were you doing there? What were you doing, period? With Johnny Vanilla's ring in your pocket and a ring for Gloria as big as the Drake? As big as the Trump Tower, for Christ's sake. What were you being, Oscar, Bulls tickets from Johnny Vanilla, "a good cop" to Big John D'Amato? What were you doing and why didn't I, your trusty boss, even know that you were doing it?

Oscar had been the fall guy and I felt like a chump. And I'd look like a chump, too, if I sullied his name after the fact, trashing Gloria's memories of perfect love. Gomez had put me in a pretty spot. Let him rest in peace or look like a bad guy myself.

Unfortunately for Gomez, and for me, unfortunately for Gloria and little Zach, In order to be a good cop you have to be willing to look like a bad guy. That was Elliot's homicide rule number six.

Chapter thirty

———◼———

I wanted to solve the crime. Crimes. I wanted to save the girl. I wanted to perform all the heroic deeds a man should perform: solve the crime, save the girl, save the day. I wanted to be a hero, and I was a little too exhausted.

Salt bath or no, I wasn't sleeping well. I was rehearsing what I needed to do the next day instead of giving myself the sleep I needed to do it.

I'd told off Oscar Gomez, but he was still hanging around. Salt bowls or not, I'd catch sight of him hunched up in the corners, saying, "Hey, man, avenge me. Solve my crime." The little fuck.

I wasn't getting anywhere solving his crime. I wasn't getting anywhere in a lot of areas.

Romance was in the wings, but it was staying there—which made me feel we were getting old. We were getting old, at least I was. This case was aging me. It was Chabrol.

As I've said, I remembered putting the ring into evidence, remembered the sports update, remembered Chabrol filling out the ticket. "Just like a pawnshop," he joked.

I liked Chabrol, liked the way he kept one ear plug in so that the beat went on even when he was talking to you.

"Terminally hip," Jamie would say.

Accurately, it would seem. Every day for a week I'd told myself I needed to see him. "Hepatitis or something," his replacement had said. "Something bad." Whatever it was, we didn't seem to be getting him back, and so I finally paid him a visit.

Chabrol lived in Pilsen, the terminally hip place to live, half artists and half Latino. I guess he considered himself a little of both. His place was one of those funky, rambling old apartments with a gas space heater and a kitchen big enough for golf. His was on the third floor, so he enjoyed access to the roof, which was where I found him. He'd made a goddamn Eden up there, a verdant jungle paradise right in Chicago, and he'd gone there to die. Amid the flowering plants and trees, he was stretched out on a canvas lounge chair, looking wizened and shriveled. His skin had gone to greenish-gray.

"The Big Lizard waits for you, my man," Chabrol greeted me.

"The Big Lizard waits for all of us," I answered.

"No shit." He was propped on one elbow, grinning, and the grin took everything he had.

"Take care of my cats, man. Make sure they find good homes. They like music and a little hash now and then. Oops. You the boss."

What I'd always liked about Chabrol, I liked still. Even dying, he was his own man, and clearly, Chabrol was dying.

"I had a good run, man. Don't look so shocked. I been HIV positive six years. That's a good long run. Almost thought I was gonna beat it. I told the orishas, good work, you got this thing licked, mama. No way."

As Chabrol talked a big calico Persian sambaed slowly over to his side. She waved her tail so slowly, "Like a fan dancer, eh? This one is Meme." Chabrol reached to pet her and I saw how quickly the disease was wasting him. His arm was a covered bone, little more.

"I need to ask you something."

"It's about that goddamn ring, right?"

"It's disappeared. So's the paperwork. That's what I need to ask about."

"Never should have touched it."

"It's just a ring."

"Who told you that, boss? Not Gomez. You saw what it done to him."

Here was the story I was after.

"He told me you said go get it. He said give him the paperwork and all. I should have called you, but Gomez, he said fine, fine, so I gave him the ring, and I knew the minute I touched it, that second time, that is. I just knew."

"Knew what?"

"I knew what it done to me. Just sittin' there cooking out its vibes. I was beating this thing before that. Beating it. Keeping a positive attitude, eat right, stay real even. Hell, I even fell in love. The partner kind. Stay with me, baby, forever. I am yours. Plant a garden, get a pair of matching rockers, grow old, and smile. That kind of love, boss. The right guy. And then come the darkness after all. That was a bad ring. It belongs to somebody *muy malo*."

He sounded like Myerling. He looked like Myerling would be seeing him very soon.

"Where's your lover? Is he taking care of you?"

"He's taking care of business. Don't you worry. I got about a week. You don't hear from me, you check up here."

"You should be in a hospital—"

Chabrol waved me off. He wasn't having any of my guilt or foolishness. He just wanted me to see about his cats, the Persian and a ghost-gray Russian blue. I saw it now tucked in the shadows under his lounge chair.

"You just leave me alone, boss. Otherwise it just get messy. And you see about Meme and Blue."

I said I would, promised I would, then picked my way back down the fire escape, through the window, through the kitchen, out the door, down the three flights of stairs.

I could have called somebody, the paramedics, he had insurance, we cops are well covered with insurance, but I decided to leave Chabrol to paradise.

And so, lying in my bed, with Oscar muttering to me from the corner, with Chabrol communing with his African saints, his orishas, across town, I found myself picking up my new bedside Bible, thumbing through the Psalms. "Lo, though I walk through the valley of the shadow . . ." I hadn't read half of it before I slept and dreamed.

In my dream, Chabrol was wearing a long white robe. He carried a crucifix, like a missionary. Next to him, at his side, walked a snow-white dog, shepherd or wolf, with hyacinth eyes. I didn't see his cats, but they were there somewhere, I knew. There was drum music, a reggae beat, and even in the dream the air smelled of jasmine and hashish. A Rasta cop, that's what Chabrol had been. In my dream he was entering paradise. It was the sound of a wolflike howl that woke me.

The bedroom corner was light enough that Oscar Gomez had vanished. I checked my watch: five-forty. Fair enough. And then that wolf howled again.

I wasn't dreaming.

The howl became a whimper and the whimper repeated itself until I got out of bed to find it. Barefoot, in my shorts, gun drawn, the full folly, I opened my door to a note from

Violet Winters. The note was on the same lavender linen stationery. This time a piece of it was pinned to a large, old-fashioned kennel, not the kind you could see in a pet store window. First I read the note. "Get a dog, you told me, and so I did. I got a dog for both of us. I kept the mama. This pup is yours."

"Oh, shit." Just what I needed with four murders to solve. Violet Winters could just take her goddamn puppy back. The whimper again. The last thing I needed was a puppy.

"Good morning," I said. "You might as well come in for a while till we call your owner back and she comes to get you."

I hefted the kennel and dragged it across the threshold. This was a big puppy. And not mine, either, I told myself.

That was before I saw her face. Safe inside the apartment, on the spot where Oscar Gomez died, I opened the door latch and said, "Come on out." She did that.

"Oh, Jesus. Aren't you a beauty."

It was a younger, smaller version of the dog from my dream, the shepherd she-wolf with hyacinth eyes. Oh, she was glad to see me.

"What's your name?" I asked her.

She was licking my fingers and face. I had squatted to greet her. She was licking my cheeks, my eyes, a wriggling ecstatic fur ball of canine love. Maybe I did need her after all.

"Daddy!" she all but said. I named her Paradise.

Dr. Violet Winters really was the head of pediatrics at Children's Hospital, exactly like her business card said. I found it in my bedside Bible, deep inside, as if it had been used as a bookmark. Missing little details like this can scare a homicide cop. Then I thought, maybe she left it there herself. The morning I told her to keep the pajamas.

I had tried her at home and then I tried her at the hospital number, filing both in memory. While I was listening to the ringing and thinking what a bad service she had, I pulled the Bible away from Paradise, who was lying on my bed, teething on it, and that's when I saw the card.

"Pediatrics," a voice said.

"Dr. Winters, please."

"Oh, I doubt she's in so early. Just a minute."

"Dr. Winters here."

"Detective Dog Daddy Elliot here."

She laughed. "Oh, good. I had to tear myself away to come to work. What do you think?"

"She's just what I needed in the busiest and most chaotic period of my life."

"I thought the little guy would like her."

"Zach? I bet he will. That had crossed my mind, right before she started teething on the Bible like a good Christian puppy. I found your business card, by the way."

"Didn't want you to forget me."

"Not likely, but a good precaution, Doctor."

"I meant the other little guy, although Zach, too."

"If you're talking about my inner child, I'm going to puke."

"Come on, Elliot. Don't be such an old fart. How does she make you feel?"

"Like I'm ten years old and can't wait to teach her sit, lie down, roll over . . ."

"What did you name her?"

"She came named. Paradise."

"Isn't that funny? I'm calling her mother Salvation."

"Now, that's catchy."

"Sally for short: I got mother and pup from this guy on the street. Outside the Haymarket Mission near the old Salvation Army, remember?"

"I'd forgotten what a nice neighborhood you live in. Yeh. I know the Haymarket. A friend of mine runs the women's side."

"Salvation is big and black and looks like a real hellion."

"Not in my Bible—what's left of it. The puppy's at it again."

"They still look mother-daughter. You'll see. What do you say we take them to the park?"

"Oh, absolutely. And then maybe to a ball game. Don't you work at that hospital?"

"I'm the boss."

"A wonderful thing in a woman, I'm sure. Why didn't I get your full professional glory before this?"

"Because you're a sexist pig, Elliot. One of your more endearing traits, so old-fashioned."

"Which park?"

"Seven o'clock tonight by Buckingham Fountain."

"They allow dogs in that park?"

"Elliot, you're a cop."

"You don't think it's mean? Letting them see each other again, then tearing them apart?"

"We survive it all the time."

"Just barely, Doctor."

"Then I'll see you at seven?"

I got off the phone. For a homicide cop in the middle of an unsolved crime—make that four of them—life seemed surprisingly viable. Paradise drank me in with adoring eyes.

"You'll need a collar, leash, your shots, of course, and a chew bone so you don't eat my holster."

Chapter thirty-one

My working agenda was: touch base with Myerling, check in with the lab for the hair and fibers on Gomez—not ready yet—and contact Zachary's therapist, Dr. Hauser. Zachary was slated for more therapy that afternoon, and I had yet to meet the woman. This bothered me. I called Dr. Hauser's office and wheedled and bullied my way into a morning appointment.

As far as therapy goes, I'm an agnostic. I neither believe nor disbelieve—the least comfortable of the spiritual positions, as the Jesuits had apprised us. As I would gladly tell Dr. Hauser, I believed in contacting my feelings, but my experience was that when they were strong enough, my feelings contacted me. It was the specter of my unacknowledged feelings damaging Zachary that brought me to his therapist's office.

Dr. Hauser kept me waiting twenty minutes "while she made some phone calls," then came to the waiting room and led me back to her office. Perhaps because her specialty was children, Dr. Hauser wore a jumper with a sort of pinafore top that gave her the fashion look of an oversized kindergarten student. Her hair was chin length, blunt-cut, and streaked with gray. She wore no makeup except the Crayola-bright slash of lipstick at her mouth. She looked like a child's drawing of a grown-up—thirty pounds overweight and barely between the lines.

We talked, if you could call it that, in Dr. Hauser's office. She had bright primary colors—which I hated—and Snoopy posters, which I thought were out of date. Garfield the cat was what kids were into now—or were last week.

I hated her office. I hated her questions. I hated my feelings, and I hated, above all, what had happened to my son once or more than once by persons known or unknown "with a power advantage," as the incest literature so delicately phrases it.

"What are your feelings about your son's attack?" Dr. Hauser began. She was an earnest woman, prematurely plump and middle-aged. I doubted she had passed thirty yet. I reminded myself that Crutcher thought of her highly.

"My feelings? They're terrible, what do you expect?"

"But what are they?"

"Well, rage, of course, and shame . . ."

"You feel it was Zachary's fault?"

"Of course not . . . I guess I feel it was mine."

"How would you feel if it were somehow Zachary's fault. Not fault, exactly, but if he knew the man, knew him as a friend? If there was more than one incident?"

"Do you know something I don't? Has Zach told you anything? Are you withholding information, Doctor?"

"No, absolutely not, Detective. It could have been anybody, that's my point. It could have been a friend or relative."

"Bullshit. Not just anybody is a child molester, Dr. Hauser."

I heard what I was saying, and could not believe it. I was speaking as Zachary's father, not a cop. As a cop, I knew that often the nicest people were child molesters. Ministers, priests, teachers, counselors. Male, female, gay, straight, pillars of the community all. "The last person you'd ever expect."

Mothers did it, fathers did it, uncles, older brothers, and baby-sitters did it, the postman did it, the gym teacher, the man who ran that wonderful children's theater troupe did it. Hell, viewed sociologically, child abuse was practically a cross-cultural fad.

On a conscious level, all that Zach remembered, or said he remembered, was that he'd "got grabbed." Except for that "blip" crossing Clark Street after the game, no more had been revealed to him—or to us.

"Are you being straight with me, Doctor? I've got a little problem with trust here. My ex-wife asks for me to not see my son. You support her in this. The theory is I—or my job anyhow—am bad for him. Then it turns out he gets molested while I'm absent. Let me tell you, I think he was primed for something to happen. Maybe he missed me. Maybe he would go off with any guy who paid him some attention."

"Zachary entered therapy due to your divorce. He was having trouble handling that."

"Maybe you made a mistake, Doctor, and Zachary's paying for it. Is that possible?"

"Anything is possible, Detective. That's my point. I was just exploring, playing what-if. I was asking you what if he went along with it?"

"It still wouldn't make it Zachary's fault."

"Would it make it yours?"

"That I should have been more alert, you mean? That I should have known? I guess so. I'd feel worse—even worse, if that's possible—if I found out we knew the bastard."

"You think a child molester wears a sign?"

"What?"

"They don't."

"Don't what?" I hoped Dr. Hauser was less confusing to Zachary.

"Child molesters don't wear a sign."

"Well, of course not, but—"

"But you should have known? Even though you weren't seeing your son?"

"I guess so. I mean, now I hear he was having nightmares that had nothing to do with me or my job."

"Have you cried?"

"Of course I've cried, Dr. Hauser. I'm the 'new man.' You may think you see before you Archie Bunker in blue, but I am as sensitive and liberated as the next guy—who happens to be Rambo." My sarcasm offended me, if not her. Even worse, my throat was thickening with rage.

"I get these pictures," I told her. "And the case I'm working on—the son of a bitch who died—I wish I'd killed him myself. He was into all that—"

"All what?"

"You should have seen the pictures. Little kids, tied, bound, as young as Zach—I'd like to find the bastards—" I could have gone on, would have liked to actually, but Dr. Hauser cut me short, changing the subject.

"Yes, I'm sure. It must be quite an upsetting coincidence. Now, where were we? Oh, yes. What are your feelings about Zachary's progress? I think he's doing quite well."

Dr. Hauser's cheery, matronly manner really teed me off. Or something did. I heard my chest heaving like a bellows.

"I want my son back," I managed to spit out between gasps. "I want him happy. I want him whole. I want you to tell me he will be okay."

I looked straight at Dr. Hauser and gave her my bottom line.

"Let's regress Zach and get this thing over with. Let's find the son of a bitch who hurt him, lock him up, and give Zach whatever he needs to heal. I want you to put him back together again, Doctor. I just want him to be okay."

"Children can recover, Detective Mayo. Children are resilient. They heal. Sometimes it's their parents who stay broken. Who stay angry, bitter, vengeful. You may have to choose, Detective, between being a cop and being a father. Solving the crime, using regression to do it, may be at Zachary's expense. It's my clinical opinion that regression may be too aggressive a tactic."

"Why? He may not be able to handle what he finds?"

"Exactly. Your son is very fragile. He's just suffered a huge loss. More upheaval could be catastrophic for him. That's my opinion. Now, you can change therapists, you can go with a more radical approach, but I'm not sure that's in Zachary's best interest."

"Dr. Hauser? I know you've been working with my wife—with Gloria—for a while now. You may even be friends, for all I know. I hope you'll understand when I say I think she's the one who might have trouble accepting things."

"We all want to think we can handle things, Detective."

"Right. I'd feel a lot better if I didn't feel shut out from my son's therapy, Doctor."

"Sounds like you're a little paranoid, Detective. Is that a hazard in your line of work?"

I was too angry to even reply. I stood up abruptly and

offered her my big and meaty hand. She shook it like I was offering a dirty rag.

Of course I was paranoid. Of course it was a hazard in my line of work. On the other hand, paranoia was often a worthy instinct . . . in my line of work. Let the doctor find me bitter, angry, and vengeful. I wasn't going to give her any more ammunition since she clearly saw us as adversaries. I was going to do something more useful. I was going to solve the crime.

That's what I was thinking as the elevator doors closed behind me. The tears came from out of nowhere, or out of the rage where they'd been hiding. I would have preferred doing this in the privacy of my squad car, my apartment, my life. Instead, I was doing it in a small steel box hurtling toward street level. But the tears felt good to me nonetheless. The elevator reached the lobby just as I mopped at my eyes with a sleeve.

Zachary was slated for three o'clock therapy that very afternoon. It was the kickoff of one hour, twice a week, until further notice. Dr. Hauser did not feel it necessary or advisable for me to participate. After our session, I had the sinking feeling that I had confirmed her earlier suspicions of me. I phoned her from the lobby to apologize for my abrupt departure—and volunteer my participation one more time.

"His mommy will do just fine," she said in that patronizing, matronly tone that may work on children but makes me, as a grown male, want to chew glass.

"You're absolutely sure?"

"That's my job, Detective. I have mine just like you have yours."

Did I detect some sarcasm there? Was it possible that the

good Dr. Hauser had a small problem with men as authority figures—for which I qualified? It was clear she and I had a communication gap and, no, I was not welcome near Zachary in his hour of need.

Fine. I would solve the crime.

Chapter thirty-two

It had never happened before, not once in all the years I'd known him, but when I got done driving through the boiling stew of midmorning traffic, Myerling was waiting to see me at the station. He'd heard about the results of the hair and fiber test and thought I might need "a little reinforcement." At his insistence, we went to Harry's. That meant more driving. More traffic. With its dyspeptic ceiling fan and resident flies, Harry's wasn't my preference, but I was willing to settle.

"This time can we stay here?" I asked. "I'd just as soon skip getting run down by marauding motorists in cahoots with a power ring."

Harry's was empty except for Harry. I was starving—my frequent reaction to stress—and nothing sounded better to me than fries, sliders, rings, and a malted, topped off by a chilly Coke.

Myerling asked for hot water. He'd brought his own tea bag. Harry charged him for it.

"As well he should," Myerling said.

We settled ourselves at Harry's only window, the one that

afforded us a nice view of winos casing my unmarked. My-erling's well-alarmed Town Car practically had an armed guard. They gave it a wide berth.

"So," said Myerling, "what did I tell you?" He was clearly pleased with himself.

"You told me I need spiritual protection," I reminded him. "I got some."

"And in the nick of time, I'd say."

"What a comfort you are, Harold."

"Order up." Harry had pride of ownership. He wasn't some damn waiter. Get that. You were to carry your own damn order. He'd cooked it. "I said order up."

I went to the counter to retrieve my flotilla of cardboard containers: the malt, the Coke, the rings, the fries, the sliders.

"That ought to do you."

"Ought to do me in, Harry."

"Don't bitch to me about it."

Ah, yes. Friends. Myerling was gloating by the window. I still wasn't quite clear why.

"You look smug."

"Vindicated, maybe. They did find that hair."

Myerling was referring to the hair and fiber tests finding a goat hair in my apartment. Since Gomez's mother kept a goat, not to mention chickens, this didn't particularly sur-prise me.

"His mother's got one. She keeps it in the backyard."

"Ah." Myerling looked almost disappointed in me. "You're assuming it's that one."

"Myerling, if it leaves shit like a horse, has four legs with hooves on them, I don't assume that it's a zebra."

"Zebras have cloven hooves, Elliot."

"Like something else you won't mention. You get my point."

"I want to give you another number for me. In an emergency."

"I've got your other number, remember?"

I dug in my wallet and triumphantly pulled out the yellow Post-it with Zachary's doodle and Myerling's number on it. I shoved it across the Formica at Myerling, who turned white.

"Where'd you get this?"

"You gave it to me. Remember?"

"Not the number, this." He jabbed a finger at Zachary's doodle, an awkward star.

"Zachary did it. It's a star, or maybe a badge."

"You shmuck. It's an upside-down pentacle."

"Oh, of course. I should have known. Same way if there's a goat hair on Gomez, it's not his mother's goat, it's some dark, satanic goat. My son draws a star and it's a pentacle, not a star."

"You might call it a witch's star . . . if it were right side up, that is. Pentacles, new moons, spirals—that's all goddess religion stuff. But this is upside down."

"Christ, Myerling. Maybe, maybe not. Which way does it go?" I took the paper from Myerling and inverted it. Now Zachary's star was right side up and Myerling's number was inverted.

"Look at the stickum. You write on those pads with the stickum at the top." He snatched back the little sheet and reversed it. Zachary's star now pointed down.

"All right. What's the big deal?" My fries were getting soggy and so was my mood. Worse, my cop knew something was a big deal. A shrink might call my feeling "resistance." The idea of Zachary idly scratching satanic symbolism did not merely make me uncomfortable. It terrified me.

"The big deal is, pentacle reversed is satanic symbolism. So, of course, is the goat."

"Harold, look, I thought this wasn't necessarily satanism. That's what you said."

"That's what I meant. The goat is Bacchus. Dionysus. Pan for that matter. Pleasure in sexual excess."

"Thank you for sharing that, Harold. That makes me so much more comfortable with my son's doodling it." I shoved the five-pointed star away from me.

I knew where my unease came from. I was seeing the clearing in the woods, the five-pointed star, the three young bodies from twenty years ago. Had we used the word "pentacle" back then? I didn't think so, but neo-paganism wasn't a fad yet and talk of the goddess religion wasn't cocktail party chat. As I remembered, we'd called it a "star" and thought it was a random choice of design, like a flower.

"I can think sex murders. I can think satanism. I just can't think sex murders and satanism and Zachary in the same sentence. It makes me ill."

"That's what I've been trying to tell you," Harold said. "Evil is *live* backward. It will make you ill. It will make you sick unto dying."

"So now it's some kind of voodoo? Harold, pick your theory and stick with it, okay? Paganism, satanism, voodoo, A, B, or C. Not all three."

Myerling gave me a look of infinite sorrow.

"It's something so dark, you can get lost in it, Elliot. It's something you need to take care with."

"Cut the drama. Let's just stick to the facts and see where they lead us. Okay?"

"I am asking you to be careful, Elliot."

"So pray for me, Harold. I've got murders to solve. You can save my soul."

I left Myerling sitting in Harry's. I got in my car and I drove. First north, along the lake. Then south, back along the lake. I was pacing, just using a car to do it. Every time I thought back to the state park murders I felt frightened again, a rookie again, a young cop that no one believed. It had been a dark time for me. I could feel that darkness settling back on me now.

I'd gone to work on that crime full of zeal and imagination. "Too much imagination," I had been told. My theories and findings were dismissed. "Five children, not three? Three's bad enough. Where do you get five? From a tracker? From a bent leaf? C'mon, rookie. Get real. . . ."

Maybe I had been too honest, I thought now. Maybe the other cops, fathers then like I was now, could not bear to put children and sex and Satan and murder into one thought.

A sex cult? Was that what Harold was hinting at? A Dionysian sex cult with multiple murders. That's what I had believed twenty years ago, finding those children in the park. The expression "blood lust" had seemed literal to me. No one had believed me. Was that why I could not believe it now? Or did the nagging sense that there had to be something more mundane come from two decades observing human nature? Lust was real enough, I'd grant you that, but when it came to crime, lust wasn't half the motivator money was.

I checked back in at the station. I had a message to call Ricky Noonan, Judge Ricky Noonan, ASAP, IMPORTANT, the desk sergeant said the message read. I could have gone back in and called him, but the station room was stifling. I decided to stop by and see Ricky Noonan. It was still early. He might not yet be at lunch.

I caught Judge Noonan in chambers: carry-out Chinese in greasy cartons, a ritzy lunch, almost as healthy as Harry's. With their high vaulted ceilings and air of imperial Rome, Noonan's chambers still impressed me, but then, Noonan himself was impressive. It was remarkable how a guy from the neighborhood could clean up with the help of a few Armani suits and a good haircut. Noonan was my age, or nearly, but had the body of a twenty-five-year-old, thanks to the East Bank club where the weight room referred to social standing, not just bodybuilding. Whole careers are built there, I'm told.

Noonan still had his Irish face and his Irish charm, but it was a smooth version, like Jameson. If I make it sound like I'm judgmental—heh, he's the judge. And a good one. And what did a little social-climbing hurt—even in Chicago, where the top was just more money instead of more class?

"That was quick," he said. "I only called you twenty minutes ago."

"I'm just like Chinese. Order in."

"Want some?" He offered me a greasy carton. "What's this about Stoufley? I thought you were laying off that line of inquiry. I thought we agreed."

"Ricky, are you telling me how to run an investigation?"

Noonan looked uncomfortable. "I ran into Courker at the ninth hole. He told me about the keys. It made me a little uncomfortable, Elliot. I mean, I trust your good judgment and all . . ."

My cop was wide awake. What the fuck was this? Ricky Noonan was shaking me down, which meant somebody was shaking him down. I dodged the question.

"I find it hard to picture portly Courker trudging over hill and dale in the summer sun."

"Yeah. Huge mother, isn't he? He rides a cart."

"So what's the scoop, your honor? Who's got their panties in a knot?"

I got the notion that Ricky Noonan was under pressure. Courker was just the cover story. Courker had been thrilled to loan me his keys. Thrilled enough to do a little harmless bragging to Ricky Noonan, who was now questioning my procedure.

"Guess that Stoufley stuff was pretty grim," Noonan said. I was right.

"Nothing you haven't seen before. Warhol shit. Artsy-fartsy S&M. Helmut Newton stuff."

"Pretty sick?"

"Sick enough."

He was wondering about that fourth cabinet, but he wasn't going to say it.

"Anything else?"

"Yeah. I could have used an order of pot stickers after all, but I'm trying to watch my girlish figure. It's not like yours."

Ah, vanity. There's a distraction. Ricky patted his washboard stomach, flat with ripples. He posed like a bodybuilder.

"Here comes de judge!"

"Not bad." I gave him a manly slug in the arm. "Anything pops up, I'll let you know. It was a dead end anyhow."

"Great, Elliot. I knew you'd understand. What can I say? We street kids can't be too careful when we're playing with the Gold Coast boys."

So that was it. Judge Ricky Noonan had political aspirations. He didn't want to cross anyone rich enough to help him along. Did this mean he'd cover up a crime if someone asked him to?

That brought me to Elliot's homicide rule number seven: Don't rule it out.

Chapter thirty-three

It was two-thirty when I left Noonan's chambers, retrieved my unmarked from parking hell, and headed back to the station, home sweet home. Hot and muggy had given way to hot and muggy and wet. The city was enjoying the kind of summer rain that felt like a bad sauna. It matched my mood.

I was a little pissed at Courker, pissed at Ricky Noonan, very pissed at Gloria and Dr. Hauser, and mainly pissed at me. Courker and Noonan were dicking around with my investigation, stepping on my turf. Gloria and Dr. Hauser were usurping my son, Zachary, and I was the one giving these idiots permission.

"Marshmallow man," Jamie called it. "What you're really depressed about is Zachary." I called Jamie from a curbside phone, caught him on the run. "Lunch with some art dealer. Hot shit, El. Look, you got bigger fish to fry than whether Dr. Hauser likes you."

"Thanks, Jamie. What are friends for?"

He laughed at me and hung up, too busy to get out the bandages. That was when I decided to stop by the house and walk the dog. If I couldn't get sympathy from my best friend, maybe I could get some from Paradise. After all, wasn't I her lord and master? And, apparently, no one was missing me at the station. With the heat, there were plenty of new murders, lots of nice gang shootings, and domestic violence.

What did they need me for? Let me play the Lone Ranger awhile longer. I was bad company. No one was reluctant to leave me alone. Besides, I'd been operating for six months now without a partner. It was just me and my shadow while they got everybody shuffled and sorted out.

Some new honcho was working with a computer program to mix and match us according to our skills. I'd said what I thought about that horseshit and everyone had given me a long leash ever since. I'm sure the new guy had found compassion on one of his computer chips, which registered healing time because of the stuff with Zach. Did they think I didn't know it was an open secret by now?

Feeling thoroughly sorry for myself, I parked my car in the tow zone in front of my building and slogged through the soupy damp, past the planter with its plastic azaleas and into the lobby of the high-rise I now called home.

Bobby, our building manager, waved to me from the desk. He was a slight, faintly effeminate young man with the barest remnants of a southern accent and an old-fashioned, pencil line mustache. He had hungry eyes, and once told me he found my job description "thrilling." I tried to be polite in passing. He tried to be something more. I got the uncomfortable feeling I was his hero.

"Glad you're here. That puppy made quite a racket when your maid was in."

"What?"

"I'm not saying get rid of it or any anything. I'm just letting you know."

"Thanks, Bobby. What time did she leave?"

"Oh, I'd say she finished about an hour ago."

"Thanks."

Now, I didn't have a maid, but I saw no reason for our building manager to know that just yet. Let him think I'd come up in the world. And let me thank Paradise for barking.

When I unlatched the door, she set to again. With admirable strength of character, I'd reluctantly shut her in her kennel.

"She'll feel more secure," Dr. Winters had promised me. "And your apartment will stay intact."

As it turned out, I'm sure my intruder felt more secure. And my apartment had not stayed intact. Even if Bobby had not forewarned me, I'd have known someone had been in my place. Myerling would say I could "feel the energy." My cop never bothered to put language like that on his reactions; he just got visceral, fast, like he was doing right now. Cuddly puppy or no cuddly puppy—my place felt creepy, no other word. My cop was using my stomach lining for a trampoline.

"It's too bad you can't talk," I said, wrestling with the pup, giving her a lesson in how not to behave. I could feel my intruder as if she still stood in the doorway.

She? It was, for some reason, hard for me to picture a "she" rifling through my apartment. Should I do prints? Oh, all right.

The balcony door was open. I'd done a quick check on entering, gun drawn, room by room, all two and a half of them, but I had not noticed the open door. A mistake like that had killed many a cop. My intruder might still be with me. I crossed to the door. There was nothing on the tiny balcony but wind and yesterday morning's paper. Which I hadn't bought. I stooped to pick it up, still expecting the intruder to loom at me, even from the space beyond the balcony's edge, but no. And it wasn't my usual paper. It wasn't the *Trib* or the *Sun-Times*. It was the *Chicago Reader,* an underground alternative paper, open to the personals. I took it inside, closed the door, and went to get my print kit.

As you work your way up the ladder, you may gain in knowledge, but you lose in skills. I was as bad at prints as I used to be good at it; you'd have thought I was diapering a baby, talcum everywhere. I got a nice set off the toilet flush, another set off the grip on the balcony door, a couple more on my top dresser drawer. There were more, but you do learn to be selective. I took one last set off my answering machine. My intruder had listened to my messages.

I hooked an old belt to another old belt, looped a third around the puppy's neck and called it good enough. Grabbing the intruder's paper, I locked the door. On our way out through the lobby I stopped to have a word with Bobby.

"Bobby?"

"So it's you and the little noisemaker." He addressed the dog. "What a pretty girl you are. I wish I had eyes like that."

"I don't have a maid, Bobby. Description?"

Bobby's eyes did full moon over Georgia. He looked somewhere between excited and stunned.

"Really. You mean I walked in on a robbery?"

"Maybe. I didn't know you walked in."

"Not walked in, really, rang the bell because of the noise, and he answered."

"He?"

"You can't fool me. She said she was the maid, but she was no maid at all if you ask me. I can spot a queen a mile away. Am I shocking you, Detective?"

"Yes, Bobby, you are."

As I knew, this response delighted him. He couldn't wait to

go on. Neither could Paradise. She was quietly peeing on the floor. I dropped the paper as damage control.

"Tall brunette. Dynel wig. Pale eyes, I thought they were lenses, lilac. Good gabardine uniform, nicer than you see these days, ortho shoes."

"Bobby? You may have missed your calling. Most witnesses say, 'Oh, tall, kind of skinny . . .'"

"But you couldn't miss it, Detective. This one had style. Bad wig or not."

I thanked him and made my escape before he got around the desk and stepped in Paradise's piddle.

"Oh, Detective?"

"Yes."

"Will you be keeping your apartment?"

"Hadn't thought about it."

"Oh. Well. If you do decide to give it up, a friend of mine is looking—"

"Sure thing." I was looking, too. The piss-soaked paper at my feet had a circled personal ad. I stooped to pick it up. It read like an ad for the fountain of youth.

"Enjoy youth and vitality. Feel young again. Call NEW-LOVE."

It sounded like a pitch for a spa, or maybe a male escort service. More to the point, it sounded like a clue.

"Detective?"

"Yes, Bobby?"

"Want me to get your locks changed? I know you may be a veteran of such things as murders and break-ins—"

"Get them changed, Bobby. Hold my keys with you at the desk."

Chapter thirty-four

———■———

Paradise enjoyed her first ride in a cop car. She peered out the side window and cast me an occasional glance as if to say, "Can you believe it?" No. We were driving by kids playing at open hydrants. The west end of the projects, where a YMCA, an old people's home, and the Cabrini Green projects all converged uncomfortably on what was once an innocent corn field.

Chicago is an ugly city, Magnificent Mile or not, and I was in an ugly line of work. There were days, driving Halsted south, catching our sawtooth skyline bold against the lake, that I felt a rush of civic pride, a "Yes Chicago" jingoism. More often, working the neighborhoods with their shingled narrow homes, and yardless, nearly treeless streets, I thought they could have done it differently, and they could have. San Francisco's crowded streets wore pastel skirts: pink houses, aqua, yellow, cream, and powder blue. San Francisco was a girlie town, or used to be. It flirted with you. Why not Chicago?

Because Chicago was a man's town, brute ugly in places,

mainly tans, greens, grays, and browns. Serviceable, sensible, strong, as masculine as an army barracks, standard-issue male. That was Chicago, a brutish town bristling with enough testosterone to render sports a necessity instead of a pastime. All that aggressive energy had to go somewhere. Better the sports arena than the streets. And so the bars had outsized televisions and the beers came in manly mugs and the civic greeting was a shout: Hey, man! How you doin'? How 'bout those Bulls?

"The big time. Grow up to be big and strong like your mommy and you can have a life in crime."

I took a maze of back streets, a scenic tour of what has come to be called "The Clybourn Corridor," and arrived at Area Six reassured that Chicago still had some factories working, even if they were cheek by jowl with yuppie clothing shops and pet stores where they sold kittens for three hundred dollars apiece. I got to the station, if not refreshed, at least no longer angry.

"I'm growing my own police dogs," I told the sergeant at the desk. "Watch her a second." I was trusting Paradise not to piddle in the sacred confines of the station.

"She's pretty."

"Nonsense. She's a fierce, dedicated fighting dog, all strength and gristle."

Paradise was looking as ferocious as Thumper, all eyes and legs.

"I've decided to leave police work and become an animal trainer," I told the sergeant. "I hear the success rate's about the same." Paradise was quietly piddling on the sacred floor of the station.

The sergeant was not amused.

I ran into Lynch in the men's room, where I'd gone for

paper towels. I caught him with his head in the sink. He came up sharply, catching his head on the faucet.

"Shit. Sorry, sir. Just trying to cool off. Guess you know the air's out."

I hadn't noticed.

"You heard about D'Amato?"

"What about him?"

"Tax troubles. Gomez told me to tell you."

"Why didn't he tell me himself?"

"Got me. Then he died and I forgot. Thought of it today because *The Untouchables* was on cable last night—and they got Capone for tax stuff, remember?"

"Yeah. Nobody likes paying taxes."

Lynch shot me a look to see if I was kidding. I wasn't. I felt bad for anybody who had tax problems, Mafia or not. I understood why my uncle Eliot had been so reluctant to bust Capone on tax evasion. Who hadn't cheated, just here and there, on their own returns? Am I disillusioning you? I think the government has disillusioned us all. I think that's why we hate to render unto Caesar the things that are Caesar's. We know that Caesar will only start another useless program or ship off arms to someplace we've got no business meddling with.

Big John D'Amato was having tax problems. Everybody did, I suppose. Tax problems seemed to be a particular bear for Chicagoans. Maybe it's that taxes are the feds, not local. Locally we Chicagoans seldom run across any problem we can't fix, one way or another.

"This town's so crooked, the only time it breaks is when you try to straighten it," the local wags put it. If John D'Amato had tax problems he couldn't fix, even in Chicago, then he had serious trouble.

I got the prints in and asked the computer jock to run a

major. "Yes, sir!" he said. All business. It hit me that he was Chabrol's spiritual counterpoint: terminally unhip, earnest, sincere, hardworking, solid white-bread. Like an import from Dayton, Ohio.

It was three-thirty o'clock. Zachary was mid-session, three to four, twice a week, fathers not welcome. After meeting Dr. Hauser, I had my doubts about her healing Zachary. I had read somewhere that empathy—a.k.a. love—was the healing variable in therapy. That being true, I thought that Paradise might be better help than Dr. Hauser. I hadn't told Zach anything about my new acquisition. I was saving her for a surprise that night at the park. In the meanwhile, I had a phone call to make.

The bull pen was quiet. Lynch was toiling away a few desks from me, but since Gomez had died, the workplace seemed somber and subdued. I caught Lynch's eye, signaled "shhhh," and dialed "NEWLOVE" as directed by the ad. A voice answered. It was velvety and soft. Androgynous, muffled, and sinister.

"Hello," I said, "I'm calling about the ad—"

"Hello, Detective! So good of you to call. Congratulations."

I signaled frantically to Lynch, who picked up silently.

"Congratulations on what?"

"Your progress, of course. You're getting smarter. This was a clue."

"Were you in my apartment?"

"Maybe. Maybe not."

"Why go to all that trouble? Why not just call me on the phone and say you want to help?"

"Spoils the fun."

"Breaking into my apartment was fun?"

"Of course it was! It was also a lesson. I wanted you to see how vulnerable you are. How vulnerable certain other people are."

Across the room, Lynch was nodding energetically, "yes." This was the voice he'd described to me, the crank call about a secret cult.

"Have you decided to help us out?"

"Maybe. Maybe not."

"Why did you want me to call you?"

"To get to the other side, Detective."

A chill stalked my spine. Violet Winters had jokingly used the same words "to get to the other side" to describe her motives for chasing me. I asked, "Violet? Is this you?"

"Oh, very good, Detective. Very good," the caller cackled. "Accuse an innocent victim when no one else springs to mind."

Lynch held up a sign. "It's a man," he had penciled.

"Look, fella," I said into the phone. "Keep your clues and your sickness to yourself."

"What about your son, Detective?"

"What about him?"

"He's the clue you're looking for."

"What do you mean?"

"Look for the crime behind the crime, Detective."

With that, the phone went dead. Lynch was staring at me. I was staring into space. My son was molested—column A. Child pornographers were getting killed—column B. That's how I'd been seeing it. Call me late to the party. It had never occurred to me that Zachary and my unsolved murders were truly connected.

How stupid could you be to involve a cop's son? How stupid could a cop be to rule out that involvement?

Stupid on both counts is the answer, but I was getting smart.

Chapter thirty-five

After nearly fifty years I can say with real clarity, I hate Chicago. No—I should say I hate the Chicago that has come to pass. The romance is gone for me. I remember the smell but I miss the stockyards. I miss Comiskey Park. These days, white collars have replaced blue, and if we are still the city of broad shoulders, it is thanks to health clubs. This Chicago baffles me. What does a guy from the Midwest need with a BMW to drive to LaSalle Street? What does he need with designer clothes? All right, I do hate this Chicago.

Water is all that saves it. The lakefront, its bosom of blond beach, the Chicago River looping through like a necklace of Chinese jade, and Buckingham, tossing her watery curls.

Buckingham Fountain is one of Chicago's glories. Tiered as a wedding cake, festive and frivolous, it's like an earring on the earlobe of a longshoreman, a little frippery for the city. My son wasn't the only Chicagoan for whom the fountain was a favorite, but he was the Chicagoan I cared about.

I took Zach to the park with me that evening—a romp with Paradise and Salvation.

"Wow" was what Zachary managed to say, laying eyes on Paradise for the first time. "Oh, wow. Dad, wow!"

"Wow" seemed to be the reaction Paradise was having, too. She wagged her tail so hard that her whole hind section looked hinged, swinging like a gate. Zachary took Paradise by the leash and headed straight for the fountain's edge.

"Be careful!" I shouted.

"No sharks in here, Dad," Zach shouted back. Okay, so I was an old killjoy—he at least sounded cheerful.

When I spotted a tall cowgirl with a familiar-looking dog striding toward me, I felt cheerful myself. If ever there was a Marlboro woman, Violet Winters was it. I wondered if cowgirls were a common sexual fantasy. Maybe we should have the Marlboro Woman on billboards. When Dr. Winters in cowboy mode planted her haunch next to mine, Chicago abruptly felt like a habitable place.

"So what did Dr. Hauser say? Did she fill you in after his session?" Now, there was a sexy opener. Clearly, Dr. Violet Winters was joining me as Dr. Violet Winters.

"No pulling punches with you, is there? Dr. Hauser said the session had gone as she expected. . . . I would not call that filling me in."

"I've been thinking about Zach—you said something about a doodle before?"

"No, I didn't."

"Sure you did. You said Zach's doodling disturbed you."

"Ah. I must tell you nearly everything."

"I listen well, Elliot. It's my job."

"That's a line straight out of Dr. Hauser."

"Sorry. It's just that I was thinking—"

"We all think. Look, Dr. Winters, you don't have to play therapist with me."

"Ouch. Sorry. I guess I just take an interest."

Dr. Winters looked out across the glowing evening green. Her flank was still next to mine, but the energy was gone. It was Zachary who had her attention.

"He looks okay." That was me, wishful thinking.

"That's the scary part, isn't it?" Straight for the solar plexus, the doctor.

"What do you mean?"

"That's how everybody can pretend it never happened. That's how it keeps on happening. The kids handle it, or seem to, the grown-ups are glad to have it go away. That's what happened with me. I don't know what happened with my brother."

When she didn't elaborate, seemed lost, in fact, to the idyll of the dogs and the light and the playful boy, I finally nudged her.

"Your brother?"

"I had a brother, but they put us in separate foster homes and we never saw each other again. It was as if he never existed. To be fair, I had a part in it. I was amnesiac. I couldn't remember my name, much less his."

"And then?"

"I was supposed to be happy."

Zach gamboled on the grass, the dogs dancing at his heels. He looked so young, so green and hopeful. No wonder so many parents chose to forget.

"I was thirty before any of it came back to me. I was thirty-three before I knew I had a brother. Then I used to imagine him, what he was like."

"Which was?"

"Wrong probably. The last time I saw my little brother was twenty years earlier, and he was already older than we are now."

"Meaning?"

"Did you ever notice how vice feels ancient?"

She was right about that, of course. I'd never put it in words before, but the words she used felt right to me. I thought of Chabrol dying in the sun, the boy hookers parading near the park—these things were ancient. Arriving at a murder scene, looking into the face of a junkie or a wino, watching the practiced walk of a hooker, there was a sense that you were seeing something older than you knew.

Virtue, decency, integrity—these things, by contrast, could seem brand new, like man had turned a corner.

"So you think Zachary might have locked away a secret of that magnitude?"

"It happens. I've had clients who were cult survivors. This one man remembered nothing, nothing at all, about his childhood before age ten. Then he started dreaming about torture, handcuffs and leg cuffs, chains and whips—rituals that sounded like something out of the Dark Ages. He'd be taken to this dark room and tortured. He thought the dreams were symbolic. Of course, he would. His father was a psychology professor at Northwestern."

"They weren't symbolic?"

"They were memories."

"How did you know?"

"In most cases, the hard evidence is vanished. The only way to know is to trust yourself. That wasn't good enough for him. He had a recurring dream of this secret room. A room filled with devices of torture—that's easy enough to interpret as a symbolic dream, isn't it? Well, he decided to take it literally. He went home to his family's summer place and found it. He took Polaroids."

"Every picture tells a story, don't it? Did he get well?"

"Yes. That's why I'm so interested in Zachary's doodles. If

they are a memory, he needs to release it. Give him some paper and pencils. Encourage him to draw."

I wasn't listening, or didn't want to. Zachary was laughing and tumbling the puppy in the grass. The sun was gilding our sawtooth skyline. Dr. Winters's thigh was resting against mine. I gave it some friction and hoped for some heat.

Violet Winters cleared her throat and moved her leg away. "I said you could try paper, see if he did any doodling."

"He did doodle. Has."

"Does Zach's doodling disturb you?"

"That must be it, Doctor. Zach's doodling disturbs me and I repress it. Maybe the next time I'm in my thirties, I'll remember."

"Sarcasm. From the Greek. To cut or tear flesh."

"You sound like a Jesuit, Dr. Winters. Sorry about the tone."

"It's understandable." She patted my leg, but not from any interest.

"Fuck understandable."

I felt like a four-year-old. Not my chosen mode with an attractive woman. Now she patted my shoulder.

"Poor Elliot. Was that so bad? I've had incest kids draw stick figures with blood on their swords. You'd almost think the drawings were staged. A little girl draws herself with a big red spot in the middle. Her daddy figure has three legs, and one of them has a dart on the end. A boy molested by his mother draws her with teeth between her legs."

"All right." She had made Zach's doodle sound innocent by comparison.

I took out my wallet, found the yellow Post-it pad with Zachary's doodle on it. I watched her eyes widen just as Myerling's had.

"Harmless little doodle," I said. At least it wasn't a man with a bloody sword.

"Harmless, my ass," said Dr. Winters. "Didn't the Jesuits verse you in the classics?"

"Ovid, *tres Gallia*. I don't see where it applies."

"I'm afraid you will. On the good side, this little doodle is a pentacle, and a lovely symbol of the goddess religion. On the bad side, it's used by a lot of neo-pagan hedonists."

I must have looked blank.

"Sex cults, Elliot."

"That seems to be a popular theory. Myerling talked about the same thing."

"Then maybe you should listen. . . . Salvation!" Dr. Winters scrambled to her feet. She clapped her hands for attention. She whistled. "Paradise. Zach. Let's get out of here. It's getting dark. Sorry to preempt you, Elliot. I just got the willies."

"Good timing. I just got the hungries."

Taylor Street was an old Italian neighborhood, tarted up for the tourists now, banners on streetlamps, valet parking. The restaurants were still good if you could get into them, elbow your way past the yuppie crowd, *Trib*s folded under an arm: "See, three stars. It's supposed to be super. Let's stay, Steve. Please?"

So Steve or Jeff or Stan, some nice boy working hard at keeping up, working harder at pleasing her, would wait in line and seethe as the locals slipped past and were seated according to a pecking order that still said Italians first, everybody else last.

That was Taylor Street to me, long waits and yuppie crowds, although most of the time the door knew me, or smelled "cop" and let me in. Dr. Winters, Zachary, and I decided to go to dinner on Taylor Street. Salvation and Paradise decided to come along.

"Taylor Street," Dr. Winters suggested. "Garlic gets rid of vampires. It should get rid of the willies, don't you think?"

"The Hub," I counteroffered. "Better yet."

"Yeah, Dad. The Hub. The Hub."

"I yield to the men," said Dr. Winters. "I've never been to the Hub."

The Hub, a.k.a. Torano's, a.k.a. the Vernon Park Hub, was located near but off Taylor Street in more ways than geography. A guy's joint, run by Tommy just as it had been run by his boxer father before him. The Hub was still, stubbornly, a neighborhood joint—unlike most of Taylor Street. Legend had it, and legend in Chicago tended to be true, that the sauce at Torano's was made fresh each morning by the widow of the man who had cooked for Capone.

"Capone sauce" I called it to Jamie, but not out loud. (Tommy liked me, liked me as well as he could like a mick and a cop.) Once a month, maybe more, Jamie and I ate there together and got good tables. Me because of my job, Jamie because of his. After all, he'd been a boxer, and a good one, before he exchanged his gloves for a paintbrush and stepped into the ring as an artist.

"You've never been to the Hub? Jeez!" Zachary was staring at the doctor in amazement.

"I always heard you needed an Italian stallion to get safe passage."

"What does she mean, Dad?"

"She means she's happy to give it a try."

I knew what Dr. Winters meant, or thought I did. She meant she was tall, blond, and beautiful, and wanted to eat when she had dinner, not be the dish. The Hub was a joint where an unaccompanied woman might be distinctly uncomfortable, a place where blondes of all sizes were preferred to their brunette sisters, a place where blondes in minks and a Town Car outside signaled "I made it."

Which was the message the guys at the Hub were busy sending each other, true or not, over their plates of calamari, mostaccioli, the best chicken Vesuvio in Chicago.

"Elliot, my man," Tommy greeted me, slamming into me a time or two like a playful bull. He looked like a bull, Tommy did—short, wide, powerful, a big man no matter what his height. But not as big a man as John D'Amato.

"Brought the family, eh?" Tommy took in Violet, Zachary, and me and made his call. I wasn't displeased. I missed having a family—even missed having Gloria, Zach's and my unhappy family.

I looked around at the families in the Hub, one or two kids, brunette guy, blond wife. It seemed to be standard issue. All Italians got blond wives, at least the second time, blond mistresses, at least. You could say opposites attract, but a high percentage of these blondes had been the bottle's bright idea.

Zachary stood with his fist tucked in mine, looking up at the vintage boxing shots, black and white beauties, that graced Tommy's wall. That was Tommy as a youngster, gloves up. And his dad as a young man, kneeling, gloves up, next to a handsome boxer dog. That shot was my favorite. Zach liked fighters because of Jamie, liked to think he had the inside dope. He could tell you about Ali, both Sugar Rays and Big George Foreman. He and Tommy usually bantered but not that night. Zach hovered against my leg. No playful jabs and feints, not this time.

He had seemed all right, playing with the dogs, but now he was gone. He wore a vague, slightly glazed look. "The inner movie," I called it. You often saw it on crime victims. You're watching them and they're watching it, playing something over and over as if this time they'll get it to turn out right.

"Hey, Zach, let's go check on the dogs," Violet suggested. We'd left them in the car and Tommy's guy, no dummy, had given my unmarked a place of honor right out front. "We can let these guys find us a table, and we can get some air."

"All right, but can Dad come with?" Zachary asked.

My cop woke up. Was Zach being shy, or did he sense something I'd forgotten? Dr. Winters entered my life as a suspect. Had she graduated (or been demoted) from that? Trust her with my son? She had the credentials that said "Trust me," but you learn that those don't always count. Then again, maybe Zachary was just feeling loyal to his mom.

"Stay here," I said. "Tommy's almost got our table."

Violet flashed me a look that said "Thanks a lot, buddy." I realized then what she had known since entering the restaurant: She was the focus of considerable interest. Sidelong glances, even a wink or two.

"Maybe I'll get some air just for me, if you don't mind," she said. She stalked to the door.

It was like catching a glimpse of tooth and claw. I remembered the time Ringling lost a tiger in the Loop. They called out half the force "to get it back alive." A Bengal tiger, the full catastrophe, nine feet long, four feet high at shoulder, not a nice mascot like Tony the Tiger, who eats Frosted Flakes, not people.

Luck of the draw, I got the job. I started with the cat's trainer. "What's the trick?" I asked him. Except for a necklace of tooth marks around one shoulder, he'd survived two decades in the ring with them. "What's the trick?" I wanted to know. What he told me was this: "Never forget what they are."

The same went double with suspects.

Tommy had our table. I went to the door and called Violet back inside. She was chatting with the dogs through the car window. I ushered her inside.

"I needed the air," she told me.

"Nice to have you here," Tommy told Violet.

"Nice to be here," Violet said, moving past him.

"Go ahead," I urged Zach. Tommy had his big battered hand on my shoulder to detain me.

"I hope you find him. I hope you get the son of a bitch," he whispered hoarsely. "Son of a bitch hurt little Johnny."

He was talking to himself as much as me. He was talking, of course, about Johnny Vanilla.

I was halfway through my mostaccioli when Big John D'Amato came through the doors. It was family night for him, too, at least for his second family, the one he had with his mistress, Alice. Big John was a portly man with Gleasonesque bulk and more than a passing resemblance. Alice was a tall, golden blonde, slightly overripe, like a Wisconsin cheese. Their ten-year-old daughter was between them, making them a perfect domestic trio, except on paper, at the courthouse, where the records on him were not inclined to be marital.

Passing like the pope through the sea of diners, Big John gave me the smallest nod, imperceptible, really, except to Tommy, who like all good restaurateurs was hypervigilant and missed nothing.

I was eating slowly and methodically, digesting information as well as carbohydrates. Violet set Zachary to sketching on his place mat. He drew a rocket man with cape, a rocket ship, and then, almost as an afterthought, added a sky for them to fly through, studded liberally with Satan's upside-down stars.

While Zach and Violet doodled, I made a slow and methodical meal. "Mosta" and "ciolli"—that's the way I liked to eat, especially at the Hub, which rewarded such dining with increments of better and better flavor.

"He thinks that way," Zach told Violet. He liked her, I could tell. "Mom says he chews on things like a cow."

"Food for thought?" asked Violet.

"Something like that."

I was thinking, thinking Johnny Vanilla's grisly death had not put Big John off his feed. No matter how close they were, Big John devoured his sausage, mostaccioli, and sauce with gusto. Alice wore a look of motherly pride as he ate the Hub's special salad and more than two full chickens done Vesuvio style. Suddenly Big John was seized with a coughing fit. Tommy leapt toward him but was waved away: It would pass.

I thought I knew the cause of Big John's indigestion. Jerry Delancey had just joined our diner's club. Delancey was a pale, spare, ginger-colored man, entirely innocuous-looking. Even his eyebrows seemed to beg off with no comment. They were so pale, his eyes seemed to float in his face, discs the color of cat's-eye marbles in my youth. He wore a nondescript tan summer suit and a light blue shirt as watery and dim as his eyes.

Delancey was a self-made man, and what he'd made of himself was a slum lord's delight. Possessed of no visible character, a fondness for gossip and a predator's sense of the weakling, Delancey turned a one-man racket. No matter how straightforward your dealings with him, he always had something cooking on the side. Delancey was a jackal, or better yet, a bottom feeder, browsing and nibbling on the leftovers of somebody else's kill.

Big John coughed into his napkin. I signaled for the check. Jerry Delancey trained his eyes on the room, sweeping the crowd like a mounted machine gun moving on its pivot. I wanted out of there.

There are worse men, I'm sure, than Jerry Delancey. I've known a lot of them. But there aren't many who could get to me the way he could. It's this. I trained Jerry Delancey. I taught him to be a cop, a good cop—only to have him decide to take it private. I don't mean moonlighting. A lot of cops do that. I mean greed, always playing the middle.

Even as a cop, Delancey was never content with what you paid him, what you gave him, always wanting an extra slice, as if there were a pie and everybody else had a bigger piece than he did.

So I wasn't surprised that not long after he went private, hiring out as a protection, a good deal of police procedure suddenly seemed to go public. Patterns we'd worked hard to uncover suddenly changed. Jerry Delancey was sticking it to us for living up to his low expectations. He'd make us pay, and get paid by somebody else for his inside information. A real sweetheart.

"Hi, Elliot," Delancey greeted me as I was trying to slip out. "Found anything solid on Johnny Vanilla?"

I swear, every fork in the restaurant stopped on cue.

"We got some things," I said vaguely.

"One of his girlfriends, you ask me," Delancey volunteered.

"I'm not asking, Jerry."

"And we used to be such good friends."

I hustled Zach and Violet out of the Hub.

"Who was that?" Zach protested. Violet was fussing with her purse. It would not close.

"Can we let them out?" The dogs, he meant.

"I don't think so—" But the minute the door was opened, Paradise preempted my directive, diving past Zach straight for freedom, squatting abruptly to leave a large, splendid piddle. I laughed. Then I spotted something on my car—a long, mean scratch fender to fender, the kind somebody made on purpose, by hand, with a key or pocket knife.

"Thanks for watching my car, chief." I was in no mood and pointed to the scratch. I stepped right in the young guy's face, probably one of Tommy's workout partners. Real smart. "Tommy pays you guys to watch these cars—or am I wrong?" I tapped him on the chest—so. "Somebody pay you to sleep through this?"

"What is it, Dad?"

"Dad's busy, Zach, just a minute."

I was suddenly livid, boiling over mad.

"Elliot?" It was Dr. Winters, sounding a little too much like the voice of reason for my blood.

"Just a minute." (That to Dr. Winters.) "Is it because we're talking about civic property, a lowly unmarked instead of one of these ginzo palaces that it's okay to scratch the shit out of it, have a little joke?"

Tommy's valet parker began turning a little darker to match my mood. His jacket said his name was Joey. He was fifteen years younger than I, easy, and he moved on the balls of his feet like an athlete—Tommy's sparring partner, it came back to me.

"Elliot, maybe Zach and I—" Dr. Winters again.

"Will you stay out of this?"

"We certainly will. Zach, come with me."

Dr. Winters took an astounded Zachary by the hand and

marched him back toward the restaurant. He followed her like a lamb. My son, the easy mark, the compliant victim, the poor little bastard.

He was a sitting duck. Hadn't I taught him don't talk to strangers? "Violet? Violet!" She'd deflected my attention. Goddamn woman. Make that women.

"Look, man, what can I say? I'm sorry. I didn't do it. We're short a guy tonight. Maybe I'm parking somebody and somebody comes by and does it. Think about it. Who'd do this?"

He had a point: Jerry Delancey.

I fished in my pocket and came up with a twenty and stuffed it in his hand. Violet and Zach watched this like I was the comic relief.

"Come on, you two."

"Yes, captain. Yes, captain, sir." Violet saluted me. I felt like booting her in the butt. Nothing like a broad with a sense of humor.

Zachary wrestled with the dogs in the backseat, and I lurched the car into traffic.

"Our first fight. Doubtless the first of many," Violet said with some satisfaction.

"Don't count on it. Zach. Quit riling up the dogs."

I felt like a riled-up dog myself. Jerry Delancey was the proximate cause, but that went about as deep as the scratch on my car. Solving a crime is like falling for the wrong woman: It leads you on, teases you, screws with your sleep, gives you false hope, shoots holes in your self-worth, and titillates you all at the same time. This may sound sexist. So shoot me. Murder is the ultimate femme fatale.

I drove toward Halsted Street north. We were having a long, Technicolor summer evening, thanks to the pollution, which produced neon sunsets. There was one stretch of Halsted that gave the Chicago skyline a chance at the appelation "handsome." Whenever I saw a movie shot in Chicago, I looked for that view of the city, west to east, but they never got it, always shooting from out over the lake for the generic postcard Chicago.

"We'll drop the doctor first," I told Zach.

"Oh, Dad, you're no fun," Zach said.

"Oh, Dad, you're no fun," Dr. Winters echoed. She slid some folded papers into my hand. I stuffed them into my pocket, glad Zach was enjoying Paradise and too busy petting her to see this transaction. I knew what the papers were. Zachary's doodles, his "pictures."

A case like Nesbitt-Vanilla-Stoufley-Gomez—because I now saw this as one case all interlocking at some subterranean level—came with its own pictures. The ones that got me this time weren't the crime scenes, terrible as they were. The ones that got me were the ones in Nesbitt's file.

It's an odd thing about images. Things you don't even realize you noticed stick with you, and the strangest things. Take Nesbitt's files. A single image haunted me: One little boy was wearing Fruit of the Looms with the label showing. Don't ask me why that got me. Maybe some murky psycho-schmyko thing about fruit and innocence. Maybe my famous Jesuit stuff: Abraham and his son, the first fruit of the vine, the sacrifice of innocents. Whatever it was, all I could think was the poor little bastard. A ten-year-old coached into a coy, come-hither look, over his shoulder. "Prematurely sexualized" the shrinks call it.

Back when we still called it vice instead of sex crimes, I worked it. The first time I saw a teenage hooker, at a juice bar on Belmont, I couldn't believe my eyes. The kid was twelve—maybe.

We staked out the juice bars because with their aura of

nonalcoholic wholesomeness they were a prime cruising ground for pedophiles, mingling with the unsuspecting kids who were sent there by their unsuspecting parents, everybody operating on the mistaken information that they were safe and drug free—not true.

Pedophiles and sex offenders of all stripes loved the juice bars. Sharks to fresh meat. The kids would crowd in from the suburbs—gang kids knew better—and belly up to the bar feeling racy and grown-up, feeling risky and also safe. It was a juice bar, after all.

The same kid who knew better than to talk to a stranger with booze on his breath struck up a nice conversation with the man who was buying a banana smoothie. What was the danger in a little conversation? And so you'd see them pair up, the nice kid from the suburbs and the nice man from the city.

The eyes have it. You get to know the look. "Hungry eyes," I call it. You watch a sex offender, you see him eat with his eyes.

Come on, I can hear you saying, all men do it. We turn our eyes to follow a pretty face or a firm butt. Maybe we do, but it's not the same. You and I may glance, the sex offender dines. The shrinks tell you it's a compulsive disorder, and after you see it, you believe it. It gives you the willies, canceling whatever liberal notions you've got left.

I know that most sex offenders were abused when they were kids, and I know that most pedophiles are "stuck" at the age when it happened to them, so what. So what if they can't help it? The fact that it's compulsive makes it all the scarier. You should watch the guys trying not to watch the kids, to not look too close or too long, to not look like what they are, sexual addicts getting a hit off flesh and fantasy. Watch them buy a kid a banana smoothie—there's a name for you, Dr. Freud. Watch them get aroused just on the act, on the interaction of fantasy in the flesh.

Most of the kids are unwary. They go off with the nice man. He gives them cash or drugs or the idea they're really cared for. Some of them creep back, chastened and shocked. "He wanted to, he tried to, he did to me." Not that they often tell their friends. Other kids get hooked on the "friendship," the daddy figure who makes them feel grown-up, who makes them feel . . . his cock.

I gag thinking about it. But these guys think about it all the time. Their eyes are like cameras, stealing a shot here, a shot there, shooting up on images.

Some of the kids like it, the money, the attention. Somebody starts them early and they continue on their own. "Prematurely sexualized." It will scare the shit out of you if you see it. When some little kid puts the make on you, looks you over just like a woman. The first time that look surveys you, your soul shrivels up. You can feel it try to hide. There is something about that child's come-hither look, something so old and at once so knowing, you come away scorched, blistered.

I hate child molesters. Hate the scummy way they make me feel. Maybe I should feel compassion, say, "There but for the grace of God," but something stops me. Like the kid in his Fruit of the Looms, I just don't get it. They want what?

And what they always want is more. Bust a pedophile and you bust a pack rat. If they don't have an actual kid, they have pictures of kids, hundreds of pictures of kids. You've read about it in the newspaper: Schoolteacher found with cache of pornography.

"Child pornography." The words do not begin to tell you. To their dubious credit, Nesbitt's pictures did. "Dirty pictures." "Filth." We toss the words around, but I'm talking about an experience. Nesbitt's dirty pictures made you feel unclean.

"Knock, knock. Anybody home?"

"Dad? Heh? Are you with us?"

It was Violet and Zach, trying to get my attention. I gathered they'd been trying for some time. I saw that I had driven the whole of Halsted Street, passed my favorite scenic view of the skyline, without seeing—or hearing—anything but the pictures in my head.

"Sorry. I was out to lunch."

"No, Dad. You were out to dinner."

We laughed over Zach's little joke. As it happened, I dropped Zach first, not the doctor. Zach's doodles were still burning a hole in my pocket, and I wanted to talk with her about them.

Chapter thirty-six

When I pulled up outside of Gloria's, the sunset was done and a light rain was flecking the windshield. I hurried Zach up the walk and into his mother's house. Gloria and I exchanged pleasantries like we were meeting at the old Berlin Wall and exchanging spies. By the time I was back to the car, the flecks were a torrent. It was like standing in a waterfall.

"I love these," Violet said, grinning wildly.

The car became a tiny submarine plunged underwater. The wind was so fierce that the trees bent at their waists, waving like sea plants.

"It's fantastic," Violet breathed, aglow.

"Right." I was dripping wet, less than comfortable, a lot less than thrilled.

"It reminds you," Violet said.

"Reminds you?"

"Of the power of things, that's all. It makes it all so clear."

I understood to be quiet, that I might learn something if I

held my tongue. Dr. Winters reached under the dashboard to the little shelf where I had crumpled Zachary's doodle.

"It looks so harmless," she began. And it did: a simple five-pointed star, a page of them. "It's hard to believe how a symbol can work on the mind."

"What do you mean?" I asked.

"Think of the power of the cross, the power of the swastika."

"Where are you going with this?" I asked.

"Well," she said, "this star is clearly a symbol like that for Zachary. And maybe for other people. I find it spooky myself."

"I had a crank call about a secret cult," I told her. "And Myerling mentioned some kind of sex club. I'm afraid I found both ideas hard to credit—don't you?"

I asked her as an afterthought. She wasn't supposed to answer the way she did, with a question of her own.

"How open-minded are you, Elliot?"

"I want to solve a crime, not be hoodooed into suspecting the wrong people."

"Oh, Elliot. You act like you're a straw in the wind. I don't find you all that suggestible."

"Depends on the power of suggestion," I said. "Weren't you the one just talking about the wind? There's a power of suggestion." Just then the wind sent a large limb careening against the power lines, showering sparks. I thought about power surges, about Zach's whole street going up in flames.

"I'm calling the power company," I said, and shifted into gear. I pulled into a minimall and used a pay phone just outside the Payless shoe store—which featured an entire window full of tennis shoes sporting tiny little stars.

The power company said a crew was on the way.

Violet was not about to be distracted. She touched my arm as I went to shift into gear. "Elliot, why is that image bothering you so much?"

Sheepishly, I took Zachary's doodles on the paper place mat from my pocket. I lay it on the dash between us. Violet smoothed her hands several times across the paper. Her eyes looked genuinely stricken.

"This must be very hard for you," she said. "He's so innocent. It's hard for you to imagine. As a parent, who can? But as a police officer—you're really caught between both roles, aren't you?"

"I don't know what you're talking about," I snapped. "My son was hurt, molested, just a few weeks ago. It only seems like forever. And I haven't solved it—or anything else for that matter."

Violet was not about to be thrown.

"We were talking about the power of a symbol. You've seen this one before, haven't you?"

And now that she mentioned it, I was seeing it again—as I had for the past twenty years—a circle of stones with a star inside and three children's bodies.

"It's from an old crime," I told her finally. "A crime I didn't solve. I was just a rookie with a theory, and nobody wanted to hear it."

"That must have been very hard for you—not being believed."

"It almost cost me my career."

"That wasn't the hard part."

"Don't play shrink with me, Doctor."

"I'm just trying to help."

"Why is it women define talking as helpful?"

Even to my ear I sounded like I was dodging the issue.

"But it is relevant. Everything may be connected," Violet insisted. "Zachary's doodle, your associations with his doodle—"

"I don't want to put Zachary and my associations in the same ballpark."

"That doesn't mean you shouldn't," she pushed.

I snapped the car into gear. "Well, thanks. Enough of this psycho-schmyko. I know I'm cutting this a little short—"

"You won't trust my intuition because you're afraid to trust yours."

"Yeah. Well, look where it got me."

"The darkness frightens you. The shadow of the old crime makes you doubt yourself now. It throws you back to being a much younger man—a man without the strengths you have now."

"Save it, Doctor. I'm not feeling very strong." (Now, why did I tell her that?)

"No. But you are. And your son loves you, Detective. You will not let him down." I felt something in me jerk and straighten as the remark hit home.

"You go for the jugular."

"No, I go for the heart."

"Same difference. Hostile enough for you?"

I drove her home in the gusting winds of the dying storm. We drove in silence, and not a comfortable one. I didn't want to talk about anything. I saw no way to connect Zachary's doodle to the scene in the woods where I first saw the ritual pentacle twenty years before. I saw no need to tell Violet Winters about the decapitated bodies of innocent children. It was ugly enough remembering myself.

I dropped Violet off with a special admonition to take care of herself. I drove myself home, thinking. One thing was true:

I was scared of the darkness these crimes conjured for me. I was so scared I was avoiding a line of inquiry I knew that I should make. Those inquiries involved Oscar Gomez and his spiritual beliefs. Whatever they were, I hoped they did not involve his mother's goats and did not involve my son.

Chapter thirty-seven

———◼———

Oscar Gomez's mother, Maria, lived with her goats and chickens and religion in a small dark house off Western Avenue. It looked more like a grotto than a residence—flickering candles, Sacred Heart pictures, Madonnas in several sizes, one magnificent Guadalupe in the silken clothes of a queen.

Maria Gomez did not give me a royal welcome. Who could blame her? Her son was killed in my stead, the very same son who had already been living in sin with my ex-wife. Thanks to me, her Oscar was burning in hell, purgatory at best, and her mother's heart was as barren of spiritual ideas as her tiny, fetid home was fecund with its reek of spices and incense.

"What you want?" Maria wondered, darkly glowering.

"To help avenge Oscar," I told her. "To solve his murder and get justice." Maria crossed herself.

"And how is she?" "She" was clearly Gloria.

"She is very sad."

"*Puta.*"

"Please, Maria, just a few questions. For Oscar's sake."

"Bien venido." She opened the door to her hellish little shrine and let me in. I took special care to admire her Mary statues and candles. I even crossed myself—twice.

"Was Oscar also religious? These statues are very beautiful."

"Oscar was a good son."

"But not religious?"

"Oscar was modern." Maria spat out the word.

And of course Maria was not. Why should she be? I glanced out the window to the backyard, filled with huts and hutches, rabbits, chickens, and goats.

"I see you keep animals, Maria. Did Oscar help you with your animals? Somebody did a good job on that coop."

"Oscar."

"Is that a goat? You don't often see goats in the city. Aren't they a lot of trouble? I always heard—"

"They were Oscar's goats."

"Ah-hah. You were a good mother to let him keep them with you. What did he use them for? Milk? Wool? Do they even make wool?"

"They were his pets. He loved them."

"Funny, the things you don't know about a person. Will you be selling them?"

"Maybe. Oscar, he gave them away to his friends. Who knows?"

"Did you know his friends?"

Maria glared at me.

"Maria, I'm going to ask you a hard question. Do you think it's possible Oscar was involved with bad people?"

"Muy malo," Oscar's mother spat out. She crossed herself and pushed me, physically, toward the door.

"Maria, thank you."

"Devil keep you."

"What?"

"*Malo. Muy Malo.*" With that, she slammed the door.

Bingo. Bad people. A web, a network, a grid of bad people with Oscar Gomez in the middle somehow, in to his chin, in despite his mother's prayers. What kind of bad people? Johnny Vanilla, for one kind. Were the people who murdered children in a park another kind? *Muy malo?*

I crisscrossed from Western over to North down to Division, then realized I needed to see Harold Myerling. I called him from my favorite 7 Eleven. He was still at work and invited me to come by.

Harold kept me waiting fifteen minutes, and when he came out to meet me, he was ash gray and damp with sweat. We talked in his waiting room. He was sparing me the corpses.

"Harold. You look like hell."

"Sometimes it's hard."

"Bad case?"

"Kid."

"Gang thing?"

"Coke bottle."

"Throat?"

"Rectal hemorrhage."

"Jesus. Runaway?"

"Throwaway. He'd been taken in by one of Crutcher's children's shelters, but they couldn't seem to keep him contained. Evidently he kept going back to the street. He was— what's your phrase? Prematurely sexualized. Probably made good money at it, too . . . What came back on prints from your place?"

"Nothing."

"Do me a favor. Run a set off the Coke bottle for me, would you?"

"I would. Harold, you were right about Gomez and the

goats. He kept them at his mother's. She said he gave them to his friends."

"I'm sorry, Elliot."

That's when it hit me: he meant about Zachary. If Oscar had been involved with bad people, people worse, perhaps, than Johnny Vanilla, it was possible he had been involved with the same bad people who had hurt my son.

"He's alive, Elliot. He'll heal. Not like this poor little guy."

"So how old?"

"Maybe twelve. Maybe not. You just came by to tell me I was right about the goats?" He raised an eyebrow.

"I needed your memory."

"Ah. Well, then."

Harold showed me into his office. There, under the watchful gaze of his totems, I asked him to reconstruct the crime we'd worked on together two decades before. The crime that kept coming at me in flashes ever since these murders had begun. The crime I had never solved and never quite forgotten, either. Yes, all right, the crime the pentacle had recalled.

"The boys in the park near Marion."

"Ah, yes. Decapitated. Genitally tortured. There were, what, three of them?"

As Harold talked, it came swimming back to me. The unreality of the bloodsoaked leaves under the tall, stern trees. The ritual circle with its carefully scribed star. The bodies, one each to three of the five points. The faint shifting of the wind as it talked about what it had seen.

"Actually, there were more. One got away. Or we never found him. The other we tracked—"

"That was your theory back then, but nobody would listen to you. I thought you were right. You said we had a witness, maybe even two. You read the tracks. You lost one set and followed another to a cliff with a river down below it."

"I was younger then. A nobody. A whippersnapper. I read the crime scene one way. The others, my elders, read it another."

"They didn't believe you, I remember," Harold repeated. "You came home hopping mad, calling them amateurs."

"I was the amateur. . . . Could a child survive? The cliff must have been fifty feet above the water."

"A child could survive. Where are you going with this, Elliot?"

"Just a hunch."

"Then I will pay close attention."

I wasn't about to tell Harold an intuition I'd had growing on me since the case began. If I believed in psycho-schmyko—and that's a big if—I would have almost said I was picking up on someone's wavelength, someone other than myself who was revisiting the scene of that crime.

Chapter thirty-eight

The next day, I went to the Hub to eat.

Snitches have their beats. That's what makes them reliable. They have a territory, a home base for all their arcane knowledge. Jerry Delancey ate at the Hub. He ate there every day, or nearly. Part of being a good snitch is being an accepted fixture, a regular. To a regular, gossip of the day is served up along with specials.

"You hear Tullio got a label deal?"

"No shit. He's good, that guy. He's good."

"You hear Angela Remo broke off with that accountant she was dating? The boy from New York?"

"Good for Angela."

I took a deuce one over from Delancey's usual table. He wasn't there, but a cop could do a lot worse than chicken Vesuvio, mostaccioli, and special salad.

"So how are you doing, Detective?" Trudy, my favorite waitress, asked me. She was a still-pretty redhead who in the years I'd known her had dated a procession of unseemly men. She meant "on Johnny's case," and I knew it.

"Getting there," I said.

"That's good," she said. "Tough."

"He was into some weird stuff," I said. Made it fact, not question.

"That's what I heard," Trudy said. "Well, what'll it be?"

"Somehow talking about sick sex kills the appetite, Trudy. You order for me."

"Well, I like the Vesuvio."

"That's good. It's in the plan."

"And shells?"

"Shells are good—but I think mostaccioli, and a special salad."

"So they found all that stuff, oh?"

"You know how it is. Murder doesn't leave you a lot of privacy."

"Well, the girls always used to say he was weird. Somebody said he was into whips, handcuffs. I remember. It was Angela, before she got with that accountant she just broke up with. Nice boy, but Jewish."

"I'm surprised she told you about the stuff with Johnny."

"Oh, she didn't tell me. Jerry Delancey did. You think I'm bad? That guy's a world-class gossip."

"Trudy, Trudy. You're dating Delancey?"

"He likes me."

"Everybody likes you. What is it with you and these deadbeats?"

"Maybe I like staying single and they give me a good excuse. Anyway, I'm not sleeping with him. We go to dinner. It's nice to eat somewhere else once in a while."

"Hey. Am I your conscience?"

Trudy laughed at that and pinched me on the arm. She placed my order and I attacked the bread basket. I'd gotten what I came for. Even in his absence, Jerry Delancey had served me well. I had my appetite back, and lots of food for thought.

Big John D'Amato had tax problems. This surprised me, and I took it to mean a snag in his system of payoffs. With a good enough accountant, no one should have tax problems, particularly on moneys that come in under the table and officially don't exist. What D'Amato had was a leaky boat. Somebody was dropping the dime on Big John's activities, or all would be smooth sailing.

Was it Johnny Vanilla? Could he have been crazy enough? Sure, but what would trigger it? That was the key question. I thought maybe the answer was weird sex.

When Trudy handed me the bill, I traded her a large tip and asked for Angela Remo's address. Trudy looked at the tip, looked at me, and paused.

"It's a tip, Trudy. I've known you—what?—fifteen years? Buy yourself a meal out without Jerry Delancey. If I were pumping you, I'd just ask." Trudy gave me the address.

"She still lives there. With her mother," Trudy told me. "Top floor, I think."

"There" was the upper half of a two-flat. It was five blocks west and two south, a neighborhood that used to be solidly Italian and was now more than half black. I rang the bell and tried to look friendly, trustworthy, whatever I would need to look to get what I was after.

But Angela Remo did not want to talk to me. She saw me, registered "cop," and ran up the stairs. A moment later, her mother appeared. She was a short, squat, strong-featured woman. Her daughter was thin and lovely, but she shared her mother's dark, fiery eyes. Angela had nothing to say, her mother told me. I worked on her mother, Rosanna. She owned the stucco two-flat that she occupied like the Alamo. She was a citizen. I got on well with citizens.

"Come on, Mrs. Remo, your daughter's not a suspect. She's an innocent young girl who got tricked. She should talk to me. It's wrong that your daughter can just be preyed on that way. You should have come to us with the whole thing."

I can be a charming guy. I can be gruff or reassuring or anything you need me to be. I can make you want to talk.

"He was a monster," Rosanna finally spat out. "What he did to her—" I nodded like I knew the whole story.

"She should talk to me."

"So many drugs. She didn't know her name. And then the pictures. I thank God my Angela went to the priest and he helped her. She's a good girl, but . . ."

"She needed spiritual protection?"

"He had a spell on her, that Johnny. I swear to you. She was caught. I feared for her life. The bruises! Terrible. Even you, Detective, you don't want to know."

"But I do want to know. It's my job."

"My daughter has forgotten. So should you."

Rosanna Remo said all this through her chain lock.

"Tell her to talk to me."

"How can she talk? He made movies of her, drugged her, and took dirty pictures, hit her—"

"I'm glad you're telling me this, Rosanna." Oops. My cop groaned.

"Telling you what?" Rosanna closed like a clam.

"Please tell Angela if she changes her mind . . ." I passed a business card through the chain lock.

"She won't talk," Rosanna said. "She doesn't even remember."

I thanked Rosanna Remo for her time. I could feel her dark Sicilian eyes willing me to never come back, to leave her daughter alone. I planned to do exactly that. After a little while. I drove north thinking about the implications of what she'd said.

I've always wondered what a father felt like when his daughter was chosen Pet of the Month. When his Mary or Sarah chose to display her labia in living color, maybe fingering herself into the bargain. Knowing your daughter was the image your pals jerked off to—could that possibly create paternal pride? I couldn't see it. My bet was Big John D'Amato felt the same way, even if Angela Remo was only his niece. The things Johnny Vanilla had done to Angela, the things he'd had Angela do to herself—those couldn't be things John D'Amato approved of.

"Should have kept your hands off her." That was one way to read the blood message of Johnny's death. "You should have cleaned up your act," read the dick in the sink.

I didn't think I'd ever prove it, but I liked the way it fit together. I thought it made sense. Like all cops, I play the game of what-if?

What if Johnny Vanilla was out of control? It certainly sounded like he was, according to Esther and Rosanna Remo. What if he and Jack Nesbitt shared a pornography habit, not just a few kinky tastes? What if they got off on getting each other off?

I wasn't sure about any of this, but I had my dark hunches. Playing what-if, I kept getting back to the same point: Nesbitt and Vanilla intersected, not just at sex, but at money.

Johnny was doling out Bulls tickets and maybe a whole lot more. If Gomez could buy Gloria a rock as big as an ice cube, Johnny Vanilla was rolling high and fast. Maybe he'd lost control. Maybe he'd killed Jack Nesbitt just for the high. It had been done before. More often than civilians care to know.

Pornography is a high. Violent pornography is an

extremely potent high. You don't believe me, go to an adult bookstore. You're looking for the trance, the flat, dead eyes that are watching the inner movie even when they're watching you. Usually the deadest eyes ask for the S&M packets: sex and violence, a doubleheader. A shot and a chaser. The guys who are into it are really into it, so far into it they can't see their way out.

"It got a little out of hand," I remember one man explaining to me as he led me into the living room where his lover, still handcuffed, was newly dead, strangled. "It was our little game. It made it better, you know? I just went too far. I thought he was enjoying it. He came like crazy."

What do you say to someone like that? How do you fit his values into the known world? When it's all about sensation, all about the high, how do you begin to show them how low they've gone, how far they've sunk from human grace?

Faced with this knowledge, is it any wonder cops develop compulsions? We wash our hands too many times, get hooked on Gregorian chant and nine hundred push-ups. We control what we can in the face of the uncontrollable. Just like the people we arrest, we get our habits. We use ours to respond to theirs.

Back at the station, I had an interesting message. Just like I thought he would, Jerry Delancey felt a need to call me. I'd been on his turf and he "just wanted to be of service." That's what he said.

"Come on, Jerry. Charity's not exactly your long suit. You're trying for points against a rainy day."

"What if I am?"

"Then say so."

"I thought you might be interested about John D'Amato."

"What about him?"

"His tax troubles."

"We're doing this on the phone so you're not seen with me, right, Jerry?"

"Come on, Mayo. What'd I ever do to you?"

I didn't answer. The answer was too long and it embarrassed me. Jerry Delancey had hurt me. I'd thought better of him than petty chiseler. I'd invested my time and knowledge in making him a good cop, and he let me down.

"Mayo?"

"What?"

"Not all of us are bucking for sainthood."

"So I gather, Jerry. So spit it out. What's the deal with Big John?"

"Vanilla fucked him over and created a little cash flow problem."

"Theories are a dime a dozen, Jerry."

"Blackmail is a little more expensive."

"Vanilla was being blackmailed?"

"You're warm but not hot."

"Come on. You're shitting me."

"Let's just say Johnny made some foolish mistakes and needed some quick cash."

"We all do, Jerry. Thanks for the tip."

I wondered who'd put Delancey up to it. Maybe it was Myerling's poltergeist, the trickster who wanted to deflect me from my work. While I considered it entirely possible John D'Amato had killed Johnny Vanilla, I did not believe Vanilla had tried to blackmail Big John. Johnny might be dumb, but he wasn't suicidal.

Somebody wanted me focused on Big John D'Amato and not somewhere else. That someone had sent me two messengers: Oscar Gomez with his news of Big John's tax troubles, and now Jerry Delancey, with his tales from beyond the crypt of Johnny the blackmailer. If you asked me, which nobody was, money was still at the bottom of it. Money got Johnny Vanilla killed.

I straightened up my desk. Sometimes that helped me think. I thought some more about Delancey's hot tip. Conclusion? I didn't believe it. It was a diversion. I was being positioned into thinking D'Amato was responsible for Vanilla's death and Vanilla was responsible for D'Amato's tax problems. That made the killing a simple case of tit for tat—it also made it too easy to look no further.

Maybe I should sleep on this, I thought. I headed home to try.

Chapter thirty-nine

In the years of my married life, I did not suffer from insomnia, although Gloria claimed I caused her to do so. I slept soundly, if restlessly—not a knack I had any longer. In my new bachelor digs I very often spent my nights on the Naugahyde couch. I came to know David Letterman and a lot of New York eccentrics—eccentrics by Chicago standards, anyhow. I came to regard even a couple hours of unbroken sleep as a reprieve from the desecrated old movies Ted Turner was replaying for the nation, beautiful movies I had loved as a child. Turner's "colorized" touch-ups, vanity surgery on film, only reminded me of the age I had become since seeing them on State Street in the movie palaces now divvied up into shopping malls or rock and roll emporiums.

I would get a good night's sleep, I promised myself, but first I would check my messages. I did that. Right after I threw out the milk I'd let sour on the counter.

The light was on and there was a message from Judge Ricky Noonan. We were talking a lot, Ricky Noonan and I. He'd left his message on my home machine. The private line

I'd kept for emergencies. The number I'd given just three people: Gloria, Jamie, and Zach.

I wondered where he'd got the number. Then again, I knew
he had his ways.

"Elliot. This is Richard Noonan. Please call me."

It was his formal judge's voice. "Please call" meant CALL
NOW.

He left a number and I called it. I told his machine who I
was and Ricky intercepted the call.

Ricky Noonan had Delancey's knack for being in the middle of things, but he didn't have Delancey's motives. Ricky
Noonan—Judge Ricky Noonan, and a good one, I thought—
actually liked people. They caught his interest. He found
them fascinating, enjoyable, basically good. It was a trick of
the lens, of course. Ricky Noonan was basically good, good
was what he knew and what he looked for. As a judge he
wasn't lenient, but he was punitive with regret. Because he
liked people, people liked him. Even criminals liked Ricky
Noonan. John D'Amato liked Ricky Noonan. Liked him, perhaps, a little too much. For that matter, I liked Ricky Noonan
a little too much.

Ricky wanted to meet somewhere "private that doesn't
look private," if I knew what he meant. I knew exactly what
he meant, and told him that a place like that had to be public—out in the open, surrounded by people, nothing to hide.

"You're right. I know you're right." He settled for a Cubs
game. I hate Cubs games. Like so much of the new Chicago,
they felt canned to me. I guess I'm a sap. I still remember the
old Sox, Comiskey Park and the way the wind sounded sift-
ing through the trees. Baseball used to feel like an afternoon
in the country, not an afternoon of MTV.

———————■———————

Ricky Noonan and I were meeting at the Clark and Addison gate. We'd sit in the sun, in public, and he'd tell me, or ask me, what he had to.

I got there early. Vendors were hawking pennants, T-shirts, hats, glasses. Pennants, T-shirts, hats, glasses. Without Zach, I had no itch to buy. This was where Zach had had his "blip," something had triggered a memory. I scanned the crowd. What? I saw a tall blonde with a ponytail that looked like Dr. Winters from the back—but she was a boy, it turned out. That was my blip. What was Zach's? A bright satin jacket? A T-shirt? It could be anything. Even a repetition of the same colors, Dr. Hauser said. Now, that was helpful!

"Thrilling, isn't it?" Was he kidding? Ricky Noonan, civic booster, in designer jeans, a soft Hawaiian shirt, million-dollar sneakers.

"Yeah. Real thrilling." Small talk wasn't on my agenda. Go Cubs. Go to hell . . . I was a real delight.

A lot of my attitudes are atavistic. Let me rephrase that— primitive. I blame it on fight or flight, the adrenal flooding that a cop's body gets accustomed to. We're addicted to our jobs, addicted to drama in general, conditioned to viewing life in dramatic terms: life or death, now or never, me Tarzan, you Jane. Either or, this or that, categories, choices, boxes. It's built into cop thinking. We're binary beings: guilty or innocent, safe or dangerous, life or death.

I mention all this in relation to Ricky Noonan and the Cubs because when you're wired for drama, normal can be pretty hard to metabolize. I don't act appropriate in normal. I don't know what normal is, really. I only visit there.

Example: It's Christmas Eve. I get a call at home. I go. Some drunk maniac has shot his wife and son and daughter. He planned to shoot himself but botched the job, so now he's armed, dangerous, wounded, and gibbering. What I remember is the cheap pine paneling spattered with his family's blood. I get the gun and the story: I was depressed, I guess. (Well, I guess!) We weren't making it. It's Christmas. There aren't any presents, the wife and kids are disappointed, so . . . (So you kill them?)

Try going home from this to normal. Try wrapping the choo-choo train and tricycle, thanking your wife for the necktie you'll never wear and the subscription to *National Geographic*. Watch her open her card saying you've bought her the dishwasher of her choice. See her eyes well up as she thanks you and you feel dead inside. You're getting pictures. The two kids under the barren Christmas tree. The dead young wife, a pretty brunette just like your wife. Try to get rid of the pictures, snap back to "normal." Normal can feel pretty strange after that.

So I hate Cubs games. They win, they lose, I don't care. I hate the fancy new scoreboards, the glitz. I want to tear someone's head off because—because it can make you angry to see people chopped, diced, mutilated. It can make you angry to get fingers in your mailbox, corpses in your living room, corpses in your dreams. It can make you particularly angry when you are dripping sweat in the middle of a lot of loud, mildly drunk sports fans who keep cranking up the volume, inning by inning.

"Dog?" Ricky was queuing up for the works. "Dog 'n' suds."

"Why not?"

I could not get Dr. Winters and Zachary off my mind. Climbing out of the car the night before, she'd pressed something in my hand. "Good night," she had said, leaning over to kiss my cheek and whisper, "You may want to show Dr. Hauser." What she handed me were more doodles, stars galore on the paper napkins Zach had doodled on during the meal. I had them folded in my pocket even now.

"What do you know about satanism?" Judge Noonan asked me.

"That the nuns used it as a scare tactic."

"I'm serious." What he meant was scared.

"Tell me more."

"Something funny's going on. I'm getting pressured. I don't like getting pressured, and I really don't like not knowing why. I told you about my visit from Courker?"

"You certainly did."

"I guess I was just passing the hot potato."

"I put it down to political aspirations, keep the Gold Coast happy, et cetera."

"Oh, sure. Political aspirations, yeah, we all have that."

That's what I meant about Ricky Noonan—no hidden agendas, no shadows.

"As I recall, Courker was worried about his keys, Ricky. I gave them back. What does that have to do with satanism?"

"Maybe nothing. Probably nothing."

All around us people were cheering. Noonan and I were like inattentive altar boys, missing our cues, bobbing up late, down late. I really hoped no one was watching.

"But? C'mon, Ricky."

"But I got this in my mail." He handed me something wrapped in a handkerchief. "Don't look at it now. Go to the men's room or something."

"See you in a second." I went down a tier to the men's room. It was empty, but I took a stall.

When I unwrapped the handkerchief, it had Gomez's ring in it, or Johnny Vanilla's, or one just like the ring that killed both of them, according to Myerling and Robert Chabrol, who claimed to be dying from it himself. Dull, golden, heavy with filigree: Zachary's upside-down star. I nearly dropped it in the toilet. I wanted to. I certainly didn't want it in my pocket, near what was not yet a missing dick. I wrapped it back up and put it in my wallet behind my badge. That had a star, too.

"Well?" Ricky Noonan wasn't eating his dog, wasn't drinking his suds.

"It's a ring."

"No shit, Sherlock."

"I know what it means. I think they know I know what it means."

"They?"

"Whoever sent it to me."

"Just for curiosity, how do you know so much about power rings or whatever you call the thing? That doesn't strike me as routine information."

"I suppose not. Lay it at my politics again. A friend of mine was looking for a good re-election issue—"

"The governor?"

"Maybe. He thought cults were hot."

"I'll say."

"Cults, youth gang, drug lords . . . Anyway, I went to Las Vegas to this conference on ritual abuse."

"That sounds like fun. Some people would say Las Vegas is ritual abuse."

"I learned a lot."

"Like?"

"Like what that ring means. Who might wear it."

"It was Johnny Vanilla's."

"You're shitting me."

"Afraid not."

"Johnny Vanilla's?" This news made him blanch.

"That's right."

"The papers didn't mention it."

"They didn't know. It was missing—along with a finger."

Ricky Noonan was turning white. The Cubs were winning for once. The crowd was rising, "the wave" was passing through, and Ricky Noonan looked seasick.

"Something I should know, Ricky?"

"It was a death threat, wasn't it?"

"I'd have to say yes, Ricky—or blackmail."

"Why the fuck you get me into this, Elliot?"

"I didn't know I was. I just wanted your permission to go look at Carson Stoufley's stash of Jack Nesbitt's dirty pictures."

"Any ritual stuff?"

"You tell me. What would I be looking for I might have missed?"

"Bondage, S&M, the mark of the beast."

I almost choked on my beer. Ricky Noonan and I were in the fifth inning on a shake and bake afternoon and he was talking about stuff that sounded like the night of the living dead.

"Meaning?"

"You know, six six six. And the sign on that ring . . . Come on, Elliot. There's more of it than you can imagine. Sex cults, satanism."

"I'm a cop."

"There's still more of it than you can imagine. The runaway kids, the 'throwaways'—they end up there. There's a network. A whole underground. There's—there's more than you know, Elliot. More horror than you know."

I felt sorry for Ricky Noonan. He was at the edge and staring straight down.

"What should I do?"

"Get yourself some protection."

"Swell, Elliot. What do you suggest? Hire Jerry Delancey?"

"Maybe some spiritual protection."

"Novenas, Our Fathers, scapulars, that kind of thing?" Ricky sounded desperate. It was one thing to be threatened, another, a worse thing, not to know why.

"Whatever works, Ricky, and call me. You've got the private number."

"Sorry. I was showing off a little, I guess. Wanted you to know I had clout."

"No problem. Anything gets hairy, just call me."

"You didn't have to say 'hairy,' Elliot."

"It gives you pictures?"

He nodded, miserable. Ricky Noonan and I had talked about pictures years ago when he was sitting on a particularly grisly murder trial. He'd done an excellent job, a star job even, but it pained him.

"Terrible pictures," he said. "Bad as I've had them."

"Remember the drill? You make your list of alternatives. You substitute those—" My helpful hints weren't settling his nerves.

Ricky Noonan looked so miserable, I thought of telling him about Father Bremner, suggesting he pay a visit. Then I decided, no, hold that information. So much of being a cop is how much to tell when. Telling Noonan about Johnny Vanilla and the ring had been a calculated choice. I felt satisfied with the result. No, I would not tell him about Father Bremner and my "spiritual protection," I decided. I didn't want Ricky Noonan thinking I was scared. What I would do, I decided, is call Father Bremner and ask him to add Noonan to his prayer list.

I left Ricky Noonan shivering in the sun. The Cubs were winning.

Chapter forty

I went straight from Wrigleyville and the Cubs to Carson Stoufley's playground. I'd left Ricky Noonan sitting in broad daylight surrounded by cheering fans. Barring a sniper, he'd be fine—temporarily. I had no doubt Noonan was a judge with a death sentence. Just like him, I didn't know why. Missing the why, it was hard to figure the where and when. Motive was what made crime comprehensible. Get the motive and you get the trail. That's why serial killers are a police nightmare. They just like killing.

I'm not saying that whoever killed Nesbitt, Vanilla, Stoufley, and Gomez didn't love their job. Certainly "Here's Johnny" in Revlon red indicated a certain joie de vivre. What I am saying is that I saw all four killings as motive-linked.

I'd been going with a pairs theory. Nesbitt and Stoufley linked. Vanilla and Gomez linked, the Vanilla killing a Mafia copycat of Nesbitt's death. Copycat killings take advantage of a spectacular crime to accomplish another one in the relative privacy of the slipstream. Now I thought my pairs theory was wrong. All four killings were linked and I, quite literally, held the key.

Now, I know I told Ricky Noonan that Courker had his keys back, and he did—one set. I had another, newly minted. I was going back to Carson Stoufley's. Not exactly kosher, but Ricky Noonan hadn't played square with me, either. I was going back because my cop kept telling me to. If they were pressuring Ricky Noonan, I'd missed something.

When I got to Carson Stoufley's place, it was late afternoon. A Mexican was barbering the hedge next door on the left, and I met the prying eyes of a blueblood, blue-haired neighbor on the right. I was going into Stoufley's as she and her Bedlington terrier were starting out on their evening rounds. We nodded to each other, mutually curious. I actually preferred being seen. I doubted my blueblood would approve of practicing satanists, sex cults, or any cults at all. Her ewe-faced Bedlington looked too precious to her to be a sacrificial lamb.

Stoufley's entry hall was dank and chill. The cacti still stood sentinel, but there was a faint smell of rot in the air, as though the tropical plants were running rampant in the dark and quiet, breeding jungle right off the breakfast room. I half expected to hear drums. Correct that: I did hear drums. Faint but unmistakable, a throbbing bass sounded from the floorboards like a huge, outsized heart. I crouched and laid a hand to the ivory flank of Stoufley's marble foyer. Yes, the vibration was real, emanating unnervingly and unmistakably from Stoufley's cave below my feet. Did I say the house was supposed to be empty? Ah, yes, the house was supposed to be empty. I made my exit, stage left.

Slipping into my unmarked where I'd left it a half block down on Astor, in a spot the fire hydrant provided for me, I encountered the Bedlington appreciating the convenience of the hydrant as much as I had. His owner stared at me. I stared back. The little dog barked.

"You're a friend of Carson's?" his owner asked abruptly.

"Aren't we all?"

She didn't answer that.

"Aren't we all?" I pushed her. The little dog pushed me back. It growled. "Aren't we all Stoufley's friends?" I asked again.

"Hardly," she answered. I decided I liked her and wanted to know more.

"Detective Elliot Mayo, Chicago's finest," I introduced myself.

"You mean Chicago police?" she sniffed.

"It's a slogan."

"I hate slogans."

"As a matter of fact, so do I. You also hated Carson Stoufley?"

"Loathed, despised, reviled," she answered. "Have I made myself clear?"

Her name was Isabelle Hubbard, "Izzy" to her friends, where Carson Stoufley was not numbered. Izzy owned the manse one west of Stoufley's, and she and her dog, Jaspar, agreed to grant me an interview. I left my unmarked guarding the hydrant.

"I don't, ordinarily, talk to police."

"I know what you mean. We're so unsavory."

"But this whole thing makes me furious. I'm livid, absolutely livid."

Izzy Hubbard did not look livid. She looked eighty if she was a day, and cool as Katharine Hepburn. She wore a finely figured silk shirtdress with delphiniums on it, a sapphire and diamond ring with the same deep blue, and probably had blood bluer than all of it, at least for Chicago. Did I say before her hair was blue? It was actually a light lilac color. I know that because it matched the blooms on the huge bouquet on top of the grand piano.

"My mother loved lilacs," I told her.

"They're fake. Very good fakes. This is July. Why should I care what your mother liked?"

She was quite a character, Izzy Hubbard. Ordinarily, I would treat a Gold Coast dowager with kid gloves, but boxing gloves seemed more her style. Feisty and colorful, she liked? Feisty and colorful I gave her. I was following the rules.

"Find out what they eat and feed it to them" was Elliot's homicide rule number eight. It applied to questioning witnesses and suspects. It applied to any of the number of exchanges where a cop wanted something for nothing.

"Carson Stoufley was a pederast," Izzy Hubbard informed me succinctly.

"No kidding."

"A pederast," she repeated.

"Homosexual, certainly," I agreed.

"Any fool could see that," snapped Izzy. "Homosexuality is not what I am talking about. Pederasty. That's what I'm talking about." She was genuinely angry, and I liked her very much.

"It wasn't 'seemly'?" I was baiting her.

"Seemly? Who cares about seemly? Buggering young children isn't about seemly. It's about decency."

I thought for a minute she was going to cry, tears of sheer fury. She had no idea how much I agreed with her.

"It all began years ago, but he was a young man himself then—relatively."

"He got older, they got younger?"

"It seemed that way. I suppose the truth is, he got older

and they stayed the same. I never really knew any of them after Frederick. He was the first. A lovely boy. I honestly thought he was Carson's nephew. Can you believe my stupidity? Carson had dozens of nephews over the years."

"You were telling me about Frederick."

"I'd have to say, I became fond of him. Overly fond. I just loved that little boy, and later, when I realized, it just killed me to think that all that time—when I was teaching him piano and he was teaching me about blackstrap molasses and crawfish—"

"Pardon me?"

"Carson had some story. The boy was from Appalachia, some little hillbilly, a 'poor relation,' Carson said. Brought north to the city to be offered advantages. What hogwash! It makes my blood boil. Of course, after Frederick there were others. Dozens of others, as I've said. All the same age Frederick was when it started."

"They fixate."

"I know all about it. I know that they were abused themselves, supposedly—in Carson's case I doubt it—and I know they fixate on boys the age they were when—"

"When it happened to them."

"I can finish my own sentences, Detective Elliot. I am not senile yet, thank you."

"So why'd you strike up a conversation with me, Izzy?"

"I wanted to smear his good name, I suppose." She enjoyed a chuckle. "I think that's it. I wanted to smear his good name and get even."

"What happened to Frederick?"

"Oh—what happens to any of those boys? They go on to a life of it. You know that."

"Not always."

"Always doesn't matter to me, Detective Elliot. That's what happened to Frederick."

"Ah. I'm sorry."

"You're sorry?" she hooted. "Why should you be sorry? You work vice, don't you?"

"Technically—"

"Will you be quiet? You probably knew Frederick, working vice."

"How's that?"

"The last time I saw Frederick—in the flesh, that is—he was standing at a bus stop on Wabash Street, right in this neighborhood, mind you, wearing high-heeled pumps and a wig."

"And you're sure it was Frederick?"

"Of course I'm sure. He was like a son to me. He was—" She broke off, overwhelmed and angered to be overwhelmed. "He was a lovely child, Detective," she finished up. "A lovely, lovely child."

I left Izzy Hubbard grieving. I was thinking about Dynel wigs. Was it possible her Frederick was now my maid?

The prints were back and I had lots to think about. I'd run the ones from my place through the full wash and rinse cycle and come up empty. You'd almost think my "maid" was just a maid.

The same thing happened when we ran prints from Johnny's, Nesbitt's, and Nesbitt's revisited for Stoufley. Speaking of which, I had a hunch.

I figured Izzy Hubbard wouldn't tattle on me anymore. I also figured I'd been a cop long enough to know that if an itch didn't go away, I had to scratch it.

Carson Stoufley's archive room was that kind of itch. I'd gone through three cabinets with Courker and one without him. I'd worked my way through the gate, door, inner door, cavern, archive, and cabinet keys on Stoufley's key ring. There was one key more. Of course, it could be a key to a cabin in Wisconsin, but I doubted that.

I wanted to go back to Stoufley's but I wanted to wait until dark. I had time to kill and a dog to walk, so I headed home.

When I got home, Paradise was pleased to see me. I'd left her on papers in the kitchen and she'd amused herself by making a sculpture out of my kitchen trash. She piddled with delight on seeing me.

"What the hell is this, Paradise?" Even I heard the joke.

She cocked her head like "What did you expect me to do? Bored silly all day?"

I was a fool to keep her, I knew that, so I told myself she was really Zach's dog and I was keeping her for him. I don't know about you, but I find my minor self-deceptions funny. I like to think I'm on to them. Gloria might tell you this is not the case.

Paradise started barking. Good puppy. Someone at the door. Gun drawn, nerves humming, I got my door open just in time to see the hallway elevator door closing. A manila envelope, a large one, lay on the floor outside my door.

I didn't think it was a letter bomb, but it should have been. The first photo was of Violet Winters, at her current age, in her own apartment, tied up, tied down—being peed on. I gagged. The second photo was worse, if you could calibrate that. This photograph was blurry, but unmistakably Zachary. He was naked.

It knocked me sideways.

Outside, the streets were purpling with night. To me it felt dark already. I abruptly understood exactly how frightened Ricky Noonan had been. It was one thing—and a scary thing—to be pressured when you knew the reason why. It was another thing, and far scarier, to be pressured when you did not know the reason.

"Do you have any enemies?" I would have asked someone else. Everyone has some, that was my experience. If not at first, at least on second thought.

I had lots of enemies. Men I'd sent to jail, women I'd widowed, and kids I'd orphaned, all in the line of duty. For that matter, I had Gloria. And Gomez, I would have said, before his death made me sentimental.

Still, for a man with so many enemies, I wasn't a man you expected to see crossed. My job was to protect and serve, and my job returned the favor. Nobody singled out a cop. Nobody drew fire that way.

Then I got it. I was being invited to dance.

The photos, the notes, the visit to my apartment: These were invitations. This was personal. Suddenly, I found myself thinking about Noonan again, about how I didn't want Ricky Noonan to turn up dead. You can call this transference. You're right. It's a cheap but effective trick. Cops worry about other people instead of themselves. It gives us the illusion of invulnerability.

"Doesn't your work scare you?"

"No."

"What about your partner, worry about him?"

"Yeah. Yeah, I do worry about him. All the time."

So I was worrying about Ricky Noonan. I took Paradise for her walk, came back up, gave her some dinner, settled in on the couch with a Coke classic, and called Jamie.

For some reason, I told Jamie I was going to go back to Stoufley's to poke around.

"Social climber," he laughed.

I left Jamie chuckling into his paint supplies and got off the line. Paradise gave me her unloved-child routine, but I put her into her kennel.

I left for the Gold Coast.

Again tonight, a big summer storm was moving in. I could see it lighting-up banks of cloud over the lake. It wasn't raining yet, but the light show was impressive and the low drumrolls of thunder were advancing like tanks.

It was quiet at Carson Stoufley's, very quiet. Even the thunder sounded muted. I left my unmarked in its slot by the hydrant, walked down the block like I owned it, and unlocked Stoufley's, bold as brass.

I said I had a hunch. That's just shorthand. I get hunches, and then later see the logic to them: Noonan was being pressured by someone, someone who knew something about Carson Stoufley, something I didn't know yet. Or didn't yet know I knew. Therefore, I had to go to Stoufley's or Ricky Noonan might end up dead.

The door opened easily. The musty jungle scent enveloped me again. Something skittered across the floor. I hit the lights. Someone stared back at me: a tiny human face, or nearly. It was a baby monkey, and it was lonely and starving. I held out an arm. It jumped at me like I was Daddy. I caught it midair, and a wave of jungle came along with it. That funky smell was monkey.

I'd heard they bite, but this one just cuddled. I tried to get her down, but she wasn't having any. She clung like an anxious woman. "Save me, save me," she gibbered, clamped to my neck. I'm a cop. I save people. Someone must have told her that.

The truth is, the monkey relaxed me. My gut said the house was empty, and so did she. I set her down, but she attached herself to my leg.

"Oh, all right, baby."

I headed for the cavern below me. No drum music seeping through the floor. No sense of anything living waiting to pounce.

I opened that basement door and knew immediately that what waited below was death. I drew my gun, but not because I expected to need it. I flicked on the electric sconces, and there was death staring me in the face. All I had to do was read the writing on the wall. "BYE BYE" was written in red letters. "BYE BYE" was written in blood. That was chilling enough, but a pentacle was daubed next to it.

Gun drawn, monkey gibbering, I descended the Gothic stairwell. The drums were gone, but the sound of them seemed to linger in the smell of campfire that remained. Somebody had had himself a real ritual here: drum music, fire, the works. I crossed the round room I thought of now as "ritual space" and unlocked the small wooden archive door. Monkey and I entered. The floor was littered with photos. Some of them were now spattered with blood.

The fourth cabinet, the locked one, had been hacked open. The photos from it seemed missing. Kicking through the debris on the floor, I saw nudes, more nudes, bondage, biracial love, but no severed torso, no children.

The unused key on Carson Stoufley's key ring was small and silver. It wouldn't fit a door. It might fit a drawer or a jewelry box. Turning to leave, I saw a drawer.

I've told you about the stainless steel table. That table had a drawer, the kind you might keep instruments in, instruments of terror. The key fit the drawer. I opened the drawer. It was empty except for a single sheet of paper. "I found them, Carson," the paper said. It was lilac linen paper. I took the note.

Monkey was tugging at my collar. I closed the drawer. I

locked it, tiptoed through the porno, closed and locked the archive door. We had found Stoufley's head in a bucket at Nesbitt's studio, looking like John the Baptist: the severed hero's head, matted hair, staring eyes. I found Stoufley's body in the basement. At least, I found what I assumed to be his body. Turning to go, I had looked straight across the ritual space into the large black mouth of the outsized fireplace at the other end: There was a body hanging on that spit. Blackened, burned, charred almost beyond recognition—but not quite.

Chapter forty-one

———■———

Jamie met me at the door with his customary sawed off shotgun and a drink.

"We've got unexpected company," Jamie said, nodding at Violet Winters, who was standing some ten feet behind him. He handed me the glass.

"Do I need this?" I asked.

"Yeah. Maybe."

"My skylight was open when I got home," Violet said. "Salvation was unconscious. Somebody came and went. The Midnight Welder. I found this." Violet handed me a manila envelope. It matched the one I'd gotten at home. Stepping over to a standing lamp, I opened it up. Another photo show.

It was Violet again, this time with some man's gun in her mouth, and I mean gun, not a metaphor. Her eyes looked gone, glassy, doped out of this world. It wasn't even clear if she was conscious.

In the photos, facial bruising was already evident, although as with all beatings, the bruises would worsen the second

270

day. I remembered the shiner and the mysterious drunk Violet couldn't remember.

"I'm about to be blackmailed," Violet echoed my thoughts. "Then again, so is she, evidently."

I noticed Salvation. She was still groggy, lying flat out under Jamie's drafting table.

"Find anything else? Anything out of place?"

"I found the phone."

"And called him?" I was jealous.

"She called looking for you, champ," Jamie volunteered. He looked as close as I'd ever seen him to guilty. He was probably flirting with her before I got there.

"Hey. Do I look jealous?"

"Yes." Violet giggled. The giggle did it. Now I was pissed.

"I brought you a little present," I told her. "Actually, I brought it for Jamie, but I've decided he doesn't deserve one."

"Like I said, she called for you," Jamie reminded me.

"Back in a minute," I said.

I ducked outside to my unmarked, where the baby monkey awaited. It was wrong to take her from Stoufley's, I knew that, but the alternative was letting her starve or blow the whistle on myself: Go get this monkey I mysteriously discovered.

"A little baby," Violet said with clear delight when I reentered Jamie's, Baby in my arms. "A rhesus baby. Come to mama, sweetheart."

"Where'd you get that thing?" asked Jamie.

I shot him a look: Shut up. No questions.

Baby crawled straight into Violet's outstretched arms. I could have done the same thing myself.

"Looks like you may be needing some protective custody," I said.

Jamie hooted. "What a great line, and with a straight face, too."

"This is business," I snapped. The great pretender.

"Right." Jamie jabbed me, then petted the monkey.

We were both posturing for the doctor's benefit. She was not impressed.

"Come on, you two. Knock it off."

"That goes for you, too," Jamie said. Baby had decided he was irresistible. She jumped across from the doctor's arms to his.

"Aw, shit," he said, clearly delighted.

"You shouldn't have named this Tattooed Zoo unless you meant it," I warned him.

He was scratching Baby's head. It looked like true love, you asked me.

"You need a safe place," I pushed Violet. "So does your ferocious guard dog."

"They could stay with me," Jamie offered. I wanted to kill and thank him.

"I would be so grateful," said Violet, a little quickly I thought.

What's wrong with my place? I wanted to ask, but the answer was obvious. People got killed there. I kept my mouth shut and fumed.

"He's thinking it over," Jamie joked, "trying to decide if I'm safe with you."

"Oh, you're safe," Violet shot back. "I'm either a yes or a no. In your case, I'm a no. You're Elliot's friend."

"I am Elliot's friend." Jamie put her in her place. "I didn't proposition you, I offered to protect you. For my friend. And take this goddamn monkey back."

"You two are hilarious," I told them, feeling fond and momentarily in control.

Have I mentioned that Jamie's idea of an ideal woman runs to professional strippers? When he warned me off Violet, he was operating from his own rules of the road.

"You want to see Jamie jump over the roof? Tell him your I.Q.," I volunteered, still testy.

"Obviously, I'm a moron if you're my idea of a good time."

"She's got a point, Elliot."

"Actually, you can both stop staring."

The doctor's cleavage had suddenly become an issue. The monkey was busy feeling her up, looking for a good time or a free meal.

"We need a bottle," said the doctor.

"Scotch, gin, tequila?" Jamie kept a bar for visitors.

"Baby bottle."

"Oh, sure. Hundreds of them."

"We'll improvise. You have milk?"

"You two work it out. Give it a banana like the movies. I'm going back to work."

"Elliot?" The doctor's voice was soft and low.

"What, Dr. Winters?"

"You look like death warmed over."

Little did she know.

The rain was pissing down. Chicago is not an ecological high spot. I got into my apartment building feeling like I'd just spent an hour in the sauna fully clothed. My plan was a nice shower and a good night's sleep. Then I noticed my message light blinking.

Zachary had left a message on the private line. "Hi, Dad. It's Zach. Please call me." I decided it was much too late to call him. I got extra papers for Paradise—I refused to walk her in the rain—and I heard a message from Myerling as I walked back in. And one from Father Bremner. Things were definitely heating up in the spiritual protection racket. It was midnight, but I called Myerling anyway. He was waiting for my call.

"I got Chabrol tonight," he told me. "Right after you left, actually. He came special delivery with a note to you."

"Everything does, these days. What did the note say?"

"I'll tell you at Harry's."

"You don't sleep, do you, Myerling? You want to meet at Harry's in the rain?"

"You won't sleep, either, when you see this."

"Thanks, Harold."

We agreed to meet in fifteen minutes at Harry's. That made it one A.M. in a dangerous part of town. Maybe Myerling never thought about things like that. Maybe death was so familiar to him that it no longer counted. I found that lately it did for me. Maybe it was meeting Violet Winters. Maybe it was the fifteen-year depression of my marriage lifting. Maybe it was wanting to be there for Zach. Suddenly it seemed I had things to live for other than merely doing my job. I hoped that didn't get in my way.

When I got to Harry's, he grimaced like he wasn't so glad to see me. "Hey, Detective, it's raining cats and dogs. I was closing."

"Sorry, Harry. I told a friend I'd meet him."

"What the hell. I can polish the silver," Harry joked.

I was guarding our table at the window when Myerling pulled to the curb in his Town Car. He got out looking like he'd been dry cleaned—he had an expensive raincoat on, bone dry, and he was carrying a big, shiny, funereal black umbrella. He tapped the glass with his umbrella and gestured me to come outside. I shook my head no. Reluctantly, Myerling came in.

"Hey. Fold that thing up. Umbrella open inside is bad luck," Harry told him.

"We won't be long," I told Harry.

Myerling leaned his umbrella against the window and sat down. "It wasn't AIDS," he said.

"What?"

"Chabrol. It wasn't AIDS."

"But he wasted away."

"That's right."

"Poison?"

"In a sense."

"Don't start. I know you're going to say voodoo or satanism or some shit."

"Starvation."

"Bullshit."

"I'm telling you."

"But why?"

"You tell me." With that, Myerling handed me an envelope. "Detective Mayo." The writing was thin and spidery—Chabrol's, I assumed. I opened it. A single sheet of paper, a single sentence: "I could no longer bear the darkness," it read. At the bottom, for good measure, there was a wobbly pentacle.

I passed the sheet to Myerling.

"What do you make of this?" he asked. "A confession?"

"Okay, maybe. But of what?"

"You tell me."

My cop stirred and poked me. He was asking me to violate Elliot's homicide rule number nine: Never tell anybody everything.

"I'm not sure I can do that, Harold."

"Ah." He seemed resigned, not surprised. He asked Harry for another cup of hot water. He unwrapped one of his personal tea bags and dipped it up and down, up and down, up and down.

I reached in my pocket. Ever since Noonan gave it to me, I'd been carrying Johnny Vanilla's ring. I took it out and placed it on the table. Harold pulled back like it was radioactive.

"I thought I told you to get rid of that thing." His calm was gone.

"I did. I gave it back to evidence and Judge Noonan gave it back to me again. He thought it was a death threat. It came in his mail. I checked evidence. It's identical."

"What's your objective?"

"What's that mean, Harold? To solve these fucking things."

"But you've got yourself a poltergeist."

"Don't start with that shit again."

"Think about it, Elliot. You've got something nobody sees that moves things around. A poltergeist is a mischief-maker. They just distract people, scare them a little. Keep them rattled."

"You're telling me I'm dealing with a ghost?"

"Don't be so literal." Myerling dipped his tea bag some more.

"You ever going to drink that?"

"When I'm ready. Who's your mischief-maker?"

I could have kissed him. I bolted from the table so fast, Harry jumped.

"I love you, Myerling," I said. "I talk to another coroner about cause of death and I get 'blunt instrument' or 'strangulation.' I talk to you, I get negative energies, poltergeists, power rings—"

"Don't act like you're such a straight arrow," Myerling shot back. "You think I don't know about your little kits?"

As a matter of fact, I didn't think he knew about my little kits. Have I mentioned them? I think of them as a little quirk left over from my days in boy scouts, my good luck bag.

On the drive home, I remembered my promise to Chabrol to care for his cats. I'd get on it tomorrow. Tonight, for the first time in weeks, I planned to sleep and believed I actually would.

For once I did.

Chapter forty-two

There is nothing like a night's sleep to change your world view. Outside my window, Chicago was the city of light. The river glinted like a mythological silver snake. The winged Mercury atop the Sears, Roebuck Building struck me as an angel of good tidings. I was an intelligent man, expert in my field, and I was about to crack this case. I could feel it. I was coming up in the world. Sure enough, checking my mail in the lobby, I had two magazines, and a heavy embossed envelope of creamy vellum.

"Anything interesting?" Bobby asked.

"I've come up in the world," I replied.

Bobby was smiling at me from behind the desk. I'd tipped him twenty dollars for his trouble with my locks, and that seemed to have moved us across into daily chats. He was an okay kid, I'd decided.

"What is it?" he asked. "Your invitation to the Academy Awards?"

"Something like that."

I didn't know that our new intimacy should include sharing my mail.

"I've got a letter opener," he volunteered.

"I'll get it at the office."

Once outside in my car on the way to the station, curiosity got the better of me. Waiting for the left turn onto Clybourn, I gouged open the creamy envelope. Yes, it was an invitation.

> *Dr. and Mrs. Malcolm Crutcher,*
> *on behalf of the Doctors' Fund*
> *for the Children of Chicago,*
> *invite you to attend a day of*
> *Information and Inspiration.*
> *The Palmer House*
> *9 a.m.–5 p.m.*
> *Luncheon served.*

Included was a handwritten note from Crutcher. "Sorry for the late notice. Thought you'd be interested—and valuable. Malcolm."

I checked the date. Late notice, all right. I had exactly twenty minutes to make it to the Palmer House.

I pulled police privilege, hit my lights and siren, U-turned right in the middle of the Clybourn, North, and Halsted intersection, and headed back to the Loop.

The Palmer House was a remnant of Chicago's glory days as a town of beef and brawn. All done up in gold and gilt, the hotel looked like a Roman palace—or an upscale bordello.

In the lobby, just as you entered, a hand-calligraphed sign welcomed the guests of the Doctors' Fund. A table stood to one side, staffed by three expensive-looking young matrons in Lord & Taylor florals. They were handing out programs and checking names off lists, filling out name tags and smiling great, artificial Revlon smiles of welcome.

"I've already got a name tag," I said to a blond matron labeled Sharon. I tapped my badge. She smiled nervously.

"Detective Mayo? Let me see . . ."

She rifled her pages, checked with her neighbors, excused herself, checked at a second, smaller table, and then returned, all relief and knowledge.

"You're on the special list," she said.

"What does that mean?" I asked.

"No donation necessary."

For the first time, I noticed the arriving guests were handing over checks—large checks—as they picked up their name tags.

"This is quite an event," I said to Sharon.

"Oh, yes. So critical." With that she gave me a conference badge, a schedule of events, a packet of information tied with a ribbon. It would take all day just to read it. "Better hurry," Sharon urged me. "You're at table three." She made it sound important.

I followed the drift of the crowd—a well-dressed, well-heeled crowd—until it surged into a handsome convention room. Table three, out of perhaps sixty, was well to the front. I had nearly reached my table, when I heard my name.

"Elliot!"

It was Dr. Winters, in her professional regalia, waving at me from table six. Good for Crutcher, I thought, managing the separation of church and state. His wife might not care for Violet Winters, but she was his respected colleague nonetheless.

"Dr. Winters." I waved a casual hand as though seeing her there was the most natural thing in the world.

Table three was round, well appointed, and graced by a huge floral display. It seated six.

"I'm Marnie Leader," said the handsome black woman to my right. "Child Services."

"I'm Norma Kottlisky," offered the woman to my left. She was a soft-spoken redhead in her late middle age. She offered me a genuine smile and the friendly gaze of her large emerald eyes. "Private practice," she added.

"You're too modest, Norma," Marnie Leader chided her. "She's an expert on child abuse, incest, and domestic violence."

"I am," Dr. Kottlisky allowed mildly.

"Sounds like a terrible job," I managed.

"Yes, just like yours. Dr. Crutcher told me you worked homicide but had a special interest in children."

"I have a son, if that's what he means."

"I think he felt you could help our cause," Marnie interjected.

"Which is?"

"The children. We're a coalition aimed at pooling information and resources to aid children in need."

"Sounds admirable." I was wondering what I was doing there, but Dr. Kottlisky had the answer to that, too.

"Malcolm and I were talking about the need to stay reality based," she said. "So many charities have all the money and spend it in all the wrong ways."

"I'm sure that's true." And I did remember seeing an article revealing that only one tenth of a typical charitable donation actually went to aiding its intended recipients.

"Here we go," Dr. Kottlisky said.

Where we went over the next six hours was through a boggling array of speeches, panels, and handouts. Between talks,

I learned that Malcolm Crutcher, in addition to chairing the Doctors' Fund, served as a board member on an abused-children's shelter and was a principal in better hospital care for welfare cases, donating a fourth of his caseload to charity.

"He's quite an inspiration," Marnie Leader told me, nodding across the room during a break to where Malcolm Crutcher was glad-handing a table full of pretty donors.

"Yes, he is—and he certainly knows it," Dr. Kottlisky observed dryly.

"He's not your hero?" I asked.

"I don't believe in them," she said firmly. "Now, what are you doing here, just following Malcolm's agenda like a sheep?"

"Yes," I said, deliberating on how much to tell her. "He operated on my son and has been a sounding board for me about his therapy as well."

"A sounding board? I think Malcolm is quite a gifted surgeon, but I do wish he'd stick to his specialty instead of straying over into mine."

"Which is?"

"I never know quite how to put it. Spiritual healing, I almost want to say. My approach is far more holistic than Malcolm's. I don't think you can just stitch up the wound and pretend there's no emotional scar tissue."

"That's quite a phrase, 'emotional scar tissue.'"

"Yes, well, that's my experience. Victims need a chance to heal at depth, not just repress things and muddle on."

"I don't suppose you know Alice Hauser?"

"Oh, dear God. Don't tell me—?"

"What?"

"Now, Norma," Marnie chided. She'd been paying avid attention to our exchange.

"We have differing philosophies," Dr. Kottlisky said finally. I got the gut feeling she'd have said much more if it weren't for Leader's restrictive presence.

"Who else is supposed to be at this table?" I changed the subject.

"I believe we've been expecting Mrs. Crutcher and two of her major donors. Perhaps they got caught up shopping."

I liked Dr. Kottlisky, liked her for her wry humor and honesty.

"Maybe she thought we were the kitchen help," Marnie Leader sniped.

"She's very social," Dr. Kottlisky agreed.

"I've met her."

"Then I'm sure you know."

"I think I'm going to table-hop," Marnie Leader informed us.

I nodded politely, but felt a relief. When Leader left, Dr. Kottlisky turned to me directly.

"Where were we?" she asked. "Talking about your child?"

I was grateful she had opened the door. I told her about Dr. Hauser's conservatism, Dr. Crutcher's opinion that regression might be stirring up needless and dangerous trouble.

"Oh, posh," she said. "Malcolm's just shoving everything under the rug. Surgeons are such prima donnas. I suppose they perform enough miracles, they forget they're not God. Surgery can't fix everything, and he hates to admit that. Regression is really a form of psychic surgery. With the help of hypnosis we can go back in, retrieve memories, even relive them—but without the pain. We can program the patient to watch them like a movie. We can even work through a traumatic event to have a different outcome, if not in reality, at least in the mind. In the patient's psyche we can effect a release, if nothing else."

I was suspicious. It sounded too good to be true, more like some New Age wishful thinking than science. I said as much.

"There's nothing New Age about it," Dr. Kottlisky chastened me. "Hypnosis is age-old. Dr. Mesmer just popularized it, not invented it."

"There really was a Dr. Mesmer?"

"Yes. That's why we say 'mesmerized.' "

"This gets worse and worse. I feel like you're telling me to brainwash Zachary."

"In a sense I am. The process can be very cleansing, but I'm not Zachary's doctor—"

"All right. I get it. I'm not allowed to forget and neither is he."

"I'm just saying heal first, both of you. Then forget. Until you remember and heal, it's not forgetting. It's repressing."

"All right. You've made your point and found an open ear."

"Have I really been so pushy?" Dr. Kottlisky gave me a charming smile. I saw Violet Winters making her way toward our table. Dr. Kottlisky saw her, too, and her face wreathed in smiles. "Excuse me," she said. "An old, dear friend . . . Violet! You look wonderful!"

The two doctors were clearly delighted by each other's company. I left them to their girlish hug, excused myself, and headed to the gold-swirled lobby to call Dr. Hauser. My plan was to insist that she do regressions with me standing by. She wouldn't hear of it.

"I would also like to have a consulting doctor who knows Zachary—"

"I'm afraid that's not possible."

"Dr. Hauser, I'm afraid you don't understand. Zachary is my son. As his father, I do have rights. Additionally, he may have been involved in a very violent crime."

"Molestation is a violent crime, Detective, perhaps not to you—"

"Look, Doctor, I will not have this come down to a pissing match—"

"I'm afraid I must insist. Regressions are not a part of my treatment plan for your son. I will not have a power struggle with you, Detective Mayo." She hung up on me.

She didn't ask, "Why, Detective? Why regressions?"

She did not say, "Maybe we can work together on this. Here's my thinking and what is yours?"

She said no.

Back at table three, Dr. Kottlisky was working her way through a large shrimp cocktail. Dr. Crutcher approached and kissed her on the cheek. She batted him away, smiling.

"I'm not one of your patients, Malcolm, you can skip the bedside manner with me," she chided, but still colored prettily.

Crutcher straightened up and greeted me with a vigorous handshake.

"Great you could make it, Detective."

"Great to be asked. Very enlightening."

"Next year, we'll have to get you up there. Give them a dose of reality, not just theory."

"Speaking of a dose of reality, Malcolm, I suggested to Detective Mayo that I thought regressions could be very useful."

"Now, Norma, you're to stay out of this. Zachary is not your case, and you know I think your mumbo jumbo with hypnosis is a lot of dangerous hocus-pocus."

Underneath Crutcher's affable delivery I sensed a will of steel. Dr. Kottlisky sensed it, too, but shrugged it off.

"Variety is the spice of life, Malcolm," she baited him,

casting their differences as a matter of taste. Crutcher accepted the détente.

"Oh, all right. You two enjoy yourselves. Oops! I'm due in the lobby for the *Trib* photographer."

With that, Crutcher left us. I watched him make his way, smiling and nodding, through the crowd.

"Quite the social butterfly, isn't he?" I commented.

"Quite the politician," Dr. Kottlisky corrected me.

I saw Dr. Violet Winters waving to me as she made her way toward the exit. It was Tuesday, her afternoon for surgery. I settled in for an informative—and endless—afternoon of speakers.

When the day ended, I took my packet of literature, stopped by the station to tag base, then headed home. I'd come to a decision about changing therapists for Zachary, and I wanted to sleep on it.

That's exactly what I did.

Chapter forty-three

—■—

Cops like cop joints, the joints that really like cops. We go back to them—bad food, rotten coffee, we'll tolerate anything if you're nice to us. The best cop joints are either pancake places or Greek. Don't ask me why. My favorite is the Golden Angel. My favorite waitress there is Betsy—Kewpie-doll smile, bleached blond hair, weighs in at two fifty, easy. Betsy loves me. After all this time, she knows my habits. After nine hours sleep and mopping up Paradise's paper route, I went to the Golden Angel.

"Two over easy, double toast, bacon, and sausage," she sang out when I made the door. I got the flagship booth.

"Saving it for you. Knew you'd have a breakthrough."

"You and God, then, Betsy. You and God."

"I see you finally slept. That's a good sign. Must have been alone for once. Should've called me."

Betsy brought me my O.J. She also brought me somebody's leftover *Tribune*. I glanced at sports, then noticed Malcolm Crutcher, his wife, Ilene, and my tablemate, Marnie Leader, all smiling at me from the Metro section. "Children's

Coalition," the cut line read. The Crutchers looked suitably handsome and charitable. Marnie Leader looked proud and happy, little caring that she was included in the shot to prove their good intentions toward the inner city, right there in black and white.

Betsy stopped to refill my coffee. "He's a good-looking guy," she said of Crutcher. "She looks like, what's her name? Mrs. Trump."

"And you look better than either of them."

Betsy and I had been flirting for at least twenty years. She kids me about my hot sex life now that I'm single. No matter what we tell you, most cops have terrible sex lives.

"In and out real fast, just like a burglar."

"What am I, the scene of the crime?"

"This a hit-and-run or something?"

"You frisking me, or is that your idea of foreplay?"

These are just a few of the jokes. There're a couple hundred more. Girls on the street tell them. More than a few cops have gone with street girls, but AIDS changed a lot of that.

Some cops drink. Some fool around with narcotics. For others it's the girls. Sex is their fix. What they do to come down, the way they medicate their job-related stress. The girls know what they're talking about when they talk about cops.

I hear we're rotten lovers. We come too fast or too slow. Can't get it up or can't get it off, get into kinky stuff, wanting the wife to learn a few street tricks to keep our interest up. No wonder we cops flirt. Sometimes that's all we get. I told Betsy she looked better than her teenage daughter. And she did. For her part, Betsy told me she was glad my new girl-friend was giving it a rest.

"What new girlfriend?"

"Red dress, red spikes, sound familiar?"

Have I said that cops are gossips? We talk like our life depended on it, which it just might. Switching shifts, there's the cop-joint overlap, a kind of relay for the state-of-the-street information.

"Adele, that sweet-faced street whore from Tennessee, jumped out a window last night."

"No way. She was pushed."

"No witnesses."

"Of course not."

"The video shop got its front window bashed again. That's two."

"Mustn't have paid his dues this month."

"Somebody should warn him three strikes you're out."

And so on.

The grapevine had me with a hot new girlfriend. More than that, I was sure. Betsy brought my eggs and a second napkin. I'd written on the first. One of the things I like to do is make lists.

> laundry
> dog food
> cats
> kit

"So? Is it true about the girl?" Betsy had her own agenda.

"It was a red dress, yeah."

"But are you seeing her?"

"She's a suspect, Betsy."

"As long as she didn't do it. Did she?"

"How 'bout some more O.J.?"

"Shoot. I thought when you showed up, you were at the talk-about-it phase."

"Getting there. Unlike my O.J."

"Yes, boss."

What Betsy called the "talk-about-it phase" was the closing part of an investigation for me. I've thought about it a lot, and most investigations look like dog bones.

At the beginning, there's a fat, fanned-out part where you're gathering information, you're talking to everybody. After that you're in the pipe, the long, skinny middle part of the bone. You're thinking, thinking. You don't want to talk then. You're mulling, brooding. You're . . . "Unbearable," Gloria always told me.

Part three, you've got a theory, maybe even a plan, you're setting your traps, talking or walking people into them. In part three your talk has a purpose. Several, in fact. You're still fishing, of course, but you're also generating a lot of smoke. I don't know about all cops, but I learned how to do part three from my mother.

"Ah . . . Elliot?"

"That's my name, Mother."

"That's a lovely sweater on you. Your sister was right about the color. Does what's-her-name, Ann, like it, too?"

If I bit, Mom knew I was dating Ann. . . . Betty was back with my juice. Okay, we'd talk a little. My lead, though.

"You want to hear something weird, Betsy?"

"Sure."

"I miss Gomez."

"No kidding! I thought when he took up with your wife—"

"My ex-wife."

"Well, now, but when they started, even I hated the little creep."

"And you don't miss him at all?"

"He was funny."

"Yeah. He did have a sense of humor."

"No. Funny."

"I know what you mean."

"Do you? I mean the way he was with women. And that religious stuff of his. His friends, he always said it was. I think he was into all that voodoo shit. The seven powers or the twelve powers or whatever. I know they're like saints and all, but—"

"Yeah. Weird, huh?"

"Same as Chabrol. Now, him I miss. He's the one told me they're like saints, not Gomez."

"How about a check?" I glanced at my watch, made a show of late.

Always quit when you're ahead, before they know you're fishing. I'd probably pushed it a little with Betsy. I started with her because a good waitress, like a good cop, is skilled at reading people. I wanted to see if Betsy'd come up with something I'd missed. She'd come up with the same things I had: weird sex and weird religion.

Oscar Gomez—and/or his friends—were practitioners of island religion, Voudun, an eclectic mishmash of African spiritual traditions and Catholicism. I would say "voodoo," but the word conjures all sorts of terrors. In reality the religion encompasses aspects of freemasonry, the Cabalah, metaphysics, and theosophy. It also—and most controversially—entails animal sacrifice. Then again, so did Judaism. What were a few chickens and goats among friends?

That depended entirely on the friends.

Chapter forty-four

———■———

I checked my messages from the Golden Angel and returned an "urgent" call from Ricky Noonan. Ricky was glad to hear from me. He'd been having little accidents, electric shocks, whenever he touched a light switch, his car stalling out, static on his phone.

"Is that normal?"

"Doesn't sound normal." I did not tell Ricky that such accidents were common to victims in Voudun.

"That's what I thought."

"What do you want to do?"

"Whatever you say."

He was spooked, and more open-minded than usual. I told him about Father Bremner.

"I can drive you," I told Ricky. "We could talk on the drive out."

"I'd rather drive myself. Maybe it will unwind me a little."

"Let me give you the directions. We'll meet at nine unless you hear from me."

I gave him the directions—twice, to be sure he had them

right. I gave him Bremner's phone number just in case he got lost.

Poor Ricky. He did sound wound up. Father Bremner, on the other hand, was completely unflapped. You'd have thought he was expecting my call. He probably was. I told him about Ricky's little accidents. Father Bremner said he'd see us both that evening—at nine, if that was okay by me.

I noticed the coincidence.

Like most cops, I'm more than a little interested in ESP. Like most cops, I hate to let on. (My cop is a form of ESP, at least of intuition.) We wouldn't want to say this in public, but ESP keeps us alive. It's the funny feeling that tells you "don't go through that door" or "he's carrying." It's a sixth sense, some heightened combination of street smarts and gut. It's whatever you want to call it, and I sound as weird as Myerling when I talk about it. So bear with me.

Basically, I'd say there are two kinds: sending and receiving. Now, when I listen to my cop, I'm receiving. You might call them gut feelings, or hunches. But they're messages. Like I said, that's receiving.

When I'm in part three of a case, I use another kind. I send. The closest I've ever come to hearing it explained is Native American ritual. They dress up like the animal they're trying to catch. They woo it in the spirit world, call to it, invite it to the hunt, promise it an honorable death. It all sounds silly, but I know what they're talking about. I do it with killers.

I'm not saying I rig horns to my head. Gomez did that for me. I don't wear war paint or don a bear rug and jump up and down. But I do collect what you might call power items. I make a little kit. You can think it's strange—it is strange—but it works. I had a few errands to run and then I would start on my kit.

First I dropped Xeroxes of Zach's doodle at Dr. Hauser's

office with a note saying, "Please advise." Then I drove to Chabrol's. I climbed to the third floor, looked for the key under the mat, found it, and got a swipe from a cat's paw. The big Persian gray.

The cat might be starving. The place might be gutted or a wreck. Street people might be living there. It could even be empty. Gone, just like Chabrol. I did not know what to expect—but not this: beauty.

And that is what I found, opening Chabrol's door.

Someone had frescoed the walls of Chabrol's apartment. They glowed with luminous tropical hues. In the central mural, Chabrol was entering heaven. As you might expect, heaven looked a lot like a Caribbean island. Entering the garlanded gates, Chabrol was wearing a long white robe. A white dog walked by his side. Yes, it was the image from my dream.

The mural didn't scare me, although perhaps it should have. Instead, I felt oddly comforted, as though Chabrol or someone, some power or powers, were watching over me. In short, I felt spiritually protected, standing there. I've heard men do that in the presence of great art, and sometimes at the site of great battles, too. I had the feeling Chabrol's apartment, his life, for that matter, and certainly his death, had been a combination of the two.

"Here, kitty-kitty-kitty." Chabrol had left an outsized carrier with directions near his door. "Here, Meme, here, Blue." I read the note.

"They belong together," said Chabrol's spidery hand. "Meme is spoiled and prefers chicken livers. Blue is easy. They're good with furniture and are current on all their shots. Thank you."

I collected the cats with less difficulty than I'd imagined. Then I looked around and made my choices.

Under his window, the one looking east toward the lake, Chabrol had a small altar. I call it an altar, but you might have seen it as a knickknack collection, nothing more. I took a hunk of quartz, a blue feather, and a candlestick. I also took the piece of Chinese silk they were arranged upon. Nodding to Chabrol, the Chabrol who floated above me like a risen Christ, I took the cats, my selections, and I left. I was making my kit.

I stopped at the Occult Bookstore. It was a small, shabby storefront operation, but it had what I needed. For $29.95 I acquired a ritual knife with a "ruby" in the handle. I also got a black goat's-head T-shirt and a nasty little book on witchcraft printed in Gothic type. More for the kit.

I was getting there, all right. I could feel it. When the Indians explain it, they say you have to think like a deer to track one. . . . To catch a killer, you have to think like one, too. That's why cops get strange. They have to cross over, mentally, to some terrible territory. When the Indians talk about the shaman climbing up the tree of life to find what he needs, I know what they mean. I don't call it climbing, though. I call it dropping down the well. It feels like a descent to me, a climb down, down into a sort of netherworld like those engravings by William Blake, souls whirling through a cloudy soup.

Are you with me? The process is hard to explain. It's a journey, I suppose. When I try to put language on it, it sounds ephemeral, but I think of it as a specific kind of signaling. I gather my "power," I "drop down the well." And it draws the killer to me. That's the point.

Maybe it takes another cop to understand. Or a hunter. Or a killer. Or a woman in love. You set a trap. You issue an invitation and make it tempting. You join the dance.

After the Occult Bookstore, I stopped at St. Angela's

Church. For a dollar I lit two candles, one for me and one for Ricky Noonan. I was out the door, nearly at the car, when it became necessary to light more. I went back, fed a ten spot into the alms box, and lit candles for Zachary, for Violet, for Jamie, for Gomez and Chabrol, even for Gloria and Cousin Charles. The candles I lit were red, blue, and white. Not for patriotism, but for Jesus, Mary, and Joseph, the Holy Family. I'd understood that family was what solving these killings was about for me.

After St. Angela's I went to the adult bookstore. I picked the one on South Halsted with two big-breasted girls painted on the front. The girls were just a come-on; gay anonymous sex was the payoff. I knew exactly what I wanted, and it wasn't a blowjob. Whether I could get it was another question. As I've said, I look like a homicide bull. That look was all right. The question was, could I act like a sick one?

The guy at the counter read me for cop the minute I made the door. As if by osmosis, there was a stiffening in the browsing males cruising each other in the bookstalls. The stiffening was not in the groin. Cop-cop-cop, the message was flashing. In some stores, they actually do flash a light. Here it was the drum-drum-drumming of the counterman's nails on the counter. I left without scoring, or thought I did until I bumped into another customer on the stairs going out. He dropped his plain brown bag and ran like demons were chasing him. Perhaps they were.

I picked up his purchase, tucked it under my arm, and double-timed the two blocks back to my unmarked. Safe in the car, doors locked, I checked out the score. I was right on target.

Kinder, a commercially produced German kiddie porn video, marketed with a sex education sticker across the front.

The glossies followed suit. They should furnish barf bags with the stuff.

Elliot's homicide rule number ten: When a case heats up, so does coincidence. In this case, the dirty pictures. My Jesuit side had done its research on all of this. I knew enough to say thank-you to Dr. Carl Gustav Jung for articulating the fact that there's more to coincidence than mere coincidence.

Jamie calls it the yellow Jeep syndrome. Buy a yellow Jeep, you see them everywhere. Maybe there are more Jeeps, or maybe we just focus on them. Selective perception. Jung believed we draw them to us. So did Goethe. So do I. Track a child pornographer, dirty pictures fall at your feet. I'm not discounting the enormous amount of work we do. If you don't do it, nothing happens—or a lot less. What I'm saying is that you chase apples, and oranges are delivered.

I wasn't thinking about any of this as I sat in my unmarked with those dirty pictures in my lap. The cats were meowing, one of them, anyway. The Persian, Meme, had a tiny, whiny mew. Blue was the strong, silent type. I knew I should take them straight to the ASPCA and get it over with, but I'd promised Chabrol, so I headed for Jamie's.

One dog, one monkey, two cats. Two dogs, if you counted Salvation. The phrase "my life is a real zoo" was acquiring resonance. I got out of the car carrying the cats, who were both now mewing loudly.

"You're pushing it," Jamie said as he opened the door. I bulled my way past him into the studio. "If you're wondering if the doctor is in, the doctor's at the hospital. The dog and the monkey are with me. Now, get those cats out of here. You're pushing it."

I knew if I gave Jamie one inch, he'd come back at me. I kept my back to him, set down the cat carrier, and began opening its locks.

"This place is a zoo."

"You asked for it. Besides, monkeys are good luck."

"Sure. So are cobras."

"I promised a dead man. I'm superstitious."

"You promised a dead man what? To give me his cats?"

"To find them a home."

"This is not a home."

"Sure it is. 'Tattooed Zoo.' A zoo is a home for animals."

"And I'm going to turn into one, you pull any more shit. Your girlfriend, her dog, two cats, a monkey. Whose monkey is it, anyway?"

"You don't want to know. Yours, I'd say. She likes you. Here are the cats. Meme and Blue. Meme likes chicken livers. Blue's easy, so you two should get along. He's the bruiser."

I headed out the door to my car. My car was gone. Its taillights were just turning onto Adams, three blocks up, right under the elevated train tracks that gave downtown Chicago its nickname, the "Loop."

Nobody steals a cop car. Nobody except a very crazy person or a kid. I'd left the unmarked unlocked while I carried the cats in.

Somehow, I didn't think this was a kid. I'd invited my killer to dance, called to him, as I said, and he'd accepted my invitation more quickly than I'd expected. He'd been waiting.

Waiting on any number of levels: to ambush Jamie, to ambush Violet or me, I was surprised he hadn't taken me out while I was ferrying Meme and Blue, just made Kitty Litter of all of us. I turned back and pounded on Jamie's door.

"That you?"

"Yeah."

"I didn't hear you drive away."

"Careful. You're getting street ears."

"Always had them. So he got your car?" Jamie was laughing.

"Among other things." I was thinking of the kit I'd been assembling. Maybe he'd take it as an homage. Maybe—I had a sudden hunch and took off at a trot.

"Hey," Jamie shouted. "Hey. Be careful."

I heard a train coming. Three short blocks. I was running now. Not exactly a wind sprint at my age. I made it to Adams, and there was my car, just twenty feet from the corner, parked at the hydrant just where I always left it. I turned right and raced for the elevated stairs.

I wasn't as fast as I needed to be.

When I made it to the platform, the train was leaving. The doors were closed and they weren't going to open again for anyone but God. I say I was too late, but maybe I was right on time. As I stood there huffing, staring at the square back window of the train pulling out, somebody waved at me—a tall, thin somebody in a Cubs jacket and hat. I trudged down the stairs and back to my car.

My unmarked smelled like cat piss, that's what I thought at first. It had a high, sweet odor in it that I blamed on Blue and Meme until my nose got serious. I knew that smell. I knew I knew it. The car was fine, none the worse for its little ride. The kit was still there, intact. Nothing was missing and something was added: that smell. Jesus, it was disturbing. Where did I know it from?

I turned on Harrison, heading to 90–94. I was very late for Ricky Noonan and Father Bremner. I thought of calling but decided not to take the time. I was off the clock. Not that you ever really are, on homicide. I turned off the cop talk and turned on my AM-FM. I kept it on LOOP-FM. Like mine, the station manager's musical tastes ran from vintage Sinatra to vintage rock.

Instant paydirt. The Righteous Brothers. For me, the world divides into those who love them and those who don't count. "One of the greatest of all times," the pitch was winding up. . . . And: "You never close your eyes anymore when you kiss my lips . . ."

I don't know about you, but I time-travel on music. I was in eighth grade back at Bridgette Hannerhatty's house. Bridgette was my very first love. The first girl I ever felt up. The first girl I ever danced with. Slow dances were our thing—what do you expect? Down in the basement rec room at some kid's place. Friday night, lights down low, hands down lower, mitts cupping Bridgette's ass, face buried in her neck—Heaven Scent. That was the eau de cologne that Bridgette Hannerhatty wore—I bought it for her, so I know— and it was a terrible, sweet, sickening perfume if there ever was one. So sickening, so sweet, so terrible that I knew with absolute certainty, twenty years later, that Heaven Scent was the odor stinking up my car.

Why would anyone be wearing that perfume these days— or ever? Why would that same person take my car for a joy-ride? It all began to seem very personal to me. If I was court-ing the killer, on some level the killer was courting me.

I had the long, slow crawl up the Edens Expressway to ponder this. It was a Friday night, and the road was clogged with construction and vacationers on their way to the Wis-consin Dells. I pulled into the retreat house sixty minutes past my ETA. Heaven could wait, and I hoped Father Bremner could, too.

Chapter forty-five

F ather Bremner answered the bell. It was well past ten
o'clock.

"Well. Here's one of you," Bremner greeted me.

"Ricky didn't show?"

"No. Did he have the number?"

"Number, address, enough directions to launch a space
shuttle."

"Ah."

I was waiting for Father Bremner to tell me what Ricky's
no-show meant. I found myself thinking of him like some Zen
elder.

"I've saved some brownies for you," he said instead.

Father Bremner led me into a kitchen the Hilton would
have envied. I must have raised an eyebrow.

"We do seat two hundred on a full retreat weekend," he
said mildly.

I was interested in the brownies and trying not to think too
much yet about why Ricky Noonan was missing.

We walked to the library, where a well-laid fire flickered brightly. It smelled like Christmas even in July.

"They're so comforting," Father Bremner said. "I think they talk to us on some primitive level. We need symbols to feel safe, don't you think?"

"I make these kits," I told him, "to catch killers with." I told him about the feather, the candle, the ruby-eyed dagger, the silk. "Is that odd enough for you? . . . Where do you think Ricky is?"

"We'll know something about your friend soon enough— you were telling me about making kits. It's ritual, of course. It alters consciousness. So does the Mass. So does the black mass, for that matter. How's your brownie?"

"Fine."

I was feeling uneasy. I knew Ricky Noonan wasn't there for a reason. I was putting the pieces together, but not fast enough. I was assembling both my kit and my puzzle and I could almost see it, almost, but not quite yet. I did not feel hopeful for Ricky Noonan.

"So, Elliot. You were talking about ritual."

"Was I? I thought you were talking about ritual and I was talking about the Cubs."

Defensive. Humor did not deflect him.

"Go on."

"I hate calling it ritual. I know it is—privately I think it is— I'd have called it something else. . . ." Where was Ricky Noonan?

"Go on. We can't alter your friend's decisions. Please tell me some more about your rituals. Rituals do interest me. I don't suppose that's surprising."

So I told him about shamans and thinking like a cougar, a killer. I told him about my dream, my dog, and Chabrol's mural. I told him about the missing ring, the way its clone bobbed up everywhere. I told him I was the common denominator between the Zachary-Gomez-Violet Winters assaults. I talked about not being able to protect anyone well enough. Finally, I talked about being scared. Where the hell was Ricky Noonan?

"Of course you're scared. That's why you do your ritual. To alter consciousness, as I said. It allows you to act. I suppose there are other reasons for ritual, but most of the time we do them for our fear. Do you know the definition of faith? 'Fear that has said its prayers.' Your ritual is a prayer."

I was thinking about the ritual of pornography. The effect it induced in its users, the way Ted Bundy told us on death row that his use of violent pornography triggered him to kill. I told all this to Father Bremner.

I talked about the way the targets of serial killers, those lucky enough to have escaped—murder interruptus—all spoke of the dead-eyed state of their abuser, using words like "gone," "not there," "no one home."

"I know where they go," I told Father Bremner. "When they're not there."

"Of course you do. That's part of the burden of your work, like an exorcist's, you could say."

"I call it 'dropping down the well,' that's how I get there. But 'there' is not a place. It's more a dimension—"

"What the aborigines might call dream time."

"I don't want to go this time."

"Of course not. But you will go and you will let them know you're not afraid."

"How do I do that? How do I do that when they're threatening Ricky Noonan? How do I do that when I'm worrying about Zach?"

"The boy can stay here with us."

I felt ten years younger. A thousand pounds lighter.

"You might call it a vacation to him. We stock our lake. I could teach him to fish. That's another subject that interests me. When I get in a certain . . . space . . . as you say, I feel I call the fish to me. By the way, who do you pray to?"

He didn't wait for me to answer. Right then I was praying to St. Jude to find the lost Ricky Noonan.

"We always think saints are so distant. Let me show you mine. . . . You have finished your brownie, haven't you?"

He led me down the echoing corridor to his small office at the far end. It was a modest but friendly room, less seigneurial than the library. Bremner crossed to a mission desk, endearingly solid and plain in design. He opened the center drawer and took out what looked at first like trading cards.

"My saints. Some you've heard of—" He thumbed through. "Jude for police and lost causes. Margaret of Scotland because she founded hospitals and the story is so good—a shipwrecked Hungarian princess fished from the sea and married by the king. She was as much prime minister as wife. Ah. Here's Dr. Connelly."

Bremner showed me an obit photo pasted to a cardboard square.

"Friend of mine. Wonderful doctor. I pray to him when someone ill comes to me for counseling."

"You mean you have friends for saints?"

"They tend to get right on it. Some of them feel they owe me still."

I could feel myself relaxing as the old priest talked. His spiritual life was so casual, so matter-of-fact, so sensible. I had come to him for spiritual protection and found myself being given a set of spiritual tools.

"Who could help you on this case?" he was asking now. I knew immediately—Gomez and Chabrol. They both prayed to orishas, the ancestors. For all I knew, they might be waiting for my call.

"I've got a couple guys," I said.

"You see, we're not in this alone," said Father Bremner. "We can call in our friends. Sometimes, they've got a vested interest in helping us." He grinned at the card of his friend Dr. Connelly, then put his saints back in the drawer. There was a knock at the door.

"Come in." A fair-haired young priest stuck his head in the door.

"A call for you, Father."

"Thank you, Father. That would be your friend, I suspect."

Bremner opened a file cabinet, took out a phone, and plugged it into a wall jack.

"I meditate here, so I keep the phone unplugged." He picked up the receiver. "Hello?" He nodded to me and mouthed "Noonan." "I see. Well, he's right here."

I got on the phone. It was Ricky Noonan. (Thank you, St. Jude.)

"Where are you? You lost?"

I thought I could hear a soft whooshing sound in the background, like wind. I could see Father Bremner open his desk drawer and take out his saint cards. I sensed that he was praying.

Silence.

"You lost? Ricky. You lost?"

"Maybe."

"You want directions?"

It had been my thought to get Ricky together with Father Bremner, calm him down, and then pick his brain. There were things Ricky Noonan knew that I needed to know.

"I don't think I'm going to come. What's he going to do?

Tell me to say novenas? I haven't seen a priest in years. I mean, what's he going to do? Hear my confession?"

"Where are you?"

"Maybe five miles from you. I just feel funny. I think I'm going to head back to town."

"Ricky, where are you?"

"Five miles or so. This picnic area thing. Near a woods."

"We'll come get you, Ricky."

"You don't want to do that." Ricky's voice sounded suddenly different, not his own.

"Ricky?"

"The line went dead?" Father Bremner asked me. "I'm afraid we may have lost him."

"I told him we'd come get him. Could we do that?"

"We could try." Father Bremner grabbed an old leather jacket from the hook on his study door. He looked like a French resistance fighter in World War II. We took the unmarked. I floored it, fishtailing down the long gravel drive onto the two-lane, siren off, toward Noonan, five miles away, straight good road under a full moon. "Hold on, Ricky," I prayed.

"It's like fishing," Father Bremner interrupted my thoughts. "That's what they called Peter. The Fisherman. He left his boat and his nets to be a fisher of souls. It's the same process, really. When you pray for somebody, you can feel their soul like a great shiny fish. You toss the line out, you bait it with grace, and you can feel them thinking about it, considering the risk of being hooked, the risk of changing, giving up the river or the sea for God's plan. The hook of God looks like death to them. They don't know it's life everlasting. They think about it. They even romance the thought a little—and then they shy away. You can feel it when they do that. You can feel them decide no, and swim away."

I understood what Father Bremner was telling me. I'd
heard it in Ricky's voice on the phone. I knew it from the
calls we got at the station sometimes: the man on the ledge;
the man with the gun. Firemen had told me the same story.
You're there. You've almost got them, and they just let
go. . . .

"You know just where he is?"

"Yes."

I knew exactly where, a highway picnic area on the edge of
the forest preserve. I'd dreamed about it. No! Myerling had
dreamed about it, dreamed about me running through the
woods. I noticed the place when I was driving by. If I hadn't
been running late, I might have stopped there just to think. A
sylvan, isolated picnic glade. Tall trees, windy grasses. I had
been drawn to it, but I was late and then I'd remembered
Myerling's dream.

I turned into the picnic area parking lot, relieved to see
Ricky's car. Twenty feet away, the phone was dangling at the
end of its silvery cord. I pulled my gun. The trunk and the
driver's door to Ricky's car stood open. The car was dented
and scraped along both sides.

A narrow gravel jogging path led into the woods. I saw
Bremner cross himself. I started out at a jog. I'd known Ricky
Noonan since kindergarten. I wasn't going to let him down—

The woods were luminious, nearly bright. The full moon
cascaded light down like a fountain. Even under the canopy
of trees the ground lay silver. I mention this because as I ran,
everything seemed to slow down and gain in clarity. I could
hear something moving in the woods to my right, something
large. It was a deer, and I knew that without seeing it. Ricky
was ahead of me. I could hear his pounding heart clear as my
own. It was futile, his taking off into the woods. He must
have been desperate.

Boom.

It sounded like a shotgun. I did not stop running. Ahead of me, off to the right, I saw a clearing, a campfire site, the kind boy scouts use. A stone-built barbecue pit, some picnic tables, all under a circle of trees, all under that moon.

Ricky Noonan, what had been Ricky Noonan, lay in the center of that circle. The shotgun lay off another five feet. It was an execution. I had no doubt of that. By his hand or another's. What did it matter? Either way, they'd killed him. He lay facedown.

"I'm sorry. I know he was your friend."

I whirled on Father Bremner, gun drawn. How had the old priest gotten behind me so quickly? Bremner crossed directly to the body. He knelt down, crossed himself, and began to pray. We were two professionals, I realized, with our jobs to do. He was saying the prayers, preparing Ricky for the after-life, just a little late.

I heard something moving in the woods. This time it was not a deer. Something had been watching us. Someone.

"You shouldn't have done this," I shouted at it. "You shouldn't have done this, damn you."

What I heard was laughter. I knew it was dumb, but I crashed into the woods in the direction the sound had come from.

Undergrowth, thicket, brambles, roots—I pushed, fell, crashed through them all. I did this for a quarter mile, maybe more, when I stopped. The woods lay behind me, a nasty little swamp lay ahead. Ricky Noonan was dead. I couldn't change it. I started back.

When I got to the little clearing, Father Bremner had fin-ished with his prayers. He was sitting quietly by Ricky's body. The glint of something nearby caught my eye. I knew it would be the goddamn ring. I knelt down and fished my lighter from my pocket. It was the ring.

"An inverted pentacle," Father Bremner said. He wasn't even looking.

Ricky, alone or with help, had blown his face off. I laid a hand on his back and said good-bye. Standing up, I stepped on the goddamn ring.

I used Ricky's dangling phone to call the murder in. I called it a murder. They'd call it what they wanted. Father Bremner and I sat in the unmarked and waited for the sheriff to arrive. We were out of my jurisdiction.

"I was afraid this would happen," I told Father Bremner. "That's why I wanted him to talk to you. I thought maybe you could—"

"Pull him back?"

That was exactly what I had hoped. I didn't believe Ricky Noonan was a bad man. I thought he was a frightened man, maybe a greedy man—but weren't we all, one way or another?

What I thought was that Ricky Noonan had gone along with something or looked the other way or allowed something to pass, and it had gotten away from him. I'd thought it was politics, and it probably was, on his end. The poor son of a bitch.

The country cops arrived like a parade. Siren, the whole show. They must have been bored. The sheriff was a tall, pear-shaped guy with a hostile attitude.

"I hate it when you city cops bring your messes up here," the sheriff said as we walked him toward Ricky's body.

"I do, too. You guys are always so helpful."

The sheriff and I were not going to be friends.

"You said on the phone you knew this guy?"

"Since kindergarten. Now he's Judge Ricky Noonan."

"Shit. You brought me a judge?"

"I didn't bring you anything. Ricky did this all by himself. We didn't help him."

"We?"

I gestured toward Father Bremner in his bomber jacket. "The father and I were at the retreat house when he called us."

"That true, Father?"

"As he said."

Why didn't he just call me a liar and get it over with?

"So, you said a suicide?"

We'd reached Ricky's body. The big sheriff reached down and flipped him over. He yanked back.

"Where's his dick? You guys got it?"

Poor Ricky. I hoped his head went first.

"Out here we usually save gelding for our animals. You city guys are sick fucks, pardon me, Father."

I read the guy's name tag in the glare of the headlights: three squads and an ambulance. Luntz. Like dunce. He and his men had driven to the crime scene and they cased it now, cherry tops still turning. What clues they hadn't driven over they were now trampling.

"You see this?"

A young cop had scooped up the ring. His prints would be all over it.

"What is it?" Luntz asked. He was going through Ricky's bloody pockets.

"Evidence, you putz." I said this softly, but Luntz heard it loud and clear.

"We won't be needing you two," he said.

"Really, we'd like to stay—"

"Hey! I found a Cubs cap." The young cop was in the bushes where I'd heard a noise.

"Unrelated," Luntz snapped.

The rookie looked disappointed and tossed the cap to one side. I saw Father Bremner quietly stoop to pick it up. He gave me a high sign. It looked like a blessing.

We stood to the side after that and let the country boys work. By the time they were done, the moon was a flat, pale disk losing to the sun. I drove Father Bremner back to the retreat. He would take Zachary fishing, he told me. I went back to the city to do some fishing myself.

Chapter forty-six

———■———

Paradise had shredded the papers and pissed on the floor. There was a pissy message from Jamie on my answering machine: "The doctor will see you now. Phone home." I did better than that. I scooped up Paradise for a reunion with her mommy and drove to Jamie's for my doctor appointment.

I rang the buzzer. It was seven A.M., the end of Jamie's normal workday and the beginning of the doctor's. Why not drop by for a nightcap or a cup of coffee? Jamie answered the door. He was in his painting clothes. Baby was perched on his shoulder.

"You sure know how to pick them. Dr. Pain-In-The-Butt's climbing the walls just like the monkey—but the monkey likes me." He called over his shoulder. "It's for you, dear."

"What?" Violet interrupted our little chat. She was in her denims and cowboy boots, looking terrific. She smiled at me, glared at Jamie.

"Hi."

"You look awful, Elliot. Don't you ever sleep? Are you eating?" She looked me over like a horse.

"Are you my mother?"

"No. And I'm not your ex-wife, either. She's calling all the time. She and Jamie have these heart-to-hearts."

"Yeah. That's another thing," said Jamie. "Gloria's calling a lot."

"How's Zach?"

"She says he's fine, but she sounds like a mess."

"Of course she's a mess. She was in love with that little bastard." This from Dr. Winters.

"You didn't know Oscar long enough to dislike him," I chided her.

"Oh, I had two minutes and I'm a quick study. I need to talk to you." She gave my arm a little tug.

"Well," said Jamie. "So much for small talk. The doctor will see you now, I suppose."

"Come on, Jamie. This is business." He sounded like a jealous wife. I told him so.

"Screw you, Elliot."

"Screw you, Mr. Art Star." This, again, from Dr. Winters.

"Why, Violet, sweet shrinking Violet. What a mouth you've got on you." It crossed my mind Jamie might have made an unsuccessful play for her, best friends or not.

"Violet, be nice. This man is your host."

"You stay out of this, all right?"

"Like the man says, you're my guest."

"Hardly my idea." Violet was fuming.

"What is this? The Bickersons? Can't you two play nice?"

"I could, but shrinking Violet here is a castrating bitch."

"You are a sexist pig."

"So what."

"What's going on here?"

"He asked me to pose. Can you believe it?"

"Sure. You're a pretty girl—woman—whatever you want to be called."

I was exercising my option for a little male bonding at Violet's expense. I wasn't about to lose my friendship with Jamie over a woman, especially one like her—uppity, difficult and now angry.

"Screw you, Elliot," she said again.

"What's that? Line of the night?" Jamie was not going to let up.

"Will you stay out of this?" I told him now.

"Come on, Elliot," she interrupted us.

"Ricky Noonan's dead," I told Jamie.

"Jesus fucking Christ. Ricky Noonan?"

"I asked him to meet me for a little talk. Instead, he killed himself—or somebody killed him and made it look like he did it. His car was dented up on both sides like somebody had played kiddie cars with him."

"Poor Ricky. Where was this?"

"Couldn't happen to a nicer guy."

We both swiveled toward her.

"You know Ricky Noonan?"

"Well . . . yes. Sort of."

"Sounds like you fucked," said Jamie, "but it didn't work out."

"As a matter of fact, we did, and no, it didn't," said Violet. "Did it for you?"

I thought Jamie was going to deck her.

"Come on," I said to Violet, "before this gets ugly." I hustled her out the door.

"What about the dogs?"

"Keep them. We won't be long."

"Fuck, no. You keep them, Elliot, and you keep her."

With that, Jamie shoved both dogs out the door, followed by a purse and duffel bag I took to be Violet's.

"Let's take them to the park," Violet said—unfazed by Jamie's temper.

I chose the part of the park south of Buckingham. There were two matching rows of trees bending toward each other. They made a long green tunnel, a sort of chute for running the dogs. We let them free, then I confronted her.

"That was crap, what you said back there about Ricky Noonan."

"Was it?"

This stopped me for all of two seconds.

"I know Ricky since he was five. He was a nice guy. A swell guy."

"You ever fuck him?"

"What is it with you, Doctor? All you can think of is who's doing whom?"

"Sometimes." To my surprise, her eyes had filled with tears. "He swung both ways. That's all. You didn't know?"

She was serious.

"No, I didn't know. He was a judge, for crissake." Even to me, I sounded naive.

"Which made him an automatic straight arrow? Come on, Elliot."

"Well . . . I knew Ricky a long time."

And he never married. I'd taken him for one of those Irish bachelors committed to a life of revolving doors and ladies, everybody's favorite uncle.

"Don't feel bad, Elliot. I didn't read him right, either, and I've got a good sense of it, most of the time."

"So you did . . . ?"

"Stop acting like I'm the Whore of Babylon. You said your-

self what a nice guy Ricky Noonan was. One of my col-
leagues at the hospital fixed us up."

"How long?" I sounded miserable.

"Will you stop it, Elliot? I dated him. I dated him for a
while. Then I found out and I thought he should have told
me."

"You mean AIDS."

"Yes, among other things. Like I told Jamie, it didn't work
out. I thought he just didn't find me attractive."

"I'm sorry. Look, I'm a jerk."

"A jealous jerk?"

"Yeah. I guess so."

"Oh, goody."

She'd slipped her hand in mine, a slender, fine-boned hand
almost as small as Zachary's. I felt a swelling of my protective
instincts. Among other things. Then she had to ask me.

"Did you look at those drawings?"

"I gave them to Dr. Hauser. Who is pretty much my idea of
a bad time. Talk about humorless."

"She's a good doctor. Conservative, maybe, but good."

"Jesus. Is there anybody you don't know?"

"Why wouldn't I know her? We share a specialty. Be fair,
would you?"

But I wasn't in the mood, and I liked to feel in charge. It
was hard to feel in charge with Violet Winters. She was always setting loose the hounds of heaven; Paradise and Salvation were gamboling on the lawn. Dark mother, pale daughter.

"Come on," I pushed. "How do you know Dr. Hauser?"

"Well, Elliot, Chicago's a big city, but it's actually a small
town. We're both doctors, we're both children's specialists,
we are on staff at the same hospital."

"Okay."

"You're worried about Zach, aren't you?"

"Of course I'm worried. God knows what happened to him. Hauser won't do regressions, and we may never find out. He was torn. Bleeding. That's how they get AIDS, you know? Tears in the lining. You know that, Doctor. Of course I'm worried about Zach. If I find the son of a bitch who hurt him, I swear to God—"

"You're yelling." An understatement.

"Fuck, yes, I'm yelling, Doctor. You'd yell, too, if it happened to you."

"It did happen, Elliot. I suppose I did yell." She said this soft and level.

"I'm sorry . . . You don't remember?" I was asking for Zachary, too.

"No. Not really. It's not like regular memories. You don't remember. You wonder. You have a funny feeling. You think maybe you made it up. You've got the evidence of a probable crime. But you're missing the memory. Your reactions are the memory."

"Like a murder scene without the body." I felt like a glib jerk.

"Oh, I've got the body, all right. And the body remembers, whether I do or not. Take me at certain angles and I cry—I don't know why. Hold me down too hard and I bite and fight you. Hurt me by accident and it might turn me on. Make love to me just perfectly, and suddenly I'm gone. I'm buzzing around the ceiling, an out of body experience. Oh, yes, and I get 'blips.' They're these little snippets. Sound like a good time, don't I?"

"I know what blips are. My son gets them."

Then we were holding each other. We were kissing. I felt that I could kiss Violet Winters for a long time. Like high school. The kiss that lasts forever.

That's when it registered. Her skin smelled faintly, ever so faintly, of Heaven Scent perfume. I pulled back. Let her think it was ethics.

"Sorry. Didn't mean to be so . . . needy," she said.

"That's okay."

"I really am a barrel of laughs, aren't I?"

"It's all right," I said.

Kissing her had been something more than all right.

Chapter forty-seven

———■———

I had anticipated trouble getting Zach away from Gloria for his "country vacation," but none materialized. I probably could have said, "Look, I'm taking the kid forever, okay?" and she would have agreed.

"Go ahead, Elliot. It'll be good for him. I just can't seem to quite . . . function yet."

Gloria sounded like she was talking to me through water.

"You on something? Sometimes what they give you to cure the pain is worse than the pain." Even to my ear, I sounded a little too all-knowing—Dr. Mayo.

"Grief. Grief is what I'm on, Elliot. I'm sorry if that offends you." I could hear her starting to wind up.

"It doesn't offend me, Gloria."

"Right."

"Look, I'm sorry you lost Oscar. I'm sorry we all lost him. Could I pick Zach up in about three hours?"

"Sure." She hung up.

I placed a call to Dr. Hauser to tell her I was worried not

only about Zachary but also about his mother. Dr. Hauser did not receive this information kindly.

"Yes? And why is that?" She acted like the call was a manipulation of some kind.

"She sounds a little erratic to me—fragile."

"Your ex-wife has remarkable reserves, Detective. Don't patronize her."

It was dawning on me that Dr. Hauser was the kind of feminist who gave the term a bad name. To her, I was a man and therefore an enemy. I hoped this attitude did not apply to young boys as well.

"I just thought, since you were seeing her and Zach, you might keep an extra eye—"

"That's my job. Don't patronize me, either."

I gave up on trying to communicate with Dr. Hauser and made another call, this one to Gloria's sister, Theresa. She, at least, was glad to hear from me. I asked her to meet me at Ann Sather's, a Swedish restaurant on Belmont. The place had great homemade cinnamon rolls and a comforting, homey atmosphere. I thought we could both use some of each.

I parked in the lot hidden behind Ann Sather's and came in through the alley, pausing to admire the window of a floral shop. A large, golden gilt angel's wing, seven feet across, hung in the window, suspended amid twining ivies and snowy-white lilies. I found the wing oddly moving, like the window had a message for me. I caught sight of myself, reflected back with the wing seeming to grow out of my own shoulder—I had to smile. As a cop, I had always wanted to save people, to be their guardian angel. I was glad that Zachary had an angel now. Even if it was a fantasy, he needed one. We all do.

Inside Sather's, I ordered cinnamon rolls and coffee for

two. Theresa came in a moment later, wreathed in hellos that did not hide her anxiety. She was dressed in bright Guatemalan cottons and her dark hair frizzed in ringlets around her face. She looked like a happier, freer version of Gloria.

Theresa was younger than Gloria by five years, but she might as well have been Gloria's mother. I liked Theresa and always felt she did her best to like me despite my difficulties with her sister.

"I'm worried about Gloria," I told her over the rolls and coffee. "She sounds awfully nervous to me."

"It's been quite a blow. I go to see her and she can't sit still."

"She's probably pretty angry."

"Well, sure, but there's something—" Theresa was groping. "I don't know, maybe guilt about the separation. Something. I haven't felt like she's leveled with me in a long time. Months."

"Didn't Gloria tell you Zach was molested?"

"What?"

"Maybe repeatedly."

"Oh, my God." Theresa ground a cinnamon roll to mush with a fork. "When did you find this out?"

"The night before he was scheduled for corrective surgery. Oscar came and delivered the news."

"That's strange. Why Oscar?"

"That's what I thought—"

I think Theresa and I came to the next thought simultaneously.

"Unless—"

"You don't think?"

"He wanted to be very sure—"

"To act innocent?"

"Oh, Jesus. That would explain a lot, wouldn't it? Maybe

that's what Gloria doesn't want us to know or want herself to know." I reached out and patted Theresa's hand. It was trembling.

"I'm just thinking, what a nightmare. To find out your kid was abused and the man you love—sorry, Elliot—was the one who did it. No wonder she couldn't see it. Who'd want to believe it?"

"I'm taking Zach out to the country for a few days. I thought maybe you'd be able to spend some time with her—"

"If she'll let me."

"You two have a falling out?"

"Not exactly. But there's been some . . . distance. I didn't like Oscar."

"That makes two of us—although I was getting fonder of him toward the end. He seemed to really care about Zach. Christ, I can't even think about it—"

Theresa was very quiet. "Theresa?"

"Nothing. I just spaced out. I was thinking."

"Thinking?"

"Thinking that in all my years at family services, I have never met any family member of a sex abuser who could really believe the person they loved would do that."

Now my hands were shaking. I signaled for another cup of coffee and tried to get a sense of what I felt about Oscar as a sex abuser. I felt like it just might be true.

Theresa spoke up. "Do you think Gloria has a drinking problem?"

"Maybe a pill problem, too?"

"You think so?" She winced but wasn't surprised.

"Yes."

Theresa was silent again. She stirred her coffee.

"I guess I do, too. I've been calling it situational, I've been calling it depression, but maybe she's just been really careful around me. . . ."

"We need to make a plan," I told her. "Just as soon as I get Zach out of harm's way."

"I'll take care of her. Don't worry so much, bro."

I left Theresa staring into her coffee cup. I kept thinking I had missed a piece in what she was trying to tell me, but I was late to pick up Zach, so I let it go. Zachary came out the door wearing his Cubs cap. He bounced down the bungalow stairs and gave me a high-five, casual as that. He was lugging a duffel bag of clothes.

"Hi, Dad. How ya doing?"

"Hey. Let me look at you. The hat looks good."

I didn't know whether I should be glad Zach was wearing the cap I gave him or not. Ever since talking with Violet Winters about non-memory memories, I'd been going over Zach's recent reactions. Clues, she had said. Was the baseball cap a clue? The only reaction I'd seen in Zach was when he froze up in the street outside of Wrigley Field. Was the ball cap a reenactment, or did he just like Daddy's gift?

I hefted Zach's duffel bag and tossed it into the backseat, when Gloria, still in a bathrobe, came hurrying down the bungalow stairs. She was, and still is, a pretty woman. But not just then. Her dark hair was tangled and dull, her lovely dark eyes were circled. She clutched a toothbrush in one hand—Zach's, it turned out.

"Make sure he brushes his teeth."

"Mother!"

Zach couldn't wait to be off now.

"Mom. I be cool."

I had to grin. Zach used street talk to get her goat. I understood the impulse. I'd always rebelled at Gloria, too.

We drove north toward Father Bremner and Zach's safe

place. The traffic on the Edens was moving, and Zach and I buzzed along listening to LOOP-FM. Somebody with great taste was playing the Shirelles.

"What's he really like, Dad?"

"Who?"

"This priest."

"Obi-Wan Kenobi from *Star Wars*. Merlin. A kind of wizard."

"He does tricks?" Zach sounded excited.

"Sort of. He just knows a lot. It's kind of magical. You'll see. Think of it like summer camp."

"But you said I'd be the only kid there."

"A special summer camp—just for you. He's going to teach you fishing."

"Really? Like *Jaws?*" Gloria had rented him the video and probably ruined his swimming for life.

"More like Moby Trout. Actually, more like Moby Blue Gill or Crappie."

"Crappie! That's funny. Why do they call a fish crappy?"

"Because it tastes like shit."

"Aw, Dad."

I wished I were going on Zach's country vacation. I wished I could sit on the end of a wooden dock with Father Bremner and listen to him talk about fishing for souls. The main thing was that Zach would be safe. I could do my job without fearing he'd turn up hurt or missing.

At Dr. Winters's "strong suggestion," we'd run the AIDS test when Zach was in for surgery.

"You want to know, Elliot."

"Do I? All right. I do."

The test came back negative—thank you, Jesus, Mary, and Joseph—but we would repeat it in six months.

"What do you think of Dr. Hauser?" I asked, heading off

the freeway onto the two-lane. We would pass Ricky Noonan's woods very soon.

"She's okay. How much longer do I have to see her?"

"Just until you feel better."

"I already feel better. It's not hurting anymore. I can run and everything. Pretty weird I could hurt myself there."

"Pretty weird, but it happens."

Just as Dr. Hauser had warned me it would, just as Violet had described it, Zach's denial system was moving in to occlude his memory. He sounded like he had no idea, on a conscious level, what had happened to him.

"Is the lake over there?" Zach, uncannily, was pointing toward the forest preserve where Ricky Noonan had died.

"No. No, it's not. That's just a swamp."

"I hate swamps. Oscar and I watched *Swamp Thing* and it was too scary."

"I bet you miss him."

Zach looked at me warily, like there had to be a trick somewhere because we were talking about Oscar. Then I saw a tear slipping out of the corner of Zach's eye.

"It's okay. I miss him, too." I took Zach's hand.

"Dad? Dad, this is awful." He was really sniffling now, heading into sobs. I pulled over at the first turnoff.

"Let's just talk a little."

"I—can't—talk—Daddy—I—can't—"

"Zach, there's nothing that you can't tell me. I'm your daddy."

"Oscar was like a daddy, and they killed him. It's my fault. It's my fault. I didn't mean to do it, Daddy. I didn't mean to kill Oscar."

I took him in my arms. He felt light and frail as a bird.

"You didn't kill Oscar, honey. That wasn't your fault. That wasn't anybody's."

"No. Mommy said if I'd been different, Oscar would still be alive."

"Your mother didn't mean that, Zach."

"Yes, she did. She said Oscar was trying to help me when they blew him away."

I didn't know where to start. His fault? Blew him away?

"Your mommy's upset. When people are upset, they say things they don't mean."

"She meant it. She said she wished they'd killed you instead. She said they were trying to."

Zach's sobs escalated into a storm. He was crying in great heaving gasps. He could barely drag enough breath in to cover his exertions. I held him against my chest and stroked his hair. Cradling Zachary, I realized that we were undertaking something new. He could come to me and I would meet him now.

It hadn't been that way for a long time. I admitted that as I held him. Unhappy in my marriage, wary of his mother and her discontent, I had avoided my wife, burying myself in my job, burying my love there, too.

Holding my son, I knew work was no excuse for leaving a child. The good cop takes the crime home with him, talks to it over dinner. The good cop can make a bad father. I don't like to say that, but I know it mainly to be true.

Now my son was crying over Oscar Gomez. Not a good cop, but perhaps a good enough father. Gloria certainly thought so. I still preferred to think so despite my recent suspicions. I told my son it was all right to love us both.

"I'm sorry about Oscar," I told him.

"Dad? Is Oscar in heaven?"

"Of course he is. Why wouldn't he be in heaven?"

It wasn't a real question. I didn't expect Zach to answer.

"I didn't think people that did that could go to heaven."

"People who did . . . ?"

I had to be very careful or I would blow this. Part of being a good cop is knowing how to get people to talk. Civilians don't believe this, but most of the time, people want to talk. If you've got them at the station house, they figure it's over. They want to tell you how they did it and why. As a cop, your job is to let them talk. Make it easy. Lean in and listen. You get an instinct for it: when to press, when to drop back. It's a minuet, a dance, a gift when you can do it. Evidently, I could not do it now, with my own son.

"Never mind," Zach said now.

"Okay, but it was an interesting question, who gets into heaven or not. What might keep you out."

"You aren't supposed to worship strange gods before me." Zach recited the First Commandment.

"I remember that! So you did learn something in Sunday school. I always hated that it was on Sunday, didn't you? That was supposed to be the weekend. Why couldn't they make it Monday school?" I was stretching for some humor to keep him talking.

"Oscar worshiped strange gods. I saw him."

"Saw him?" I was acting too interested.

"Never mind. I don't remember very much about it." Zach sensed a trap and was pulling back. It was his story, and he'd tell it when he was ready . . . if he could still remember.

"Let's get out of here. Feeling better?" I tousled his hair, threw the car in reverse, and nearly backed into a sheriff's car pulling into the turnoff.

A tall, pear-shaped officer with a Beefeater face climbed from his car.

"Do I know you?" he asked.

Yes, he did. We'd met over Ricky Noonan's dead body.

"We met the other night." I signaled shhhh, kid.

"What a mess. Somebody said he was a friend of yours?"

"What, Daddy?" Zach was getting too interested, and I was trying to contain my resentment at this lunkhead talking murder in front of a kid.

"This your boy?"

"Yeah. Zach, this is Officer"—I remembered—"Officer Luntz, a friend of mine."

"Sorry to disturb you, but we got this call about a guy and little boy. They come here in droves, know what I mean?"

"They who, Daddy?"

"I assume I know what you mean."

"Some little old lady called in. Just wanted to make sure you weren't cornholing this little chicken here—"

I lost it then.

"I think if you don't get out of here—" I said. Quietly.

Officer Luntz blinked.

"You're talking in front of my kid."

"Well, so are you, asshole." Luntz slapped my unmarked with the flat of his hand. I was close to snapping, but Zach tugged on my arm.

"Let's go, Daddy," he said.

We went. I pulled into the retreat house with the sense of relief a pony express rider might have had at a way station. We'd made it.

Father Bremner greeted us with brownies and milk. Zach took to him like a long-lost grandpa. I stayed fifteen minutes, then said good-bye. I felt a whole lot better heading back into the city.

We were down to a waning moon. The road was as straight as an Indian's part. I pulled my energies into me as I drove. I know guys who claim driving does more for them than meditating. I say driving is meditating, that we're Americans, and the highway, the last frontier, offers our version of a transcendent experience. Driving the dark, straight road approaching the forest preserve, past the swamp, I had the sensation I could feel the darkness moving toward me. Just as I passed the last of the woods, a lone deer loomed alongside. It came sailing out of the forest, leaping into view like a mystic figure, so large and strong, it seemed it could not be real.

The deer kept pace with me, racing the car on the shoulder of the road, neither passing nor falling behind—a visitor. What Myerling or Father Bremner might call a sign. I checked my speedometer. Forty-five. Was it possible?

Just as I reached the freeway, the deer veered off, arching back toward the woods it came from. I was glad to see it go. I headed south, back to the city, where the creatures of the night had just two legs.

Chapter forty-eight

━━━■━━━

They all had a motive for killing Nesbitt. No one liked him. I had Lynch, Daley, and Chaworski running down all the leads pertaining to routine procedure. They talked to the neighbors, to the employers, to the friends. There was a consensus: Jack Nesbitt was a rotten guy.

What about the other deaths? Where was the motive for them? Except for Isabelle Hubbard, Carson Stoufley was liked and admired by one and all. Ditto for Ricky Noonan. Ditto even for Oscar Gomez. Such a bunch of nice guys to get murdered. You'd have thought we were collecting character references for their entry into paradise. Even Johnny Vanilla. Sure, he was a rat with women, and some people said that, but overall he was viewed as an okay guy. It occurred to me that maybe the horror of the crimes made anybody seem too nice to be killed that way. They couldn't all be sweethearts.

Take Oscar Gomez, possible child abuser, sex addict for sure. Dead, his Latin temper gone. I'd all but forgotten the smashed wall. His roving eye was gone. Gloria mourned him like a loving spouse and faithful husband. Even Zachary, feeling guilty with Gloria's help, acted like he'd personally killed the Stepfather of the Year.

I was thinking about all this as I made the elevator ride to my place. I was coming up with a theory that went, somebody is getting even. Either the crimes are all connected, or somebody is getting his rocks off, or both. My hunch was that somebody knew all of them somehow. But who could that somebody be?

Paradise was so glad to see me, she wet herself. She made a nice big puddle on the spot where Oscar Gomez died. Somehow, I was never able to think of that part of my apartment any other way. Unless that changed, I would be moving soon.

Speaking of Oscar Gomez, I had a long, blurry message from Gloria on my phone machine. Sounding small and shaky, she went on and on about how she missed him. What a great guy he was, no matter what Zachary says . . .

No matter what Zachary says?

I played the message back just to be sure. What a great guy he really was, "no matter what Zachary says."

I felt a trapdoor open as my consciousness dropped through it to new and terrible conclusions. Bye-bye, Denial. Hello, Nausea. My speculations with Theresa were beginning to sound a hell of a lot like fact.

I laid out some fresh papers for the pup, then raced out the door. I made it back to our marital home a lot faster than I had to divorce court. Fifteen minutes, door to door. I was ready to kill Gomez, but he was dead. When I came through the door, it looked like somebody had killed Gloria.

The place was torn apart, lamps knocked over, pictures smashed, broken glass on the floor and the rug, plants tipped over. Gloria, lying facedown dead center of it all.

"Gloria. Gloria." I knelt and shook her. She was warm.

She was breathing. Thank you, God. "Gloria. Wake up." Still nothing. Then a moan. She was drunk.

Grief can make a mess out of anybody, and it had done a thorough job on Gloria. Matted hair, wrinkled clothes, eyes swollen, no makeup—the works. Her skin was the color of cream of mushroom soup. She couldn't focus when she looked at me, and the bottle lying next to her used to hold gin.

"Poor Oscar," she said finally. She meant, "poor Gloria without Oscar."

"Come on, Gloria. Get up."

"I—don't—want—to."

"I don't care, Gloria. We're going to get you a nice, cold shower."

"You're so mean. You were always mean."

"Into the shower, okay?"

"No."

She went limp in my arms. I dragged her, lugged her, hauled her down the hall.

"I'm not taking my clothes off for you."

I was wedging her into the shower, turning it to cold. She slid to the bottom. Good. It was safer, anyhow.

"I'm making coffee."

On the way out of the bathroom, I snagged her pills. Gloria liked pills a little too much, but who was I to critique? Maybe a little Valium was a normal thing, like she said it was. I was hypervigilant on the issue, counting my drinks and my once-a-year drunks, worried about turning out like so many cops who made those drunks once daily. My worry about my drinking was a joke with Jamie. He called me a "Christmas drunk," like that cactus flower that blooms only once a year.

I snagged Gloria's Valium and flushed them. Even in her stupor she spotted what I was doing.

"You can't. I need them!"

"You're not supposed to drink on them."

Gloria began banging on the sliding glass shower door. "Will you get out of here? Will you get out of here?"

"Yes. I'll make you coffee."

In the kitchen I found a pound of that black jet fuel espresso that Latins love and made Gloria a pot. I did the dishes while I was standing there, not because I was nice, but because they helped me think.

Gomez had made that pretty speech to me about how he loved kids. How he really, really liked Zach. I couldn't believe he was a child molester. No, I could believe it, I just couldn't stand the thought. Theresa was right, though. If Gomez was the molester, a lot of things dropped into line. Gloria's off-the-wall remarks about how maybe Zach had been complicitous. Zach's guilt about Gomez's death. If he was being molested, he probably wished the SOB dead. If Gomez was a molester, then was Zach's "blip" just a fiction? Now I wanted to do a regression with Zach. I had to know.

Dr. Hauser and I had discussed hypnotic regression. She'd told me that it had been unnecessary and inappropriate from her perspective, but what did "inappropriate" mean? That it wouldn't work? That it wouldn't help? That Zach couldn't handle it? That she couldn't do it? I'd do it without her if it would help my son.

Gloria came into the kitchen wearing one of my old robes.

"I kept it," she said sheepishly.

I took this as a manipulation. She was just sober enough to scheme.

"Have some coffee." I handed her a cup.

"Oscar's coffee," she said when she sipped it. She was ready to cry some more.

"What did your message mean?"

"Oscar was a very good man. He loved Zachary. He would never, ever hurt Zachary. No matter what."

"No matter what Zachary said?"

"Yes."

"Why would Zachary say anything?"

"Don't you play cop with me, Elliot."

"So level with me, Gloria."

"You're just twisting everything around. You're just trying to hurt me, Elliot. Oscar loved me. He loved Zachary—" I got the feeling Gloria had told herself this many times before. It was a mantra for her. I had an idea.

"I'm sure Oscar loved you," I told her, changing tactics. "You're a lovable woman. Your message just worried me, that's all. You sounded so out of it, I got scared. Come on. Pull yourself together a little and I'll buy you dinner. Somewhere nice."

Gloria brightened like a little girl. She always loved treats, and I could have had a much better marriage if I'd just remembered to give them to her.

I took Gloria to Chez Robert. I hate frog food. She loves it. Over the escargots, the Poisson en Croute, and the strawberries, I got the story. It was hard for her to tell me, I knew that. She had wanted Oscar to be her Prince Charming, not a flawed or difficult man.

Yes, Oscar had a temper.

Yes, he was a yeller.

Yes, he even was a hitter, sometimes. A spanker, really.

Yes, Oscar loved Zachary.

Yes, Oscar even read him bedtime stories.

No, Oscar would never do anything like that. He loved kids.

"Dr. Hauser mentioned we could use hypnotic regression," I told Gloria. "Then we might know for sure. I'm not saying

Oscar would do that, but maybe he had a weird friend, maybe—"

"Dr. Hauser told me she opposed regression," Gloria said. "I told her as Zach's mother, I'm not sure I want him to go through that."

"I know what you mean," I told her truthfully. "As his dad, I want to spare him. As a cop, I want to know what he knows—especially now . . . I think we owe it to Oscar, too."

She bit. "What do you mean?"

"They were after Oscar that night. Not me. I think that Zachary may know who Oscar's killer is. You told me, Zach's teddy bear was here the whole time, under the bed. Gloria, listen to me. Oscar went to my place to meet somebody. He was tricked. The killer was someone he knew, someone Zachary might have met."

"Oh, my God." Gloria looked truly shaken. "Who would have wanted to kill my Oscar? He was so—"

"I'd like your cooperation to try to find out. Even if it means regressing Zach—"

Gloria nodded. I called for the check.

The story I told Gloria was a setup; I admit that. But for all I knew, it could have been true. Maybe Oscar did know his killer. Maybe he was meeting him at my place, perhaps to kill me, but they had a falling out.

Gloria and I were now agreed on hypnotic regression with Zachary, Dr. Hauser or no Dr. Hauser. Regression might prove Oscar guilty of the crime I cared about. If it didn't, it still might solve a murder.

And, according to Dr. Kottlisky, heal my son.

Chapter forty-nine

D r. Winters had entered my life as a suspect, evolved into a suspect with a strong motive—one of the very best, revenge—and had then abruptly transmogrified into a black-mail victim, bruises, damaging photos, and all. On the basis of reasonable doubt I was protecting her as innocent. Either that, or I was sheltering a suspected criminal.

Either Dr. Winters was my killer or she was what Myerling called my poltergeist, my distraction.

"Not necessarily a ghost, Elliot," he'd explained. "A mischievous entity. A visitor. A distraction. Typically, you get a poltergeist when a situation is unhappy. A miserable adolescent may attract one. In fact, there are those who think a poltergeist is nothing more than the negative energy of adolescents. I'm not inclined to view it that way, but I agree they like to keep company."

"Misery loves company?"

"You might say that."

I was miserable and Dr. Winters was keeping company with me. The whole situation lacked clarity. Particularly when you factored in the satin baseball jacket Dr. Winters was wearing slung over her dangerous red dress. The last time I'd seen one just like it, its owner was waving to me from a fast-receding train. Any cop will tell you that the worst part of the process is when you have enough pieces but you still can't see the picture. That's where I was at. And then she shows up with the jacket.

"Here's what I want to know," I said, guiding the doctor through the door at Jacky and Johnny's. "Where'd you get that jacket?"

"Like it? I think it's hip." We headed for a back booth.

"Like I said, where?" We took the darkest spot they had—good necking territory, but the mood wasn't high romance. Violet could see that I was serious, and I could see that she was cornered.

Cornered shows even when they're very good. She was—good.

"I've had it from . . . I don't remember." We ordered scotch doubles just to get rid of the waiter.

"You're bullshitting me, Violet." She looked me straight in the eye. Like I said, she was good.

"Well, sure," she said. "I mean, you want me to confess it's an old boyfriend's?" The drinks came and she signaled a toast.

I went for the throat shot instead.

"An old boyfriend who kills people?"

Violet went white—or at least pale. She was protecting someone, and it was his jacket.

"I thought you trusted me," she said, giving me the lamps.

"I need to know who you're protecting, Violet. I need to know why you were in my ear, why you waved to me from the el train, why you're doing everything you can to keep me from solving these murders. I need to know, Violet, what your story is."

"So you brought me here to see if you could trigger a confession? Show me the crime scene, tell me the horror of it, the lake of blood, the stomach-churning way it made you feel? I know a lot more about that than you think, Elliot. I know a great deal about murder. But I wasn't in your goddamn car and I don't know what you're talking about. As for the jacket? I just found it, all right? It was in my hall closet. Somebody must have left it there after a party. Why? Is it yours?"

We were in a corner booth, far as we could get from where we found Johnny, not that his death seemed to hurt business any. This was Chicago, remember? Murder sites are a tourist attraction.

"I think it's my killer's."

"I think you're nuts. I think you've gone around the bend. Giving me hell about a jacket. Christ, Elliot, all women get irrational crushes on certain pieces of clothing. All people. What about men and their ratty old hats?"

"Whose jacket?"

"Fuck yourself, Elliot. Save us both a lot of time and trouble."

Violet's voice was low and deadly. She was angry at me and she was firing back, and she didn't miss a shot. She was cornered, yes, but she was also a fighter. And her choice of weapons got me right in the gut.

"I'm a doctor, Elliot. A children's doctor. My specialty is abuse. That means beatings, burns, mutilations, reconstructive surgery for sexual assault. That means I've seen lots and lots of children suffering just like Zach did, ripped open, damaged, torn apart. You are right, Elliot, that puts murder in your heart. That puts murder on your list of options. And you know what else? It makes you lose patience with the authorities, with the whole system and the way it doesn't work, with you, Elliot, because you don't know how to stop them. It takes a gun."

"Go on."

"Those sons of bitches whose killer you're so intent on finding? Your victims? Your precious victims—Jack, Carson, Johnny, what's his name, Oscar, Ricky—they're your murderers. They deserved to die. You do know that. You do, right?"

"Go on. Get it on the table."

"You want to know who the killer is, I just told you. I'm not hiding anything. I'm not protecting anybody. I'm just telling you the bastards all deserved to die."

My cop was crouched and listening closely. There was something here, something dark, but it was not what she was selling. I pulled another thread.

"Whose jacket?"

"Leave it alone, would you? I told you. I don't know." She showed her décolletage, but even that didn't work.

"Whose jacket, Violet?"

"It's mine. I've had it since I was a kid."

"Violet, it's real simple. Either you tell me or I take you in. Now."

"You know I didn't do it."

"Then you tell me who did."

I was bluffing, but Violet didn't know that. I was employing Elliot's homicide rule number ten: Do what's called for.

What was called for just then was leaving the restaurant. I tabbed our drinks, hustled her into her jacket and out the door.

"Come on," I told her, "we're taking a little ride."

"With a stranger," she joked lamely.

I knew exactly what I was going to do, and I knew it wasn't ethical. I knew I'd feel bad about it later, that it was rotten and unfair, and knowing that, I did it anyway because I thought it might work.

While she made nervous small talk, I drove Violet Winters up Halsted Street past Cabrini Green to one of those deserted factory streets that angle off west. Nobody's on them at night. They're empty and isolated. Turning the unmarked onto one of them, then into a narrow alley, I pulled Violet from the car.

"I want to show you something," I said. "Come on."

I dragged her to the rear of the car. I unlocked the trunk.

I unwrapped the silk that covered my killer's kit. I took out the ritual knife. I wanted to scare her, scare her badly. It worked. When I showed her the ring, she started gibbering.

"Where have you seen this? Where have you seen this, Violet?" I demanded.

She was pulling away from me, struggling, but I had her.

"Where have you seen this?" I repeated.

Her eyes went round and white. I thought she might faint. She went limp in my grasp, sinking to the broken glass and concrete of the alleyway, whimpering, "Don't, don't."

I had expected to shock her, but I hadn't expected this. She was curling into the fetal position, whimpering, "Don't, don't. Please don't hurt me. Please don't hurt Freddy. Don't. Don't."

She was helpless as a child. In fact, she was a child. She looked at me in wide-eyed terror, one hand reflexively at her mouth. She was biting at her fist the way a child does to control its crying. I understood then. She wasn't my killer. She was a victim.

"What did you see, honey? What did they do to you?" I talked to the child she had become. I took her in my arms. I rocked her. "You can tell me. You can tell me, sweetheart. You're safe now. You're safe," I crooned. I felt like a son of a bitch.

"They cut me," she sobbed. She pulled her dress up and showed me a scar on her thigh. "They cut me. They cut Freddy. They hurt him. They cut him real bad, bad."

"Where is Freddy, honey? Where is he?"

"They took him away." She rocked back and forth, back and forth. "They hurt my brother. They hurt him. They hurt him."

She was sobbing, gasping for breath. I tried to calm her, tried to bring her back.

"Where did they do this, honey?"

But she was gone. We sat in my unmarked for over an hour. Two blocks to the east, the elevated sparked and roared. A few blocks west, the Chicago River slid by in silence. We waited in the DMZ of the city for Violet to come back to herself. Her sobs gave way finally to gasps. Her gasps became deep breaths. I held her, waiting it out.

"They always tell you to say you're a survivor, not a victim." Violet finally spoke. "I tell people that myself. I think that works for most people. I think that gives them hope."

"Aren't you a survivor? You look like one to me—a doctor, a specialist."

Violet dismissed her career with a wave of her hand.

"Sometimes I think I'm just a clever invention, a system of adaptations. I was resigned to that until I met you, Elliot."

"What are you saying?"

"I'm saying—I'm saying I care for you. I'm not numb anymore. And it hurts."

She looked miserable and beautiful, her face a visage of grief and hope. It scared me to see this mixture. It looked a lot like love. I'd been feeling it myself.

"Let's get out of here," I said. "I have work to do."

My mind was racing. Violet Winters had a brother named Freddy. Freddy something. Carson Stoufley had molested a young boy by the same name. Was Violet Winters's brother who I was looking for? Yes, if he existed.

"Violet?" I wanted to be careful here. "I have to ask you something very hard. Are you sure—is there a Freddy?"

She didn't answer. I was afraid I had pushed her back into that abyss, but it was something else—anger—that kept her from speaking. When she finally answered me, it was from a great, controlled distance.

"There is a Freddy," she said. "And he's not me." Her voice was low and gravelly now, shaking with rage. "You don't think that occurred to me? You don't think when this started I knew it could have been me? What do you think I do for a living, Elliot? What do you think I've done for fifteen years? You think I don't know about the mind? The way it keeps secrets? The way it compartmentalizes? The way it hides things from itself? Why do you think I've spent all these years working with abused children? I spent them because I was one of those children. I know what the mind can hide. Yes, a mind could hide a Freddy. I've seen it. I've seen children so abused, they have other children inside who take the pain for them."

"Multiples?"

"Yes."

"But you are not a multiple?"

"No. I'm just complicated. Does that make it any simpler?"

I drove her to Jamie's. I'd talked him into taking her back, invoking our friendship. I waited until she was safely inside.

Chapter fifty

—■—

What they call it is a repetition compulsion. Somebody did it to you, you do it again and again. You do it to change the outcome, or you do it because you're stuck there. Either way, you do it and do it because somebody did it to you. Repetition . . . compulsion. You have to do it, want to do it, do it whether you want to or not.

Victims often become perpetrators creating victims who become perpetrators. . . . That's the way they—the therapeutic community, as they like to be called—excuse sexual disorders in court.

I understand their point. I know it's meant to move us toward compassion, and I think it does do that—but so what? The once-victim is now a perpetrator, and what's being perpetrated is horror and pain. I know I sound reactionary. I sound cold and without sympathy. I know that. But I also know that somewhere the cycle has to stop, and that part's my job.

I got to Eden Adult Books at eleven P.M., prime time in that place. I didn't know exactly what I was looking for, but I did know I'd find it. I took a packet of insurance with me.

There were half a dozen men in the place when I entered. I went straight to the desk and to the point. The guy at the register was blond, nervous, and thin. He had changed his hair color since my previous visit.

"Hi," I said. "I'm interested in some specialized information."

"Yes?" He looked me over.

"Your name is?"

"Henry . . . Henrietta. What we have is all on the racks in plain view."

"What can you do for me . . . Henrietta?"

"What do you have in mind?"

"Actually?" I leaned closer. "I'm police, I got some child pornography from a regular client of yours, and what I want is some cooperation—now."

Henry/Henrietta gasped. It was a thrilled little gasp that turned my stomach. I was getting angry, but my cop was hissing, "Easy does it. Easy does it."

"You don't seriously think—?"

"Can it. Henry, I do. In fact, I know." With that, I opened the envelope of sodomy shots dropped outside Henry's store.

"You could have got those anywhere."

"So maybe you'd answer a few questions."

"Questions?" Henry did dumb as well as I did ballerina.

"It's not a new word, Henry."

"Well, yes, it's just—"

As we "talked," the men drifted toward the door. One by one they slipped out, except for a short, well-muscled young man in a black T-shirt who rocked back and forth in the far corner behind the last book rack. Eyes closed, ecstasy nearing, he wasn't going to let a mere cop disturb his home run.

"Henry? You cooperate and we won't close you down."

"You bastards."

"I'm looking for somebody named Fred."

"Oh, me, too. Although I wouldn't turn down a john, either."

I didn't laugh. I just shuffled the photos.

"Okay, okay. What does he look like?"

"I don't know."

"What's his whole name, then?"

"I don't know."

"If I solve this little riddle you don't run me in?"

"He's involved with this stuff." I shuffled the kiddie porn photos again. "Who is he, Henry?"

I left the question out on the counter to dry. I turned and watched the man's face as he crossed home plate. It's a strange feeling, watching another man climax. In the movies, it's always the girl. In my bedroom, it was always the girl. The recipient of an anonymous blowjob in the corner of Eden Books was my first visual experience of another man's sexual satisfaction. He looked silly, grimacing like he was trying to get the lid off a jar.

Henry was polishing his counter. I did not make small talk.

"Fred?" he said after ten years.

"Fred." I didn't elaborate. I waited.

"Maybe I know. There is one guy."

"Good."

"You want to see him?"

I didn't answer. Let Henry do the talking for me. He did.

Slipping out from behind his counter, he crossed to a video rack. Eden must have had a thousand videos, all glossily packaged: girls with breasts the size of headlights; young men flexing and grimacing. Henry knelt and selected several from the bottom row. Their packaging was out of date, the lettering from a fifties B movie. He patted the covers clean and smiled fondly. He handed me three tapes.

"There you are . . . Freddy. Freddy Fury," he announced with satisfaction. "Poor Freddy. Nobody wants him anymore. And he was the biggest thing, the biggest thing for a long time."

I looked at the tapes and looked again.

"He's something, isn't he?" Henry asked, segueing into his sales spiel. "Began as a young star and really went the whole distance. A great star. Really, really something else."

He certainly was. Flexed and grimacing on one video, flexed and batting his baby blues on another, Freddy was Dr. Violet Winters with a dick.

"What's the scoop on him now?"

"Oh . . . he's retired."

"Retired?" I left the question on the counter. Henry knew it wouldn't go away.

"Key West, I think. Maybe Miami. No, I heard Key West. You know, where faggots go to die. Maybe not in front of the camera, but that has other satisfactions, I'm sure. He was a great artist, always breaking new ground. Always. I admired him."

"How much?" I nudged the video stack.

"For you? . . . There really hasn't been much demand." Henry shoved the videos into a plain brown bag stamped EDEN in red letters. He reached for the kiddie photos.

"I'll keep those."

"I thought we had a deal."

"We do. I'll keep those."

"You bastard." Henry hissed the last word. Over in the corner where the man was zipping up, he glanced at me with interest.

I took the videos back to my place. I fixed myself a deep

scotch and told young Paradise to cover her eyes. I told my-self it was anthropology I was embarking on, not some sick sexual fantasy of Violet as a man.

Before two minutes had elapsed in *Stud Love,* Freddy Fury had his pants down. He beckoned, look. I looked: His penis didn't get to me, but his eyes, his beckoning eyes, were Vio-let's eyes.

I switched off the tape.

I think we underestimate the pornography factor. I know we do, and I know why. Pornography in some form has been part of everybody's life. There's at least one pinup in every-body's past that he's got a fondness for. Maybe you were lonely the summer you were seventeen and jerked off a thou-sand times to Miss July. You develop a fondness for the girl. You'd know her on the street. You root for her for Playmate of the Year. When she doesn't win, you think they're wrong. Maybe you date a girl with her ponytail. You've got a "type," and your type is Miss July. That's innocent enough, right?

Yes and no. It's still a progression from photo to real-life matching girl. Now let's factor in some violence. Let's say your Miss July had looked scared. It wasn't *Playboy* or *Pent-house,* but some other porn—*True Detective*—you'd found, and she was tied up and luscious and terrified. The "and terrified" is part of the kick for you. Now you know your type, and you know what it is you want to do with her—scare her silly, then come on her face. First you do it in your head, then you do it in your bed. That's progression, too.

A place like Eden Books, "Chicago's Oldest and Boldest," has served some customers for decades. They come in first as the timid kid with a fascination, and then they progress. They meet people. They meet their addiction. They begin to know what they want, and to want more and more of it. They meet like-minded men. They grow, as the title says, older and bolder. They progress.

We talk about criminal progression all the time with crimes like burglary. We can see it on a guy's rap sheet. He tries petty theft, starting small. He likes it. He gets good at it. He tries something a little more ambitious, mastering the skills to pull that off. As a criminal, he's grown. He's progressed. The same sequence happens with violence. Murder doesn't often start with murder. You look back and you see the guy's got a taste for violence. He gets off on it. Assault, bar fights, assault with a weapon . . . You see the progression. Not always, but often enough. Too often. He's got a taste for violence, we say.

With the pornography, the progression is the same: a taste for something becomes an appetite for something more. "A little light bondage" becomes snuff films over time. People think I'm kidding because they want to think I'm kidding. He's not talking about me, they say, and maybe I'm not. But maybe I am.

I've seen it. There's something very dark that happens, and it grows darker over time. They don't want to fantasize about Miss July. They want to do it to her. A certain way. With force if they need to. They think about it all the time. First this, then that, then . . .

It's a triggering process, a ritual, as Father Bremner would say. Sexologists say the same thing. (Elliot's Fancy Facts.) They see the criminal progression in terms of addiction and levels of addictive behavior. The levels move from light to heavy, or light to dark, in Myerling's terms.

When I arrest a sex offender I know that I am catching him mid-stride. There's a progression he's gotten away with and that progression will continue once his jail time is done.

It's a joke with us, a sick joke, about pedophiles. I call

them "librarians." You bust a guy and he's got a whole library that goes down with him. Say he's thirty-five when you catch him. He's got images going back twenty years. A photo of a friend, an ad from the Sears catalogue, some amateur Polaroids, his first glossy eight-by-tens, his video collection . . . Video rigs have made pornography an acceptable "date" among sex addicts and criminals. Think about the progression and how it works: They think about doing it, they do it, they film themselves as they do it, they watch themselves do it over and over and over . . . Jeffrey Dahmer was like that.

Ted Bundy said that violent pornography threw a switch in his mind. I believe him, but most people don't. They don't want to. It's too scary. Of course it is. It's scary for me.

I suspect all of us have this addict potential inside us. I know I daydreamed for hours about Jane Barkin's white bra strap when I was a horny thirteen years old and she was the neighborhood beauty waiting tables at Salvatore's Pizza. I figure if I can get hooked on a bra strap—and some men can—then what if it's black lace, black leather, black and blue . . .

That's the way it goes. An image or a series of images takes hold and becomes a loop. Pornography addicts are real scholars. They pore over their images, catalogue them, sort them, label them.

I remember a schoolteacher accused of molesting a senior boy. Innocent, he claimed. I didn't think so, and I will tell you why. When I interviewed him, he got out his file on the kid, and on the front there was a Polaroid. "It's not a very good one," the guy said. My cop went crazy, so I got a search warrant. I took Gomez and Lynch. We found a whole library. The guy was guilty as hell. He had photographic records of his own progression, his star pupils in Polaroid poses starting at about ten until they were too old to match his obsessions.

When I opened those files of Nesbitt's, I knew what I was looking at. The negatives were "missing" because someone was using them, growing sick off the intersection of Jack Nesbitt's talents and his obsessions. Perhaps growing very rich as well.

My thought until Stoufley was killed was that he had been the one. Now I figured he was just a piece—you'll pardon the expression. I began to realize the murders were almost beside the point. Terrible as they were, they kept pointing me somewhere further, somewhere even darker. The killings were only a series of ghastly clues.

Chapter fifty-one

---■---

My cousin Charles opened the door in a ratty plaid bath-robe. So much for the clichés about gay men being fashion plates.

"It's your cousin."

"I know that, Elliot. Got a tax problem?"

"Come on. You're the one who blew off Thanksgiving at Aunt Fran's."

"Are you coming in?"

"That was the plan."

Cousin Charles lived in a brick bungalow just like the one I'd ceded to Gloria. I got mine from my folks. He got his from his folks.

"Coffee?"

"I guess so."

"It's good coffee, Elliot. Not everything is a crime."

My cousin had eleven months on me which he used like eleven years. Older and wiser was Charles's self-image, and not just with me, I was sure. A "master accountant," he liked to call himself, and he had enough arcane knowledge to beat

Uncle Sam consistently. For this and his likable disposition as kindly resident curmudgeon, Charles had been a family favorite—until AIDS.

"Sorry about Thanksgiving, Elliot. I just get so tired of them boiling the silverware."

"They're old, Charles. They don't know any better."

"You're telling me they don't read? Sorry, Elliot. It's not you. Twenty years they pretend I'm not gay, then AIDS hits and now I can't come by for dinner."

Charles had a point. He usually did.

"Shit, Charles. As far as they're concerned, Gloria and I aren't divorced. You know how they are."

"They certainly are."

We were seated by now at Charles's kitchen table, a cozy little booth. His kitchen featured red and white checked curtains and a set of red and white checked vintage Betty Crocker cookbooks, prominently displayed. Charles made good coffee.

"Eggs?"

"Why not? It's midnight. Sorry about my timing."

"Elliot, you never were real thoughtful. Scrambled with chives?"

"Why not?"

I let Cousin Charles fuss. He was good at it, and I appreciated the wifely ministrations.

"I assume you came for advice?"

"I came for scrambled eggs, Charles."

"And I'm dating Marilyn Monroe."

"Okay. Let me think."

"Spit it out, Elliot. You never were tactful."

"Well—"

Talking to Cousin Charles about Freddy Fury had seemed a good idea in the abstract. In the execution, it seemed pretty much undoable. Cousin Charles seemed as prissy as our aunt Fran, not too likely an expert on gay pornography. And while his sexual preference was open between us, it had always remained comfortably vague.

"I'll make it easy," Charles said abruptly, cracking eggs with enthusiasm. "I notice you have an Eden's shopping bag. You're not a late bloomer, are you, Elliot?"

"Hardly."

"No. I didn't think so."

"So you know this joint?"

"Elliot, everybody knows the Eden. Chicago's 'oldest and boldest.' What's in the bag?"

I shook the videos onto the table. Charles wiped his hands on his apron and turned to look.

"Oh, my," he said fondly. "Fred Fury."

"You know him?" On some silly level I was scandalized.

"Everybody knows Fred Fury, Elliot. Everybody of, shall we say, a certain age. He was one of the first real stars—and a Chicagoan! I remember seeing him in the bars on Clark Street and on lower Wells in the old days. He had such presence, you had to see him to believe it. He practically glowed in the dark. They say all great stars have that. I heard that George Hurrell thought it was something in the skin. He said Marilyn had the faintest peach fuzz everywhere that caught the light. Oops! Your eggs."

I was probably gaping. This was a side of Cousin Charles I'd never seen. He talked about Freddy Fury like a teenage girl with a crush on a football star. And the movie-star stuff. With me, he'd always talked the Cubs.

"I've got another envelope, Charles."

"What is this? Show-and-tell?" Charles was whisking the eggs. He kept at it as I dumped the kiddie porn onto the table.

"Oh, my God. Oh, Elliot. Put them away. I hate that sort of thing."

Charles's voice had scooted into my aunt Fran's range. He was genuinely, terribly upset.

"Sorry, Charles."

"How can you look at it? It's dreadful. Dreadful. Oh, dear. Excuse me."

He wiped his eyes with his apron, then had a full-fledged wheezing attack. A child asthmatic, Charles had always endured taunts of "sissy." "He's a sensitive soul," my own mother used to say, neatly skirting his sexuality. Charles truly was a sensitive soul.

"I know some people are into that, but it just breaks my heart," Charles was saying. "I tell myself it's none of my business, and it isn't, but, oh—excuse me." He dabbed at his eyes.

"What did Freddy Fury have to do with this stuff?" I asked. "It's important, Charles. I wouldn't ask you if it weren't. I can't afford to ask much on the street. They'd hear me coming."

"Let me get these eggs." Charles was up to the butter, the skillet, the chives. "I remember something."

I let Charles cook, shuffling through the glossies just to spoil my appetite. Most of the shots were grainy and workmanlike. A cheap-paneled room, a young boy, and an adult male. The boy looked young, serious, and slightly dazed. Three shots, of the twelve, stood out from the rest. They were artfully lit and particularly lascivious. Cropped close in on the sexual act itself, they were at once erotic and deeply disturbing. The young boy in these photos, the boy giving head in close-up, looked luminously intent and rapturous, as though sucking cock were a sacred mission, as if he'd been trained to it by birth.

Charles served me my eggs. He glanced at the stack. The glossy, artier shots were on top.

"Why, that's it," Charles said. "That's his stuff, the way it looked."

"What do you mean?"

"He was a real artist," Charles said—Henry's words, too.

"I thought you hated this stuff."

"I do, Elliot. With the children. I really can't bear it. But the style of Freddy's work, the look—there was always a certain romance to what Fred Fury did—in front of the camera or behind it." Charles turned over a video box and pointed to the credits: FURY FILMS.

Fred Fury had moved from actor to writer, director, producer. He had moved from victim to perpetrator. Had he moved to murderer as well?

"Thanks, Charles. Great eggs."

My cousin looked at me quietly. I didn't need to be told how vulnerable he felt, how much courage he'd just shown me. Why?

"Sorry about Zachary."

That was why.

"Thanks, Charles. So am I."

"Any leads?"

"Not that go anywhere—except maybe here." I tapped the video stack.

"Elliot?"

"Mmmm?" I waited as Charles weighed his words.

"I heard Freddy was HIV positive."

"Ah." I waited again.

"They say now it's AIDS."

I felt my stomach whirl into its own black hole, although Zach had tested negative. I believed now that Fury was connected to the crimes and therefore to Zachary.

"Where would I find him? If you knew that I'd be a happy man."

Charles looked at me like I had just asked him to slash his wrists. Step in front of a train. Maybe I had.

"I've known him twenty-five years. I'm his accountant," he said finally. "I'll find him for you."

Chapter fifty-two

———■———

At the station, my war of containment was failing badly. I had a stack of messages that could fill a mattress. Lynch was dealing with the press, and it showed on him. In two weeks he'd gone from eager to cynical. Like me, he was Black Irish, pale skin, dark hair and eyes. His circles were beginning to look like shiners.

"Get some sleep, kid."

"The press is the nightmare, isn't it?"

Poor Ricky Noonan. Suicide or murder, these were not the headlines he'd been seeking: "Judge Falls Victim to Satanic Cult."

"What is it? Somebody bullying you about our methods?"

"I didn't know Judge Noonan was such a hero."

If you think a celebrity murder is a mess, double what happens when it's a judge. It has to do with people's associations. A judge is an archetype, like Daddy, a civic father-figure, an icon of strength and safety. That's why people are so outraged when a judge is crooked. Not to mention when a "good judge" is murdered—and Ricky Noonan had the reputation of being a very good judge.

"Don't believe everything you read. Ricky Noonan was a good guy and a good judge, but he was not Plato."

"Guess you read that lady's stuff."

"In the *Trib?* Yeah. She had the hots for him, clearly. Not every judge looks like—who was it she said? Robert Redford?"

"Yeah. Did he? I thought his hair was—"

"Maybe she meant Paul Newman. Get some sleep. I'll tell them to fuck off."

"That columnist called."

"Lynch. In Chicago our columnists have names."

"That's what he said, too."

"I'll handle it."

I called the Big Name. I told him I needed him to divert attention so I could get my job done. I also told him he should have been a cop, he was that close in the theories he'd spouted to Lynch. Thank you, God, he bought it. Did I mention his theories involved Carson Stoufley and a jealous woman lover? A certain woman writer who had defected to the paper across the street?

Journalists. They probably had a special place in heaven for them—about the size of a dime.

Do I sound bitter? You should have met the old guys, newspapermen, they called themselves. They hated the new journalists with their psycho-schmycho insights. "Stick to the facts," they would snarl. "What's wrong with the facts?"

The Big Name Columnist no longer believed in facts. His specialty was insight. Failing that, he went for innuendo. Hey, who could blame him? It kept him from having to leave the office. Myself, I can't see phone reporting. I say, watch the picture without the sound. It's a guy's body that tells you the story.

The minute my phone cleared from the Big Name, it rang again with Myerling.

"Got a minute?"

"For you, Harold, anything."

"Good. Meet me at Harry's."

"Come on, Harold, use the phone," I teased. "We're old-fashioned. What do you have to tell me that I have to see you to believe?"

"Elliot? Meet me at Harry's, okay? Sherlock Holmes didn't use the phone."

Holmes was a hero of Myerling's, invoked only on solemn occasions.

"Okay."

I got off the phone and told Lynch to forget about that nice little nap he was heading home for.

"Sorry, kid. It's back to the switchboard for you."

"Yessir."

"Lynch?"

"Yessir?"

"Use my name. I'm not your daddy."

"Yessir. Elliot. Sir, okay."

"Okay?"

"Yessir."

I gave up. I was old enough to be his daddy. I felt old enough to be my own. I drove to Harry's with geriatric care.

Harold Myerling had a bribe waiting for me: shake, rings, fries, malted, cheeseburger. Mine, not his. He and the bribe were at our window table. Behind the counter, Harry was swabbing up for the night. Even though they were name-sakes, Harold and Harry had never liked each other. Harry resented Harold for his prissy tea bags and hyperchondriacal cleanliness. Harold resented what Harry's food could do to the body. I was just that likable guy in the middle of it all.

"Hi, Harry! We keeping you open?" Harry grunted an acknowledgment and he jerked his head toward Harold. "Hi, Harold." I nodded toward the food. "What if I'd been late, Harold?"

"I'd have been in full possession of a cholesterol death kit."

"Very funny—right, Harry?"

Harry pretended he wasn't listening, but if he wasn't listening, I'm Queen Elizabeth. I knew someone was paying Harry off. Who?

Myerling was dipping his herbal tea like a bad mechanical toy. Mr. Robot. "I had a dream," he said.

"So did Martin Luther King. You see where it got him."

Myerling dipped his tea bag some more.

"Okay. Tell me."

"I dreamed about Judge Noonan. He had X-ray eyes."

I waited for more. Myerling dipped his tea bag.

"So?"

"So I thought I should tell you."

"That's it? That's the whole dream?"

"We're at the funeral. They put him in the ground, but even through his coffin I could see his X-ray eyes. Like an old movie."

My cop was throwing body blocks against my stomach wall. I told it, okay, I'm listening. I get it.

"You finished?" Myerling nodded toward the missing onion rings, the vanished fries, the burger and shake I'd inhaled.

"Yeah. I'm finished."

"Me, too."

I thanked Harry and we walked outside to the curb, where my unmarked was chatting up Myerling's Town Car.

"What do you think it means?" Myerling wanted to know.

"It means no more garlic before you sleep, Harold."

"Funny you should mention garlic. Garlic wards off vampires, and that's the image. Like the old one, Nosferatu? The burning eyes. X-ray eyes, like an old movie."

"You said that."

"Okay. Be a pissant, Elliot. I won't ask if you're taking your baths."

Harry was watching us out the window. I wanted to wrap it up.

"So you called me over to hear about X-rated eyes?"

"Not X rated, X-ray."

Myerling and I both got it at once: X-rated eyes, like in an old movie. Porno films!

"Say good night, Harold. The eyes of Texas are upon us."

"That's what I thought. Take your baths, Elliot."

The talk with Harold made me edgy. I headed home, realized I was in for a sleepless night, and pointed my car east, toward the lake. For a change of pace, I drove Lake Shore Drive south, toward Indiana, and I focused on the black of the lake, the white lines of the highway, instead of on my problems. Sometimes, when I'm driving, say when I'm executing a tricky left merge, an answer will come to me. Not this time. What came to me was more insomnia, the kind that talks to you all night. I headed home to keep it company. Then I had one last brainstorm.

"Let's take the dogs to the park," I suggested to Dr. Winters from a pay phone on Division.

"It's the middle of the night, Elliot. Just ask Jamie. He's snoring."

"He's snoring? How could you know he's snoring?"

"Calm down. He's in the other room. Not that it sounds that way. You ever heard his snore?"

She was right. Jamie snored like a diesel breaking down.

"Are you saying you don't love me, Violet?"

"I'm saying I've got an early call. Surgery at six A.M. Vaginal repair. She's three."

"Thanks for the details, Violet. You won't come out and play?"

"No. I'm lying here. Salvation is at hand, and you sound drunk or high or something."

"Did Ricky Noonan like movies?"

"Now, there's a change of subject. I don't know. Let me think—yes. He had about a million old-movie videos. One of his habits was having an old movie on during sex."

"Spare me the details. Sweet dreams."

"That's it?"

"Yeah. I think so."

"You on something, Elliot? You sound wired for sound."

"Onto something. Same effect. Save me a dance, Violet."

I got off the phone. God bless Harold Myerling.

I wondered who had told him about Ricky Noonan's X-rated eyes. A dream, he said. I remembered the time Harold got sloshed and told me he communed with ghosts. Ricky Noonan was a good Catholic boy. Maybe Harold was communing with him and he'd confessed.

Chapter fifty-three

———◼———

I went to see Peter Abramson, state's attorney, at nine A.M., after three hours sleep. On the way, I bought myself the morning papers and a cup of coffee at the Golden Angel.

"You getting anywhere?" Betsy asked as she poured my coffee.

"Older, Betsy." And I felt it, too.

The papers were making Ricky Noonan's death out to be a suicide. It was and it wasn't, if you asked me—but nobody had. Until Betsy did.

"You think that judge killed himself? Want a doughnut with this?"

"I'll take a doughnut."

"I can see you're being secretive. All right. I loves you anyway." Betsy flicked a wipe rag at me and sent me on my way.

I headed for the state's attorney's office and an intricate and delicate piece of negotiating. I wanted to investigate Noonan's death as a murder. I did not think this would be an easy sell. Everyone thought it was a suicide, just like the papers said. Even Myerling agreed that the angle and impact were consistent with suicide. Personally, I had no doubt Ricky Noonan's death was a suicide—I just thought it was induced. Ricky should have insulated himself from whomever he thought he was protecting. If he were alive, I'd have told him that. I talked to Peter Abramson instead.

We talked in Abramson's snappy office, the one with Art Institute prints and the tufted leather couch. The one with the good fake Oriental rug. The one all done up as a launching pad for a young man on the rise. I say we talked, but I talked while Abramson worked the Sunday *New York Times* crossword puzzle.

"Judge Noonan did not just step into the deep end," I told Abramson. "We're not talking about somebody who was chronically depressed. He was threatened. I want into his place."

"What are you saying, Detective Mayo? I thought the findings were for suicide."

"And they were. What I'm looking for is why."

"We don't do psychotherapy here. Just investigations." Abramson looked proud of his snappy answer. His snappy suit. His snappy self. He filled in his little boxes with a number two pencil.

"I have reason to believe Ricky Noonan—excuse me, Judge Noonan—was connected to the deaths of Jack Nesbitt, Carson Stoufley, Johnny Vanilla, and Oscar Gomez," I continued.

"Really?" The voice was politely disbelieving, but Abramson's look said: You idiot.

"No, I want you to look like a jerk so you'll never be elected. For God's sake, Abramson, I'm offering you a career maker."

It was no secret to me that Abramson, just like Ricky

Noonan, harbored political ambitions. I knew that from Noonan himself. Now Abramson cocked his rat-terrier head and thought about my possible value to his political aspirations.

"You're serious there's a connection?"

"Yes."

"Judge Waldo won't go for it."

"He'll cooperate if you ask him nice. Noonan was his friend. Tell him you're trying to clear him. Tell him you don't want his name besmirched. You'll both be good Samaritans."

"Ah . . . I'll see what I can do."

"Clear Ricky's name and you're a hero."

"Right."

"Papers are looking for an angle. A friend on behalf of a friend is a nice story."

Abramson took a millisecond before he bit. I knew he was seeing headlines—and votes. I also knew the last thing my work would do is clear Ricky Noonan's name or promote Abramson's precious career. You say what you have to sometimes.

"I'll get on it."

"You're a good man." Okay, so shoot me.

"You're sure on this?"

"Reasonably. But we're reasonable men, aren't we?"

Peter Abramson liked to think he was. And I knew he'd persuade Judge Waldo to help clear his friend's dishonored name. Let Peter Abramson fantasize that he'd be the hero and Ricky Noonan would be his ticket to stardom. My real agenda was a little different. I thought Noonan's death did interlock with Johnny Vanilla's. I thought Judge Waldo's search warrant might tell me how. And I didn't think the how would make Ricky look good. Did I lie about this to state's attorney Abramson? You bet your ass. A lie of omission in the service of a greater cause than his little political career.

From my perspective, things were coming along nicely. Thanks to Peter Abramson, I had my warrant to search Noonan's place. I had my son safely tucked away in the country. My cousin Charles was indulging in a little nepotism and getting me the home address of my number one suspect. Yes, the mystery was unraveling.

I left my unmarked parked illegally next to the planter filled with phony plants. I started across the lobby and was nearly to the elevator before I registered that Bobby was not at his post. I found him behind our reception desk, unconscious, a visible bruise above his right eyebrow. I bent close; he was breathing.

While I was kneeling there, out of sight, I heard the elevator doors hiss open. Stay put, said my cop.

I stayed put, listening to the tap, tap, tap of a woman's high heels, the squeaky suck of the front door opening, the tap, tap, tap of heels down the front stairs. When I poked my head out to look, I saw a tall redhead entering a Yellow Cab.

Bobby stirred at my feet.

"How are you doing?" I asked him. Bad, was the answer.

"Detective Mayo?"

"In the flesh." Why did I mention flesh?

"You're okay?" Breathless concern.

"Me? What about you?"

"Oh, it's all right. The line of duty, you know." You have to picture Garbo delivering these lines.

"So what happened?"

"I heard the car. I went out from the desk. She comes storming inside—"

"She?"

"—and she demands to see you. Of course, I say no, as per your instructions, and she coldcocks me." I got it: my hero.

"Thanks, Bobby. Take care of that bruise."

I took the elevator up to my place. I had no illusions about safe havens. My apartment door stood open. I drew my gun and entered.

What I can tell you, rationally, is that the draft came from the open balcony window. What it felt like, hitting the apartment door, was that I had suddenly stepped into a meat locker. Despite the summer's heat, my place felt cold, damp, and dead. Paradise started whimpering. Daubed on my wall, in dull red brown, was a message for me. ONE BY ONE, it read.

"Here we go," I said to Paradise. I didn't know quite where. She thumped her tail. I scouted for dead bodies.

I was beginning to feel like a murder weapon myself. I was only grateful that Zach was safely out of town, fishing with Father Bremner. . . .

Oh, Christ. My phone machine! What if he'd called? My phone messages were a who's who of the people I cared about—Zach, Gloria, Jamie, Violet, my cousin Charles.

I crossed to the phone machine. Just as I feared, I had a message from Zachary.

"It's really cool up here, Dad. Father Bremner and I caught a giant trout."

I also had a message from Cousin Charles. "Check the hideout," Charles said. What the hell did that mean? What hideout?

At the front of the tape there were old messages from Gloria, Jamie, and Violet. One by one, they'd all checked in. One by one, they were all targets now. I heard a sound behind me and whirled around, gun drawn.

"Holy shit," Bobby was standing in my doorway, staring at my blood-daubed wall. "Is that blood?"

"Or a good imitation."

"Oh, my God." He sounded thrilled. Clearly the scene of the crime was his idea of a good time. Not mine.

I was calibrating how nearly I had missed my mystery caller.

I wondered if the miss was intentional. Yes, I decided. I was wanted alive. I was being goaded, even led to solving these crimes. I was also distracted, misled, sabotaged.

"Bobby, I'm calling the boys from my office. Wait for them here, would you?"

"Do I need a gun?"

"No, I don't think so." He looked disappointed. "They'll have those," I added.

I called Lynch at the station and asked for them to come right over. "Be sure and print my phone machine," I told him. "Our killer paid me a house call."

The phone at my favorite 7 Eleven was out of order. I called Father Bremner from an Amoco station on Ohio Street. The line was bad, but he could hear me.

"I'm downtown. Look, I think you and Zach are in danger. Do not let him out of your sight."

"And you, Elliot? Are you in danger?"

"No," I said. "And that's not the point. Thanks."

Father Bremner's question hit me as almost silly. My danger was not the issue to me. Zachary's was, Father Bremner's was, Jamie's, Violet Winters's, and Gloria's was. And now, last but not least, my cousin Charles's was.

Gloria. She was the most defenseless. And if they wanted to find Zachary, they'd go to her. I had to get to her first.

From the Amoco to my old brick bungalow was the longest, slowest thirty blocks I'd ever driven, and I drove them very fast. I squealed to the curb and was up the walk, buzzing the bell, before the motor stopped.

"All right. All right. Who is it?"

I was relieved to hear Gloria's drunken voice.

"It's me, Gloria. Elliot."

"Go away."

"Let me in, Gloria. You're not safe."

I heard the slide bolt scratch and the chain rattle. Gloria opened the door looking the way I thought she would in twenty years.

"What is it, Elliot? What do you want?"

"I want you to take a little vacation."

"I'm on a little vacation, Elliot. Can't you tell? You and Theresa, such busybodies. You should have married her."

Gloria wore a gaudy chiffon peignoir over a shortie gown. Oscar's taste, not mine. She'd been drinking and was drinking still. The gin on her breath was hot and bright as the fumes from glue.

"Make yourself a drink, Elliot. I got one drop left."

Gloria swirled the gin in her glass.

"I'm packing you a bag, Gloria. You're going for a little ride."

"Fuck you . . . Don't you want a drink?"

I left Gloria in the living room and went to what was once our bedroom. I could have packed right off the floor, but I settled for the leftovers in her drawers. I knew the head of Haymarket Women's Mission. Roxy Sue was an ex-teenage hooker I'd taken off the street into detox ten years earlier. She'd made it, gone to Roosevelt, then gotten her counseling license. I'd helped her out a little along the way. Now she could help Gloria.

"Put this on." I handed Gloria a floral muumuu she'd worn when she was pregnant with Zach.

"Where are we going?"

"The doctor."

"I've already been to the doctor with Zach."

"Just get dressed, Glo."

"It didn't happen to me, Elliot. I don't need therapy. Dr. Hauser says so."

I yanked the muumuu down over Gloria's nightie. She teetered into me and rubbed her breasts along my chest. I felt a wash of tenderness, not lust. Poor Gloria, she was doing the best she could.

"Hold me, Elliot."

"Let's just get you finished here," I said, patting down the floral fabric, smoothing back her hair.

"Nice Elliot. I remember you."

"Here we go. Bring your drink if you need to."

"Sweet Elliot."

I got Gloria, her drink, and her suitcase out the door, down the stairs, and into the car.

"Buckle up."

"You buckle up, Elliot."

I buckled the belt across Gloria's lap.

"I miss him, Elliot. I miss my Oscar."

"I know, sweetheart. Now, hold on to that drink."

I got to Haymarket before Gloria finished her drink. That was fast. She didn't ask where we were going, and I didn't need to tell her. I just wanted her safe.

"Zach didn't like the doctor," Gloria said just as we pulled onto the mission's street. "Oscar said he was wonderful, but Zach didn't like him."

"Dr. Hauser?"

"Oh, she was okay. The other one."

"You mean Dr. Winters, the one at the hospital with me?"

"No, he liked her. But so do you, right?"

"What doctor, Gloria?"

But Gloria had nudged herself into a crying jag and wasn't answering any questions.

"Don't, Elliot. Don't start." Gloria began sobbing. I jumped out to hustle her into the mission. She was right. I didn't need to start with her. I needed to warn Cousin Charles.

Just down the street from detox, a parking lot had a pay phone. I called Charles. He did not answer his phone, and neither did his machine. I tried Jamie's. His machine was on, as it often was when he was working. I could not tell if he or Violet were there.

Ladies first, I told myself, and headed for Jamie's place. I wanted to be certain Violet was safe, then I would go to Charles's.

Chapter fifty-four

———◼———

"Imagine meeting you here." Violet Winters opened the door. She was in her cowgirl mode.

"Where's Jamie? Are you okay?"

"I'm fine. It's nice to have a little solitude. He left me armed and extremely dangerous. I think he needed to get laid." She waved me in. Salvation didn't bark at me.

"Is this a professional visit? Don't tell me."

Dr. Winters collapsed on Jamie's leather couch. It looked just like my fake one, but it smelled good. So did she. I collapsed next to her fragrant shoulder.

"What's that perfume?"

"Not perfume. Oil. Night Blooming Jasmine."

"Very exotic."

"So am I."

She rubbed a blue-jeaned leg against my haunch. She was playful and coltish, like a teenager. This just made me angry. Didn't she know she was in danger? Then again, so was I. She was a suspect and I was more protective than suspicious. I moved into twenty questions.

"What did you wear as a kid?"

"Clothes. And you?" She poked my ribs. "Lighten up."

"Come on. Perfume. Evening in Paris? White Shoulders?"

"Nah. Those were too classy. I wore Heaven Scent. It smelled like cat piss. Perfect for when I wanted to feel rotten. I lost it last time I moved over here."

"Do that often?"

"Move?"

"Put on perfume just to feel rotten."

"I used it for a while when I was doing my therapy. It was unconscious until my therapist pointed it out. I guess I wanted to remember my brother."

"Don't tell me he wore it, too."

"We used to play dress-up, switch roles. He'd borrow my perfume, dress up in my clothes. I'd put on his baseball jacket and practice chewing gum."

"Good all-American family."

"I know it sounds sick now, but we were just kids. We were dressing up, that's all." Violet looked wistful.

"I'll take that drink." I got to my feet.

"Too much for you, Elliot?"

It was. I crossed to Jamie's bar and poured myself a stiff scotch.

"Things started coming apart in my thirties. That's when I started having the dreams."

"The dreams?" I didn't want to know them.

"Hooded men in white. Ghosts or Ku Klux Klan. Too many horror movies. Too much reading about civil rights, maybe . . . Whatever they were, they scared the hell out of me.

"I stopped wanting sex. Then I suddenly wanted it wildly, with the wrong people. I was afraid I'd hurt myself. I was hurting myself."

"Go on." Not that I wanted her to.

"I was getting in the wrong beds and I couldn't tell you why. It's about then I met Ricky Noonan. I hate to even think about him."

"C'mon. He was a nice guy. Maybe a little too ambitious, but overall, a nice guy."

"Your version. There was stuff about nice Ricky Noonan you didn't want to know. And somebody, like Ricky himself maybe, should have told me."

"His alternating current?"

"That and the rest of it."

"The rest of it?"

"It's a wavelength, a darkness. I could sense it in him and he could sense it in me. We started to fool around with it. I got scared. You might say Ricky and I were mirrors, and what I saw frightened me. I didn't know how far we would go or when we'd stop. It was a power game really. I went for help."

"And help was what? Therapy?"

"The works. Call it three years in hell and let it go. I came out with a name for what ailed me and a professional specialty in abused children. I've been more or less fine, at least functional, ever since. And then along comes you. You had to remind me there was a difference between functional and happy. Not that you are exactly a barrel of laughs right now."

With that, Violet Winters crossed to Jamie's bar and opened a bottle of Perrier. She calmly emptied it over her head.

"What the fuck are you doing?"

"Cooling my jets."

"You're also irrigating Jamie's floor."

"It needs it. He's knee deep in shit."

"What does that mean?"

"He's with some art fan who sent him a love note and invited him out to play. He's into some pretty sick stuff if you ask me. His porn of choice is *True Detective*. He's got a whole stack of them hidden under the couch. You ask me, your friend Jamie should be a suspect, not me."

"Look," I said. "There's some things you can't fuck with, Violet. Jamie's my friend. My best friend."

"Did you know he keeps a stack of *True Detective*s?"

"The hell—"

"You really don't know what he does, do you? I mean, look at his paintings, for chrissake. If they don't look like assaults, I ain't know what does."

I had to admit she was right. The paintings were assaults—but did that mean Jamie was capable of killing, castrating, and mutilating men? Did something happen to him in the juvenile home that caused his sexuality to twist and darken?

"He knew all the victims," Violet pointed out. "And he had access to Zachary."

"What's Zachary got to do with this?"

"You tell me. Zachary doodles an inverted pentacle, the same pentacle we find with Ricky Noonan, with Gomez—"

"I never saw Jamie doodling any pentacles," I managed, as if her first line of conjecture was comfortable. "Just stars."

"Jamie's not Mr. Mental Health," Violet repeated. "You know where he is tonight? Out with some red-haired hooker type—"

I thought I knew which red-haired hooker type.

That's when the doorbell rang. I made it across the room, gun drawn, just in time to open the door and let Jamie bleed on his own rug.

"Bitch cut me," he said, falling over.

Dr. Winters was elbowing me aside, issuing orders ("Lie still, don't talk, call 911") to Jamie and to me. We obeyed.

"Help me get his pants down."

"His pants?"

"You heard me. Hurry!"

My friend Jamie Hackett had nearly been de-balled. Dr. Winters held together a gaping abdominal wound in her left hand and sliced-up scrotum cradled in her right. "I got you," she said to Jamie. "You're going to be all right."

"Promise?" Jamie was gray.

"I promise, you son of a bitch. You're lucky you're fat. Fat saved you."

"Yeah. I'm a real sumo wrestler." With that, Jamie passed out.

"It's the shock, not the damage," Dr. Winters said to me.

The ambulance was shrilling its throat out down Dearborn Avenue. I went out to greet it, and found Jamie's car covered with blood.

Fuck this bastard. This was too personal.

Rage in my throat, I helped the medics load Jamie into the ambulance and told him I'd be by in a couple of hours.

"I'll ride with him," Dr. Winters said, but I grabbed her arm, too roughly.

"No. I don't think so. You'll ride with me."

"Where are we going?"

"To the bottom of this mess."

When teaming up with a suspect feels safe to you, you know you're on dangerous ground.

Chapter fifty-five

I didn't need a search warrant to search my cousin Charles's. I had an invitation. All I needed was the key he kept in the drainpipe by the back door.

"I'll go first," I told Violet. "He could be in here."

Despite his sartorial habits, Charles was quite the little homemaker. I opened the back door to the scent of lemon oil furniture polish mixed lightly with an air freshener and Spic and Span. I did not smell trouble.

"I don't think he read *The Feminine Mystique*," Violet said as we passed through the kitchen.

"Don't be catty," I chided.

"He's your cousin?" Violet asked. "You never told me you had a gay cousin."

"Why would I? There are lots of interesting things about Charles beyond his sexual preference."

"Like his lemon sponge cake recipe?"

"Like the fact that he's been missing for hours—maybe longer."

"Should I hope we find him?"

"No."

"Is that because he's a suspect or a victim?"

"Just let me work, okay?"

"What are you looking for?"

"I'm not sure."

"Elliot? I'm going to make coffee while you decide."

"What a nice little woman."

I checked out the modest "dining area," spent ten minutes on the living room, and proceeded to Charles's bedroom, maple furniture and the kind of twin beds favored by the Hays Office in old movies. Nothing smacked of sex—of any kind. I looked under the bed, through the bureau drawers, in the closet. Nothing. Ditto for the guest room.

"Coffee's ready." Violet was doing Betty Crocker.

"I'm almost done."

Violet appeared with a mug of coffee for me. I was standing in Charles's entryway, worried that I hadn't found him, relieved that I hadn't found him. Violet joined me with a coffee mug of her own.

"What's he keep hidden behind the bureau?" she asked.

The bureau was a three-drawered oak number with a mirror and hat rack attached. It served as a spot to tie your scarf on the way out of the house, sort your mail on the way in. A bulky piece, it backed up against—and obscured—the small door leading to the oddly shaped storage room beneath the stairs.

Of course! The hideout!

How could I not have remembered the hideout? Charles and I had played there as kids. It was the perfect hideout— five feet deep, ten long. We'd even slept there in our sleeping bags, pretending it was a cave in western Montana.

Charles had the heavy bureau blocking its entrance. I went through its drawers—folded linens—then shoved it aside. I entered the hideout, nearly stooped double. I was surprised to remember the exact placement of the single light switch, but I was more surprised when I hit the light. There stood an old chest, low, flat, standard olive drab. Frederick Fury's name was stenciled on the top. I opened the trunk.

Frederick Fury was an organized man, even in his compulsions. Filed neatly in his old trunk, just behind his tax files, he had hundreds of photos of a certain sexual act. I leafed quickly through them, realizing with sinking heart they were leading deeper and darker with every few shots. What is it with evil, I wondered, that could move a man to submit himself to such degradation and to ask it from others?

I was about to close the trunk, when I noticed that the top inner lid had gaffer's tape reinforcing its edges. It was an old trunk, but still . . . I took out my pocket knife and scraped at a corner. Sure enough.

The half-dozen photos were old and yellowed. If you didn't know what they were, the first few looked as sinister as cast photos from a bad amateur production of *Julius Caesar.* My cop did a very slow somersault: dressed in togas, five young children smiled at the camera. In togas and hoods, a circle of adults stood behind them. From there, the photos moved into true horror: one shot of three bodiless heads; another of three headless bodies; a third shot of "young talent" applied to oral sex. The "talent" was Freddy's and may have saved his life. The fifth child was Violet.

I took the photos and switched off the light. I left the hideout in the darkness I'd found there.

"What is it?" Violet asked me. "You look shaken."

I brushed her aside, shoved the bureau back into place. I was shaken.

"You're not talking? I thought maybe you'd find your cousin in there."

"So did I. Where's that coffee?"

"Right here." She held the cup toward me. "Can I see what you found?"

"No!" A real bark.

"You don't have to shout at me. I get it I'm supposed to be your docile female companion."

"Good." I glared at her.

"As your docile female companion, I want to suggest we drink our coffee in the cozy kitchen."

Talk about docile—I followed Violet numbly into the kitchen. She settled us at Charles's breakfast nook and patted my arm.

"Drink up," she urged.

"I'm starving," I told her. As usual, appetite was my response to carnage.

"Shall I?" Violet asked, starting to her feet.

"No, Doctor," I snarled. "I'm the new male. I know my way around the kitchen."

That's how it happened that I dove into Charles's refrigerator looking for sandwich materials and left the stack of photos on the table near Violet.

"Oh, my God," I heard her whisper. "Oh, Jesus."

"Don't look!" I warned, whirling to snatch the photos away, but it was too late. Violet was rocking softly back and forth, her arms wrapped tight around her body.

"I remember. I remember," she was saying. Her pale skin beaded with sweat.

"Remember what?"

Violet's eyes were dark and flat, focused past me, past the time we were in.

Her hands were shaking. They were damp, then wet. I held them tight as a tremor coursed through them, through her whole body.

"What is it, honey? Tell me."

The shaking got worse. She didn't, couldn't, answer me.

"What is it, honey? You can tell me. It's all right. What did you see? What did you see?"

Violet didn't answer me. She didn't speak at all. For at least five minutes I held her hands and waited. For what, I didn't know. She was coming back to me, coming out of the flashback. I watched her carefully, watching her face until she watched me back, behind her own eyes again, finished with the inner movie.

"Can I hold you?" I asked.

Violet crept into my arms, and then the sobs came. They came for a very long time. They'd been wanting to come for too many years.

Chapter fifty-six

———■———

Post-traumatic stress disorder, they call it, and Violet had it in spades. She curled her fist in my hand just the way Zachary did. Even her body language was the coltish, unsure walk of a suddenly sprouted girl.

"I don't know how to bring you back, Violet," I told her.

"I'm right here," Violet protested, but she wasn't.

I'm a cop. Half my job is to solve crimes, but the other, more important half is to protect people. I felt I was failing Violet Winters badly. Her memories had battered her.

"Violet? Is there someone I could call? Your old therapist?"

"You met her. Dr. Kottlisky. I guess you could call her."

"Let's try reaching her from Harold's."

I drove her to the coroner's. Harold Myerling received us without surprise. I was beginning to think there was something to his and Father Bremner's talk about the spiritual life as a sort of psychic network.

"She's having some kind of flashback," I told him. He led us into his office, where African masks, power baskets, and his various degrees adorned the walls. He ushered Violet to a hardbacked chair, sat her down, and clapped his hands sharply three times. She barely seemed to hear him.

"Abracadabra?" I asked lamely.

"Entities," Myerling pronounced. "Thought forms." As if it made sense. "They hate this."

"You mean memories, Harold? Not ghosts."

"Light that, would you?" Myerling ignored my question and nodded to a small bunch of gray-green twigs lying on his desk. I struck a match and they lit, emitting a heavy oily smoke. I waved them around as Myerling mimed.

"Smudging," Myerling explained. He was waving a vial of sharp-smelling oil under Violet's nose. I didn't recognize the scent.

"Mmph!" She drew back abruptly, her eyes focusing for the first time. "What is it?"

"Vertiver," Myerling said. "It's grounding. Here, hold these now and breathe slowly. In and out. In and out."

He handed Violet two stone balls, one clear, one dark. She took one in each hand, balancing, like Justice. Myerling moved on, wrapping her now in a bright golden square of silk, a lopsided sari.

"How do you feel?" he asked. He was snapping his fingers in the air near her ears.

"Better. This black ball is getting heavy, though." Violet held out the ball and Myerling took it.

"That's good," he said. "It absorbs negativity. Now how are you feeling?"

He laid a hand on her forehead, felt her pulse. He looked pleased. Violet herself looked better, almost with us again. Myerling had a real bedside manner.

"How are you feeling?" he repeated.

"Like I've seen a ghost," Violet said softly. "I was just gone." She shook her head. "So gone."

"I'll vouch for that," I said. "Welcome back." I felt like a flippant idiot.

"Elliot." Violet reached for my hand and smiled up at me. Her eyes were clear. When she smiled at me, I knew relief. I'd have understood her hating me.

"My past isn't your fault, Elliot. Tell him that, Mr. Myerling."

It would have been easy to let her believe that. I wanted to believe that myself, but it was not the truth.

"Some of it is, Violet." She looked at me sharply. "Your memories and my life do intersect. . . . Harold, I'd like to talk with her about the crimes in the park."

"It's a risk."

"Violet, I would like to call Dr. Kottlisky. We might want her here."

"You can call her, Elliot, but I know I need to go back again. I've been dreaming again."

I thought of Zachary and his months of terrible dreams when I was gone. It was Zachary's justice, Zachary's healing, I hungered for, as much as Violet's.

"She had these dreams, Harold—men in white robes, some kind of ritual."

"Some kind of ritual abuse," Harold said.

The minute the words were out, Violet met my gaze with a look I can call only tranquil. It was as though she had fallen from a great height and survived. What I saw in her eyes was knowledge.

"I know," she said. "On some level I have always known. Let's call for the doctor."

I tried the number Violet gave me for Dr. Kottlisky. I left a message on her service, then realized the doctor had given me a card the day we had lunch at Malcolm Crutcher's gala. I fished her card from my wallet.

"Hello. This is Dr. Kottlisky." She answered on the second ring. She had the lilting, musical voice you would want in a fairy godmother.

"Dr. Kottlisky, this is Detective Mayo. I sat by you at a fund-raiser?"

"Why, yes, Detective. How nice to hear from you."

"I'm with a former patient of yours, Violet Winters. We're at the coroner's—"

"Oh, my God—"

"No, no. She's fine. That is, she's not fine. That is, I think we need you—"

"Let me talk to her," Dr. Kottlisky interrupted. I handed Violet the phone.

"Doctor? The dreams. They're back. I think I'm ready now. Could you come? Please?"

"Of course."

Violet handed me the phone back and I gave Dr. Kottlisky directions to Harold's morgue. It would take her half an hour to drive, maybe longer. We settled in to wait. There was no small talk, more the urgent communiqués before battle.

"Violet, I wouldn't ask you to do this, but I think that you have the key."

"I'm sure I do. And I've used it to lock my memories away."

"I'd rather anyone have to go through this than you."

"I know that, Elliot. . . . What did you mean, you were there?"

"Harold and I were both there. We were called in to help— not that they let us. I've never forgiven myself for being backed-down. We could have found you, brought you back. I knew—I—knew—" I couldn't speak. "All those years—"

"Let me explain," Harold interrupted. "Elliot always said

there were five children. He said there were two unaccounted for."

"It's not your fault, Elliot. Tell him that, Harold. And tell those entities to stay the hell away."

"Stay the hell away, entities."

Was it my imagination, or did the room actually brighten? It wasn't my imagination—or Harold's powers, either.

"Ah. The sun's out," Violet said. Myself, I was glad to see it. If we were going back into that terrible darkness, we would need light to see by. "If the two of you could leave me alone for a few minutes—just until Dr. Kottlisky gets here, I'd like to try to get ready."

"I'd rather stay with you," I told her.

"I'm fine. I just want some quiet."

"You're sure?"

"Elliot, I said I am fine. Now, leave me alone . . . all right?"

"I'd rather—"

"I am not going to kill myself and take your clues to the grave. Don't worry. Now, get out, all right?"

Harold and I left Violet alone in his office, sitting amid his power masks and symbols of spiritual protection.

I had a few questions Harold could answer for me. We ducked into the small room where he kept his chemicals. I handed him the photo collection I had retrieved from Charles's hideout. I wondered if Charles had ever opened the trunk himself. I wanted to believe he had not.

"You like hell," Harold remarked, "and I mean that literally."

"Jesus, Harold. Don't you ever just weep? Wait till you look at these."

"And I will, but first, you look at this."

Harold handed me an open Bible and pointed me to the Fortieth Psalm.

I waited patiently for the Lord;
And he inclined unto me and heard my cry.
He brought me up also out of an horrible pit,
Out of the mirey clay, and set my feet upon rock.

I read about the mirey pit and God's rescue while Harold spread Freddy's photos on his desk. I saw him working with a magnifying loupe.

"The rings," he said. "I was right about them."

I finished the psalm and crossed to the desk. I was feeling steadier, if not better.

"Here." Harold stepped aside. "A cult, like we thought."

I looked through the loupe and sure enough saw the gold rings on the fingers of each of the togaed men. "Hey, Harold," I said. "Noonan, Vanilla, Nesbitt, Stoufley—one to go. A ring for each of them. But who's the last man? We've got five identical rings."

"No. I told you before. They only looked alike. One of them felt different. One, the first one, was a power ring. The man you're missing is the leader, and he took this picture."

"Some leader. Like that son of a bitch Jim Jones. That's a spiritual leader?"

"Ah, Elliot. After all these years, you still underestimate it."

" 'It.' You mean, 'evil'?"

"Evil, the shadow, the lie—call it what you want. The man you're looking for, the leader, has some kind of rationale. He sees good in the evil he is doing. True villains do not believe they are evil, Elliot. They believe they are doing a good. And in their upside-down universe, they are. The man you are looking for thinks he's a saint."

"Come on, Harold. You're into your shit again. One of the rings feels different. What am I supposed to do with that? I need facts, not feelings."

"Was I wrong about spiritual protection for you?"

"No. It was a good idea."

"Then listen to me. When we talk about these things, they're more than theory."

"You're telling me my Bible really moved?"

"You're telling me it didn't? It's called 'spiritual practice,' " Harold interrupted me, "because it can be practiced. It's not just theory or superstition, you know. When I talk about this stuff, I am telling you what I experience, not what I imagine."

"Well, God help us then," I said—not reverently.

"Oh," said Harold. "He will."

"Good," I said, "because I'm going to need him. If Dr. Kottlisky will let us, we're going back in that pit."

There was a light crunching on gravel and Harold peered out the window. "She's here," he said. "She is beautiful." I looked at Harold in surprise. Since the death of his wife, Ruth, ten years before, I had never heard him express interest in a woman. Yes, I supposed, Dr. Kottlisky was beautiful. She was a petite, elegant woman with soft, lush auburn hair—but I was focused on her strengths, not her beauty. Harold might have seen them as the same thing. I saw her as a member of a rescue team.

"Bring that Bible," Harold suggested to me. We left the little supply room and met Dr. Kottlisky at the door to the morgue.

"Hello, Detective. Hello, Doctor . . . Where is she?" she asked.

"Waiting inside," I told her. "She said she wanted to be alone to get ready."

"Let's go to her. That girl has been alone a long time already. I'm so glad to see she has allies now."

It struck me that Dr. Kottlisky's language paralleled Harold's, that she, too, saw us as engaged in a sort of crusade. Her eyes flicked to the Bible.

"Good idea," she said.

"A little spiritual protection," Harold murmured. He and Dr. Kottlisky locked eyes. A look of recognition passed between them. Here? I thought. Now? As naturally as if she'd always known him, Dr. Kottlisky folded her arm into Harold's and together we went inside. We found Violet sleeping, curled on the couch. She reminded me of a child, the way they sometimes drop asleep to avoid anxiety. I reached over and shook her gently by the shoulder.

"Wake up, Doctor. Wake up."

"Come on, dear," Dr. Kottlisky interjected.

Violet's eyelids fluttered. "Are we going?"

"Going where?" the doctor asked her.

"Back to . . . I'm not sure, but I am ready."

"Into the mirey pit," Harold said softly.

Violet rubbed her eyes, sat up, and looked from Harold to Dr. Kottlisky and back again.

"Hello, dear," said Dr. Kottlisky. "How are you feeling?"

"Ready," Violet answered again. "You were right that we weren't quite done when I left you, you know."

"Everyone moves at her own pace," the doctor told her.

"What do you need from us?" I asked.

"We'll make a circle," Dr. Kottlisky began. "Violet, we will do what we always did. I will count you back. You will never lose touch with me or with your adult self or with your allies here. You are completely safe and protected. You will have consorts, fellow travelers—you will not be going back to that place alone."

At the words "that place," I felt a hammering in my chest. I was frightened by what we were about to undertake.

"Doctor?" I interrupted her. "There's something you may need to know," I told her. "I was there. Not when it happened, just afterward."

"All right. Good. I'm glad you told me." Dr. Kottlisky glanced at Harold with surprise. "And you? You were there, too, weren't you?" Call it a hunch, an intuitive hit.

"I was there, too," Harold said. "We were young men then."

"Well, well, then . . . As a group, we are all gathered for a purpose. How interesting that it will take a circle of us . . . Shall we start?"

We did as the doctor directed, standing ranged around Violet's couch like a circle of protective sentries. The minute that image came to me, I winced. The ritual had occurred in a circle as well. Dr. Kottlisky's soft voice reassured me.

"Violet, I need you to know you are safe and protected with us. You will never be alone. We won't leave you." Dr. Kottlisky looked at each of us. "Is there anything else you want to say before we begin?" she asked.

I found I did have something I needed to say.

"I love this woman," I told her. "I need to know that what we are doing is safe. I need to know that she will heal."

Violet interrupted me. "I am a survivor, remember?" She reached up and squeezed my hand.

"She is healing," Dr. Kottlisky assured me. "It's part of regaining her health to go back."

"This will be a regression?" I asked Dr. Kottlisky. I wanted to be sure we were talking about the same thing.

"That's one word. I prefer 'a journey.' "

Just for a moment I wanted to bolt from the room, grab Violet by the hand, and flee. I remembered where we were going to. The park with its strange, fearsome terrain, its grotesque outcroppings of rock—the Devil's Needle, one outcropping was called, and rightly. I remembered the acrid smell of dead and dying vegetation, the loose, shaley terrain with its danger of copperheads, coiled and invisible in the leaves, which were golden and rust from the autumn chill, golden and rust with blood. I remembered the dreadful circle with its slain innocents in the points of its awful star.

"Elliot."

I snapped back to the room where they were waiting for me.

"I'm ready," I said. Harold was quietly lighting candles. I saw he had lit a braid of ceremonial sweet grass as well.

Now Dr. Kottlisky took Violet by the hand and asked her to stretch out fully on the couch where she had been sleeping. She covered her with a blanket Harold had folded at one end.

"I will count you back," she said. "We will start with where you are, safe and warm, here with us, at your present age, thirty-seven. We will take that safety with us, surrounding you and cocooning you, as I ask you to close your eyes and visualize a staircase. It has one step for each year of your age. As I count, you will descend the staircase. You will go slowly back, safely. Safely. Thirty-seven . . . You are moving down. Thirty-six . . . You are growing younger. Thirty-five . . ."

I tried to meet Harold's eyes, but he was concentrating on Violet, lying as still as one of his charges. Am I the only one who is frightened here, I wondered. Where do they get the faith? A dark alley, a blind staircase with a killer crouched at the top—those risks of my job were nothing compared to this. Suddenly I noticed the weight of the Bible, remembered the words of the psalm. I felt a sense of purpose stealing over me. Yes, I was ready, too.

"Nineteen . . . eighteen . . . You are completely safe. . . . We are going back. . . ."

"Oh!" It was a gasp, a sharp intake of breath from Violet, as if she had been punched. We all jumped. Violet's breathing quickened.

"You are safe. . . . We are with you. . . . You are protected. . . . Nod if you are ready to move on."

Violet nodded her head.

"Seventeen . . . sixteen . . . fifteen . . ." Violet was twisting her head from side to side. I thought I saw a tear sliding down one cheek.

"Fourteen . . . You are safe. We are with you. We are going back to the park. . . . You are thirteen . . . twelve . . ."

"I see it." A chill ran over me at the words.

"What do you see?"

"A park."

"Are you there yet?"

"No. I'm packing . . . Jack is taking us. We are going to make a movie, he says. In a park. We will have costumes. I love costumes. We will be stars, he says, little twinkly stars. . . ."

Violet's voice was clear and young, a child's voice, telling. It took me a while to know what was happening. The transformation was complete and eerie. Before our eyes, Violet's voice and manner were turning younger and younger. A girl again.

"Mom wants us to go. She's excited. I got a special suitcase, a pink hair dryer, and a new little stuffed dog, blue and white, named Winky. I don't know why."

"And your brother?" Dr. Kottlisky was gentle and very calm.

"Freddy wants to stay home. He hates Jack and doesn't like the others, either, but they give him money."

"What others?"

"Jack's friends. His playmates, he calls them."

"Who are they?"

"We aren't supposed to know their names. It's a secret club, Jack says. That's why they have special rings. Pretty rings with stars on them."

I felt a tremor surge through me. I knew which rings, and I knew which stars—the upside-down pentacles Zachary doodled. I knew what Violet was describing and I knew that my son was also its victim, two decades later.

"Uncle Jack told Freddy we were going to make a movie."

"Do you make a movie?" I asked her. At the sound of my voice, Violet appeared confused.

"It's all right," Dr. Kottlisky told her. "I told you that you would have guardians. They can ask questions, too. He is a protector. A friend. Now answer his question. Do you make a movie?"

"I think so. Everybody wants to make a movie, especially Jack and the leader."

"The leader? Isn't Jack the leader?"

"Oh, no. Not Jack. Huh-uh."

"Go on, dear. You were telling us about the movie—"

Violet nodded, eyes closed, hands balled into fists. "They're saying it is just like dress-up. We have dresses, pretty white dresses. They have dresses, too. Long white dresses with hoods on top. We've got little ones . . . oh! Oh! They're making us watch things! They want us to watch! They have a goat. He's a baby goat. He's black and gray and white. Oh, no!"

Violet was growing agitated, twisting her body side to side, shaking her head so tears flew from her squinted eyes. "They're killing it!" she sobbed. "And the chickens! Two chickens! Oh, no! They make us watch. . . . They make us watch more!"

Suddenly Violet's body grew rigid. I could see her eyes racing beneath her lids.

"Watch what?"

"They make us watch them hurt the other kids, they cut them. They're cutting them!"

"They cut them?"

"Yes."

"Do you know where you are? Where they took you?"

"To the woods. They took us to the woods. We're supposed to lie down on this circle. They have this knife, this bad knife, all twisty like a snake!"

I knew now why Violet had collapsed at the sight of the kris. I was lucky I hadn't pushed her into madness.

"It's all right, dear. You're safe," Dr. Kottlisky reassured her.

"I'm not safe. I'm lost. I'm lost. It's cold. I can't find Freddy. . . . I'm lost. I don't know where I am. . . ."

Violet started sobbing.

"They said it was a movie. They said it would be fun. We'd have costumes and other kids to play with."

"Was it a movie? Violet, did you make a movie?" I pressed for the answer.

"Yes . . . no . . . I don't know. I got away, but they kept Freddy. I couldn't get him. They took him away. . . ."

"Who?"

"Uncle Carson."

"Who else?"

"Uncle Jack. All the men."

"Where was your mommy?"

"She was sick. She couldn't take care of us. She gave us away. . . ." Violet was retching. She heaved and shook.

"You are safe. You are safe," Dr. Kottlisky said. "You can remember. You can tell us."

But Violet dropped silent. She sat frozen except for two steady streams of tears that ran straight as string down each of her cheeks. She was watching the inner movie, I knew that. But what was she seeing?

"Violet?" I tried to reach her.

"Shh." Dr. Kottlisky motioned me "shh" with a finger to her lips.

"Go on, dear," she urged. "What do you see?"

Violet frowned in concentration. "They are letting Freddy hold the camera. They say he can if he touches them."

"If he touches them where?"

"On their pee-pees. The leader likes Freddy. He doesn't like me."

"Is that how you get away?"

"Maybe."

"Do you run away, Violet?"

"Maybe."

"Does Freddy?"

"No. He touches them and they let him hold the camera. He's safe now, they tell him. But I'm not. They are doing something to the camera. They drop something. I run. I run away. I run and I run."

"You are right to run, Violet."

"They are killing them! They are killing them!" Violet suddenly shrieked, her voice skittering high with terror. "Run! Run, Freddy! Run!" Violet was gasping for air, sobbing, hysterical.

I gestured stop. Stop! Dr. Kottlisky shook her head "No."

Even as she spoke, the wave seemed to pass and Violet grew steadier.

"You're all right, Violet," she insisted. "You are safe. We are with you. . . . Where are you now?"

Violet did not answer. She was silent for so long that I thought we had lost her. Then she spoke.

"I got away," she said flatly. "I left Freddy. I left my brother there."

"You were right to run, Violet. Freddy chose to stay. That was safer for him. You both did what was safe for you. Freddy was right to stay and you were right to run. Can't you see that? You didn't abandon each other. You saved yourselves."

On the couch, Violet's tensely hunched shoulders began to drop. I could see her working with this idea, trying it out.

"You needed to run. He needed to stay," Dr. Kottlisky repeated firmly, persuasively. "You both did what felt safe to you. There's no guilt. There's no guilt anymore, Violet. You were wise. You were very wise. So was your brother. You saved yourselves. That was smart, Violet. Both of you were smart. Both of you survived. Just different ways . . ."

There was a softening in Violet's tense features. A slow smile stole across her face. Maybe with the help of suggestion she really was able to work things through.

"I am going to move you forward now. . . . I want you to go to the next significant point in time. . . . Where are you now, Violet?"

"I'm down by the river. They see me . . . I'm cold."

"Do you tell them who you are? What happened to you?"

"No. I can't remember. I can't remember—"

She didn't remember running, terrified and bleeding, through the woods. But I remembered her tracks, the way they had led to a cliff over a small river, the way I knew the child had to have jumped.

Violet began sobbing softly again.

"Are you okay?" I asked.

Violet shook her head side to side: no.

I didn't try to reason with her, didn't try to tell her she'd been right to run away, right to leave her brother and the memories behind her.

"Violet?" She didn't seem to hear me. I reached for her hands, cold. "Violet?" I held them in my own. Harold and Dr. Kottlisky sat quietly back, content to let us be.

"The mind is a powerful thing," Dr. Kottlisky told her. "It was protecting you."

Slowly and carefully, Dr. Kottlisky worked at bringing her back. As we watched, Violet's face took on its familiar adult expression, alert and wary. Her lids fluttered. She was with us again, an adult now, remembering.

"I didn't remember that knife, those rings—I didn't remember. I didn't remember the animals, the chickens, and the goats. I didn't remember Freddy."

Violet Winters remembered her name three months after they found her, bruised, bleeding, nearly naked, crouched and shivering on the riverbank. She had jumped more than fifty feet from the cliff above, landing in the shallows, just deep enough to break her fall, just swift enough to carry her down stream as she struggled to the bank.

Violet remembered her brother Fred and his name, three years after they found her. Her new parents told her there was no finding her brother, and the memories she had of him retreated as her new life advanced.

This is what she told us as we sat in Harold's office. I invoked grace. I wanted to hear this story clinically, like a good cop, but it was hard. No, impossible.

I knew what she didn't—that her brother was Fred Fury and the probable killer I was seeking, the probable molestor of my son. I wanted to find the son of a bitch and kill him. Harold and Dr. Kottlisky knew that. I could feel them willing me to go easy with her.

"Elliot, I saw my brother," Violet said with wonder.

"You miss him?" I finally asked.

"The Freddy I remember doesn't exist anymore," Violet said. "It's years since that Freddy went away."

"And he never found you?" I was thinking of her satin jacket, still wondering if she was hiding him, even now.

"Funny. You could say he found me. His memory found me, eventually. Even though I was in good hiding."

I asked what she meant.

"Tell him your story," Dr. Kottlisky urged. "It is a success story, you know. In the end."

Violet told us then about her three foster homes and eventual adoption.

"You could say I was very lucky. I was also very pretty, bright, and presentable, which improved my odds. I was placed in a home, a good one, miraculously enough, and I was so grateful, I set out to be the perfect child."

"Meaning?"

"I got straight A's. I never talked back. I wanted them to keep me, and they did. I graduated as valedictorian of my high school class, won a scholarship from the St. Xavier nuns for my hard-luck story and my grades, even though I was officially Baptist. I was dean's list all the way through college, top of my class in med school, and the perfect, indefatigable resident after that. In short, I was pretty much perfect. Then it all began to fall apart. I began to have the dreams—I guess I should say the memories—I couldn't sleep. I thought I would shake apart."

"And that's how we met," Dr. Kottlisky put in.

"You were a miracle worker," Violet told her.

"Nonsense. You worked like hell. . . ."

"But I didn't remember everything. Not until today . . . Have I remembered everything?"

"I think you've remembered all that you need to. The mind is a good doctor, Violet. Trust it. You did good work today. You were very brave."

"But am I finished?"

"None of us is ever finished, dear. But, yes, I think you've faced the worst."

"So where do we go from here?" Violet asked me.

"Perhaps it might be better for you to stay with the doctor—" I began.

"On the contrary," interrupted Dr. Kottlisky. "She's done her work with me. Violet is not the fragile flower her name suggests. She belongs in her current life—belongs with you, it would seem, Detective."

"But I have work to do—"

"We both have work to do," Violet insisted. "Zachary was molested, but so was I. It's my crime we are solving as much as yours, Elliot."

I glanced at Dr. Kottlisky. She nodded her okay.

"Then we're going for proof," I told her. "We're going to solve the crime that hurt you and my son."

I thanked Dr. Kottlisky and left her to talk with Harold. I had the sense they had years of conversations ahead of them. I bundled Violet into my car. She seemed fragile, but gaining.

"Where are we actually going?" Violet asked me.

"Into Harold's dream," I told her. "He dreamed about Ricky Noonan and X-ray eyes."

At the Amoco on Ohio, I called Peter Abramson and checked on my search warrant. All set and waiting. Good. I called the *Trib*'s Big Name Columnist, an old neighborhood guy, and promised him a hot scoop if he'd pull his microfilm for me on the state park murders twenty years ago May. If I died, I wanted someone on the story.

Then I drove us to Ricky Noonan's.

Chicago is a two-layered city: the city and the undergrid of a city, a whole separate set of streets one hundred feet below the surface. I went into the underground at Canal and came up five minutes later a block from Ricky Noonan's place on the Magnificent Mile.

"Nice work," Violet said, sounding with us again.

"In another life I was a cabbie."

I showed badge to get into Ricky's condominium and assured one Mr. Don Curry, the building manager. He bowed himself out, looking worried. He didn't ask for a warrant.

"What are we looking for?" Violet wanted to know.

"X-rated eyes. According to Myerling's dream, Ricky's got something forbidden here. Nobody's supposed to see it. The only question is where. Where would Ricky Noonan hide a secret so terrible, he died to protect it?"

"How's your stomach, Elliot?"

"Why do you ask?"

Violet went straight to Noonan's bedroom, straight to a handsome ebony bureau, straight to its third drawer, right-hand side.

"Here." She reached in the drawer and tossed me a pair of black leather men's underwear featuring chains and a cut-out crotch. "I went looking for a handkerchief one night."

"I bet Noonan shit a brick when you found those. What did he say?" Poor Ricky Noonan.

"He said they were a joke gift from one of his old law clients. He had to say something."

My cop poked me: remember. Remember what? Then I knew. Johnny Vanilla, Mr. Sex Himself, had once been a client of Ricky Noonan's. He'd handled Johnny's divorce from Esther. And handled it well. Maybe Johnny Vanilla had given Noonan the S&M gear. There is a "bond" in bondage.

"See if you can find anything else. I'm checking the library," I told Violet.

"You mean the TV room? Ricky never read anything, but even the nights I was here he'd hole up in there for hours, watching videos."

Of course! X-rated eyes. Suddenly I knew, or thought I knew, what I was looking for. A film.

Ricky Noonan's library had everything you'd expect a judge's library to have, and then some more: a saltwater fish tank, Audubon prints, outsized globe nearly the size of the real thing. The nine-foot walnut shelves held rows of glossy leather-bound legal tomes, a row of tony first editions, another row of hardcover crime books, the kind favored by Book of the Month.

On impulse, I pulled out a book. When I pulled the book out, something rattled. The book wasn't a book at all. It was an elaborately disguised videocassette.

"What did you find?" Violet stood in the doorway.

I pulled out a second book. Same thing. I reached next for Truman Capote's *In Cold Blood*. It held a video, too.

"I don't know. Some video."

"Let me show you the setup."

Violet moved aside an Audubon print to reveal a wall-recessed television and VCR.

"Let's take a look." She took the cassette from my hand and popped it into the VCR.

In the late seventies, something called "snuff films" began surfacing in New York and Los Angeles. They were advertised, rightly, as cinéma verité. They were actual footage of the torture and murder of women. Most of them came from South America, some from Germany and Holland.

What Ricky had hidden behind the burgundy leather of his specially bound edition was in cold blood, all right. Violet and I watched, horrified, as the murder proceeded.

"They're really going to kill her," Violet said.

The door buzzer sounded. I flicked off the set and went out to the intercom.

"Yes?"

"You about finished up there?" It was Mr. Curry sounding hot under the collar.

"Just about."

"I'd like to lock up and show you out."

"Give us another ten," I told him.

Back in the library, Violet was holding out another film.

"I found it," she said. "*The Wizard of Oz*. Ricky always said it was his favorite. 'My autobiography,' he called it. He said we'd watch it together someday. Then he'd snicker, this really ugly little snicker—I'll bet— Do you suppose a judge thinks of himself as a wizard? I mean, they both wear robes and—"

We were both laughing, so it took us a minute to see the screen. When we did, I gagged.

"Oh, Jesus," Violet said.

Onscreen, dressed in togas, carrying willow branches and wearing crowns of fake gold leaves, three young boys proceeded to walk solemnly along an archway of trees. The togas were open down the sides, so there was the occasional flash of flesh.

"You don't want to watch this," I told her. "You really don't."

I knew what it was. So did she.

Violet pointed to the screen. Where the three young men had walked a moment earlier, two young children walked now, a boy and a girl—snowy-haired blonds, innocent as Christmas angels. Violet and her brother, I guessed.

"Stop it," she said. "Make it stop." She was shaking violently.

I pushed freeze frame. Violet buried her head in her hands. She was rocking back and forth, shaking, shaking.

Onscreen, the image was frozen on the two children dressed in ceremonial white, walking side by side below the canopy of trees. At my side, Violet began sobbing softly. I stroked her back. I slid Ricky's video under my shirt.

"Even when I remembered, I never thought it could really be a movie," she said. "I thought they just told us that. How did I ever get away?"

"You were the girl," I told her softly. "Maybe they weren't as interested in you. And maybe you didn't really get away."

The intercom sounded again. I wondered who was paying off the building manager, and how much he'd lose for every minute we dawdled.

"We're leaving now, Violet," I said. I held her arm and led her out the door. She was a little wobbly on her feet.

Down in the lobby, we parade-marched right past Don Curry. He had picked up the phone before we cleared the revolving door. It occurred to me that visiting Ricky Noonan's had been smart and dumb. Whoever Don Curry was reporting to—probably the same someone Noonan had died protecting—would know we were there.

Chapter fifty-seven

———■———

Walking Violet Winters into the night air, I explained to her she was now in my protective custody—no matter how it might seem. I emphasized protective and custody.

"I'm a hostage?"

"Something like that."

"How romantic. I'd like to stop at my place," Violet said. "I could use a change of clothes and to water my plants—that is not a metaphor."

I took the bag of Fred Fury porno films off the passenger seat and told Violet to fasten her seat belt.

"Maybe you should level with me, Elliot. Tell me what you know. Let me help."

"You have helped." I wasn't about to tell her who her brother had turned out to be and that we were really looking for him.

"You're patronizing me again."

"Okay. Guilty."

"So tell me," she pressed.

"I'm not sure that's such a good idea—but getting the hell out of here is.

"Violet?"

"Yes, Elliot."

"I can't tell you what I don't know. What I do know, or at least suspect, is that whoever brutalized you and your brother may be doing the same thing to other children twenty-five years later. I also think, sometimes a victim becomes a perpetrator."

"Fuck you."

"What's the anger for?"

"You think that I just might be a multiple personality, willing and able to chop men's dicks off? Yours, for example?"

"It's still a possibility."

"Thanks, Elliot. So's nuclear war."

"I'd be equally upset by both."

That line made her laugh. It made me laugh, too.

When we arrived at her building, I parked, grabbed the bag of films, and we walked past the sleeping Doberman and wide-eyed surveillance cameras. The guard was nowhere in evidence. Violet called the key-operated elevator. We rode its whir to her floor.

"Don't try to seduce me, Doctor."

"Don't try so hard not to be seduced. That's a seduction, too, Elliot."

At her door, she punched her seven-digit entry code. God, she was pretty, especially when she laughed and shook out her pale, pale hair.

"I remember this place," Violet said, unlocking her door. "I used to live here. Jesus Christ, Elliot. Look!"

I did look. A poster-sized photo of Violet giving head was tacked to the wall in her entryway. I could barely look at it. On the other hand, I couldn't not look. Looking is my job. In the photo, Violet appeared dazed, and not with lust. She looked barely conscious. I wondered what drug they'd used, some super Mickey Finn.

Violet ran for the bathroom. I could hear her retching. I felt like retching myself. I heard the toilet flush, heard Violet padding toward me.

"I don't remember any of this," Violet said. She was back from the bathroom, several shades of pale. "How could they do that to me? It's like necrophilia."

"I'm sorry."

"Fuck you." She was fighting back tears.

"Big deal, Violet. What's a little blackmail between friends? At least we know what your blackouts were now. At least you weren't killing people during them. You were just giving head. That's all."

That broke her up. She started laughing, really laughing, doubled over, rib-ache laughing. I'd never heard her do that, and it sounded nice.

"You're okay, Elliot," she managed between spasms.

"You're okay, too." I grabbed her in a friendly bear hug and she turned to me with lots of little kisses, joke kisses at first. Then we were into the real thing.

I had my hand on the small of her back, and the arch of her against me felt the way it looked in the movies. This was it, True Romance. Kissing Violet Winters under that blowjob blow-up poster felt as new to me as high school love. I'm reluctant to say that maybe being in over your head from murder and blackmail feels the way teen kisses used to, but it's true. I waltzed Violet Winters away from that poster, kicked off my shoes, and sank to the floor right in the middle of the living room. I didn't care about killers. I didn't care about crime. What I cared about was her collarbone and the way kissing it led me to her breast.

"This is where I came in," I said, kissing a snowy slope. Kissing it again.

"So do that," said Violet Winters. "Come in."

I believe in strong coffee, love at first sight, and second chances. With Violet Winters, I was enjoying all three. I woke up in the middle of a good Persian rug, with a good mug of coffee beside me—but no sign of Violet. My wallet was open, badge out, and my pockets were emptied on the parquet floor four feet away. I felt like I'd just been rolled and the take was my heart.

"Violet?"

No answer.

"Violet?" Maybe she was out walking Salvation.

"Maybe you should be talking to me instead."

I whirled at the sound of the voice, and a man stepped forward. I say man, but what I saw first was Violet Winters, my lover now, dressed as a man. He/she moved toward me stiffly, gun in hand. He/she looked very thin and deathly ill.

"I see by your notebook you were trying to pay me a little visit. Took you long enough, Detective. I've been expecting you since your little visit to Eden Books. I'm Freddy Fury, Violet's brother. . . . And you're not Sherlock Holmes."

"Where's Violet?"

"Out of harms's way."

"If you hurt her—"

"You'll what? Don't you think you've hurt her yourself, Detective? Screwing her on the floor like some goddamn whore." Freddy did sound brotherly and protective.

"It wasn't like that." I told him.

"Drink your coffee."

I wanted to say, You son of a bitch, did you fuck my son,

kill my friend Ricky Noonan, blackmail your own sister? If so, you deserve to die.

I said it. What the fuck?

Freddy Fury laughed at me. "I see why she likes you," he said. "I could like you myself."

There was something so lascivious in his tone that I must have recoiled. Freddy laughed.

"A little homophobic, are we? Don't worry, I didn't spit in your coffee."

"AIDS?"

"What else? I'm a pornographer. Safe sex just wasn't as erotic to my viewing public."

"A simple case of aesthetics."

"I see it that way."

"You would. Oh, and thanks for all your little clues. Nice stationery." My sarcasm surprised me.

"Hers, actually. We got it when she was fourteen."

"That's a gun you're holding. I never pull one unless I'm going to use it. I say we skip the preliminaries and you just kill me, cut my dick off, send somebody a note about it. Either that or blow your own fucking head to little bits."

"Temper, temper." Freddy was laughing at me again, a racking spasm that turned to coughing. Reflexively, I took out my handkerchief.

"Chivalry's not dead? Too bad I nearly am."

Freddy gestured toward the dining room table, indicating a chair for me and another for himself. We sat down with the black lacquered table gleaming expensively between us.

"We're supposed to make small talk?" All I could think of was the terrible tear in my son, Zach.

"Ask your son about me if that's what's got you so mad you're trying to make me kill you," Freddy said.

"I'd ask, but he doesn't remember a thing. He's blanked it out."

"Come on, Elliot. My sister's a doctor. Do regressions if you want to know."

"I'm not sure I want him to remember."

"Funny how people deal with things, isn't it? My sister forgot everything, even me. I remembered every single bit."

"And loved it all, no doubt."

I was baiting Freddy and couldn't quite say why. He had a Walther PBK trained directly at me, and I had not one doubt he was right, and I was trying to goad him into killing me. Maybe I just wanted to get it over with.

"You could have saved a lot of time just by having your sister introduce us."

"Ah. You're a nasty man, Detective Mayo. You think my sister is lying to you. My sister lies only to herself. When she says she doesn't know me, she believes that. She doesn't know she knows me, if you know what I mean."

"You've lost me."

"Exactly. She's lost me and I've found her, and she's never found out, not all these years. I dress like her. I talk like her. I smile, I talk, I walk like her, and she doesn't even know I exist. I've had a key to everywhere she's lived for the past fifteen years."

"If you have a key, why keep breaking her skylight?"

"Crude. That's not me. That's somebody imitating me who lacks my skills. Somebody trying to scare me as much as you. Keep her, me, all of us off base."

"Where is your sister now?"

"Asleep in the bedroom, enjoying a long winter's nap, just like you did." My stomach did a long, slow somersault.

"Gas?"

"Yes. I'm afraid I started with poppers and moved on to

the hard stuff. Do you know how long you can come on anesthesia?"

"I can imagine."

"Yes. And I can remember. I've had an interesting life. That's why I want you to kill me."

I spilled my coffee and it beaded up on the slick black table. I looked into Freddy's thin face. He was serious.

"I can't kill you, Freddy."

"Sure you can. Here. Take the gun."

Freddy slid the Walther PBK across the table. I grabbed for it, but he beat me. Quick as a snake.

"You wouldn't have done it anyhow," he said. "Not yet. You're too interested in solving all your crimes to just plain kill me. But you're slow, Detective. I'm running out of time. Think about it. You know that it's not me blackmailing Violet—or Richard Noonan, either, God bless him."

"What about my cousin Charles? Your biggest fan as it turns out. Now he's missing."

"Is he missing? He doesn't return my calls. I rather thought he'd told you about me. After all, blood is thicker than friendship—or unrequited love. My guess would have been that Charles would give you my files and speed your process up a little."

"I'm not at liberty—"

Freddy cocked his head slightly, amused with us both. He laughed his dreadful, phlegm-riddled laugh.

"You are going to figure this out, Detective. That's why I picked you. I wanted someone who would solve the crime behind the crimes."

"Why don't you just tell me? I could use a little help."

"Ruins the game."

"Give me one piece. One."

"All right. One."

"Johnny Vanilla?"

"Not mine. A copycat."

"That's what I said!" I crowed.

Freddy liked the game. Liked the fact I was playing with him. Find out what they eat and feed it to them.

"Give me another piece. One more question," I goaded him.

"Okay. But you can't ask me anything you already know. It has to be something only I could know."

I thought about asking— Then I realized there was really only one question.

". . . Are you done yet?"

Freddy fired, but not with the gun. His left hand came up, canister ready, and he had me maced before I could jerk away. I tumbled off my chair, clawing at my face.

"Sorry," Freddy said, "but I didn't want to shoot you."

I couldn't see to watch him, but I knew he was gone. I heard the door click shut, the elevator whir.

Have you ever been maced? Maybe having your fingernails pulled out feels worse. I staggered to the kitchen, got the water turned on, held my eyes open, and ran water straight onto them. I did it for five minutes, until I wasn't blind anymore, just wounded. When I was done, they were bloodred, but much improved—and Violet Winters was standing groggily in the doorway.

"We just had a visit from someone," I told her. "Someone you used to know."

She wobbled a little. "I feel so weak."

"You were gassed."

"Gassed?" She slumped against the doorway. I knew I had to get it over with. She had to know.

"Your brother was here. We took a little nap, and he made sure yours lasted long enough for him to talk to me."

"My brother?" she repeated. "My brother?"

We might as well get it over with, I thought. I picked up the bag of porno films and crossed to the VCR. I cued one up. "A Fred Fury Film," the credits announced.

"Never heard of him," Violet said.

I thought of stopping the film, but before I could, Freddy's face loomed onscreen. Violet stared in stark horror. Freddy was in full drag. He was very convincingly a woman, and "It's me. He's . . . me," Violet whispered. "That's even my dress, or—"

She leaned forward, drawn in, fascinated and frightened.

"My brother?" she managed. She was off the couch, across the room, staring at the screen. I pushed eject. Violet whirled on me.

"I want to watch it."

"We don't have time."

"That's my brother. I'm sure of it. What's he doing?"

"Killing people, I think." I popped out the cassette. "Killing everyone connected to the crime in the park—all of the perpetrators of his induction into darkness, you might say."

"Why am I in danger, then? He wouldn't want to kill me."

"I don't think your brother is the only killer. We still don't know who the leader was, remember? I think the leader is just as determined to stop Freddy as Freddy is to stop him. You're Freddy's Achilles' heel—and, therefore, you're in danger."

"I think you're forgetting something," Violet said. "I think Zachary is your Achilles' heel."

"I haven't forgotten that. That's where we're going."

Chapter fifty-eight

———■———

Ten minutes across town, and then I was on the Kennedy. I was pushing it north as fast as I could. Violet, pallid as the new moon rising, sat quietly beside me. I wondered how she felt knowing her brother was alive and not well and visiting her regularly? Not very good, I suspected.

"Elliot? That was my dress in that video."

"What are you saying, Violet?"

"I'm saying that man—my brother—looked like me on purpose. The cleaners said they lost it. I don't think that's true, Elliot. Do you?"

"No. I don't think it's true." I glanced at Violet. She was staring intently out the window, chewing on her lower lip.

"But there's coincidence."

"Don't patronize me, Elliot. Lies of omission are still lies. Didn't the Jesuits tell you that?"

"What am I not telling you?"

"How crazy am I, Elliot?"

I reached across and grabbed her by one icy hand. Myerling had brought her back, but she was slipping away

413

again. Jamie was in the hospital. My place and hers were opened up like cans whenever the fancy struck. No wonder she was scared.

"You're not so crazy, Violet." I squeezed her hand and let it go.

"Are you sure? Are you positive?" she asked.

"Going sane feels just like going crazy," I assured her. Where did I get that line?

We were forty minutes north of the city and speeding farther into the country. A sickle moon rode the western fields to my left. Low, dark clouds scudded to the right. You could smell the extra ozone that boded a summer storm.

"I think I'm crazy," Violet said. "Maybe."

"Maybe not. Maybe it's just aftershock."

"Don't do that. I told you, don't patronize me, Elliot. That makes me crazy."

"Okay. What are you scared of?"

Violet reached across and took my hand again. She dug her nails in as she told me.

"When they started? The murders, I mean. I was scared they could be my doing. I knew on some level I had to want to do them. I certainly had motive with Jack and with Johnny, and I wondered—"

"I wondered the same thing, Violet. We call you 'suspects' because we suspect."

"I mean I really thought so, Elliot. I had to go back through my calendar and check. I wanted to know where I was every minute. I didn't want any blocks of time unaccounted for. I drove my secretary crazy. My head nurse was very concerned. I told them both I was doing it for a big paper I was working up. I don't know that they believed me, but we managed to track me down."

"You could have asked my help, too. I had you placed, except for that one missing evening."

"Johnny Vanilla."

Violet said it so flatly, I wanted to drive straight into a tree. If this was a confession, it was delivered like a summons.

"Something you haven't told me? Like you killed him?"

"I met him for drinks. That night."

"I thought you hated him."

"I did hate him. It was blackmail. He still wanted to bring me down for interfering with his sex life by taking away his favorite victim."

"Blackmail. Did you pay him off?"

"Fate intervened. He died."

"And you killed him?"

"I was afraid I had."

"Come on, Violet, you'd remember a little thing like a killing."

"Given my past, I'm not so sure of that. Are you? The mind is powerful. According to Dr. Kottlisky. Is it powerful enough to hide my being a murderer?"

The question hung in the air between us. We both knew the answer was yes and no. We both knew, as Violet said, that not only was the mind powerful, hers was trained in repression.

"I had reason to kill him," Violet said. She said it like facts are facts.

"He fuck you over somehow? In addition to the blackmail, I mean?"

"He fucked me."

This hit me with violence. I was jealous. I was sickened. I was very, very angry. I counted ten, then spoke.

"I thought you said you'd never been with him. I thought you said he was scum."

"He was scum."

I signaled the turn that would take me off on the long country road where Ricky Noonan had died. Violet still had my hand clutched in hers. She was ruining my palm with her nails.

"He raped me."

"What?"

"He raped me. I ran an abused women's group. He'd qualified one of the women for it and he was pretty mad when she sought help and stopped going along with his little games. It took me six months, but I got her to divorce him— Forget I said that, okay?"

"Esther?"

"Elliot, I can't. Client privilege."

"You're right. Go on."

"So one night, I'm leaving the hospital and somebody grabs me from behind. I'm blindfolded, beaten, raped—raped everywhere. I know it was him. He had this ring—"

I thought I knew which ring.

"You didn't report it?"

"It was when I was dating Ricky Noonan. I told him. I know it was Johnny Vanilla, and I did know, because I saw his ring."

"Ricky tells you not to press charges?"

"He told me it would ruin my practice and that the case would never stick. He said maybe lots of people had the very same ring—gold, heavy, with a star."

"You believed him?"

"Ricky's a judge, Elliot, and a good guy, I believed then." Violet broke off, stared out the window. "When it comes to Johnny Vanilla, I think the killer could be me. And don't forget my shiners, the photos, the whole mess. Where was I,

Elliot? Did I really make it safely home, drink a loaded scotch, and fall asleep? I hope so."

"I haven't forgotten any of it, Violet."

We were running west now, straight toward the forest preserve where Ricky Noonan took his life, alone or with help. I did not doubt Violet's story about Johnny Vanilla, and I understood her fantasy about killing him herself. I just didn't think she had. That was either an instinct for truth or rock-solid denial.

"I want you to do me a big favor," I asked her.

"You trust me?"

"Yes, or I wouldn't ask. I want you to regress my son. You can do that, can't you?"

Violet stared out the window into time, not space, before she answered.

"I could do it, yes. I do regressions, but I think you might find it difficult," she said.

"Why? Zach knows you and likes you. He might feel safe."

"And you might want to shoot the messenger if we find terrible news."

"What else are we going to find? My son's been raped; your brother's the prime suspect."

"I guess what I am trying to say, Elliot, is that I don't want to risk losing you. A regression can be savage. You saw that with me. After it's over, you may never want to see the doctor again, knowing that they know."

"I have to think of Zachary," I told her. "I can't think of us right now. It's possible Zachary can tell us who the leader is. If Zachary does know, that knowledge could get him killed. You have to help me."

"Then I will."

Suddenly, I noticed the headlights coming up behind me,

closing fast. Damn! Soon as I noticed them, the lights went dark. I pressed the accelerator.

"Elliot?"

"Check your seat belt."

"Elliot?"

"Now!"

The car that hit us first came from behind. It eased into us and shoved. I fought to keep the road.

"Brace yourself!" I snapped, fighting to keep the wheel. I'm a strong driver, and I managed to hold the road. I powered ahead instead of braking. I wasn't going to do what poor Ricky Noonan did, slow down and head for safety and certain death.

"Maybe we should—"

The second car came running straight toward us, lights on high beam, moving on our lane of road. I took the risk and held my own lane. Let them use the shoulder or hit us head-on. They were out to kill us one way or another. They swerved. We clipped their taillight. They bought the ditch.

"Who are they?" Violet asked.

"Whoever killed Johnny Vanilla. Whoever doesn't want us to get to them or to my son, who may know how to find them."

"My brother?"

"No. Whoever your brother is still after. The leader."

Freddy couldn't drive two cars at once. I had killers, plural, to deal with. I was chasing one and another ran back of me. The crime behind the crime, Freddy had said.

The next pass would be live ammo. A mile ahead, the retreat house turnoff lay to the right. I flicked off my lights and raced toward it. The sickle moon did me no favors. The road was dark and narrow.

"Angel of God, our guardian dear, to whom God's love

commits us here, ever this day be at our side, to light and guard, to rule and guide." Violet began praying aloud.

The retreat house turnoff now lay just ahead. The first car was gaining again. A shot rang out as I slid my car into the turn. Just as I did, a huge rogue deer vaulted onto the road. I heard the sickening thud, followed by the crash.

Chapter fifty-nine

———■———

As soon as I came to a halt, the light by the retreat house door blazed on and Father Bremner flung open the door, gesturing us to quickly come inside.

"Safe and sound," he said. For one terrible moment I wondered if he was one of them. Was he aware because of spiritual attainment or collusion? Had I delivered Zach into their hands? Were Violet and I walking into a trap instead of a sanctuary?

"Elliot." He met my eyes. "You're safe here. Come in."

Father Bremner was throwing the dead bolt on the door. I was relieved he was invoking more than spiritual protection. Events can have a velocity any longtime cop can tell you about.

To see it on TV, you think police work is all fast action. Cops and robbers, chase scenes, shootouts. Truth is, ninety-eight percent of all police work is the paper chase, the frustrating business of checking stories, returning calls. An investigation is a slow and tedious business. The worst of them take years. Facts accumulate and so do mistakes. Mistakes are discovered, new facts are found, corrections are made, and then one day there is a quickening, a shift, and abruptly the investigation has a velocity of its own. The pieces move into place and the gears of discovery rumble to life. I try to hurry this process. That's what I'm doing when I drop down the well. I'm shouting an invitation.

I'd sent one such call to Freddy Fury, and he'd responded. What I hadn't known then I knew now: Freddy Fury was my killer, but he was committing executions more than murders. He was meting out justice, his version of justice, for crimes done. Those crimes were the source of the velocity I was sensing now. Events were rushing toward an end, but what events and what end still eluded me—as I'd escaped them, until now.

"You were praying, I suppose?" Violet asked him.

He nodded mildly. I was thinking that deer was one hell of an answered prayer. He smiled at Violet like a long-lost daughter.

"Father Bremner, Violet Winters, Violet, Father Bremner."

"Follow me," Father Bremner was saying. "We'll sit by the fire and get our wits about us. It's a good thing Zach and I made brownies."

He led us down the long, echoing hallway to the comfortable old library with its mullioned windows and fire. In front of that fire, neatly set out on a large round hassock, were four place settings with brownies and milk.

"Aren't we missing someone?" Violet asked, taking her spot, back to the fire, the better to fight spiritual chills.

"He'll be here," said Father Bremner. "I told him to get into his pajamas and robe."

I chose my seat next to Violet and left Father Bremner to his customary one, staring into the fire.

"We used to leave cookies and milk for Santa," Violet told Father Bremner.

"For the angels and Christ the Traveler," Father Bremner said.

"What about for me? Don't I get cookies?" Zachary stood in the doorway, rubbing his eyes and grinning. "Hi, Dad," he said.

"I knew we put those brownies out for someone," Father Bremner teased. Zach came to hug me, and in passing Father Bremner, socked the old priest playfully in the arm.

"Hi, kiddo."

"Hi, Father. Hi, Dad."

"Hi, Zachary." This from Violet.

"Hi—"

"You remember Dr. Winters, Zachary? You met her at the hospital."

"Sure. You're the lady who looks like my guardian angel."

"Ah," said Violet.

Father Bremner sat back calmly. Zach, Violet, and I went through our greetings, settled into our brownies, sipped at our milk. I noticed Father Bremner had a small Bible by his chair, a large crucifix, and three vials of sacred oil—the kind they use for extreme unction. Father Bremner was alert and calm. I had the sense he was expecting a cue, and when he got it, he would begin.

The fire in the fireplace crouched and receded. Father Bremner reached for his Bible. The fire leapt up and roared. Zachary wore a look of resolution. He frowned and stared into the fire.

"You're not scaring me," he said. "I know who you are and you can't scare me anymore."

"Who is it, Zachary?" Violet asked. She moved her chair closer.

"Zachary?" I started to interrupt, but Father Bremner signaled me "shhh" with a wave of his hand. This was not my drama, and Violet and he were trained for what they were doing. Call it a hypnotic regression, call it an exorcism, call it what you will, we were there to rid my son of his demons, to hear the story he had to tell.

"Zachary, I'm going to help you," Violet said. "I want you to lean back and close your eyes. You're very safe here, Zachary. Your father's here and I'm here and Father Bremner's here, and we're all here because it's safe for you to remember now, Zachary. We're here so we can help you. You can lean back slowly and close your eyes."

My son looked first to Violet, next to Father Bremner, and finally to me. We each nodded reassuringly. Zachary leaned back then and closed his eyes.

"I'm going to count from ten to one now, Zachary, and when I do, I want you to imagine you are on an escalator and the escalator is taking you slowly and safely down to a warm, safe place with a big, cuddly chair, where you will rest and remember very safely. Are you ready?"

Zachary nodded.

"Good. Then we're starting now. Ten, we're stepping on the escalator. Nine, we're moving slowly down. Eight, we're going deeper . . ."

As Violet moved Zachary into trance, I, too, felt a calm stealing over me. The phrase "spiritual healing" came to mind. With the crimes my son had endured, emotional repair was the real solution we were after.

"Three . . . you are nearing the bottom now. You can see your easy chair. . . . Two . . ."

Zachary looked as calm and peaceful as an angel. For this alone I felt grateful.

"You are settling in your chair now, Zachary. The most safe and comfortable chair there is. You are safe enough to remember here, Zachary, to remember what happened to you. You will see and tell us everything. . . . It can't hurt you again."

Violet exuded an aura of trust and confidence—an amazing air of stability given what she had just gone through.

"Are you ready, Zachary?" she asked.

"I'm ready," my son answered.

I was the one in that room who felt unready. I was the one who needed help. I felt a rage ripping through me then as I studied my son's angelic face. What son of a bitch could harm a child? Fred Fury? Oscar? I could have killed them both at that moment, scooped out their hearts with a rusted spoon.

"Our Father, who art in heaven . . . forgive us our trespasses as we forgive those . . ." Barely audible, Father Bremner was praying. I hoped he prayed for me.

"We know you've been keeping a very hard secret, Zach. It's okay for you to tell us. No one will be angry with you."

The fire jumped again and crackled angrily. Was it just my tribal Catholic associations? Fire-devil-demon-hell? What we were doing with Zach did feel like an exorcism—at least to me.

"Oscar did funny things to me," Zachary said softly. I could barely hear him as the roar in my ears was deafening.

"What kind of funny things?" Violet asked.

"He was silly. He gave me baths. He took my picture."

"He took your picture?" Violet prodded gently. "Why did he take your picture?"

"He said it was for Mommy, but—"

"Didn't you believe him, Zachary?"

"No . . . not really. He was my friend. He took me places. We had fun—"

"He gave you money for your pictures?"

"No. But he gave lots of fun stuff, teddy bears and baseball stuff and a basketball hoop— He got us tickets, too."

"So you wanted to let him take the pictures so you could go to the games and you could buy things?" Violet sounded curious.

"That's right. He said Daddy would never take me."

I was gripping both arms of my chair and keeping my mouth shut. I did that even though I wanted to scream, "No, son, NO. I'd have found time, really . . ."

Violet flicked me a sympathetic glance. I grimaced back.

"Did he touch you on your penis, Zachary? Did Oscar touch you there?" Violet asked now.

"No."

"Are you sure, Zach?"

"No. Oscar didn't touch me there. . . . His friend did, though."

"What friend, Zachary? Do you know his name?"

"He was Oscar's friend. The big man."

"I want you to remember, Zachary."

"First they made me drink funny stuff."

"What kind of funny stuff, Zachary?"

"Like Kool-Aid, but with a real cherry in it. Two real cherries. One from each of them, they said. She was pretty. Her hair was red, but maybe it was a wig, my angel said."

"Then what happened? Where did he touch you?"

"Down there."

"On your penis, Zachary?"

"Behind. On my pee-pee and behind my pee-pee."

"Did he hurt you, Zachary?"

"The big man hurt me. They put me on the table and they all started to hurt me, but my angel made them stop."

"Where did this happen?"

"The place with music. They were hurting me, but the angel took me away."

"Your angel? You have an angel, Zachary?"

"Yes." Zachary smiled to himself. "Freddy. He told them to stop and he took me away. They were very mad. So was Oscar."

"Was Oscar there, Zachary?"

"Yes."

"Were the people friends of Oscar's?" Violet's tone was gentle, curious.

"Yes. But he was scared of them."

"Were they friends of your angel?"

"Yes. But he was mad at them and they were mad at him."

"Why were they mad at him?"

"He said he wasn't going to help them do it anymore."

"Do what, Zachary?"

"You know. Take pictures of little boys."

"Is there anything else you want to tell us about, Zachary?"

"Yes. Oscar hurt me, too. He touched me there."

"Did you hate Oscar, Zachary? It would be okay to hate Oscar for hurting you."

"I didn't hate Oscar, but Freddy did. Freddy's my angel. He said what Oscar was doing to me was bad. He said bad men did it to him when he was a little boy, and it made him bad for a long, long time."

"Did he tell you how he was bad?"

"He said he did things to people. Then he got a disease from it and died and came back to be my angel."

"Is that what he told you?"

"Yes."

"What did your angel look like, Zachary? Did he have big wings?"

"Nah."

"Did he wear a long white dress?"

"He wore a baseball jacket."

"And what did he look like?" Violet was too calm.

"Like you. Just like you. But he was a boy." Violet winced.

"Why do you call him an angel? How can you know if he didn't have wings?"

"Because he saved me. He wears a baseball jacket, but he told me he was my angel when he took me away." Zachary sounded proud.

"Zachary, where was your mommy when this was happening? Was she away?" Violet was asking my question now.

"She was drinking," Zachary said softly. "She drinks every day since Daddy went away."

Violet glanced up at me, signaling "shhh." I was screaming inside my skin. I gestured to Violet: "Hurry up—emergency."

"Zachary, it's time to come back now. . . . You're going to feel much, much better since you told us your secret. You're going to wake up and eat your brownies and then you're going to have a good, long night's sleep. Now I'm going to count from ten to one. . . ."

Violet began bringing Zachary back to reality. I waited until his eyes fluttered open. He was sucking in deep breaths, hyperventilating, and he looked a little disoriented. I told him I was proud. He looked sleepy but content. He reached for a brownie and began to munch.

"Daddy'll be back in the morning," I said. "Eat your brownies and get some sleep. In the morning we'll go fishing."

"I'll show you and your father the very best spots," Father Bremner promised. He signaled me to "shoo," that he and Zachary were fine. Violet laid a hand on my arm and led me from the room. I stopped only long enough to kiss my son good night.

"Sweet dreams," I wished him. "Sweet dreams," he echoed—almost as if he'd never had any other kind.

Violet led me into the long hall. I closed the library door behind us.

"We were lucky," Violet said. "It can take a lot more sometimes. He was a good subject."

"Can we trust what he said?"

"I think so. I tried not to lead him too much. Memories can be false, but they can also be all too true. I think that what we got was real—and most of it."

"I know who I'm looking for," I told her. "It's Malcolm Crutcher. He has unlimited access and everyone's goodwill. The place with the music. That's his house. It's right by Ravinia music park."

My mind spun at the cleverness and complexity of Crutcher's setup—his charities gave him access to a steady stream of throwaway children. A perfect cover. Who knew how many of his charges—

Violet swayed. I caught her and propped her against the wall. "Jesus Christ, I'm going to be sick."

"What is it?"

"I sent him patients. We all did. His reputation was beyond reproach. I should have known."

"How could you? He fooled everyone—he fooled me. On the board of children's homes. The big child-care philanthropist. The saint parents could depend on. He probably told himself he was doing the kids a favor, introducing them to a better life—a few trips to the Art Institute and three squares a day. Doesn't that make up for buggery?"

Violet was carefully counting in deep and measured breaths. She looked like she was going to pass out.

"Are you okay?"

"I'm okay," she said. I stroked her face.

The library door opened behind us. Father Bremner stepped into the hall. "He's sound asleep," he whispered.

"Time to go," I said.

Father Bremner ducked back into the library.

Violet touched my arm. "I just need you to get back okay."

"I'll get back," I promised. I touched her face.

Bremner came back into the hall then. He held the vials of holy oil clasped in one hand.

"Sit with the child. It will comfort you," he instructed Violet. He walked with me toward the door.

"I want you to have a gun," I told him.

"I have a protection," he said. "A gun, among other things."

"Take care of them," I asked. "Be careful."

"Take care of you, son," Father Bremner interrupted me. We were at the door. I reached for the sliding bolt.

"Give me just a moment." Bremner stayed my arm. "Protect you," he said, cracking the seal on a vial of the sacred oil.

I waited impatiently while he rubbed a drop on my forehead in the shape of a cross.

"God go with you."

"Thanks. Thanks." I slid the bolt, heaved open the heavy door, headed for the car.

Chapter sixty

It was a thirty-minute drive, less if I didn't live through it. I wasn't the real problem, and Malcolm Crutcher knew that by now. I said my own set of prayers for no visits from local sheriffs, no visits from hit-and-run wildlife, no surprises of any kind. I wanted to be the surprise. I wanted to kill the bastard and let him know who did it.

All the pieces were now in place. "The crime behind the crime" was a child pornography ring. Freddy was a defector from it. One by one, he was picking off the men who led him into the life. All right. But what about Oscar? Ah, yes. "Freddy was mad at him." What about Johnny Vanilla?

"Not mine," Freddy had said.

Of course: Malcolm and Ilene's. Malcolm and Ilene's, and they were hoping to hang it on Freddy or on Big John D'Amato. Just as he had in the restaurant world, Vanilla had wanted to move in and up. He was greedy. Malcolm and Ilene liked things the way they were. And so, "Here's Johnny" was a curtain call.

It all hung together except for one question. How could

they watch Freddy's bloody progress and not know they were the final destination? What insurance did they have?

Of course! Violet. They'd made her a suspect to deflect me, and they kept her alive because she was Freddy's one vulnerability. If he threatened them, they would blackmail her—or worse. Now that I had Violet, the Crutchers were at risk. Freddy would make his move—preemptive—before they got to him.

When I got to Highland Park, the sky was a delicate pink, the milky color of a baby's skin. I headed for the Ravinia district, the neighborhood where music floated in the air, providing accompaniment for its residents' lives, for their bright fantasies and their darker realities.

It was dawn and not a note of music was playing when I pulled into Dr. Crutcher's place, cutting the engine to coast up the drive. A floodlight burned above the circular driveway, a single light burned in a bedroom window. Timed, I supposed.

I drew my gun and slipped from the car. I began to make my way along the side of the house, when I saw the front door slightly ajar. I stepped behind a privet hedge. As I watched, the door swung farther open. Crutcher lurched toward me through the open door. I stepped forward.

"Detective! You're a little late—"

"You son of a bitch." I cocked my gun. "Innocent children—"

"But I saved them," he said, and pitched forward, very dead. A thin, snaky kris protruded from his back. Fred Fury had gotten to him first.

My son's guardian angel stepped through the door just then, rigged out in a snow-white ceremonial toga, Cubs jacket slung over one arm, not the arm that held his Walther PBK. I might have pulled the trigger, but this was Violet's brother. Thin and sick as he was, Freddy Fury wore the high holy anger of an avenging angel on his ravaged face.

"And the wife?" I asked him.

"I took her first." Dr. Malcolm Crutcher and his wife, Ilene, had been executed with a relish I could only imagine.

"This is for you," Freddy said, tossing me the satin jacket. "You may not think so, but it's good luck. Take the kid to some ballgames. And take care of my sister, would you?"

"Don't—" I started, but he interrupted with a wave of his gun hand.

"I'm going to go with you, but first let me talk." Freddy had his Walther PBK for persuasion. We were at a standoff unless I wanted to shoot him. He motioned me toward an ornate white garden bench. "Relax. I'm planning to."

With that, gun still on me, Freddy took a seat on a companion bench. We faced each other across a small oval flower bed in gaudy bloom.

"Pretty, aren't they?" Freddy asked. I have to say, he seemed like a man at peace.

"Pretty," I agreed.

"So were the children," Freddy said. "So pretty, so innocent, so beautiful and clean. Maybe that was the attraction. Not that it matters. What I did was filthy."

"Go on."

"I'm glad you're a Catholic, Detective. It means you understand confession."

"I understand guilt."

"Ah. That's a different question."

"What are you saying, Freddy? That you aren't responsible?"

"Please, Detective. I'm very responsible. I have single-handedly wiped out a pornography ring that victimized, by my count, five hundred children. Five hundred and three, to be precise."

"Holy God." Freddy's gun was aimed at me now, and my gun hand was unsteady.

"Five hundred and three, ages seven to seventeen, over a period of twenty years, seventeen states, and, need I say, millions of dollars."

"How did they get away with it?" I believed his claim and his numbers.

"Ah, well, they usually drugged them. That certainly helped."

"But when they went back to their parents—"

"The whole trick was picking kids without parents, or with parents who didn't care. Take our mother. Did Violet tell you our mother was a junkie street whore? Perhaps that's harsh. Let's call her a nice girl from Appalachia with two children and a drug habit to support. Our mother was glad to be rid of us."

"I'm sorry."

"I don't dwell on it, Detective. I'm not blaming her. I think I've made it perfectly clear who I blame. Crutcher's charities were full of kids who had mothers just like ours. What was a little sodomy when it brought a warm bed and safety with it? That's what Crutcher always said. I'm sure he felt he was doing my sister and me a favor. Things just got out of hand and she ran away. I was too frightened to run away. And now you know why."

"So Crutcher was always the leader?"

"He was the brains. Nesbitt was the dick. Jack Nesbitt told our mother he'd give us art lessons if we would do sister-brother poses for him. He may have given her money, too, I don't know. You could ask my sister."

"I'm not sure she'd remember."

"No. Probably not." Freddy grew soft, wistful. "I always envied her that. Once I found her, I couldn't see disturbing her. Do you know how hard it is for a kid to find another kid in a foster home? It took me years."

"I'm sorry."

"You keep saying that, Detective. It's not your fault. I'd say you're quite a good cop. Your son certainly thought so. Even Oscar thought so. I couldn't believe it when he brought your kid in."

"So Oscar—?"

"Crutcher wanted the protection of having somebody on the force. Who were we going to ask? You? Besides, as you may already know, Oscar had his proclivities. Johnny could influence him."

"You mean bribe."

"Exactly. What a little hypocrite. Him and his island religion. Just one more way to get high. That's all it was for him. Or maybe the brakes were gone. That's what Robert said. I honestly don't think Oscar meant to involve your son—and I honestly don't care. He did it. Just like Johnny Vanilla, he didn't know when to stop."

"I thought Johnny wasn't yours."

"And he wasn't. Johnny did himself in. He got greedy."

"That's what I thought."

"Malcolm decided he was expendable. He managed to convince John D'Amato. I don't know how."

"Angela Remo is D'Amato's niece. Vanilla defiled her."

"I didn't know that. No wonder he let Malcolm take Johnny out."

It was beginning to feel almost comfortable, exchanging information and strategy. Almost like a debriefing.

"What else do you want to know?" Freddy asked me.

"My cousin Charles."

"Didn't know—but had his suspicions. He asked me for an address. I have one for you now, 615 Roscoe, penthouse. Everything is in order and waiting for you. Your cousin loved me, Detective. That's why I told him to get out of town. Crutcher would have killed him. . . . Anything else?"

"What made you stop? If it's such a compulsion—how could you?"

"Good question. Maybe it was my diagnosis. Maybe it was finally, really, falling in love—with somebody decent, that is. Maybe it was his prayers. His sacrifice. Him for them, he said."

"Chabrol . . ." I thought of the gentleness of the man, the beauty of his murals, the beauty, for that matter, even of his death. "Him for them."

"He was genuinely good," Freddy said.

"Yes, I sensed that."

"I'm glad you could see that. 'My darkness,' he called it. I'd say compulsion and he'd say darkness. He started praying for me. I was saved. Or something."

"I'd go with the or something. You've killed people, Freddy."

"They weren't people anymore. I thought of it as containment. They wouldn't stop, so I stopped them."

He paused and looked directly at me. "I was supposed to fuck your son for them, Detective. Even with my disease."

At the mention of Zachary, I reflexively raised my gun, a stupid, foolish, totally unconscious move.

"Save you the trouble," Freddy said.

It was over then. As if he'd practiced a thousand, no, ten thousand times, Fred Fury snapped the gun to his temple and fired.

As he crumpled to the ground, as he folded to the earth like a fallen angel, his shattered skull bloomed red while the toga billowed white.

At 615 Roscoe, penthouse, Fred Fury had everything waiting for me, just as he had promised. He left a meticulously detailed diary—of his crimes and theirs. Let me tell you what I found.

I unlocked the door to 615 and encountered Freddy himself, muraled as an angel, sword of death in hand. I recognized the style from Chabrol's. I looked for the signature, and saw it, F.F., at the bottom right. My cousin Charles was right. The man was an artist after all.

Past the portal to his apartment, I found Freddy had prepared well for me. He'd left me all I needed: A list of missing and molested children. A file filled with their names, photos, and fates, if known. A second file listing regular customers, notes on their pornography of choice, their criminal involvement, if any. A third file containing Internet sites and other commercial outlets for what was a big cash business. A fourth file was addressed to me. It contained a leather-bound journal and a note on the usual stationery.

Dear Detective Mayo,

Take care of my sister. I believe she loves you. As you surely must see, there is much to love in her. Appreciate what she has made from our common history. Compare it to what I made from the same piece of cloth. This journal is my personal history as I know it. It does not excuse my life, but it does, perhaps, explain it. Do with it what you think best.

About the Author

Julia Cameron has been an active artist for more than thirty years. She has extensive credits in film, television, and theater. Her essays have been anthologized, and she is a published poet. An award-winning journalist, she has written for such diverse publications as the *New York Times*, the *Washington Post*, the *Los Angeles Times*, the *Chicago Tribune*, the *Village Voice*, *Rolling Stone*, *American Film*, *Vogue*, and many others. Additionally, she has served on numerous film faculties—Northwestern University and Columbia College among them—and has taught and refined the methods of her bestselling books *The Artist's Way* and *Vein of Gold* for nearly two decades. For the past several years her focus has been sound healing which has informed her recently completed poetry CD, *This Earth*, as well as a metaphysical musical entitled *Avalon*.